PRAISE FOR GAIL R. DELANEY

Phoenix Rising
Book One
Janus

Part Two of the Future Possible Saga

JANUS

PHOENIX RISING BOOK ONE

GAIL R. DELANEY

TO: DADDY—LOSING YOU RIPPED A HOLE MY HEART LIKE I NEVER IMAGINED I COULD SURVIVE. THANK YOU SO MUCH FOR RAISING ME TO BE WHO I AM, AND FOR BEING THE BEST DADDY IN THE WORLD. EVERY LITTLE GIRL THINKS HER DAD IS THE BEST EVER, BUT WHEN I LOST YOU, I REALIZED A LOT OF OTHER PEOPLE THOUGHT YOU WERE THE BEST, TOO. I NEVER KNEW SOMEONE COULD FEEL SO MUCH PRIDE AND SO MUCH PAIN AT THE SAME TIME. I LOVE YOU, DADDY.

TO: JENIFER—MY BEST FRIEND, MY BUSINESS PARTNER, THE OTHER HALF OF MY BRAIN, AND THE INSPIRATION FOR JENIFER IN THIS BOOK. SHE'S NOT YOU, BUT SHE'S WHO YOU KIND OF WANT TO BE.

TO: CHRIS—MY JOHN. YOU'LL MOST LIKELY NEVER KNOW ME, OR THE FACT YOU INSPIRED A HERO IN MY BOOK, BUT THAT'S OKAY. I KNOW.

TO: BILL—MY SILENT, DISTANT MUSE. JUST HAVING YOUR CHAT WINDOW OPEN WAS ENOUGH TO FIRE UP ALABASTER AND MAKE HER EARN THE TITLE OF 'MUSE.'

TO: PATRICK—THERE ARE TOO MANY REASONS TO LIST. I LOVE YOU.

CONTENT DISCUSSION AND AUTHOR INSIGHTS

Throughout the whole of the Phoenix Rising quartet, there is a prominent character dealing with the trauma and emotional recovery from childhood sexual assault.

The events are in the past, and are not detailed anywhere in these novels. Doing so would not add anything but unnecessary shock value, and that isn't the type of author I am. I write enough so the source of the trauma is clear, and the reader can understand the extent of the physical and emotional trauma inflicted on this character.

There will be times when the memories are very raw and near the surface, and I recognize this may be very difficult for some readers when it parallels their own experience. Some books delve deeper than others, but the past events come into play in all four books.

There will also be a point when children are removed from a similar situation. Again, no details. I can't even go there myself.

I don't wish to blindside anyone. I hope perhaps the journey to recovery, very unique for the characters, will be worth the read.

THE FUTURE POSSIBLE SAGA

THE PHOENIX REBELLION QUARTET

BOOK ONE: REVOLUTION

BOOK TWO: OUTCASTS

BOOK THREE: GAINING GROUND

BOOK FOUR: END GAME

PHOENIX RISING QUARTET

BOOK ONE: JANUS

BOOK TWO: TRIAD

BOOK THREE: STASIS

BOOK FOUR: LIBER

THE FUTURE POSSIBLE SAGA
STORYTELLING STYLE

The Future Possible Saga is a continuous timeline, in which any give book extends the story of the book prior to it and sets up for the next book while also telling its own story. The books must be read in order to have full understanding of the saga.

This means each book has its own story arc, but also extends the greater saga story arcs.

There will be cliffhangers, but as the author I will always provide you with a payoff within the book you're reading. Each book has its own plot, it's own storyline, and its own resolutions. Each book (with the exclusion of the final book in the saga) will have setup for the next book. These may or may not be considered cliffhangers by some. But, be aware, they exist.

The good news is the saga as told through The Phoenix Rebellion quartet and Phoenix Rising quartet is complete. You don't have to wait for a cliffhanger resolution. Just continue to the next book.

I hope you enjoy, and complete the journey with us.

"Beauty, truth and rarity,
Grace in all simplicity,
Here enclosed in cinders lie."

The Phoenix and the Turtle
~William Shakespeare

PROLOGUE

6 March 2053, Thursday
Sorracchi Research Facility Alpha
Oriental Bay, Wellington
Former Nation of New Zealand

he night sky glowed orange with smoldering balls of falling Sorracchi base ships, and the popping sound of distant fighting echoed in the air. Jenifer only heard the fighting in the sky when the fighting around them paused, which wasn't often. They'd made it past the outer perimeter security before pulse charges were exchanged, but now she and the small group of Phoenix soldiers were barricaded behind a partially crumbled cinderblock wall.

The metallic tang of ion burn-off hung in the air, and Jenifer squinted through the haze. Crumbled concrete and gravel dug into her knees as she faced the wall, scrutinizing the situation. Half a dozen Sorracchi slugs had the entrance to the facility blocked, and they returned fire with as much expertise as the Phoenix soldiers backing her up. What she wouldn't give for another two-dozen, though. With the amount of time, and lack of resources, they had going in to this War she was frankly amazed any of them were still alive.

A squadron of Death Bringers flew over their heads, the sonic boom

1

left in their wake making her ears pop. She couldn't help the urge to crouch as she watched them disappear into the burning sky. A blast from a Sorracchi weapon hit the barricade to the right of her head, sending concrete dust into her face, making her cough and sputter.

Jenifer, Elijah, and a Phoenix soldier she only knew as Malloy reached the inner hub. Jenifer stepped over the smoldering body of a Slug, nudging it out of the way with her boot, while Malloy dragged another clear of the door. Elijah put his back to the wall and checked his power level, leaving the current cell in place.

"There's going to be at least four, if not more, slugs on the other side."

Jenifer only nodded, signaling to Malloy to take up with Elijah on the other side of the door while she stood at the control panel, waiting to slap it and open the doors. She punched in the stolen security code, and with three ticks of her chin, slapped the release button. The doors hissed open and an array of weapon fire greeted them, scorching the far wall.

She had all the codes, so it was up to Elijah and Malloy to cover her as she rolled across the floor and moved from makeshift protection to makeshift protection until she was within feet of the communications control panel. Nick Tanner, the retired Earth Force Colonel who'd traveled by wormhole across the known galaxy in search of allies, had relayed that more than three-fourths of Slug communications routed through this central hub in New Zealand. And from here, all long range special messages originated. Take this down, and the slugs were deaf and dumb.

How he got the codes, she didn't know. Didn't really care. All that mattered was that they worked. The first had gotten her through the door. The second would delete all external communication ports, then they were blowing up the entire thing. No reboot.

Pulse blasts echoed in the small chamber, echoing off the metal walls, making her ears buzz. With one last glance of confirmation back to Elijah —even though she knew he'd have her back—Jenifer rolled out of her hiding spot—firing her weapon with well-honed precision at the last two slugs hiding behind the console. One flew back, the side of his head vaporized by Damocles' powerful blast, and the other fell to his knees with a circular burn mark in the center of his chest from either Elijah's or Malloy's pulse charge pistols.

Holstering her weapon, Jenifer gained her feet and went to the console. A message already streamed across the wide screen in the angled glyphs she recognized as Sorracchi.

"Either of you fluent in slug?" she shouted over her shoulder.

Malloy stayed at the door, watching the hallway while Elijah joined her at her side, zipping up his jacket. His features were pinched, his jaw tight. "I read some. Let me see."

Jenifer studied his face for a minute before stepping sideways. "You okay?"

"Sure." He leaned over the console, squinting as he scanned the flowing data. "I think they're calling for reinforcements. Looks like three —no—four more ships have been docked just outside our long range scans. Damn. That's not good."

Jenifer slid back in front of the monitor between Elijah's body and the console edge. She pulled the nearest keyboard to her, scanning the unfamiliar symbols. She didn't have to know what they meant, she just needed to remember the sequence.

"Let's see what we can do about that."

She punched the last key with a bang, and watched the data on the monitor change.

"Message halted," Elijah read, leaning his hand on the console to read over her shoulder.

"Good. Let's load up and hot foot out of here."

While Malloy continued to guard the door, she and Elijah worked their way around the circular console filling the center of the room with multiple workstations. With their charges placed, they met up again on the side nearest the door and Elijah held up the detonator, waving it back and forth.

"In the mood for a run, baby?"

Jenifer took Damocles from her thigh holster, and together the three of them ran back into the hall just as a new bunch of Slugs showed up to make their retreat from the base more challenging. It was okay. Jenifer never liked to feel she got away with killing Slugs too easily. She liked to sweat a little bit, work at it. Made it so much more satisfying.

Just as the exchange of fire started, the Phoenix soldiers they'd left along the way joined the fight, attacking the Slugs from behind. The battle was over too quickly, as far as she was concerned, and they worked their way back out of the building. Smoking Slug bodies littered

3

the hallways, but based purely on the number, Jenifer assumed some had run when the fighting got bad. Word had to travel fast that the Humans were taking back their planet with a "Shoot First Ask Questions Later" vengeance.

As a mass they ran clear of the building into the night, and Jenifer was immediately proved wrong about her theory all the Slugs had run away. A spread of ion blasts sent them stumbling back into the building they'd just rigged with enough explosives to create a small crater on the island continent.

They all took position around the exit, some standing and some crouched on the floor. Jenifer put her back to the wall and Elijah beside her and looked around the corner. She heard him breathing hard, and chuckled.

"Workin' you too hard?"

"I've never been one to complain about how hard you work me."

She shook her head and rested back against the wall so she could look at him. His attention was intent, his gaze immediately focusing in the general area of her cleavage. "Is that all you think about?"

"Sex with you? No." He grinned. "I think about what we can blow up *before* I have sex with you."

The whistle of an aircraft falling at high velocity in the sky over the building vibrated through the air, and Jenifer tracked the burning trail of fire from the west to the east before it hit the ground probably twenty miles away. The explosion accompanying the mushroom cloud made her ears pop.

"This isn't getting the job done," one of the other men said. In the darkness she didn't know who.

"Then let's party." She spun into the doorway on the ball of one foot, sliding her extended leg around on the side of her boot to keep herself balanced, and fired a quickly yet precisely aimed series of shots where she pinpointed the remaining glow of weapon fire.

The others followed her lead, firing into the darkness, chasing each blast with one of their own until the return fire stopped. "Move before anyone else comes to play!" Elijah ordered, grabbing her arm as he went past her to pull her to her feet.

They cleared the perimeter, heading toward the beach of Oriental Bay, the shouts of more Slugs carrying through the trees. The salty breeze

4

coming through the trees was a strange contrast to the heat and fire of war.

"This far enough?" she asked in general.

"We'll be clear of the blast," one of the Phoenix soldiers confirmed.

"Hit it, Elijah," she said, turning to find him in the orange and yellow glow of flames overhead. But, he wasn't within the circle of soldiers and a bitter panic stirred in the back of her throat. "Elijah?"

Jenifer ran back in the direction they came, and barely went twenty feet before she found him kneeling on the ground, his head down and his body supported by one arm, the other wrapped across his abdomen with his hand inside his jacket.

"Elijah!" she shouted, closing the space between them. She dropped to her knees in front of him, reaching for his arm. Jenifer pulled his hand free from the inside of his jacket. "Let me see." In the flash of fire overhead, she saw the deep black stain of blood on his palm. "Damn it. Why didn't you say something?"

"Never quite seemed like the right time," he said with a wry chuckle.

Jenifer held back her growl of frustration and looked back over her shoulder. "Who has the medkit?" Three men came forward, all pulling various bits of an apparently patched together and incomplete medkit from their battle vests.

"Don't worry about it, Jenny," Elijah ground out, his bloody hand wrapping around hers. But she didn't look at him, didn't hesitate to slide her hand free easily with the slick of warm blood.

"Lie back. I can't get to the wound this way."

"Jenny!" he snapped, her name followed immediately by a groan and wet cough. Whether it was from her demand or because he couldn't maintain his position any more, Elijah fell sideways and she barely managed to cushion his head before it hit the ground. "You don't have time for this."

"We'll damn well make time."

"We need to blow it."

She didn't acknowledge the soldier behind her, while fumbling with Elijah's hands as he attempted to stop her from seeing his wound. *Damn stubborn idiot.*

He looked up at her with a faint smile despite the pain lines pinched at the corners of his pale blue eyes. "Jenny, listen to me."

"No, you listen to me. I'm going to treat this wound, and when you're better, I'm going to kick your ass seven ways to Sunday for not telling me."

"Ma'am," Malloy said from somewhere behind him. "We need to detonate the explosives."

"We'll blow it when *I say* we blow it!" she shouted over her shoulder.

She tugged Elijah's jacket open and pulled his shirt free of his belt to expose his bloody abdomen, and the wound that ripped his stomach open.

Tears burned in her eyes. Something that hadn't happened in a *very* long time. She wasn't a doctor, but she'd seen enough bodies ripped apart to know maybe—*maybe*—if they were ten feet from a hospital he'd have a fighting chance. There was no hospital in sight.

Elijah took her hand again, his grip lacking the strength she associated with him. The smell of blood and ashes tainted her mouth and nostrils and she blinked hard, feeling the unfamiliar sensation of moisture on her cheeks.

"I'm sorry, baby," he said softly, his voice fading with his strength.

"Don't you apologize to me, you stupid son of a bitch!" she ground out. "If you'd *told* me back *there*, I could have done something!"

He smiled, and despite the pain clear in his features, twin dimples dug into his cheeks. Elijah raised his other hand, free of blood and gore, and touched her face. He smoothed a bit of dark hair behind her ear as she hunched over him, and ran his thumb over slick skin.

"I never figured out why you were with me." She had to bend closer to hear him, and sucked in a sharp breath when she saw the drops of her own tears hit his jacket. He tried to speak again, but pain screwed his eyes shut and his body arched off the ground. His grip on her hand tightened, and she held on.

"You made things better," she finally said, holding his hand between hers.

"Good." His word turned into a cough, and he tried to take a breath with his mouth open wide, sucking in the salty air. "You could have told me about Savannah," he rasped out. "I would have listened."

Jenifer's skin rushed cold, and for a second, she couldn't even blink. *How had he known?* His hold on her hand slipped and she held it tighter.

"Don't do this to me." Jenifer shook her head, gritting her teeth against the violent clash of anger and terror in her chest. "Don't you *dare* do this to me, Elijah!"

"Ma'am!"

Jenifer twisted around, glaring into the darkness. "I know!"

"Jenny." His rough voice saying her name brought her attention back to him. He still held her in his bloody grip, and slid his free hand into his jacket, bringing out the detonator. Resting the device on his chest, he took her hand in both of his and laid them over the detonator. "We've got to do this."

She nodded because she knew what he was saying, what he was asking. Swallowing hard, she slid her hand from beneath his to cover his and the detonator. Blinking hard, she pressed on the switch.

Seconds later, the explosion shook the ground beneath them and a dome of fire rose above the tree line. Jenifer only saw it in her peripheral vision as she kept her focus on Elijah. She leaned over him, brushing her hand over his hair—hair she loved to curl her fingers into as she moved over him. Jenifer stroked her fingers across his forehead. Sweat made his skin clammy and cold.

"I love you." His words made her breath catch, and she blinked, her mouth falling open. Elijah grinned, making her wonder if he'd expected the very reaction she gave him. "Wanted to get out while I could."

She wanted to return the words, but they stuck in her throat and her eyes burned with more tears because she couldn't give him the one thing she should be able to, even now as he died. *What kind of sick person am I?*

Jenifer sniffed and leaned over to press a kiss to his forehead. His face was ashen in the amber glow of ships burning up in the atmosphere, but he smiled at her. He blinked, but his eyes opened slowly. Elijah drew a deep breath, his lungs rattling as he released it.

"It's okay. I loved enough for both of us, Genevieve."

She didn't know how he knew her secret, didn't care. She'd let the shock sink in later. His grip on her hand tightened only by the smallest degree, then his eyes slid closed and his head lolled to the side. One final wet breath eased from his chest. Jenifer choked, fighting to breathe, and bowed her head as the night sky lit up once again.

CHAPTER ONE

8 January 2054, Thursday
Aretu and Raxo Embassy
United Earth Protectorate, Capitol City
Alexandria, Seat of Virginia
North American Continent

11 Months After the War

"*We've secured the perimeter and have men on the protestors, sir.*"
"Understood, Captain." Lieutenant Colonel Connor Montgomery stood at the top of the steps leading into the Aretu and Raxo Embassy, scanning the group of twenty, or so, people forming a protest at the bottom of the embassy stairs. They held up signs demanding the ambassadors "Go Home!" and "Get off Earth!" while others were more colorful in their suggestions.

He knew his team member's underlying message. It grew harder every day to tell friend from foe. The sign-wielders could very well just be a group of peacefully protesting Separatists, or they could be Xenos. Xenos looked like every other Human—or Areth, as the case may be—walking the streets. Except Xenos took their beliefs to the extreme, and weren't afraid to spill blood to prove their point. The saddest part was they *were* Humans, and they had no qualms about killing other Humans in their pursuit of purity for the Human race. *Kill Humans to purify Humans.*

Which was what had earned them the name Xenos. *Xenophobes* on a global scale. To the extreme.

All he could do was be as aware as possible.

A family of four walked twenty yards north of the embassy entrance. Across the street, a man dressed in rags had been slouched in a doorway for over an hour. He'd taken several long swigs from the bottle resting between his feet. Could be a drunk, could be a ruse. Maintaining a drinking habit wasn't exactly an easy thing in 2054. Alcohol had been scarce before the world went to hell; now, it was as good as gold.

Random pedestrians moved along the dank street. The afternoon thunder show had driven most inside except for the diehards. The rain had left a raw nip in the air and darkened the pavement with the quick shower. At least it helped with thinning out the crowd.

At the base of the stairs half a dozen news agencies camped out waiting for the ambassador to exit; yet another recent change. After the War, information was dispersed solely by the newly-established government. It took six months for the first independent news source to appear, and now they were anywhere "news" might happen. Or they could create it.

The talks between the ambassador and the Presidential Council for Planetary Reconstruction had been going on for three days. They were near a settling point, and everyone wanted to break the news first.

Then there was the usual gaggle of grinning females hovering outside the concrete barriers on the opposite side of the staircase from the protestors, charismatic young women who wouldn't be deterred by just a little rain. Wherever John Smith was, so were the women. Connor shook his head. He'd be the first to admit he didn't have a clue about women, but he couldn't figure out what had so many going gaga over this particular ambassador.

Connor tipped his chin toward the crowd and spoke to his 2IC, Mel Briggs, who held her post on the other side of the door. "Hey, Mel. You're a woman, right?" The answer was a half-hearted "Hey!" before he continued. "What about Smith has the women all over him?"

"Why? Need some tips, Montgomery?"

He chuckled and looked at Mel over the top of his sunglasses. "I'm doing *just fine*, thank you."

"If you say so, sir."

Connor chuckled. In truth, there was really only one woman he focused on these days—Mel. After years of working side-by-side with her, he finally had begun to see the woman who had been there all along. Problem was, he was her commanding officer. "Just answer the question, Briggs. Is it just the alien thing?"

"What *alien thing* are you talking about?"

Connor rolled his head back, grinning. "You know. Women get all gooey at the idea of being with an alien."

Mel chuckled. "No, sir. It's most definitely not an alien thing." Connor stayed quiet, waiting for her to elaborate. After a pause, she huffed. "Okay, so maybe a little bit. But, he's also powerful. He's sexy. He's intense."

"Sexy?" Connor looked at Mel again over his glasses. "Are you kidding?"

Mel smiled slowly. "No, sir," she answered, dragging the words out. "He's got those great angular features. Sharp cheekbones. Defined chin—"

"—Big nose. Big ears," Connor interjected.

"Long, lean body—"

"He's tall and skinny!"

"Those *gorgeous* blue eyes." Mel shook her head. "You could take a lesson or two from Ambassador Smith about how to deal with women. He doesn't talk, he listens. And looks directly at you the whole time with those *great* eyes—"

"Alright! Alright!" Connor held up his hands in surrender. "I get it. Actually, no, I *don't* get it but I've heard enough."

Mel smirked and shifted her stance, her hand resting on the hilt of her pulse weapon. Connor had been reluctant when Colonel Goldburg first assigned Mel as his 2IC five years earlier. Slight of build, she just cleared his shoulder, but he soon learned her size was an asset. She was assumed to be weak because of her stature, but Mel could lay out a man twice her size on his stomach with his hands and feet hogtied before he managed to say, "Hey, baby." She could drink half the squadron under the table, but could buff her nails, comb her hair and silence a crowd when she

11

walked in. With short golden-brown hair and matching eyes, and a bright smile, Mel Briggs was a looker. She also never seemed to be lacking for company, so maybe she *did* know what she was talking about.

But still, John Smith *sexy?* Even his *name* was ordinary.

Connor just didn't get it.

The small electronic earpiece molded into the canal of his ear twittered softly before he heard Lieutenant Halliwell's voice.

"We're on our way down, sir," Halliwell informed him.

Connor nodded to the three Firebirds standing ready at the foot of the stairs, and to the driver waiting outside the armored hovercar. When he heard approaching footsteps inside, he turned and gripped the curved door handle. Mel matched his move from the other side of the entrance, and in unison they pulled open the doors.

Ambassador John Smith and his son Silas moved into the dim afternoon light, flanked on each side by Firebird soldiers. Connor moved into position beside the ambassador, his hand on his pulse pistol. Silas held his father's hand, his dark eyes wide as they moved into the street.

"Good afternoon, Ambassador," Connor said as he took up position. He leaned forward just enough to grin at the young boy clinging to his father's hand. "Hi, Silas."

Seven year old Silas—although by what Connor understood, no one could be positive about the boy's age since his mother was dead, and John Smith had effectively adopted him after the initial Sorracchi attacks —looked up at Connor with wide eyes. A toothy grin spread his lips. "Hello."

"We need to talk," John said with his head turned toward Connor and away from his son. His elongated vowels and lilted accent made him sound like he was from Manchester, England rather than an alien planet on the other side of the galaxy. "Silas is more frightened now with your men hoverin' than he was after the inner-city bombin's. Is this necessary?"

"President Tanner thinks so," Connor answered, keeping his attention on their surroundings as they walked down the stairs. "He can't let threats against your life go unanswered. Both you and Ambassador Drucillus Clodianus Hiacyntus are vital to the continuation of relations between Earth and your worlds."

John snorted. "Who's been preachin' the party line to you, my friend?"

Connor couldn't help his grin. "Doesn't help when your sister is married to the *President of the World*." As pretentious as the title sounded to him, Connor knew *President* Nick Tanner felt the same way.

As they neared the bottom of the stairs, the cluster of women to their left called out to John, reaching out past the barriers as if he were some 20th century singing star. The news reporters lunged forward, shouting the ambassador's name and rapid-firing questions at him.

The ambassador turned to the reporters, not addressing one in particular, and grinned amicably. "I would prefer no' to comment until we've completed the discussions. Thank you." With that simple statement, he turned and angled his son away from the screaming crowd and toward the hovercar.

"You know, Ambassador," Connor said, reaching for the hovercar door handle. "Security would be a hell of a lot easier if you didn't attract every single female within a—"

His words trailed off as one particular woman caught his attention in the crowd of ladies who wanted to have John Smith's alien love child. While the other women blushed and cried, calling out John's name, she stood apart. She wore nondescript, unadorned clothing – a dark, heavy jacket and worn denims—much like most civilians wore since simple staples like clothing had become short in supply and high in demand. She was beautiful, with rich brown hair and as far as he could tell, dark eyes, and olive skin. But, it was her expression—the smug calmness— that caught his attention.

"John, get in the car," Connor said in a low, but stern voice. He tapped his earpiece. "On alert," was all he said.

Every Firebird within the perimeter drew their weapons. Connor stepped around John so he stood between the ambassador and his son and the beautiful woman with the cool expression. Connor stared at her through his sunglasses, and she stared right back. Then a small, almost indiscernible smile bowed her lips.

The hairs on the back of Connor's neck stood to attention and he shoved John toward the door just as she took from the pocket of her jacket a small, metallic ball with red lights blinking around the circumference.

"Grenade!"

13

"*M*r. President, wait! We haven't secured this area—"

Nicholas Tanner, President of the United Earth Protectorate, pushed his forearm against the chest of the soldier as he moved past the man without pausing.

"Let him through, soldier."

"Yes, sir."

Nick didn't look back to Colonel Ebben, knowing his chief security advisor walked no more than two paces behind him. The man's powerful baritone silenced the soldier's protests and the handful of armed men that stood between Nick and his destination stepped aside to let him through.

Disinfectant and the tang of blood tickled his nose. The emergency wing of the rebuilt-but-pathetically-inadequate hospital was in chaos. Doctors in white lab coats smattered with scarlet rushed from one wounded patient to the other, shouting orders and grabbing bandaging as they moved. A scream laced with pain so tangible it scraped over his skin ripped through the air. Nick scanned the hall-cum-triage, his hands fisted at his side.

"Nicky!"

He turned to the sound of his name, catching his wife as she threw her arms around his neck. Her body shook, her fingers gripping his shirt and catching the silver hair along his collar. Nick cupped his hand against her blond hair, looking past her to catch the eye of her security detail. The men's silent nods acknowledged they knew she was safe now, she was with him, and they could back off.

"I can't find him." Her voice was rough and strained, and the warmth of her tears slicked his cheek. "He's not with the wounded."

"He's here. We'll find him." Nick eased her away from him, laying his palm against her cheek. "I promise." Caitlin nodded her acceptance, but he didn't let her pull away. Instead, he laid his palm against her cheek and bent at the knees enough to look into her eyes. "Are you okay?"

She nodded, the greatest part of the question remaining unsaid. *Are you and the baby okay?* Only Caitlin's private physician knew about her

14

pregnancy, and with the tender state of the Protectorate and the impending threats that seemed to stalk him, Nick refused to risk their baby, so for now it was their secret.

With Caitlin held against his side, his arm holding her to him, he reached out and grabbed the nearest person in a white coat. The man instinctively jerked away and immediately launched into an angry speech about letting him work until he looked up. His eyes widened and his mouth stayed open, silent.

"Montgomery," Nick demanded.

The man with *Lorenza* embroidered on his jacket blinked.

"Lieutenant Colonel Connor Montgomery," Nick snapped again, louder.

"Y-yes, Mr. President. Right this way."

Lorenza handed the bandages in his hands to a nurse as she passed, mumbled some quick instructions, and led them several yards down the hall to a closed door. Nick led Caitlin, holding her hand. Her fingers were cold, shaking in his grip, and he knew she had to be about ready to jump out of her own skin. They'd lost so many people—and *thought* they lost so many people—since hell had come to Earth, the idea of losing someone else was too painful to even consider. Caitlin had thought Connor was dead for a long time.

Lorenza pushed open the door, and the room beyond was dark, the silence a sharp contrast to the chaos in the hallway. There were two beds, each occupied, with the soft glow of overhead lights casting shadows over their blanket-covered forms.

"Colonel Montgomery is there." Doctor Lorenza indicated the bed furthest from them, speaking in a hushed voice. "His injuries were treated quickly and he was one of the first of the injured to arrive." He took a personal access computer interface tablet from his coat pocket, the personal access computer tablet beeping as he retrieved Connor's file. "He's been sedated to allow him to rest."

"What are his injuries," Caitlin asked, and before Lorenza could speak, she cut him off by raising her hand, palm out to him. "Let me remind you I'm a doctor."

He nodded, clearing his throat nervously. His eyes darted to Nick before answering. "Understood, ma'am. The colonel sustained multiple minor contusions when he was thrown against Ambassador Smith's hovercar. No broken bones, but some severe bruising through his ribcage and along his spine. He'll be sore for a few days. No head injury. The most severe injury was sustained by his eyes."

Nick's gut clenched and Caitlin's grip on his hand tightened. But her expression never changed as she watched Lorenza. Her composure was on the surface only. No one would see the turmoil but Nick, and no one felt it the way he did. Her fear electrified the air, sparking around her.

"Diagnosis."

"Ultraviolet Keratitis. Flash grenades were used in the attack, and Colonel Montgomery was in close proximity to the burst."

Damn. "Is that bad?" Nick asked.

Caitlin explained before Doctor Lorenza had a chance, knowing exactly what he really asked. "It's not permanent. His vision will recover."

"Flash burn?"

"In layman's terms, yes. Sir," Lorenza added, clearing his throat again.

Caitlin released his hand, and took the PAC from Doctor Lorenza. The conversation quickly turned to treatment, recovery time, and really long words that made little to no sense to his military mind. Nick stepped clear of the conversation, moving to the foot of Connor's bed.

His brother-in-law's head was wrapped in white gauze, thick pads covering his eyes and tufts of dark blond hair stuck out like dirty spikes above the bandages. Red, raw patches marked his cheeks below the bottom of the bandage edge. When Nick was barely a captain, he'd been in a hanger bay when a power surge hit a welding machine in use fixing the wing of a glider. He still remembered the blinding blue-white light, and his eyes had burned for days. No amount of saline wash helped the feeling of sandpaper behind his eyelids. The doc had told him the flash burn was minimal. He'd been miserable. If Connor's burn was severe, he didn't envy the man the next few days.

Nick glanced over his shoulder, making sure Caitlin and the doc were still talking. By the looks of it, Caitlin didn't like something about what Lorenza said—whether it was treatment or medication—and the poor man had a tough argument on his hands. Caitlin was stubborn, especially when it came to younger brothers, even if they'd gown up years ago.

Nick understood. Finding out a dead brother was alive had a way of making a person protective. Kind of like finding out a son you thought you'd lost was alive. Yeah, he understood.

He looked back to the bed, set his hands on the footboard, and leaned his weight into his arms. A tight, hard knot sat between his shoulder blades and a constant throbbing pulsed behind his eyes. This was the third Xeno attack in as many months, and each attack had been worse than the one before.

As if wounded eco-systems and crumbling cities weren't enough, let's add homegrown terrorists to the list.

Connor jerked with a low moan, his head rolling on the pillow. His hands slid over the blanket, searching his surroundings. With a quick glance over his shoulder at Caitlin, Nick stepped to the side of the bed between Connor and the other side of the room.

"Easy there, buddy," he said in a low voice, setting his hand on Connor's shoulder.

Connor's head tipped in Nick's direction, and he stilled. "Sir?"

"Don't move around too much, or you'll catch your sister's attention. You're not strong enough for that yet."

Connor grinned, but immediately winced. The raw skin on his face would be sensitive to everything, including smiling. "Thanks."

"Do you remember what happened?"

Connor licked his lips and tried to shift, wincing again. "We were escorting Ambassador Smith to his transport." He paused, and by what Nick could see of his face, it looked like he was trying to piece together the details. "I saw this woman in the crowd. She threw a grenade." His words died and his hand came up, touching the bandages on his eyes.

"Temporary," Nick said quickly. "Even your sister says so."

With a long release of air, Connor let his hand fall to the bed again. "How many were hurt?"

"Three civilian deaths, five severe injuries." He grit his teeth and swallowed hard. "I'm sorry, Connor. We lost four Firebirds." With more control than he thought had, Nick tamped down the rage boiling just beneath the surface of his skin, curling in a fireball in the center of his chest.

Even with only a portion of his face visible, Nick saw the flash of raw emotion across Connor's face and his fists clinched on top of the blankets. "Who?"

Nick bowed his head and rubbed his thumb and fingers across his brow. Colonel Ebben had given him the names, but his attention at the time had been on getting to the hospital. He focused for a moment before answering. "Crosby. O'Shea, Hastings and Mandalay." He raised his head with a sigh. "Your 2IC Briggs was hurt, but she'll be fine. Not in as bad shape as you."

Connor's hands relaxed, but only enough to get rid of the white around his knuckles.

Nick shook his head, tapping his fingertips against the side railing on the bed. "I can't wrap my head around their logic. The damn Xenos want aliens off Earth, so they kill Humans to prove their point."

"I'm sorry, sir."

"Don't," Nick snapped. "This isn't on you. You did what you could. It could have been worse." A pleasant tingle brushed beneath the hair at his nape, easing some of the tension. "Your sister is coming. Brace yourself, soldier."

Nick stepped back, and his wife immediately took his place, moving between him and the bed. The stern no nonsense doctor of minutes before was replaced by the near-hysterical sister who touched Connor's face with tenderness as she fought not to cry. Nick laid his hand on her back, but his mind was already outside the room, running through the facts he knew and how he would react. He refused to resort to retaliation, but he *would* find the Xeno-terrorists, and they *would* pay for their crimes.

Phoenix had struggled for nearly fifty years to find the truth, and thousands of men and women died in the war that gave the Earth back to Humanity. For what? So Mankind could go back to killing each other? Just like it had been before the governments of the world unified under one common government in 2017, man killed man over differences of opinion. National lines had not been redrawn—and as far as Nick was concerned, the *only* good thing to come out of the last five decades was a politically unified planet, *even if* he wasn't convinced it should be unified under *him*—but there were definitely lines. Lines between Humans who welcomed the next step of Mankind joining the variety of other races and species within the universe, and Humans who wanted to cauterize, sterilize and purify the planet of any alien influence or contact.

Those were the idiots who didn't get the fact the Human Race was far from pure, modern Human beings having been *created* by a commingling of races and species. *Purifying the Planet* was impossible by Xeno standards.

Duh!

He knew the idea of peace had been Utopian at best, but he hadn't expected things to fall apart so damn quick.

"Sir."

Connor's voice pulled him out of his thoughts, and he blinked the room back into focus. "Yeah."

"What about the ambassador and his son?"

Nick paused, clearing his throat. "Both alive. You did your job, Colonel."

CHAPTER TWO

*S*ilence had finally settled in the hospital halls outside the dark room where John watched over his son. Only the occasional sound of passing footsteps or mumbled voices broke the quiet in the room. John hadn't moved since the doctor left them, not even as darkness had settled into the room, casting everything in shadows except for Silas, haloed by the light over the bed.

Silas looked so small in the large bed, the stark white blankets covering his curled body. His hands were folded beneath his cheek and a small streak of blood soaked through the bandage covering his forehead. His dark skin camouflaged the worst bruises, but John knew they were there. He had run his fingertips over the swollen bumps and felt the heat emanating from the contusions.

Even after the doctor had treated him, and given him some medication to calm him, Silas had cried and clung to John's hand. Only when he'd slipped into sleep could John step back and sit in the chair beside the bed. He sat hunched forward with his elbows digging into his thighs, his fingers laced together in front of his face in supplication.

It was all he could think to do. He'd long ago forgotten the prayers he'd memorized as a child, he was beyond requests spoken by rote, and all he could do was offer to God the terror that rolled in his chest like a storm. He couldn't describe it, couldn't ask it be taken away because he needed it. He needed guidance.

He had once thought he wanted to be a physician, but it hadn't taken more than two years in the confines of an academic setting for him to accept he was a soldier. John had been trained to fight for Aretu and the Coalition. He'd trained to protect, to serve, to give his life if he had to. Soldiers made terrible husbands, and even worse diplomats.

Today was a case in point. All he wanted to do was get his hands on a weapon and hunt down the Xenos who'd hurt his son. The fighter in him, trained to protect and act, was not trained to sit on his haunches and wait.

Waiting got people killed.

A fact he knew only too well.

John tore his gaze away from his son and bent his head, resting his brow against the pads of his thumbs, and closed his eyes.

It was a mistake because immediately his mind was filled with sounds, images, and sensations from earlier in the day. Connor Montgomery telling him to get in the hovercar. Pushing Silas into the safety of the armored vehicle. Hearing the shouts and the explosions before the hovercar catapulted sideways and rolled across the street, landing at a strange angle against the far buildings, the engines dead and the metal creaking.

And the sounds of Silas' screams.

It reminded him too vividly of Harrison Park, Chicago.

He'd held the boy to his chest as the car flew against the wall, protecting his son with his own body. He felt the ramifications of it now. His back ached and the muscles of his shoulders burned with tight knots of exertion. A bandage over his right eye covered a jagged slash. But none of that mattered.

When the smoke had cleared and the explosions stopped, one of the Firebirds had ripped open the hovercar door and helped them out. John had burned his fingers when he touched the exterior of the vehicle, the safety metal scorched with ash and hot to the touch. But, it had done its job. The energy from the pulse blasts hadn't penetrated the thick hull, and the flying debris had only dented the metal—not crushed it—protecting them inside.

But, not protecting enough.

There was a soft knock at the door before it slowly creaked open and Nick Tanner stuck his head inside. "John?"

"I'm here," he answered, not moving from his spot.

Nick stepped into the room and eased the door shut. He took three steps toward the bed, keeping his footfalls light. A familiar tension buffered the man, tinged with sadness and regret.

John learned shortly after coming to Earth only a minor portion of the Human population carried the dormant Areth DNA that gave his people their psychic Talents. On Aretu, only one in one hundred thousand Areth were without some form of Talent. On Earth, it was nearly the opposite. He sensed those rare individuals when their emotions or thoughts brushed against his psyche, a voice in the overwhelming silence.

Nick Tanner was one of the few, and his voice was louder than most even though he barely understood what he was capable of.

Nick drew in a long breath before speaking, his tone tight and hoarse. "Michael was clinically dead twice, the Bitch hurt him bad, and the Umani doctors managed to bring him back. I've never felt so useless and angry." He cleared his throat, and his voice was less strained when he spoke again. "Or so damn happy to see him open his eyes."

John rubbed his hands together, focusing on the floor as he struggled to find control of his rage. "Does it get easier?" he finally managed to ask.

"Seeing your kid get hurt? Not as far as I can tell." Nick shifted his stance, and John heard the rough rub of a palm over his face. When he spoke, his voice was slightly muffled. "Silas will be okay."

John let his hands drop to hang limp between his knees. "This time." He raised his head and squinted in the dark to focus on Nick's face. The edges of light from the bed lamp just touched his features, but John didn't need to see the deep lines around his eyes to recognize the frustration, worry and anger rolling off him. "How many of your people did we lose?"

"Four Firebirds. Several injuries, both Firebirds and civilians. Three civilians were killed." His voice was level in an attempt to disguise the gut reaction John knew he felt.

"Connor?"

"He's hurt pretty bad. But he'll be fine. Caitlin is with him."

John looked down at the blood on his shirt. It had dried and darkened to an almost black crust, making the material stiff and rough against him. Some of the blood was Silas', some wasn't.

"What about the girl?"

"She's in ICU, but she'll live."

John nodded, focusing on his hands again.

They settled into silence, and John turned his focus again to the bed. Silas hadn't moved except for the slight shift of his chest as he breathed. They could probably bring a marching band into the room and the boy wouldn't stir. The medication had pushed him into a deep sleep.

John drew a breath and forced it out through his nostrils. "Silas couldn't sleep alone for weeks after his mother died." The thought was random, and he said it aloud before considering where the conversation would go from there. "He had nightmares. He'd scream and stare into the dark, no matter how many times I said his name."

"Michael had nightmares." Nick took another step toward the bed, coming further into the circle of light. "He still does once in a while, Jackie's told me. And he's a grown man."

John braced his hands on the armrests and pushed himself from the chair, taking the single stride needed to reach the side of the bed so he could rest his hand on Silas' coarse hair. "I don't pretend to know everythin' about being a parent. But, I know I'm no' supposed to let this happen."

"You didn't *let* it happen any more than I *let* Michael live in hell for twenty-five years." Nick's voice was stern, insistent, and John wondered just how many times he'd told himself the very same thing. And if he believed it yet. "It's what you do from here that counts."

John turned and finally looked straight on at Nick Tanner, some of the anger boiling beneath his ribs forcing its way out. "And just what is it I do? No' five minutes before this happened, I told your man I didn't want so many soldiers hoverin' 'round us," he hissed through clenched teeth to keep himself from shouting.

Nick said nothing, just stared back. Finally, John slid his eyes closed and dropped his chin, drawing in antiseptic-tinged air. "I'm sorry," he conceded, curling his fingers around the safety rail along the side of the bed. He raised his head again and shrugged a single shoulder. "Being a soldier was easier."

Nick chuckled, grinning. "Hell, yeah." He set his hand on John's shoulder, patting it firmly. "You figure out what you need to do for your son, and leave the rest to me."

The inside of Nick Tanner's office smelled like fresh wood and old leather, reminding John of Aretu, and his family's farm at Devon on the Hill in Callondia.

He'd only been back to Aretu once since the Sorracchi had surrendered. Once in eleven months. And the visit had been far too brief. He'd only remained long enough for Queen Bryony to request he serve as Aretu Ambassador to Earth and to arrange for the care of his home while he was away. When his brother Conrad married Bryony and took the crown as prince consort, the family farm passed to John. A soldier he was, a farmer he was not, and since then he had trusted the estate to the care of an old family friend, Anson Barclay, which was how it would continue for as long as John could see.

John slouched further into the couch in Nick's office, scrubbing his face with the palms of his hands. He needed to shave, but hadn't strayed far from the hospital since the attack. They had only let Silas leave that day, and it took everything John had to just to come here without him.

If he couldn't leave the boy for a couple of hours, how could he do what needed to be done?

The door opened and Nick came in, followed behind by Jacqueline Anderson. For all intents and purposes, and to the staff within the Protectorate Capitol, she was considered the president's daughter-in-law although she and Michael Tanner weren't married. John smiled as he stood, greeting both Nick and Jacqueline by taking their hands.

"It's good to see you, Jacqueline," John said, and leaned in to touch a kiss to her cheek. "It's been weeks."

Jacqueline nodded as she stepped back from him, pushing her hands into her back pockets. "Yeah. Nick here has been keeping me busy with the new recruits."

"I think Jackie might be able to help us out with your security detail while Connor is recovering." Nick motioned toward the couch where John had previously been sitting. "She knows all about the attacks and the threats against your life."

John sat and leaned forward on the couch, his hands linked and his elbows resting on his legs, focused on Jacqueline. "What do you think?"

"I think if you want to stop an assassin, you hire an assassin."

Nick paused in his descent into his chair, quirking an eyebrow before he finished sitting. "Who?"

"You probably don't know her. But, I guarantee you, if you want the ambassador's ass protected—no offense, Ambassador—she's the one that'll do it for you."

"Am I to assume this person isn't exactly official?" He grinned, because very few things since the Humans fought back and retook their planet could really be termed as official.

"Assume anything you want, Ambassador." Jacqueline sat on the edge of Nick's desk, obviously comfortable and at ease in the presidential office. But, John noted the way her gaze slid to the family photos on the desk—specifically one of her with Michael and their daughter Nicole—and just as quickly, she looked away. "All I'm saying is she's the best there is if you want someone dead, or if you want to keep them alive."

"Is she Phoenix?" Nick asked. Which really meant: *Was she part of the resistance before the war?*

John had garnered through his time with Nick Tanner the right answer to the question held a lot of weight for him when it came to determining loyalties. With the major threat of Sorracchi oppression gone, most of the world population had started to come together to rebuild. But, volunteering after the winner is chosen was a very different thing to Nick than being part of the fight.

"Officially?" Jacqueline flipped her long, black hair behind her shoulder and moved from the desk to perch on the arm of the couch. She was a stunning woman, John would readily admit, lean and strong, with rich latte skin and dark eyes to match her dark hair. He knew little about her except she'd practically been raised by Phoenix, and she was raising a little girl with Michael, Nick's son. And right now she was harboring a whole lot of pain she wasn't about to let anyone see. "We've collaborated."

Nick made a small sound in the back of his throat, and rocked in the chair, the aged mechanisms creaking slightly. For several moments, the chair squeaked under his habitual rocking as he rubbed his fingers across his lips.

"She was with me when I found Jace Quinn."

Jacqueline's statement immediately stopped the rocking, and John carefully watched the unsaid communication between the two of them. It was no more than a meeting of the eyes, and a slight nod from Nick.

"I trust Jackie with everything precious to me. And if she says this woman—whoever she is—can be trusted to protect you, then I think you should seriously consider it, John." Only then, when he said John's name did he look away from Jacqueline.

"Good enough for me."

"I still need to know more about her," Nick added as a caveat. "You trust her, and I trust you, but I can't allow someone to be in meetings and hearing *stuff* without checking her out."

"Understood," Jackie said with a nod.

Practically in unison they all stood, and John again took Jacqueline's hand in his. "Thank you."

"Sure." As she did before, she slid her hand free of his and tucked it in her back pocket, looking uncomfortable as she took a step backward.

"How soon?" Nick asked.

"I'll let you know more by morning."

"Good," John added, turning from Jacqueline to Nick. "I have one other thing to discuss with you. Silas."

Jacqueline stepped back from where they stood and sat again on the arm of the nearby couch, one foot swinging. She crossed her arms over her body, cupping her own elbows, and seemed to wait for their conversation to end.

Nick didn't say anything, so John swallowed, hoping he had the courage to go through with the decision he had made sitting beside Silas' bed during the night. The idea made his chest ache, but the thought of Silas being hurt or frightened again made him angry enough to push past the dread.

"I'm sending Silas to Aretu."

"Are you sure?"

"I'm sure it's the right thing to do." He turned and paced away from Nick, rubbing his hand across the back of his neck. "As long as I serve as ambassador, or until we stop the threat, he will be at risk. On Aretu, he'll be safe." Several feet away from Nick, he turned and set his hands at his hips. "I sent word to Conrad this morning. He and the queen will take care of Silas as a member of the royal family. Silas isn't my son by blood, but he's my son, and among the Areth that's enough."

He thought he saw Jacqueline shift when he spoke, turning away so he couldn't see her face. He had a difficult time identifying exact emotions from Humans who didn't have the psychic-genetic markers, so he only knew whatever she felt was negative.

Sometimes he enjoyed the mystery, but at times like this he wished he knew.

"Okay. I'll check on our transport schedule and let you know by this afternoon when the next one leaves. I'll ask Connor to give up a couple Firebirds to—"

"I'll go." Jacqueline interrupted Nick's promise, coming off the couch to stand beside him. "I'll escort Silas to Aretu."

"You're talking four months *minimum* there and back, if not longer." Nick argued.

Jacqueline shifted her weight, again taking the common stance of her hands in her back pockets. "I know."

"I don't want to pull you away from your duties." John began.

She shook her head adamantly. "You're not. I have people who can run the classes while I'm gone. Right, Nick?"

Nick scowled, rapping a knuckle on the desktop several times "Right."

"Fine." Jacqueline's voice had lost some of its surety, but her expression still held. She nodded. "I'll work on my contacts, and then I'll be ready. Just tell me when the transport leaves."

She turned sharply, almost to the office door before Nick went after her, calling her name. John stepped back, trying to put as much distance as he could between him and the two, allowing them to speak with as much privacy as possible with him in the room. But the office was small, and their hushed voices carried.

Nick set his hand on the door, leaning into his arm to close some of the space created by their difference in height. "What about Nicole?"

Jacqueline's slid her eyes away from Nick and cleared her throat before focusing on him again. "She should stay here . . . with family."

"*You're* her family. You're her mother—"

Her hand shot up, cutting him off. He paused only long enough to change tactics.

"Jackie, I don't know why Michael left, but I know him well enough I'd bet dollars to donuts he doesn't understand what leaving did to you—"

"I'm not going because of Michael." She shook her head, looking at him. "I'm going because a little boy needs to be protected."

"And Michael has nothing to do with it?"

"I'm coming back. Isn't that what he said?" She tugged at the door, but it wouldn't open with Nick's hand against it. They stared at each other for several moments before Nick dropped his arm and stepped away. With a jerk, Jacqueline yanked open the door. "Well, I'll be back, too."

CHAPTER THREE

*J*enifer's lungs burned as she tried to draw in air, the effort akin to breathing through wet cheesecloth, and her thigh muscles ached with the strain of forward motion. The rhythm of her pace drove her down the dirt road, her own heartbeat pounding hard in her ears.

Thump-thump-thump-thump!

Sweat rolled between her shoulder blades, eventually absorbed by the already soaked material of her tank, and her long, dark hair clung to her scalp and the back of her neck. The air was thick and hot, the mid-day sun scorching what remained of the city. This was the hottest time of day, when most inhabitants of Slum City found refuge in the shade for an afternoon *siesta*.

This was when she ran. When she pushed harder, sometimes hovering on the edge of collapse when the heat beat down on her and her body cried for rest and hydration. But, she had only run five klicks out of the city, and had at least another two before she reached any of the rivers spawned by the destruction of Rio de Janeiro and the subsequent restructuring of the entire Brazilian coast.

To focus past the pain, she emptied her mind, allowing her thoughts only to dwell on the next step and the next klick, the next corner to take, the next obstacle to avoid. The pain was inconsequential.

"I've got a job for you."

Jenifer fought the urge to close her eyes as an attempt at blocking out the conversation she'd had with Jacqueline Anderson five days earlier. She ran her slick forearm across her forehead, pushing her damp hair off her brow and pushed to quicken her pace just enough to switch her attention.

It didn't work for long.

"I've got a job for you."

"I'm closing communications now."

"Don't you even want to hear what the job is?"

"Nope."

"Too bad," Jackie had managed to slip in before Jenifer turned the vid-com off. *"This job would probably really piss off the Xenos you've been chasing down there. How many of your Barrio Rats did they kill with that fragment bomb last month?"*

She'd almost regretted shutting down the channel at that point, but only because Jackie Anderson was the closest thing Jenifer had to a friend. It had nothing to do with Jackie's off-handed attempt at goading her into caring.

Jenifer ignored the replay of the conversation looping in her head until she finished her run and returned to the tiny, sweltering room she'd bunked in for the last three months. In the silence of the room, with nothing to distract her but the heat and the noises outside as the slums came to life again with the setting of the sun, she found it harder to keep the question at bay.

"Don't you even want to hear what the job is? How many of your Barrio Rats did they kill with that fragment bomb last month?"

She was in the street, headed for the only establishment in Slum City where she could get a drink. The place didn't even have a name. Since it was the only bar in town, it didn't need one. Anyone who wanted hard liquor, and had means to pay for it, knew where this place was. Where the alcohol came from, she didn't know and didn't care.

The interior was dark, as usual, and only moderately cooler than outside. Fifty-year-old ceiling fans rotated the air with whining engines and at least one had a broken blade, making the whole mechanism knock out of balance. The air stank of stale liquor, mold, ancient cigarette smoke, and body odor, but she wasn't there for the ambiance.

"Wondered when you'd drag your skinny ass in here," the big black man behind the counter boomed when she sat down at the bar. She didn't know his name, and he didn't know hers. "Usual?"

"Yeah, and don't try giving me the cheap crap you keep on the shelf. I want the bottle under the counter."

He didn't argue, slamming a double shot glass on the counter, filling it with tequila from a bottle he took from behind the counter, not from the shelves behind him.

"Leave it."

"It'll cost you."

"More than I paid up front?" she asked with a quirk of her eyebrow. When he didn't answer, but shrugged as he moved down the counter, she picked up the shot glass and slammed back the liquor.

It was nasty, and burned all the way down, but she knew it was better than the swill he kept out for the usual barflies. The alcohol landed in her gut like a ball of acid. She debated about eating one of the nutrition bars in her jacket pocket, but she only had half a dozen, and she needed to stop by Teresa's shack to drop them off. Six nutrition bars could feed the four children in the house for at least a day or two.

She took out one of the bars, flipping it in her fingers. The packaging was non-descript, listing only the required nutritional information. Typical of military-issue foodstuff. Fresh food was hard to come by, and without manufacturing plants and farms, even processed food was more than likely available only through the black market.

Her stomach rumbled, but in the end, she put the bar back in her pocket.

"I thought you learned after Beirut not to drink on an empty stomach."

Jenifer didn't turn at the voice she recognized immediately, schooling her response by pouring two fingers of tequila into her glass. She set the bottle down with a thump.

"I still drank you under the table," she said without turning.

Jackie Anderson climbed onto the stool beside her, resting her bare arm on the sticky counter. She tossed on the counter a similarly packaged nutrition bar to the one Jenifer had just put back in her pocket. Jenifer eyed the bar, and before she could refuse it, her stomach grumbled once again. Jackie just grinned, and the familiar smile released some of the tension in Jenifer's shoulders.

She smirked back, mumbled, "Go to hell," and tore open the bar. It tasted like honey-coated cardboard, but it filled the hole.

Jenifer watched Jackie from the corner of her eye, studying to see if there were any big changes since the last time they saw each other—had to be at least eight months or more. She looked the same for the most part with her long, dark hair and olive skin. Looked like she'd thinned down and muscled up a little, her exposed arms had more definition and her features were just a little sharper. The biggest difference was in her eyes. They were shadowed, hiding something very different from the near-sparking eyes Jenifer had seen last time. Course, last time, Jackie wasn't alone. She'd had a good-looking man beside her and of all things, a baby in her arms. Something Jenifer never would have bet on a year earlier. Not Jackie Anderson—dedicated soldier—with a steady man and raising a kid.

She'd told her as much.

"Must be a hell of a job for you to leave your posh digs in Alexandria to hunt me down here in the armpit of the southern hemisphere," she mumbled around the food in her cheek. "Your boy toy with you?"

The tightening around Jackie's eyes was almost unnoticeable except Jenifer knew her, and knew how to read her well. "I wouldn't have contacted you if I didn't think you're the best person for the job."

Jenifer motioned to the bartender, tapping her glass, and he came back only long enough to set an empty one in front of Jackie. Pouring out the liquor, Jenifer turned on the stool to face her friend. "Fine. You've got me interested. But I'm not making any promises."

Jackie ignored the tequila and took her PAC from her belt. Setting it on the bar, she turned it on. "I'm guessing you don't get the newscasts down here."

Jenifer chuckled, and poured another shot. They were lucky to have things like running water and a meal a day, forget the past comforts like interior climate control, warm baths, hot food, toilet facilities, and

WorldCom broadcasts. Brasilia was one of the worst slums left on the planet. Three hundred square miles of coastline had been destroyed when the Sorracchi blew up Rio de Janeiro, and refugees who had managed to survive migrated to what had once been the beautiful, prospering capitol city. The city itself had been shaken to its foundations and several buildings had been reduced to rubble. The destruction was nearly as complete as the devastation left behind on the island of Japan forty-three years earlier.

"This was six days ago," Jackie explained, turning the PAC so Jenifer could see.

The screen lit up, and a blond woman stood facing the camera, a small microphone pinned to her lapel. Behind her was a flight of stone stairs leading up to wooden double doors, a Firebird on each side standing at attention, one a man and the other a woman. A flag hung on each side of the door, one representing the planet of Aretu, the other the Council of Seven governing body on Raxo.

To the left and behind the reporter was a group of people holding up signs with messages ranging from "Get off Earth!" and "Go Home!" to "Don't make us fight your war!" and various other colorful words of advice. To her right was a group of women, none of which held any signs, but watched the embassy doorway with rapt attention.

"This is Allison Wetherly reporting from the joint Umani and Areth embassy, waiting for Ambassador John Smith of Aretu to emerge. He had a closed-door meeting today with the Presidential Council for Planetary Reconstruction to discuss the type and quantity of aid the Aretu government by way of the Defense Alliance, the coalition of galactic races of which both Aretu and Raxo are considered super powers, would provide Earth. Sources within the embassy have reported—" She stopped and turned to look over her shoulder at the doors. "Here comes the ambassador."

The two soldiers pulled the door open, and Ambassador John Smith came out with a young boy walking beside him, holding his hand. The boy looked to be maybe eight, with dark brown skin and hair trimmed close to his scalp. He held the man's hand in both his, his cheek pressed against the man's sleeve.

Even though she knew Areth aged at a different rate than Humans, at first glance she'd put him at maybe forty, with the kinds of lines around his eyes that said he smiled a lot. He was lean, which accentuated his cheekbones and the sharp line of his jaw. His hair, which was long enough to catch in the breeze without getting in his face, was a non-descript brown. His eyes . . . his eyes were a pale cornflower blue and were by far his most prominent feature. John Smith wasn't a gorgeous man—not by any standard she held, now or at any other time. And yet the women at the base of the stairs immediately screamed his name and reached for him. Jenifer thought she even heard one yell something about having his half-alien baby.

The reporter, along with several other news personnel gathered at the bottom of the steps, shouted the ambassador's name and various questions about his meeting, most of the words lost in the frenzy.

The two soldiers escorted the ambassador and his son. Jenifer knew the story of the boy. It had been widely reported after the war when Smith was named Ambassador to Earth by Queen Bryony of Aretu. The ambassador had been in Chicago—a solitary scout soldier sent by Aretu —when the Sorracchi first attacked, and the boy had been left an orphan. He'd, in essence, adopted the boy as his own, even though he was alien and the boy was Human.

The group of four reached the bottom of the stairs where a hovercar waited. The ambassador spoke briefly to the crowd, stating with a pleasant smile he didn't wish to comment on the meeting until everything was complete. But, Jenifer didn't care about his statement as much as she cared about the group of women behind him. One woman stood out in particular, with mid-length brown hair, golden hazel eyes and fine, exotic features. She stood back from the barricade, much calmer and more subdued than the other females.

"They're missing her," she mumbled. A cold ball sank into her gut, and she wondered if she had somehow missed the breaking news the Ambassador to Aretu was dead. If the Firebird didn't turn around and see the woman . . .

The male Firebird opened the door, speaking with the ambassador, when his attention shifted past Smith to the crowd of women. Jenifer recognized the immediate change in the soldier. His entire body tensed and drew to attention and he shouted something, shoving the ambassador and his son toward the car.

Despite herself, Jenifer held her breath.

The ambassador got his son inside, and just as he moved through the open door himself, the soldier pushed him hard—shouting something. The screen lit up with white light, blocking the image. Jenifer squinted, trying to make out anything past the flash bomb.

The scream of the reporter, so close to the camera, echoed over the shouts and explosions no one could see. The camera tilted and bounced on the ground, a bloody hand falling into the shot. She assumed it was the unlucky cameraman.

The image cleared a second later. Everything was tilted at an angle as the camera filmed the carnage. Boots ran past and the shouts of Firebirds mingled with more screams and the sound of pulse charge weapons. The hovercraft was on the other side of the street on its side, with what should have been the top making a sizeable dent in the building that had stopped its tumble. Bodies littered the street, mostly Firebirds. One body burned with three-foot high flames and two Firebirds ran to extinguish the flames while others fired their pulse weapons after someone off screen.

Jenifer couldn't look away, even though she wanted to. Her memories of the month before came back like the remnants of a vivid dream: the stench of blood and explosives in the air, the screams of Maria Hernandez as she cried over the limp body of her seven year old son, and little Jessie Alejandro kneeling beside her sister. Their parents had been killed during the first attacks of the war, leaving fourteen-year-old Jessie to be sister, mother, and father to Terese. Now, Jessie was just Jessie alone. She hadn't spoken since the day of the Xenos' bombing.

The Firebird who had pushed the ambassador and his son into the car lay on the ground, his face turned into the scorched pavement. The female who had worked the detail with him knelt beside him and tried to turn him over, shouting for help. Her voice was lost in the chaos, but Jenifer saw the words on her lips.

The pulse fire and explosions stopped, but the screaming didn't lessen. Somewhere off screen but near the camera, she heard the cries of a little girl calling frantically for her mother. In the distance, the sirens of approaching emergency hovers grew stronger as they raced to the scene. Two Firebirds climbed onto the smoking, scorched hovercar and pulled the door open, helping the ambassador climb from the wreckage.

His son clung to him, skinny arms and legs wrapped around his father with his face buried against the man's shoulder. Blood soaked into the ambassador's sweater, but he didn't release his hold on the boy.

The footage continued to play as the camera lay forgotten on the road, and as much as Jenifer wanted to ask why Jackie made her watch, she couldn't turn her attention away long enough. She scanned the crowd as much as the camera picked up, and finally saw what she looked for. The brunette woman she had spotted just before the explosion stood near an alley in the distance, a pulse weapon braced against the crook of her elbow. She fired no shots, which would draw attention to herself, but she watched the destruction unfold.

When she took a step back and disappeared into the dark alley, Jenifer shifted her focus to watch the way the tableau played out. The emergency vehicles arrived, and medics worked to load the injured Firebirds, treating them as best they could. She sought out and found the ambassador as a medic took his son from his arms, and even at the strange angle, the intense mix of anger and panic on his face was undeniable.

But then his attention shifted, and Jenifer leaned in, trying to see what it was he saw. He said something to the medic as they led his boy into the emergency vehicle, and then jogged away. Jenifer cursed the fact the camera was immobile and she couldn't just shift it to see what she needed to see. To see what could have pulled him away from his son.

Then he came back, carrying a little girl no more than five or six years old against his chest. Her blond hair was bloody and her clothes were torn. At first the medic shook his head, and she tried to read the words on his lips.

"We need to get you and your son to the hospital, Ambassador."

The ambassador shook his head, and even with the strange angle Jenifer had of his profile, she saw him shout at the medic. With no further argument, the ambassador climbed into the ambulance with the little girl still in his arms. Then the screen went black when Jackie turned off the PAC.

Jenifer released a metered breath and leaned back in the chair, crossing her arms over her body. Her head felt a little heavy, the effects of the shots settling in, but she was a long way from being drunk. *Too bad.*

"Okay, so a bombing. They happen every day around here. Why did you show me?"

"You saw her."

"Who? The brunette in the back who threw the first grenade? Of course I did. She should have had a mortar pulse in her head, would've solved everyone's problem."

"Exactly." Jackie clipped the PAC back to her waist. "We need someone who knows what to look for. Our Firebirds are the best soldiers there are, but they don't know what to look for to do their job."

"Which is?"

Jackie looked at her now, her expression infallible. "To keep Ambassador John Smith alive."

Jenifer shook her head and slid off the stool. "I'm done, Jacks. I did my part."

"There's still a lot needing to be done," Jackie called after her. "John is beginning a planetary tour in two weeks to recognize—"

"And someone else can do it."

She shouted the words as she pushed through the bar door into the humid night, squinting in the sudden darkness. As she crossed the street, little Elise—who only went by Elise because no one was sure of her last name—ran up to Jenifer with a toothy grin, dragging her brother behind her. Both of them held a half-eaten nutrition bar in their free hands.

"*Olhe o que nós começ!*" Elise squealed, throwing her far-too-skinny arms around Jenifer's hip. "See? Look!"

"Where did you get the bar?" she asked, crouching down to look the two directly in the face when Elise let her go.

"The soldiers gave them to us. They said they were from President Nick."

Jenifer straightened slowly and looked back to the door where Jackie stood, her shoulder against the rough jamb. Clenching her teeth, she stormed back. "You wasted your time with the bribe, Jacks. I said no."

Jackie shrugged. "What? You think we're taking them back because you said no?" She looked past Jenifer to the kids as they ran off. "We're also unloading clothes, medical supplies, and water filtration systems. In fact," she turned back to Jenifer, "Nick didn't even know you were down here. I just told him I was going along for the ride. Some of the men unloading are my trainees. We're doing a tour of Central and South America, leaving supplies from Mexico City to Bahia Blanca."

"Don't bother stopping in Buenos Aires. The tourist draw isn't what it used to be."

A "thank you" was probably the appropriate response, but Jenifer couldn't seem to force the words out. Jackie's only response to her snark was a small, amused smile. After staring at each other for several moments, Jackie stepped away from the door.

"It was good to see you," she said as if the previous conversation never happened. "Don't be a stranger."

CHAPTER FOUR

"*S*he's hard to figure out, Nick. Before the war, she would have been all over this job. I can't read her now."

Jackie stood in the apartment's small common area, arms crossed over her body, talking to Nick through the vidscreen on the wall. Nick ran a hand over his short-cropped hair, and even though Michael wore his much longer, the action of the father made her think of the son. "Okay. We'll work something out."

"I have some other suggestions, but she was the best option for the situation. Maybe one of the candidates I thought of for the Umani ambassador can be assigned to John."

"Give the list to me when you get here." The lines around his eyes pinched, yet another expression she recognized. "I wish you'd reconsider."

"I've considered it, and reconsidered it." She stepped closer to the wall. "It's fine, Nick. Really. I just . . ." She shook her head and looked around the simple, utilitarian apartment. "I need a change of scenery."

Nick huffed. "I promised Caitlin I'd try." He grinned, and she knew the heavy conversation was over. It wasn't the first time he'd tried to talk her out of going to Aretu. Both he and Caitlin had tried when Jackie dropped off Nicole and her things. She figured he might try one more time before she left, and in truth she didn't mind. Meant he gave a damn. "I'll see you in an hour."

The vidscreen went black and Jackie headed for the larger of the two bedrooms to finish packing for the trip with Silas Smith. Her rucksack sat open on the bed, waiting for the few final items she'd gathered. Her years of traveling—going where she needed to go to do whatever she needed to do—had taught her to pack light and tight, so the military-issue rucksack was more than sufficient to pack up everything she'd need for the next few months. She knew she would need to buy Areth-appropriate clothing once she was on the ship to reduce her visibility.

In a couple months, none of the clothing in the rucksack would fit anyway.

Her small bag was a sharp contrast to packing for Nicole's stay with her grandparents while Jackie was gone. Two bags of clothes for every possible change in weather, another bag of Nicole's favorite toys and the crocheted afghan she'd slept with every night since her first Christmas—even making the trip from Tennessee to space and back again. Jackie swallowed hard, refusing to allow herself to acknowledge the black hole eating its way out from the center of her chest. She thought she'd never have to feel this kind of emptiness again, not once Michael came back to her alive, if not quite whole. She'd thought when Michael asked her to never leave him, the promise went both ways.

She shoved the last of her necessities into the bag just as the door chime echoed through the quiet apartment. Jackie swiped at her cheeks, pulled the top string closing the bag, and tossed it on the couch as she passed, heading for the door. The chime sounded again half a dozen short buzzes as the ringer leaned on the button repeatedly.

"I'm coming!" she shouted. She yanked the door open. "What's the big emergency . . ." She trailed off, but quickly recovered from her surprise to lean into the doorjamb with her arms crossed. "Damn. Never expected you to show up at my door."

Jenifer pushed past her into the apartment. "Not going to invite me in?"

With a shake of her head, Jackie shut the door. "Considering the pathetic state of commercial traffic, I'm pretty damn impressed you made it from South America to Alexandria in two days."

Her guest shrugged and sat on the back of the couch, looking around the apartment. "Yeah, well, I'm not without my contacts. Nice digs. This the kind of set up you get when the president's your kid's grandpa?"

"This is military housing." Jackie tried not to clench her teeth at the dig. She figured Jenifer deserved to get a few in, given the machinations she'd attempted to get the woman to come back to Alexandria. "Everyone in this building serves in the military in some capacity."

"I would have thought the president's son would get better than the grunts."

"We're fine here." The *we* grated on her, but she didn't let it show. "Did you want something, or were you just in the neighborhood?" She wanted to ask outright. *Did you change your mind?*

Jenifer stood and walked to the small antique hall cabinet Michael had salvaged from a destroyed house on the outskirts of the city on one of his explorations. The apartments came furnished with whatever pieces of furniture could be gathered, and so furniture tended to be very eclectic. Their bed wasn't one they chose, but it served the purpose. Nicole's crib was the same crib she had slept in after she was born in Tennessee. The couch was threadbare, and the small table in the kitchen was scarred with one leg was slightly shorter than the others, leveled out by a small piece of shim. But the cabinet was theirs. He'd spent three weeks stripping it down by hand, sanding away the scars and damage, and refinishing it to a chestnut shine.

Three picture frames were displayed on the top, because photos were luxuries and they had only managed those few. One was from Nicole's first birthday just six months before, and the entire Tanner clan had sat for the photo while Grandpa Nick held the cake-and-frosting covered toddler. Michael and Jackie stood behind Nick and Caitlin, smiling into the camera. Michael had his arm around her, holding her against him, while he leaned on his cane with the other.

The other was just Nicole, sitting on the grass at the Tanner cabin in Parson's Pointe, Maine. Short blond hair reflected the sunlight and, deep dimples dented her cheeks.

The third was at Nick Tanner's Inauguration as President of the

Protectorate. He wore a blue dress uniform from his days serving in Earth Force, with Caitlin standing on one side of him and Vice President Beverly Surimoto on the other with her husband Victor. Michael stood beside Caitlin, and Jackie stood beside Michael, holding the still tiny Nicole wrapped in a blanket.

"You sure as hell don't look like the woman who broke into that Sorracchi base in Florida a couple years back."

Jackie noted Jenifer didn't mention the reason for mission—to pull out Elijah Kerrigan. She could throw back digs with the best of them, but she refused to be cruel.

"Don't let appearances fool you, Jenifer. You should know by now."

Jenifer turned on her heels, making a show of glancing through the doorways off the living space to the bedrooms and the one bathroom. "So, where are they?"

"Not here. What do you need, Jenifer? You made it pretty clear the other day—"

"What happened to the little girl?"

Jenifer cut her off with the question, and brought her attention back to Jackie, all joking and kidding gone from her expression. Jackie squinted, shaking her head. "Nicole?"

"The little girl in the video."

It took Jackie a second to switch gears in her head, but when she realized what Jenifer meant, she drew in a slow breath. "She'll live. Lost a lot of blood, she was hit with debris. It was touch and go through most of the first night, but she'll be fine."

"One of the lucky ones."

Jackie shrugged a shoulder. "Maybe. She wouldn't have had a chance if she'd gotten to the hospital any later."

"What about her family?"

"All died."

"What happens to her now?" Jenifer's questions came rapid-fire, but her expression never gave away anything more than mild interest in the answers.

"I don't know exactly." Jenifer's lips pulled tight and her jaw shifted, but Jackie kept talking. "I know it doesn't seem this way where you're coming from, but Nick is working his ass off to take care of everyone. She won't wind up on the street. He's working with both off-world ambassadors to get the resources—"

"I'll do it."

Jackie walked past her and retrieved the rucksack from the couch. She didn't care what changed Jenifer's mind, and she wasn't about to question it. "Good. I was just on my way to meet up with Nick and the ambassador."

Jenifer followed her out of the apartment and picked up a ragged, worn pack from the hall as Jackie locked the apartment door. But, as Jackie punched in the final digit for the lock mechanism, her chest tightened and she swallowed hard against the choking lump in her throat. Up until that moment she'd managed to ignore the hollow pit in her chest and the burning tears behind her eyes, waiting for her to reach her breaking point.

"Forget something?" Jenifer asked, standing behind her.

"Yeah," she choked and re-entered the code. The lock disengaged and she shoved the door, pulling her rucksack open as she went for the photos. She only grabbed the one from Nicole's birthday, holding it briefly to her chest before shoving it in the bag between her extra sweater and her tee shirts.

Blinking fast against the tears, she yanked open the top drawer of the desk and found a pad of paper and pen. With a shaking hand, she wrote *I'll be back* and leaned the pad against the photograph of Nick's Inauguration.

Jenifer still stood in the hall when Jackie pulled the door shut again, locking it for the second time.

"Everything okay?"

"Yep," she managed to say without having to clear her throat. "Let's go. I've got a transport waiting for me."

"No, Papa! Please! I don't wanna go!"

Silas' cries were muffled against John's shoulder, and hot

tears soaked into his shirt. He crouched on the floor of the transport station, his son wrapped in his arms, stroking the boy's hair.

"I know, son," he said softly, trying to keep his voice steady and sure as he felt the sobs shake the boy's body. "I don't want you to go, but you have to."

"I'll be good, I promise."

John gripped the boy's shoulders and forced him away from his chest, looking Silas in the eyes. Tears streaked his cheeks, and he sniffed loudly through his runny nose, another sob shaking him.

"Oh, Silas. You're a good boy. A very good boy. I'm no' sendin' you to Aretu because you've been bad."

"I want to stay with you."

John stroked his thumb across Silas' cheek, and leaned up to kiss his forehead. "I want you to stay with me. But, more than that, I want you to be safe."

Silas just sniffled and nodded, but his grip on John's shirtsleeve didn't lessen. Beyond Silas, John caught movement as Nick entered the bay, trailed by his security team. He rose, but kept Silas close to his side, holding the boy's hand.

"Jackie is here and will be down in two," Nick said when he reached them. "I've got something to talk to you about." He twirled his finger toward the waiting ship. "After."

Silas turned into John, burying his face against John's stomach with arms wrapped around his hips as far as they would reach. John laid his hand on Silas' shoulder, and squeezed gently.

"Somethin' wrong?"

"No, no. Just a change in plans."

The crew of the *Constellation* worked to load the final crates and boxes into the cargo bay to make the two-month trip back to Aretu, and the sound of their work echoed through the large building. Nick waved his hand at John and Silas, silently indicating he would give them some more time, and walked away to talk with Kendrick Devlin, the captain of the *Constellation*. Once again, John crouched down to look his son in the eyes.

"You remember goin' to Aretu with me." Silas nodded, using the back of his hand to wipe his nose. John reached into his pocket and pulled out a handkerchief, and Silas scrubbed clumsily at his face with it. "And you remember visitin' with your Aunt Bryony and Uncle Conrad at the palace. And playin' with Aubrianna."

Silas sniffed loudly. "Yes," he mumbled.

"Your uncle and aunt have promised to take care of you until I can come for you. I know they love you." He smiled widely. "Nearly as much as I do."

The tears had stopped, leaving behind wet cheeks and swollen eyes. Silas nodded and fell into John's arms again. This time when John stood, he lifted the boy with him. Silas wrapped his arms around John's neck and his legs around his body, his face pressed to John's shoulder.

Only then did John notice Jackie standing several feet away, watching him with a sad but guarded expression.

"Look, Silas," he said, stepping toward her. "Jackie is here. You remember Jackie?"

She laid her hand on Silas' back, and he raised his head, looking over his shoulder at her as he nodded. Jackie smiled, and the sadness she'd allowed John to see for brief moment was gone. Silas smiled back, but didn't loosen his hold.

*J*ohn Smith was a confident man.

He looked people straight in the eyes when he spoke to them. He stood straight and tall, even though he held a clinging young boy in his arms. Jenifer would bet anyone the man didn't know how to give a weak handshake.

When he spoke with Jackie, his attention was on her and not on other things happening around the dock. Even though he listened to her, he never stopped stroking and comforting his son, focused equally on the boy.

Only once did she see his attention waver—when his head turned slightly in her direction and his ministrations for the boy stopped. Jackie stopped talking, too, following his gaze to the dark area where Jenifer stood. Jenifer saw the questioning "What?" on Jackie's lips.

She stepped back further into the shadows, pressing her back against the wall. Moments passed, and he finally turned away but his features were tense.

He was obviously also an observant man. Jenifer gave him credit for suspecting her presence. Paid assassins had missed her not ten feet from them, and it was usually the last thing they ever missed.

President Tanner returned from speaking with the ship's captain, and both John and Jackie turned in his direction. The hitch of his thumb over his shoulder as he spoke indicated the ship was ready to depart. The *Constellation* was a massive, bulky craft lacking the sleekness of a cruiser or battle craft. Of Defense Alliance design, it was built to carry freight and a competent compliment, but not a luxury ship. It would get Jackie and the boy off Earth, but it was the slow boat to Areth. She'd seen these ships before from a distance, but never this close. It was half again the length of a football stadium and filled the air harbor bay, hovering above the metal floor anchored by the exit and entrance ramp twenty feet wide. The four people walked toward the craft, and from her spot in the shadows, Jenifer saw the boy's arms tighten around his father's shoulders.

While they were inside the craft, Jenifer took the opportunity to study the building. There were security gaps all over the damn place. Once she and Jackie arrived, Jackie had left her to meet with President Tanner with the intent they would catch up with Jenifer later. Left alone, Jenifer had freely moved through the facility without being questioned. If a Xeno— or a group of Xenos for that matter—made it inside the building and past security somehow, no one would question them. They could walk into the bay right now and kill both President Tanner *and* Ambassador Smith.

Here she was, not fifty yards from the President of the Protectorate— aka President of The Whole Freakin' Planet—and the two guards at the door had no idea she was there. She'd walked through a service door on the upper level catwalk wrapped around the entire bay and taken a set of stairs down to the main level. No one so much as blinked.

The *Constellation's* engines shifted from hover to preparation for flight, humming to life, no more than a low buzz in the air indicative of the superiority of Areth workmanship. Walking side-by-side, President Tanner and Ambassador Smith came down the ramp leading from the ship, the president resting his hand on Smith's shoulder. On the way to the dock, Jackie had filled Jenifer in on the trip. The ambassador feared for his adopted son's life, and rather than risk it any further, he was sending the boy away to Aretu to stay with his family. Who—lucky kid—turned out to be the Queen of the Areth and her prince consort, Smith's brother.

Must be a tough life.

Of course, her childhood hadn't exactly been the slums. But, frilly pillows and even frillier dresses didn't mean life was great and grand. She knew that for a cold, hard fact.

The president patted Smith's shoulder as the boarding ramp disappeared into the ship and the docking clamps released. Over their head, the roof peeled back to allow the ship to rise straight up. President Tanner left the ambassador alone in the center of the bay, meeting up with his security staff at the door. One went with the president, the other remaining behind to wait for the ambassador.

Smith moved back from the center of the bay, moving clear of the low-energy propulsion waves. His head tipped back as he watched the ship leave, his shoulders dropping. With a subtle ripple through the air as the engines engaged, the *Constellation* rose into the atmosphere and disappeared from sight.

The roof folded back in to block out the sun. As soon as the roof closed, and the hydraulics hissed back into place, the ambassador's head tipped forward and he crumpled—no other word came to mind for what she saw. He folded in on himself, his head held in his hands, and his arms on his bent knees as his shoulders shook.

She was supposed to meet up with the president again, but seeing the ambassador's silent grief stopped her. People gave more away when they thought no one was watching, especially in their grief.

Jenifer took a step forward, stopping at the edge of the shadow so she was still hidden, and watched. Of course, he knew he wasn't alone. The security guard was at the door, but even the guard had turned away to allow him a few minutes. She wondered if what she saw was the true measure of the man, or whether like most politicians, every action—every glance—every word—was a performance for any eyes that might see.

She didn't believe altruistic people really existed. Everyone had an agenda. Everyone wanted what they could get out of whatever they did.

No one did anything just to be kind, just to help, just because it was right.

John Smith had a long way to go before he convinced her otherwise.

He stayed in position for several minutes, only the occasional muffled sound of his weeping reaching her in her dark corner. Finally his shoulders relaxed and he raised his head. The echo of his heavy sigh whispered through the empty bay and he rose, scrubbing his palms over his face. One quick rake of his fingers through his hair, and he walked to the exit door.

CHAPTER FIVE

6 May 2052, Monday
The Day of Destruction
Harrison Park, near the Rush University Medical Center
University of Illinois at Chicago
Former United States of America

"John! John Smith!"

John pivoted toward the sound of his name as it carried through the small park. The brisk spring breeze he had kept to his back as he walked hit him in the face, lifting his hair away from his forehead. He smiled to see Chloe Founder waving at him from the trail fifteen yards away, and raised his hand to wave back.

She jogged toward him, pulling a small boy along with her. John guessed he was no older than five, perhaps six. Eyes as dark as his mother's seemed to blend into his equally rich skin. He smiled as he ran on short legs beside Chloe, and his toothy grin made his cheeks dimple.

Chloe reached John, her breath curling slightly in front of her face. "What a nice surprise," she said, near breathless. "Seeing you on our day off. Do you live near the university?"

He nodded, tilting his head to the area south of the park. "I've got a flat just over there."

"Oh, this is my son Silas." Chloe rubbed her hand over the boy's hat, shifting it on his head and he grinned up at John.

"I'm five," Silas declared, holding up a hand, and John could only assume by the way the mitten was stretched out the boy presented all five fingers.

"Hello, Five." He looked at Chloe, making a puzzled face. "I thought you said his name was Silas?"

"It is," Silas declared, laughing behind his hand.

John looked down at him again. "Well, which is it, Silas or Five?"

Silas laughed harder, and Chloe chuckled along with him, smiling brightly. "My name is Silas. I'm five years old."

"Well, glad to get that straight. Hello, Silas. I'm John."

"John and I work together at the medical center," Chloe said down to her son, but he seemed far from interested. Instead, he looked past John to a red-painted swing set positioned just off the walking path. "Go on. Play for a bit before we go home."

Silas was gone like a shot, immediately wiggling his way into one of the low-hung swings. John chuckled, tucking his hands into his pockets against the cold. He and Chloe had shared conversation over cups of coffee more than once in the break room of the medical center, so it felt natural to walk to a bench with her and sit while her son played on the swings.

"I didn't know you had a son," he said as they sat, tipping his head toward Silas. "Is he your only?"

Chloe nodded, smiling at something the boy did outside John's line of vision. But, before she could speak a thundering sound boomed over their heads, and the air vibrated, pounding against his chest like the beat of a massive drum. John shot to his feet, looking up to the cloudy sky to see five single-man ships shoot across the sky.

John's skin prickled and the hair on the back of his neck stood on end.

Death Bringers.

Chloe stood with him, tipping her head back with her hand shielding her eyes, watching the sky just as he had. "What is it? What were they? Earth Force ships? Why would they be flying so close to the ground around here?"

John kept his attention on the sky, but gripped Chloe's arm, moving in the direction the gliders had come from. "Come on. Silas!" he called to the boy, motioning he join them. "Come here!"

The boy had jumped off the swing, but stood at the edge of the sand, staring at John and his mother with wide eyes.

"What is it? John, *what is it?*" Chloe demanded.

"The end of the world as you know it. Come on," he insisted this time, pulling Chloe along with him as he swept Silas off the ground, carrying him with his other arm. "We've got to find shelter." *Maybe . . . if they could reach his ship. It was designed for atmospheric re-entry, it might withstand—*

The ground shook, and the three of them tumbled together onto the concrete pavement and another explosive boom ricocheted around them. John flipped onto his back to see what had once been downtown Chicago burst into a massive ball of red-hot light. Chloe screamed, pulling Silas against her, and John rolled to cover both of them as much as he could from the wave of heat rippling out from the destruction.

Sandwiched between them, Silas cried, screaming "Mama!" over and over again. Sweat broke out over John's body and his chest burned as all oxygen sucked from the air. All around him, he heard screams.

They've finally shown their true face.

After what seemed an eternity, John sucked in air that didn't scorch his lungs and lifted his head. Looking to the west, nothing seemed unusual. Buildings still stood, trees still held their roots. Then he looked over his shoulder. A black, rolling cloud billowed into the sky and the air smelled scorched, tangy with residual pulse charge ions on a massive scale. Through the cloud shot the Death Bringers, heading back toward Harrison Park, and John scrambled to his feet, pulling Chloe and Silas with him.

"Run!"

"*J*ohn!"

John blinked and looked to his right, where Nick stood outside the hovercar holding open the door. His shoulders were drawn up to shield his neck from the icy snow now blowing across the Alexandria streets, and his eyes were pinched at the corners as he stared into the car.

Without saying anything, John opened his door and climbed from the car. The air was raw and biting, stinging his cheeks, and he matched Nick's hunched stance to defend against the cold. This first winter since the war had been especially brutal after the loss of the WeatherNet that had once controlled the entire globe. With the ecological damage of having several cities and portions of landmasses destroyed, every bit of weather was extreme and often close to deadly.

"You okay?" Nick asked as he joined John to walk into the United Protectorate. He pulled a face and tipped his head back and forth. "Stupid question."

"No, I'm no'," John answered honestly, eating up the distance to the wide double doors ahead of them with long strides. He nodded, just a sharp jerk of his head toward the United Protectorate Capitol building. "But I will be."

If this Jenifer—her name being all he knew about the woman thus far —was half the woman she was depicted as, then this would be over soon and he would have his son back. Then and only then would he be okay.

*P*athetic.

   It was the only word that came to mind as Jenifer stood in the middle of the president's office, staring at his worn yet massive desk. Absolutely pathetic.

Not only had she beat the president and ambassador across town, but she'd managed to practically have the doors to the Robert J. Castleton Memorial Building – The Castle opened for her. Correction someone *had* opened the door for her. Granted, he was some schmuck carrying a toolbox and an armload of wood, so he probably had no clue who three-quarters of the people were in the building and wasn't about to guess if she belonged or not. All she had to do was smile, toss her hair and offer to hold the door for him.

And she was in.

The security measures for the building probably seemed sound to *someone*. Restrict entry to the building at the main entrances, issue security idents, scan for weapons and whatnot in the main lobby, etc. Theoretically, anyone who got *in*, and got past the main security checkpoints, belonged. Just like at the launch port. Once you were in, no one questioned you.

Except it was disgustingly easy to *get in*.

Jenifer sighed and walked around the desk to the chair, pushed back from when the president last stood. It was leather, and good sized, not surprising since Nick Tanner was a tall man and pretty solid in build. But the arms, and the seat along the edge, showed wear. Just like everything else on Earth, it had probably been scavenged from the wreckage of something else.

She dropped into it, and wheeled it closer to the desk. Stacks of notes and papers sat in the left corner with a cup of pens and pencils. A closed compact computer sat immediately in front of the chair, but it hummed softly to indicate it was on and waiting for use. Her fingers itched to open it, but she wasn't a fool. It was one thing to stroll into the Office of the President to prove a point, it was another thing entirely to start going through his papers and files.

The right side of the desk was crowded with a plethora of photographs in varying sizes. Some of them she recognized as the same ones Jackie Anderson had on display in her box of an apartment, but President Tanner had several others and Jenifer took the opportunity to study them before she had guests.

There were pictures of Nick Tanner with his son Michael. One looked like it had seen better days, creased and worn, with an image of Nick Tanner standing between Michael and First Lady Caitlin Montgomery-Tanner. Even in the photographs, Jenifer saw the shielded darkness in Michael Tanner's eyes she'd recognized the first time she met him. She didn't know all the details, all Jackie said was Michael had been through seven levels of hell, but Jenifer knew whatever had happened it left a deep dent.

Other than a photograph with President Tanner and his wife, arms wrapped around each with wide smiles on their faces, every other photograph was of Nicole Tanner, daughter to Michael Tanner and Jackie. Well, sort of. Jenifer wasn't quite sure how the whole set up worked. Michael had unofficially adopted the baby when she was a few days old after her birth mother died, and since he and Jackie were— whatever it was they were—they raised the girl together; whether that made Jackie the girl's mother was for them to sort out, not Jenifer.

She moved a frame out of the way to get a better look at the picture behind it, and she stopped. Nestled amongst the frames and pictures —*Oh, yes!*—was a jar of candy. Not nasty pink-and-white swirled hard peppermint stuff old people kept around, but multi-colored candy covered chocolate. *Mmmmmm.* She hadn't had chocolate in—*Damn, had it really been two years?* She chuckled and picked up the jar, inhaling deeply when she popped off the vacuum-sealed lid.

Her eyes nearly fluttered with the aroma.

Jenifer dumped half a dozen candies in her palm and tossed them back like a handful of pills, humming as she chewed. She leaned back in the chair, settling into the worn leather cushions, and propped her boots on the desk edge, following up with another handful.

The distinctive voice of President Tanner carried from the hall, growing louder as he neared the office. Instead of jumping free of the "Big Man's" chair, Jenifer just slouched lower, making herself even more comfortable as she popped another handful of sweets in her mouth.

"I don't know when she's getting here. Just let her in when—"

Jenifer swiveled the chair, shifting her feet on the desktop so she didn't have to sit up, and dumped more candies in her hand. The president stood in the doorway, his hand on the knob, staring at her with his lips slightly parted from his stalled speech. Beside him stood Ambassador Smith, one eyebrow cocked with interest. Another man she didn't know—but if she had to guess, she'd say some form of aide to the president—stared past Ambassador Smith's shoulder with wide eyes.

"Do I even *have* to say it?"

*J*ohn wasn't sure which of them—himself, Nick or Captain Phelps—was the most stunned to see the woman stretched out at Nick's desk. Completely unapologetic, she dropped the candies from her hand into her mouth, biting down with a crunch for emphasis, he was quite sure.

She brought her legs down from the edge of the desk, letting the chair tip forward. Each movement was smooth, graceful, and calculated as she set the jar on the desktop.

"It's a wonder you both weren't dead a long time ago."

"I'll call security—" Phelps began, but Nick's hand shot up, silencing him.

"Ever heard the phrase 'shutting the barn door after the cows got out,' Captain?" she said, while coming to her feet. She kept her hands flat on the desk, leaning forward with a sarcastic smirk. "Your *security* is a joke. I didn't even have to *work* at getting into the building, *let alone* your office, Mr. President."

Thus far, Jenifer—because there was really no doubt *this* woman was the expert Jackie had so adamantly recommended was Jenifer—was nothing like John had imagined. The description of her skills and qualifications had rendered a much different image; perhaps an Amazon or, at the least, a woman of broad shoulders, deep voice, and prominent Adam's apple.

Neither description fit this woman. She was tall, and that was the last comparison he would make between Jenifer and any Amazon. He had met and fought with many women in his career, and recognized in Jenifer the lean, powerful body of a soldier; or at the least, someone who *lived* as a soldier. Slightly longer than shoulder length dark hair framed her face at chin length, accentuating the refined lines of her features. Blue eyes—pale enough to almost be called grey—dared any of them to contradict her.

The most fascinating thing of all was he felt *nothing* from her. Even now, he was aware of Nick's surprise mingled with a touch of annoyance, and Captain Phelp's outright terror—probably fear of retribution for allowing this woman access to the president's office—but nothing from the woman leaning over Nick's desk, scolding him like an errant school boy.

"Security protocol is inadequate, pathetic, and weak. If we're gonna do this, we're gonna do it *my* way."

She punctuated her speech by falling back in the chair with just the smallest touch of a flourish, banging her boots onto the desk edge again.

Watching them all, she dumped the last few candies into her hand and held it out in a silent offer to share. When no one immediately took her up on it, she tossed them into her mouth with a self-satisfied smirk.

Silence settled in the room, and John shifted his attention from Nick to Jenifer, waiting to see who would break the silence. Finally, Nick took a step forward.

"Do you have *any idea* how *hard* it is to get that stuff?" he demanded with a boom.

To her credit, Jenifer just smiled wider. "Then I suggest we discuss security, so we can protect your black market contraband candy, Mr. President."

Very slowly, and very deliberately, Nick turned to face John and Captain Phelps, his smoldering gaze on the captain. "Go get Vice President Surimoto and Colonel Ebben. Apparently, *she's he-ere.*" He dragged the last word out with a singsong tone that did little to disguise his annoyance.

"Y-yes, sir." Phelps made a speedy departure, practically running back down the hall.

As if she'd decided her point was made, Jenifer came out of the chair and walked around to the front, sitting on the edge with her arms over her body and her ankles crossed. She watched him as she moved, her gaze never wavering from him. And he watched back. Nick rounded the desk in several long strides, swiping the empty jar up from where Jenifer had left it. He mumbled under his breath, but all John caught was something about Caitlin and how she was going to kill him.

John took a step toward Jenifer, extending his hand. "John Smith."

The fact he still had no *sense* of this woman both fascinated and frustrated John. Usually, if he concentrated on the person he spoke to, he could get a clear sense of them from the emotions they projected. The skill had proven useful as a soldier and especially in the first few months he lived in Chicago before the attacks, and had doubled in usefulness since taking on the title of ambassador. In all that time, he hadn't met a Human he could not get some type of sense from, even if to only some minor degree. Even those without *any* Talent could be sensed if he reached out far enough.

She looked down at his hand, and very purposefully unfolded her arms, leaning back a few degrees further to rest her palms on the desk top. Long, seeking fingers found a pen near her left hand and her fingers curled around it.

Sensory perception, or not, John understood body language as well as any properly trained soldier would. He didn't divert his gaze, but lowered his hand back to his side, sliding it into his pocket.

"I know who you are, Ambassador Smith." Her tone held a sardonic edge, and he could practically hear the unsaid scoff. *Do you think I'm an idiot?* "Need to know whose ass I'm protecting."

"Fair 'nough," he said with a nod. "Jenifer."

She said nothing, just stared back at him.

"Just Jenifer," he said, leaving the question open.

"Just Jenifer," she reiterated with the slightest nod.

He contemplated for a brief moment asking her if she was one of the few hundred known as the Emancipated, men and women who had been previously possessed by a Sorracchi consciousness but had been given back their own minds through Areth intervention. Some called them Husks. The derogatory term always made John clench his teeth because more often than not the people who used the phrase saw these people as less than human. Alien in their own way. They had been victims, only to waken often hundreds of years after their last memory in a world that didn't know how to accept them.

Because their memories were often nothing more than whispers, and in some cases, they woke from the separation procedure with no memory of themselves whatsoever, most of the Emancipated went only by a single name. No family, no surname except in the rare instance when information was still recalled. He thought perhaps because this gun-for-hire went by the simple name of Jenifer, she might be one of these individuals.

But, this Jenifer could not be an Emancipated, he realized. Jackie Anderson had told both he and Nick she had known Jenifer for many years, and they had fought together more than once in the Phoenix efforts prior to the war. It had only been *since* the war the process of dividing Sorracchi consciousnesses from their unwilling hosts—like removing a parasite—had begun in earnest.

"I don't know why you changed your mind," he said, trying a different approach. "But, thank you. The sooner this is resolved—"

"The sooner I can get the hell out of here," she cut off. "Look,

Ambassador, I *get* you want to make this a friendly little chat, but you're my job. I don't do sociable."

She pushed away from the desk and strode past him, dropping onto the office couch in a completely relaxed flounce, although he recognized the ready-for-action tension in her body. *Ever the fighter*. He glanced toward Nick, who still stood behind his desk. Nick cocked an eyebrow and shrugged a shoulder as if to say, "You got me, bud." Then he picked up the empty candy jar and scowled.

John had a passing thought perhaps it wasn't music that soothed the savage beast, it was chocolate.

CHAPTER SIX

*T*he only way to be prepared for any mission was to be informed. Not just about your enemies, but about those people in which you were expected to lay your trust. The people supposed to be your allies.

Jenifer remained silent in her spot as the office filled with people, studying each one. Even though she hadn't agreed to take on the job, she had spent the last two days researching the men and women she expected to have contact with.

Beginning with the president.

Nicholas Michael Tanner, age forty-nine, former Earth Force colonel. Retired at the age of forty-two. At the time of his retirement, he held the speed and accuracy records for wormhole navigation. A record he still held.

Nick Tanner had been married in his early twenties to a woman named Kathleen, who'd supposedly died giving birth to his son, Michael. Michael had also reportedly died. Two years earlier in '51, the child—now a man at twenty-five—was discovered to be alive in a Sorracchi facility in New Mexico where he had been kept as little more than a Human guinea pig. It was also discovered the woman who had birthed him was not dead, but was a Sorracchi scientist. Nick Tanner joined Phoenix to rescue his son.

Even before coming to Alexandria, and based on what she knew about the man, Jenifer had respected him. Which wasn't something she could say about most people, whether she'd met them or not. Jenifer was very, *very* good at reading people, and could tell almost instantly whether a person was trustworthy or not. She'd smoked out more than one friend-turned-enemy over the years, and it'd kept her alive more times than she could count. After Savannah, she had to be.

When President Nick Tanner walked in the door of the office, Jenifer knew this man could be trusted. The truth was in the eyes. She stared at him, and he stared right back. There was no hesitation, no doubt, and no deception. When she looked into his eyes, she immediately thought one thing: Nick Tanner would have her back.

She had expected to see Michael Tanner, but had learned after reaching Alexandria he was, for lack of a better term, MIA. All Jenifer was able to glean was Michael had left Alexandria unexpectedly approximately six weeks earlier, leaving Jackie with the kid. Although the people she spoke with knew of his departure, they knew very little about why, or where he actually went. He'd disappeared from his hospital room after recovering from surgery to repair an old injury. Jackie certainly hadn't offered any information, and Jenifer didn't push. Sounded way too personal for her to get involved.

Which was okay, she'd met Michael before. And while she knew immediately the man hid a world of darkness behind eyes almost identical to his father's, he was still a man who could be trusted.

As long as he trusted *you*, and in that Jenifer and Michael were very much alike. Her guess was trust didn't come easy for him, and she understood.

She hadn't met Caitlin Montgomery-Tanner, First Lady. But, the chances were fairly slim they would have any dealings since Mrs. Tanner worked more behind the political scenes. She had causes and committees, typical of a First Lady if Jenifer remembered her history lessons.

Nick still stood at his desk, looking more than just a little perturbed at the empty candy jar. She'd broken into his office, called his efforts at security pathetic, and eaten his candy, and as far as she could tell, he was angriest about the candy.

Okay, so . . . trust him, but don't mess with the man's candy. Got it.

John Smith had taken a seat at the far corner of the couch that faced where she sat, with one foot raised so his ankle rested on his other knee. For the moment, his eyes were closed and his chin tilted just slightly toward his chest. Thin lips pulled together and a deep 'v' dug into his forehead.

The information on him was sketchier and harder to come by. Jenifer supposed it was pretty easy to hide the skeletons in a closet if the closet was on another planet.

She knew he was considered old by Human standards, but for an Areth he was somewhere nearing middle age. His exact age, no one knew. He was a soldier by trade and sent to Earth close to three years earlier—before everything went FUBAR—to check things out for his government. When the Sorracchi ended their forty-year masquerade and turned on Humanity, he had been trapped on Earth, his ship destroyed. Phoenix found him by chance, but his discovery led to many revelations that ultimately helped keep the war swift and decisive.

Couldn't get much swifter than one-hundred-and-three hours from first attack by the combined Human/Umani/Areth fighter fleet to the unconditional surrender of all Sorracchi on Earth.

Well, all they could find.

Other than his familial link to the Areth royal family, not much was known. No other familial connections, no military history, no education, no training. He was a void.

Jenifer didn't like voids.

Especially if her job was *him*.

Oh, wait she *did* know something else about him. Apparently, he had become the poster boy for sex symbol on post-apocalyptic Earth. Sitting across from him, she looked him up and down. Okay, so he wasn't *un*attractive.

He opened his eyes and his gaze shifted up to lock with hers, his temple resting against his long index finger. Ambassador Smith stared, and she stared back. Jenifer wondered if he knew how easy he was to read. Fortunate for him, she liked what she saw. As far as whether he could be trusted or not, yeah, he could.

Problem was she got the distinct impression if he didn't like the way something was being done, he did it his own way. For a soldier, a good trait—see something needs to be done, and do it. Don't wait around for orders or approval or for some big wig somewhere to make the call.

That worked great on the battlefield, but not here. He wasn't a soldier anymore. As an ambassador, he didn't even carry a weapon. Supposedly, a Man of Peace shouldn't carry a pulse charge pistol, or some BS. Which meant he would have to rely on her to watch his back.

Trust and instinct were not always good bedfellows.

The office door opened and she looked past Ambassador Smith to the newcomer, Vice President Beverly Surimoto. She was petite and delicate, with golden red hair that hung down her back on corkscrew curls, held at her nape by a silver clip. Vice President Surimoto didn't walk into the room, she practically glided. And she sure as hell didn't strike fear into the heart of the enemy. Probably wouldn't strike fear into the heart of a puppy.

Jenifer didn't need to talk to the woman to know she didn't trust her.

Didn't matter if Nick Tanner, John Smith and *whoever else* was in charge of the planet thought she was perfect, the civilian balance against President Tanner's military background. The voice of reason.

In Jenifer's view, Beverly Surimoto consorted with the enemy. She didn't care the man Vice President Surimoto called her husband *wasn't* the enemy, it didn't matter he was Human—or as Human as a Husk could be—*now*. When Beverly Surimoto made Victor her lover, he was considered to be Sorracchi. Jenifer had heard the explanation that the overwrite of his consciousness as a Sorracchi had failed. And how he'd contributed to the quick end of the war.

Granted, one-hundred-and-three hours of fighting barely constituted a war, but after the way the Sorracchi had pummeled the planet before Humanity ever had a chance to fight back, the planet looked like it had gone through the apocalypse.

The point was, Beverly Surimoto had held a position of power within Phoenix. She had been second-in-command to General Robert Castleton, commander of next to the largest Phoenix covert bases. She was a leader, and she let her body overrule her head.

For that, Jenifer wouldn't trust her.

Colonel Phillip Ebben, Chief Security Advisor—aka Resident Schmuck—was the last to enter the room. After watching the video of the attempt on the ambassador's life, Jenifer had initially laid the blame on

Lieutenant Colonel Montgomery, the man in charge of the Firebirds protecting Ambassador Smith. But then she'd reconsidered. He may have been the man on duty, but he could only work with the resources provided to him. If the Head Schmuck was an idiot, then Montgomery probably was a man working blindfolded with one hand tied behind his back. He *did* see the woman, and he'd saved the ambassador's life. He wasn't *without* blame, but Jenifer didn't believe in passing the buck of blame, she believed in naming the idiot responsible.

Colonel Schmuck stood near the door with a sour expression on his sagging face, glowering in Jenifer's general direction.

Word must have gotten around about her coming on board.

Jenifer just stared back, purposefully crossing her legs and getting comfortable. *Get used to it, bub. I'm here for the duration.*

Ebben was nowhere near being on her short list of people she could trust.

Vice President Surimoto stood with the president near his desk, smiling widely as she spoke to him. Jenifer couldn't make out the words, but she heard the tone and cadence to the vice president's voice. Her tone was soft, some of her sounds slurred and rounded. Shortly after the war, she had been given her hearing by an Areth doctor, and had been learning to speak since then. Her hands still intuitively moved in the silent language she had previously used to communicate, although she kept the actions close to her body, serving more for reiteration than communication.

Although Jenifer had suspected as much, it was very clear, very quickly President Tanner wasn't a guy who relied on protocol. When everyone was inside the small office, he shut the door and went back to his desk. Instead of sitting behind it, he sat on it, shoving aside his computer to make room.

"Okay, so . . ." He clapped his hands together, rubbing them briskly before letting them dangle relaxed between his legs, his boot heels tapping the desk wood. "This was supposed to be a meeting about security on John and Ambassador Hyacinth."

Jenifer couldn't help her small smirk at the blatant mispronunciation of the Umani Ambassador's name. She'd practically choked herself the first time she tried to say it, and figured a guy would have to be pretty damn pretentious to insist people *only* use his full name—especially when his name was Drucillus Clodianus Hiacyntus.

Personally, she preferred just Claude.

"It still is, but with a change in plans." Nick motioned toward Jenifer.

Every set of eyes in the place turned to Jenifer, except for John Smith's. His stare hadn't shifted since he had looked up minutes before. Which was fine, he might as well get used to looking at her. She'd be there every time he turned around.

"From this point on, Jenifer is in charge of John. She runs the show."

Jenifer watched with amusement as Colonel Ebben's face turned a deep shade of magenta, but he said nothing. His lips turned down, chin jutting like a petulant child. Jenifer watched President Tanner's attention hold on Ebben for a few moments before his dark eyes slid away and he addressed the group as a whole.

"She's allowed wherever John is allowed, any meeting, any building, unless John makes the call otherwise." He looked between John and Jenifer. "And I assume she'll be traveling with the ambassador on the commemorative tour in a couple weeks. Any questions?"

She saw the question forming on Ebben's face, and he took a step away from the wall, but then the office door burst open and the nervous Captain Phelps stuck his head in through the opening. "Mr. President," he practically stuttered out. "I'm sorry, but—"

"What?" President Tanner demanded, already hopping from the desk and taking two strides toward the door. His tone wasn't one of anger for the intrusion, but of concern for what might have initiated it.

Vice President Surimoto and Ambassador Smith both got to their feet, moving toward the president and captain, and Ebben was near enough to the door one step brought him into the circle. Jenifer stood, but kept her distance. The small office let her hear everything anyway. An apprehensive chill danced over her skin, the tension in the room suddenly ramping up ten steps.

"There's been an incident, sir. We've received a communiqué from the Boston camps." The young man's attention shifted past the official leadership in the room, to briefly touch on Jenifer before he looked back to President Tanner.

"Speak!" President Tanner barked.

Phelps swallowed. "There's been an explosion, sir."

"In the tunnel?" Vice President Surimoto asked.

At the mention of a tunnel, Jenifer's gut went cold. She hadn't been to Boston since the war, and had only been there briefly after the attacks leveled most of the city. But, she knew the tunnel the Vice President mentioned. One and a half miles long, it connected South Boston to what had once been Logan Airport by going under Boston Harbor. Winters were cold in Virginia, and worse further north. It made sense to find shelter in a structure of size, but an explosion had to be bad news.

"Yes, ma'am," Captain Phelps finally confirmed. "Colonel Suarez reported an explosion near the kitchen facility within the tunnel massive enough to severely damage one of the tunnel walls. The structure integrity was compromised, and eventually collapsed."

Jenifer stumbled back a step, nearly choking. Something invisible but completely tangible shoved against her, pushed her back, and left her shaking inside. For a brief moment, she wanted to weep . . . no, it was more than that; she wanted to scream. Fighting for control, she drew a deep breath and forced herself to concentrate on the racing beat of her heart. She reached out behind her and found the arm of the couch, leaning on it until the urge disappeared just as quickly as it had hit her.

When she opened her eyes, she had to blink the four other people in the room into focus. Vice President Surimoto had paled, the same kind of devastating sorrow Jenifer had just felt obvious in her face. She breathed hard, clinging to President Tanner's arm in an apparent attempt to stay on her feet.

"How many got out?" President Tanner asked.

"Unknown, sir. Colonel Suarez is estimating they were able to evacuate approximately one-third of the population."

Vice President Surimoto pressed a hand to her chest, dropping her head forward. The President slowly closed his eyes and leaned his hand onto the corner of his desk. "Four thousand," he mumbled.

"I'm so sorry," Ambassador Smith whispered, barely audibly, and squeezed Vice President Surimoto's hand before he turned away from them, nearly stumbling back across the room to the fireplace. He braced his hands on the mantle with his head hung and his shoulders hunched. The grip he had on the smooth wood whitened his knuckles and his nails made a scraping sound as he curled his fingers into the wood.

Jenifer managed to push away from the couch and stepped forward, aware she was supposed to be silent in these meetings, but still needing to know. "Four thousand. Four thousand what? Four thousand they got out?"

President Tanner only shook his head.

Ambassador Smith was the one to look at her, his blue eyes moving slowly to connect with her. Tears shone there, and he made no move to wipe them away. "No." His voice was strained, his lips pulled tight so they barely moved when he spoke. "Four thousand trapped in the tunnel."

No one said it. It didn't have to be said. *Four thousand dead.*

The presidential homestead was in darkness by the time Nick's driver stopped in front and Nick wearily dragged himself from the backseat. He mumbled a "goodnight" and made his way inside, barely managing a nod to the two Firebirds standing security at the front door.

The house was small in comparison to homes provided to past presidents, both those who governed globally and the Presidents of the United States before the unification of the countries, but larger than anything Nick had ever lived in. He'd gone from military quarters as a young man, to military housing, to his cabin in Maine, and back to military quarters again in Colorado. A five bedroom, three-story house was overkill for just the two of them—soon to be three. But, it was in an isolated, rural area on a piece of property that could more easily be monitored—and if needed—defended. It wasn't his cabin, but it was home.

He shut the front door with a click of the lock and left his boots in the foyer, shuffling in stocking feet across the polished wood floor. Just inside the sitting room, he heard a soft whimper and went in to check on Dog. Nick had no idea how old Dog was since he'd been a full-grown mutt by the time he wandered onto the cabin porch years earlier. Since then, he'd gone from Maine to Colorado to Tennessee and finally Virginia, survived not one but two Sorracchi attacks, and taken a trip in space. Age had finally caught up with him. The fur around his muzzle and eyes had gone gray, and his step had lost its zing. Dog couldn't climb the stairs to the bedroom anymore, and Caitlin had made him a nice, soft bed downstairs near the fireplace.

"Hey there, boy," Nick said softly, and Dog's tail thumped on the edge of the woven basket Caitlin had lined with worn blankets and pillows.

With a rub of his head and quick scratch of his tummy, Nick left Dog to go back to sleep. Everything was silent as he climbed the stairs to the bedroom level, and the air in the upstairs hallway had a definite nip. Nick hoped one of the Firebirds in charge of his wife had thought to build fires in the bedroom fireplaces.

His question was answered as he eased open the first bedroom door he reached and felt the brush of warm air across his face. A small hearth glowed with a low burning fire, warming the bedroom decorated in pale pinks and purples. A white crib sat against the wall furthest from the hearth. Nick didn't want to take the chance of waking his granddaughter, but he couldn't pass up the chance to take a peek. As he reached the side of the crib, Nicole drew in a long breath and let it out with a shudder of her little body. He couldn't help his smile looking down at her. Lying on her tummy, her cheek pressed against the mattress to make her lips bow in a tiny pout. Blond hair whispered around her cheeks and her hand rested on the multi-colored afghan Lumpy Caitlin made for her when she was just a baby.

He risked waking Nicole to smooth his hands over her hair before stepping back from the crib and sneaking out of the room.

The master bedroom was in darkness except for the orange glow cast by the flames in the brick fireplace across the room from the foot of the bed, creating long shadows from the posters of the bed against the walls. The air smelled of snow and cold and burning cherry wood, and the white curtains stirred slightly from the wind drifting in through the crack Caitlin had left open.

He smiled as he shut the bedroom door and tugged his sweater over his head, dropping it on the floor as he approached the bed. Ever since living in Tennessee, Caitlin said she enjoyed the smell of fresh air, no matter how cold. In the summer, the windows had been wide open, but as the season cooled the window closed a little more. Just never fully shutting unless it was just too cold to take.

Shucking his jeans, he slid into the cool sheets and toward the curled form of his wife. Her blond hair, nearly as long now as when they'd met over a decade before, spread across the pillow and quilt and she lay on her side with the blanket curled beneath her chin.

Nick supported himself on his elbow and looked down at her. Part of him wished she had been awake so he could talk to her and forget about the last twelve hours, and the burning heaviness in his chest every time he thought of the lost souls in Boston. They didn't have to talk about anything in particular, just talk. But, part of him was happy just to watch her sleep. Traveling through space, when it had been just him and his own thoughts, it was moments like this he dreamed about to keep him going.

Any incentive to bring him home.

Caitlin stirred, drawing a slow breath. Her eyes fluttered open and she looked up at him, a small smile tipping her lips. She immediately slipped an arm free of the blanket and touched his cheek, drawing him down to her for a kiss. Nick was never one to argue over kissing his wife. Caitlin tasted of peppermint tea with honey, and he hummed against her lips at the rush of want hit his gut, curling his hand over her hip beneath the blanket. Gently, he rolled her onto her back and leaned over her, his hum turning into a low groan when her hands slid over his sides.

He wanted to make love to her, the final act would push away the demons of the day, but it was late and he knew she was tired. Instead, he reluctantly broke the kiss and rested his forehead on her shoulder, drawing a deep breath as he wrapped his arms around her as best he could and held her close. She smelled of floral soap and powder, mingled with fresh air and sunshine. She combed the fingers of one hand through his hair, the other rubbing across his shoulders. Soft lips kissed his neck.

"Connor heard from Colonel Ebben this evening, and told me what happened," she said softly against his ear, her fingers playing across the back of his neck. "I'm so sorry."

Nick shifted and slid further into the bed, down her body until he could lay his cheek on her stomach, the soft cotton of her sleeping gown brushing his skin. He'd lain like this before, nearly two and a half years ago, as he prepared to leave Earth for parts unknown and allies yet to be made. Just like then, Caitlin stroked his hair and let him rest beside her.

Only now, their son or daughter rested beneath his cheek. Nick closed his eyes and tried not to think of all the sons and daughters who had died today. What was worse? Losing souls to the ignorant terrorism of the Xenos, or losing them to a stupid accident?

"I love you, Caitlin," he said, his words muffled against her warm body.

"Come here."

He raised his head and looked at her along the length of her torso, her fingertips touching his jaw. Nick moved back to the head of the bed, letting his chest brush along her cotton nightclothes. She shifted beneath him, and he settled in the familiar place between her thighs, tugging at the hem of her nightgown until the fabric bunched around her hips and he felt the heat of her bare skin against him.

In the darkness of the room, lit only by the flames of the fire, her eyes sparkled as she looked up at him. Her palms touched his cheeks, her thumbs stroked his skin, and warmth spread from his chest. A quick thought clicked in his head and he scanned the dark for the wind-up alarm clock on the bedside table.

"What is it?"

Nick squinted in the dim light to read the time. Twenty-two minutes past midnight. He smiled, leaning in for a deep kiss that coaxed a purr from the back of his wife's throat before answering. "Happy anniversary."

Caitlin smiled and pulled him closer, her hands trailing over his back. "Happy anniversary. Now, make love to me."

It was all the urging he needed, and he leveraged his body weight over her. With the slightest nudge of his hips, she raised her knees and tipped her head back into the pillows as he pushed into the heat of her body. Nick groaned, closing his eyes. God let him die if he stopped feeling this way whenever he was inside her.

Tonight wasn't about burning passion, or even finesse, it was about losing himself inside her and forgetting the darkness of the day in the dark of the night. Every slow push and pull of their bodies together was a cleansing, a replacing of one thought with another.

The tension slowly eased from Caitlin's body and she relaxed again into the bed, her eyes opening. She released a soft sigh and touched his face again, her thumb stroking his lip. "I love you."

"I'm glad to hear that," he said, smiling against her finger. "Because I lost your candy."

CHAPTER SEVEN

*J*ohn tried to sleep, but his body had gone too far past tired to allow him to rest. His body ached with exhaustion, his limbs heavy. Each blink was a chore, but when he closed his eyes to sleep, his mind refused to rest. Thoughts piled on top of each other, vying for priority. Meetings he needed to prepare for over the next week, data he needed to review and compile for the agricultural reconstruction committee, the one-on-one meeting he had scheduled with Drucillus Clodianus Hiacyntus in just a few hours—all things he knew should be dealt with, it was his duty.

But they all paled beneath the heavy knot in his chest left behind by the absence of his son and the tragedy of the Boston tunnel collapse. And every painful bit of his own personal tragedies re-awakened. He had let the visceral reaction snap out of him in Nick's office, and knew he had overwhelmed Beverly with the intensity of it, and it had been a chore to rein it all in to deal with the situation. Now, with nothing more than his own thoughts to distract him, planning meetings was inadequate to push the memories aside.

Sleep was impossible.

The clock beside his bed said 3:42 when he finally tossed off the twisted and rumpled bedding and walked barefoot through the dark apartment to the kitchen, not bothering with a tee shirt despite the cold bite in the air. The second and third levels of the embassy had been designed to be living spaces for himself and the Umani ambassador. Since Ambassador Drucillus Clodianus Hiacyntus usually preferred to sleep aboard his private carrier holding orbit in the airspace over Virginia, John and Silas were usually the only inhabitants of the embassy. Silas was gone, replaced by the brash and assertive Jenifer with no last name.

He hadn't figured her out yet, but also accepted he probably never would. She was beautiful, but in a Southern Bagdaghir Desert Black Scorpion kind of way; sleek and mesmerizing, even graceful and seductive, but everything about her said, "Back off or risk being stung."

The kitchen was simple, providing only the basics, just like the rest of the apartment. A sharp contrast to the embassy accommodations provided to the seven Umani ambassadors to Aretu, which were equivalent to palaces in comparison. Even if Earth had been able to provide John with that type of living quarters, he doubted he would have wanted it. Too many years of living on a farm or sleeping under the stars. John opened the small refrigeration unit provided and removed a bottle of purified water.

He contemplated making some of the coffee in the tin on the counter, but decided against it. If he drank the strong brew, sleep would be even more impossible. Besides that, he hadn't developed the taste for coffee. It reminded him too much of the thick, bitter drink called *Kouffa* on Zibal. He'd drank it only once because Tahlia had smiled, her violet eyes practically twinkling with mischief, and told him it was delicious.

He paused, the bottle of water half way to his lips. Memories of Tahlia had been numerous, and sometimes vicious, since they'd heard the news of the Boston tunnel collapse that afternoon. It was like a new wound, everything reminded him of it.

John took a last swallow from the bottle and left the kitchen, leaving the bottle on the counter. He moved through the apartment in darkness until he reached the large windows facing out the front of the embassy onto the street below. The majority of the city was in complete darkness, barely a silhouette against the starlit night, with only the moon to cast any form of light. Even in the darkness, he saw the remaining destruction from the attack on him just a week before. The building across the street was missing an entire section of brick from the impact of the hovercar, and portions of the street were darker from the burn of the explosions and pulse charges.

He crossed his arms over his chest and bowed his head, closing his eyes. It seemed nothing was exempt from the thoughts and memories of twenty years past that were determined to keep him awake.

ARETH CALENDAR DATE: 12ᵀᴴ DAY OF SOLATICE, 3254.6
CITY OF NANTE'EK
DEFENSE ALLIANCE PROTECTED PLANET OF ZIBAL
IN THE CONSTELLATION SETTA GEMII

The ground shifted beneath his feet as another blast hit the city of Nante'ek from the Sorracchi Death Bringers that filled the sky like a swarm of dart bees. John kept running, hunching forward with his arms crossed over his head to protect himself from the flying debris.

"John!" Burgess shouted from the haven of a half-collapsed building.

John looked up, waving the dust of destruction away from his face. He nodded, indicating he would make it across the rubble-littered street as soon as possible. A whine echoed through the air as another half-dozen Death Bringers shot through the sky overhead. He prayed Tahlia had made it into the tunnels beneath the city before the firing began. His gut twisted at the idea she might somehow be caught in the middle of this devastation.

He waited for the firing to pause, then ran across the street with his weapon at his side and hunched over to stay as close to the ground as possible. "Where the hell is our air cover?" he demanded as soon as he reached Burgess. "They were supposed to be here ten minutes ago!"

Burgess sat on the ground reloading his weapon with an energy cell. A stream of blood ran down the side of his dirt-smudged face from a cut above his eye, and his hair spiked with sweat and filth. His Defense Alliance uniform was covered with dust, dirt, and blood. John assumed he looked no better. The fighting had been fierce and intense for the last twelve hours.

"Cap says they're coming, but the Sorrs set off an atmospheric storm in a perimeter around the city. They're having a hard time getting through."

John cursed and ducked as a blast hit a nearby building, sending rubble dust into the air. His lungs burned and his eyes were full of debris, making each blink painful and blurring his vision.

"We can't stay here. We're directly in their line of fire."

Then the sky lit up with the familiar blue-green glow of Defense Alliance weaponry, and the Death Bringer whine was drowned out by the combined volume of fifty DA ships breaking through the atmosphere with a boom that popped in his ears and made the air hum. A group of Sorracchi grunts, wearing the skins of their most recent conquest, cut through the alley across the street and laid down fire on John and Burgess. They both fired back, ducking behind the fallen wall with bits of mortar crumbling around them. John took down three of the five, and Burgess' aim was true on the other two.

Overhead, the show was spectacular. DA ships spun and dipped, quickly bringing to bear their weapons on the Death Bringers, and one by one, the enemy ships exploded in mid-air. Within minutes of the DA ships arrivals, the Sorrs flipped their afterburners and shot into the night sky, disappearing from the airspace over the city. Half the DA ships took pursuit, leaving the other half to fly scout over the city. Within moments, the explosions stopped completely, and an eerie silence settled on the city.

In the distance, John heard the shouts of other DA soldiers mingling with the frantic cries of the Zibal civilians they had been assigned here to protect. This was bad, but John didn't want to contemplate how bad it would have been if the Defense Alliance hadn't offered their protection. One by one, the Sorrs had been conquering and destroying planets through the nearby sectors, one by one, stealing bodies and technology to continue their war.

Now, with the worst over, John settled beside Burgess and took a hydration pack from his vest. He handed Burgess two of the pills, and popped two in his mouth, humming when the sensation of cold water burst in his throat and he swallowed, feeling the cool refreshment spread through his body.

Only when the sounds of war dropped away into the still of the night did he hear the subtle twitter of his personal communicator from its clip on his belt. He had to remove the device during battle in case his commander needed to reach him through the closed DA links and didn't want to mistake one for the other.

"Hell of a fight," Burgess said after swallowing his own pills. "We live another day, hey, John?"

John smiled and chuckled, taking the communicator from his belt as he flipped it on. The screen flashed MESSAGE—TAHLIA. "My wife," he said, holding up the device so Burgess saw the screen. "Probably tellin' me where she's bunked up so I can come get her."

Burgess rolled to his feet, dusting his hands on his thighs as he stepped into the street, waving down a group of their fellow Defense Alliance soldiers approaching from the west part of town. John took the opportunity to open the message, smiling even before Tahlia's face came into view on the video screen. But, as the image clicked on, his throat tightened.

Her face was smudged with dirt, and wherever she was, it was dark. The image shook as she tried to hold the communicator still. Her eyes glistened and she sniffed softly as she seemed to find a steady position to hold the communicator.

"John," she said in a cracked, dry voice. Her natural accent wrapped around his name, the 'n' getting caught against the roof of her mouth the way it always did. "I don't know how lon-long I can talk." She blinked and tears rolled from her violet eyes down her cheeks, streaking the dust to reveal the alabaster paleness of her skin. She was struggling with the words, and he almost wished she would just speak in her native tongue if it would make it easier to tell him where she was. Suddenly, he had an urgent need to find her.

Somewhere around her came the sound of someone crying and the whimper of a child calling for their mother.

"We are in a tunnel, John. But, the fighting—" She looked to the ceiling and more tears ran down her cheeks. "We hear it. The walls shake." Tahlia looked again directly at the screen, and the terror shone so bright in her eyes John's heart clenched in his chest. "They are falling. The walls. We cannot—we cannot leave."

A scream somewhere near her smothered her voice for a moment and Tahlia jumped, the image shaking with her. She cried openly now.

"John, John, I love you." She held the communicator closer to her so her face took up the entire screen. Hair like spun gold hung across her cheek, dirty from the dust falling around her. "Be safe, my husband. Please. Please be safe. I love you."

He clenched the communicator in a death grip, the image blurring as hot tears burned his eyes. "Tahlia," he choked.

"I love you," she whispered, her voice almost lost in her own weeping. "I love you, my John. My John."

A sickening crash preceded Tahlia's scream and the message ended.

"No!" John screamed, his voice echoing back off the collapsed buildings around him. He rolled to his knees, gaining his feet, as if somehow that would change anything. "No!"

The communicator fell from his shaking hands, clattering on the ground. Somewhere in his peripheral consciousness, he heard Burgess return with others but his ability to think or react was gone. Concern and confusion bounced off them, but the pain squeezing his heart muffled their emotions.

Someone picked up the communicator, and he heard his beautiful wife's voice speak again. "John I don't know how lon-long I can talk."

"Damn," Burgess mumbled, and the sound of Tahlia's voice stopped.

John spun on the balls of his feet. *She was trapped! He had to find her!*

He bolted into the street and headed east, pausing after running only a few dozen feet. No . . . no . . . their small living quarters were in the south. She would have gone to the nearest shelter tunnels. Near the center of the city, she had to be there.

John ran again, but Burgess' hand gripped his arm, spinning him around.

"John! Where are you going?"

"I have to find her."

He pulled away, trying to run again, but Burgess grabbed a fistful of his uniform, hauling him back. "John! You don't know where she is!" John shook his head, not wanting to hear what Burgess said. Burgess yanked at his uniform until he turned to face him, and he hated what he saw in his friend's eyes. "John, the message is time stamped two hours ago."

John shook his head.

"She's gone."

His blood pounded in his ears, muffling everything else, and he couldn't breathe. Nothing was right, nothing mattered, nothing was real. This couldn't be real! She couldn't be dead!

He blocked it out, had to or all of existence would have exploded in his chest. John dropped to his knees in the stone and dirt that were the remains of Nante'ek and curled forward until his forehead touched the broken earth and pounded his clenched fists into the gravel. His body shook with his weeping and he choked on the dust left in the wake of the Sorracchi.

*J*enifer set the final bio-rhythmic security globe along the perimeter of the ambassador's apartment and set it to sleep mode until she remotely downloaded the bio-codes and engaged the system. The furthest ring of security wrapped around the perimeter of the embassy, including the roof and all entrances. Security spiraled inward from there, through the embassy on the first level, all possible routes to the second and third levels and the hallways and entrances outside the apartment. Finally, the tightest circle monitored the entire apartment. It had taken her nearly three hours to set out all the globes.

No one would get past any level of security without her being aware of it. During the day, the system would be set to a minimal level because of the quantity of people moving back and forth. But, when traffic was lowest, and the likelihood of a direct attack in his own home was the greatest, then the system would engage.

She had set the bio-codes for the direct members of her team as well as the Firebirds assigned to the embassy. Their biological readings would not set off the alarm other than letting her know where they were if they were within the perimeter established. As part of their training as Firebirds, all soldiers' bio-codes were downloaded and kept on record, which made her job easier in respect. She'd created the system, so her personal coding was part of the system's basic core. Ambassador Smith's coding was the only step left in the process.

Ambassador Smith had been out of his room for the last fifteen minutes. He'd stopped briefly in the kitchen and then moved on to the main living space. She had been on the balcony that extended along the back of the embassy—*stupid idea. Did these people have any concept of security?*—when she noted his movement. She knew he hadn't been sleeping before that, his restlessness carried through the silence of the apartment. With the system control core clipped to her belt, she walked through the dark halls to the living area, and stopped in the doorway.

He stood at the bank of large windows facing out onto the city, his back to her. Standing in the darkness with the moonlight the only source of light, Jenifer had to admit Ambassador Smith had certain attributes most women would find attractive.

It was obvious he hadn't thought about being prepared to make a quick escape when he left his bedroom. He wore only a pair of loose fitting pull-on pants hung low on his hips. They were a rich blue color, and by the sheen on the material, possibly some type of silk or similar fabric. His feet were bare, and he wore no shirt, leaving his back exposed. He stood completely still with his arms crossed and his head bowed, pulling the muscles along his back and shoulders tight enough she easily saw the definition.

Okay, so not half bad. He was obviously fit, so he probably wouldn't be a total waste in a fight. But if someone else didn't kill him, she was seriously considering it.

"Did you need somethin'?" he asked, his clipped tone barely carrying across the room. He never raised his head, never moved.

"Yeah," she said, crossing the space. "I need you to not be so damn stupid."

He raised his head slowly, unfolding his arms to rub his palms over his face, sniffing softly before he turned his attention to her. "Excuse me?"

"I said I'd really like it if you wouldn't be so damn *stupid*, Ambassador." She took the security core from her belt, snapped one of the electrodes from the back and slapped it unapologetically against his chest over his heart. The core interface immediately came to life, several graphs recording the various biorhythmic information she needed for the globes.

"What the hell are you doin'?" he ground out, reaching for the electrode, but she shoved his hand away.

"What President Tanner hired me to do, keep your ass alive. But if you're going to make it harder for me, I'll quit in the morning." She pulled a stylus device from the side of the core and grabbed his hand, jabbing a finger with the tip. "You know, I heard you were a soldier back on Aretu, so I thought you'd have enough sense *not to stand in front of an exposed window.*"

He looked from her to the window, either oblivious to or indifferent to the fact she held his hand, squeezing several drops of blood from his finger into the stylus tube. The core twittered in acknowledgement of the data.

"I wasn't—"

"Thinking? Obviously." Finished with retrieving the data she needed, she snapped the stylus back into place and gripped the edge of the pad on his chest. Jenifer contemplated just ripping the pad free without at least pulling the skin taut to ease the removal, but in the end she remembered she hated ripping off bandages just as much as anyone else. She laid her hand against his warm skin, bracing it slightly before gripping the electrode edge and yanking *hard*.

"Bloody hell!"

"It'll hurt a hell of a lot more if you get hit with a long range pulse blast." She eyed up the window and the surrounding cityscape, as much as she could call the broken horizon a city. "I wouldn't be surprised if these Xenos went retro and took a shot at you with one of those old time projectile guns. Messy, but they'd cut through this glass like butter."

She half expected him to scramble back from the windows, but he didn't. He just looked out again.

"Where the hell is your head?" she demanded, entering the commands to distribute the biorhythm information to the security globes and engage the system.

"Zibal."

Jenifer pulled a face. "Where?"

"Boston," he clarified.

"The tunnel collapse?" He nodded, but didn't look at her. "What do you care?" This time his head *did* snap around and he glared at her, his brow tugged down over his eyes. Deep frown lines bracketed his mouth. Before he could say anything else, she clipped the core to her belt and continued. "You're a damn ambassador. What the hell do you care, really, if another four thousand *Humans* are dead? Fewer of us for your government to have to take care of, right?"

"Do you really believe tha'?"

Jenifer shrugged and turned away, walking back to the couch facing the windows. With a derisive wave of her hand, she flopped down on the cushions. "Hell, yeah. That's what it's always about."

He shifted his stance, standing heavily on one foot with his arms crossed over his bare torso. Clear as day, she saw the battle going on in his head in the firm set of his lips and the tight clench of his jaw. He wanted to say something, but debated with himself whether he'd say it or not. Typical politician weighing the ramifications. Saying only what would work for him in the long run.

She watched and waited, curious as hell what he'd say.

Instead, he dropped his arms to his sides and turned on the balls of his feet. His long strides across the floor were nearly silent, but the power in his intent was clear. Jenifer snorted, completely unsurprised by his avoidance. Typical politician. Don't like the topic of conversation? Divert. Ignore. Deny. All else fails, run away from it altogether.

He stopped short of the door and turned back to her. When he spoke, his voice was heavy and thick, and if she'd ever heard a "watch your step" tone, it was then. Good thing she wasn't intimidated by such things.

"You know *nothin'* about me, Jenifer. Until you do, I suggest you refrain from commentin' on my motives."

"I know enough." She curled to her feet and strode to him, standing just inside the perimeter of his personal space. She had to tip her head up just a little bit to keep his gaze, but at this proximity she heard every restrained breath he took. "I know you don't do anything without a reason. Right down to your *sincere* show of emotion for the lost Humans in the tunnel."

A bunched muscle jumped along his jaw as he clenched his teeth, his lips pulled together in a tight line. She didn't look down to be sure, but by the tensing of the muscles in his shoulders she guessed his hands were balled in tight fists at his side. When he finally spoke, his voice barely carried between them, it was so low and restrained.

"You've never watched someone you cared about die, have you." It wasn't a question, but a statement.

Anger flashed through her in a vicious wave, but she carefully schooled her expression to show none of it. Jenifer took a slow, deliberate step backward and removed her pulse pistol from the holster on her thigh.

"You know nothing about *me*, Ambassador," she ground out. "And since you never will, I suggest you take your own advice."

She didn't release the tight breath in her chest until she was in the hallway outside the apartment.

CHAPTER EIGHT

3 February 2054, Tuesday
Ambassador Suite, Aretu and Raxo Embassy
United Earth Protectorate, Capitol City
Alexandria, Seat of Virginia
North American Continent

*O*n Aretu, John Smith was eighty-six years old—on Earth, seventy-one—and regardless of which calendar he used, which star he orbited, John had been married to Tahlia less than a year. Their time together was best measured in weeks and days rather than months, at least then it sounded longer.

He'd spent his youth and adolescence living in his parents' home, sharing his life daily with his mother, his father, and his brother Conrad. When he left home for his brief two years of medical training, he lived in a dormitory with two-dozen other young men. Once he left behind the idea of being a physician and signed up as active military, he often shared a space with others—but the space wasn't his home, and he didn't share his life. Not until Tahlia did he share his life.

By the measurement of Earth's orbit, nearly twenty years had passed after her death before Silas came into his life, and overrode all aspects of his daily existence. In a miraculously short period of time, John intrinsically shared his life with another person. He'd spent the majority of his life working as an independent soul, and without pause or hesitation, he didn't want to think of life alone.

All this came to him in the second it took for Silas' toast to pop up and for John to remember his son wasn't there.

It would take more than ten days to forget the routine of making peanut butter toast.

He was aware of her when she came through the apartment door. Unlike her first night in the apartment, when he'd let his mind wander so deeply into the past the present blurred, he was attuned to the silence now. Just before she walked around the corner, her steps nearly noiseless despite the boots he figured she wore, he took the bread from the toaster and tossed it on a plate.

"Breakfast?"

"Thanks," she said, her tone flat. Not bothering with butter or the open jar of peanut butter on the counter, Jenifer Of No Last Name bit into the dry toast with an unappealing crunch.

Their co-existence was tenuous, but had lost the strain of the first couple of days. She was still distant, cool, and militant in her duties. He'd yet to figure out when she slept, because she was awake when he went to bed, awake when he rose, and if he got out of bed any time during the night, she'd never failed to be on patrol around the apartment. Outside the apartment, she was rarely more than an arm's reach from him. She did her job with a dedication greater than any soldier—Human, Areth, or otherwise—he'd ever known.

Today she wore the same military issue clothing as all military personnel, with the exclusion of any indicator of rank or affiliation. He knew Nick had offered her Firebird designation—"to establish chain of command," he said—but she'd refused. Green utility pants with wide, deep pockets on the outside of each thigh and drawstrings around her ankles to bring the hem tight around her heavy-duty black boots. A black, long sleeved shirt formed to her body beneath a form-fitted matching green jacket she hadn't bothered to fasten closed. A tight braid hugged her scalp to her nape, and he wondered if she was aware wearing her hair restrained accentuated the length of her neck.

She was a beautiful woman, if he could get past the cold anger in her blue eyes.

She leaned across in front of him to snatch the jar of peanut butter. "Is this real?"

John grinned. "'Suppose it is. Is there such a thin' as fake peanut butter?"

"You have no idea."

He had to force himself not to stare when she dropped the dry toast and dipped her finger into the jar, sliding the peanut butter smeared finger into her mouth. If he didn't know better, he'd swear her eyelids fluttered and he was pretty sure he heard her moan. John cleared his throat and poured a glass of the orange flavored drink. If nothing else, the woman knew how to enjoy her food.

Without another word to him, she picked up his knife and spread a thick layer of peanut butter on the toast. After eating half the slice, she picked up his glass of orange flavored powdered beverage and drank half the glass.

"Help yourself," he said with a grin.

Her blue eyes slid to him, and held as she popped the last corner in her mouth. John hid his smile when she jumped up onto the counter, her feet swinging a foot off the floor, and picked up the jar again. Apparently not appeased by her toast, she swirled a knife in the jar and brought out a thick glob of peanut butter. Without looking even remotely apologetic, she proceeded to lick the knife clean.

John had to look away, finding himself far too enchanted by her simple act of eating peanut butter. He cut a thick slice of bread from the crusty loaf he'd brought home the day before, and reached for the peanut butter jar. "May I?" he asked, holding his hand out for the knife.

One elegant eyebrow arched before she handed the licked-clean knife back to him. She smirked, but hid it by pulling her lips together as she hopped down from the counter, her boots thumping on the floor. John scraped the remains of the peanut butter from the jar and spread it on the bread, folding it in half for a quick breakfast before they left for the first meeting of the day.

They'd settled into a moderately comfortable existence together in the apartment, despite the first night when she put him in his place. And there was no doubt that was exactly what she'd done. He wouldn't make the mistake again of letting down his guard. Or of letting his mind linger on things long gone.

He also wouldn't make the mistake of having only one jar of peanut butter in the house, and wondered what she would do with a spoonful of smooth casha cream smothered in the bayaberry jam his mother made each spring.

"We're burning sunlight, Ambassador," Jenifer called through the apartment.

John tossed the knife in the sink, stuck the half-sandwich in his mouth, and grabbed his jacket off the back of a chair as he passed.

"*T*his is no' a *negotiation*, Drucillus Clodianus Hiacyntus."

John's frustration practically echoed off the cracked and faded walls of the embassy council room. He paced across the width of the small room, his hands at his hips, tension pinching his angled features.

"Would you prefer that the coffers of Raxo be laid at the feet of the Humans with no compensation for our effort?"

Jenifer stood near the wall, just a few feet from where John paced, observing the meeting between John, Claude, and Claude's entourage. She met the bored gaze of Firebird Captain Butch Calloway, who stood like a bookend to one side of the couch Claude occupied. He looked away, glaring sideways at his charge, and then back to her. Another Firebird stood at the other end of the couch, looking equally bored, and Claude's attendants, including his second wife and his third mistress, sat on the floor near the exterior windows playing some sort of game with marbles and carved figures.

The lack of security, protection, or common sense in the embassy still amazed her. Although she'd learned enough to know John had implemented some of his own rudimentary security precautions, as much as he could within the confinements of his position, she knew Claude considered his faction of admirers his security. If anyone attacked him, they would die first and would willingly give their lives for his overindulged existence.

She'd met a lot of politicians in her life, a lot of leaders and heads of state, and none of them held a match to the pretentiousness oozing off Drucillus Clodianus Hiacyntus like the silk brocade of his gold cord trimmed robes. He refused to sit at the table, but instead had taken up residence on a wide couch positioned near the head of the table. Layers of shimmering fabric flowed around him like a massive tent. Gold, burgundy and white layers spread out over the cushions from gold-fringed epaulettes at his shoulders. The top of his head was shaved smooth, a ring of tightly curled hair wrapping around his skull from ear to ear. She remembered in her ancient history lessons at one time, a nobleman's girth was intended to be indicative of his wealth and prosperity. If that were the case, then Claude had to be one of the wealthiest men in all of Raxo.

John stopped pacing to lean over the scarred table, bracing his weight on the palm of one hand while he rubbed the fingers of his other hand across his forehead. "The people of this planet are the children of Raxo. They are the children of Aretu. They are the children of visionaries and pilgrims, and the destruction visited on this planet was in retribution for a war they had *nothin'* to do with. We owe it to them to take care of them, not dangle food and medicine in front of them like some bloody carrot." He slapped his free hand down on the tabletop, making Claude jump.

Jenifer bowed her head and pressed her lips together to keep from chuckling.

Claude recovered quickly, huffing with a shake of his head that sent his jowls to wagging. "Perhaps you have spent too long away from home, John Smith. The ways of this planet have infiltrated your language and your attitude."

"There you go again," John nearly shouted, and Jenifer thought she noted his already prominent accent grew even more prominent in his anger. "You speak about the people of this world as if every part of their society and culture is foreign to you. Look around!" He threw out his arms, encompassing the world in his observation. "I look at every face on the street and I see *us*. Aretu and every nation of Raxo. We are *here*. They are *us*."

"I understand the science of ancestry, John Smith. I do not need to be lectured by you—"

"I think maybe you do."

And so the arguing began. Jenifer glanced at her wrist, confirming the hour. They were early today by twelve minutes. She had stood in this room for the last week, listening to the two of them shout back and forth, and she had to wonder why John even bothered.

Claude was a *quid pro quo* kind of politician. It was all about what he, or his constituents, could get out of the deal. Even though the initial attacks had reduced the world's population by nearly seventy percent, and only about half of the globe was actually habitable, Claude wanted his fair share.

Fair share of what?

She knew a nice pile of manure she'd be happy to share with him.

Someone knocked at the conference room door. Initially, no one moved or acknowledged the interruption. Only when they knocked again did Captain Calloway step away from his post to answer the door. It wasn't Jenifer's job to fend off everyone who sought time with the ambassadors; it was her job to make sure John stayed alive another day.

Calloway opened the door enough to speak to whoever it was in the hall, then stepped back and looked in her direction. "Jenifer . . ."

She quickly surveyed the room, scanning the draped windows and the far corners even though she'd examined the room before the meeting began. She hated the positioning. They faced the street, and while they were on the second floor, the bank of ancient, simple glass windows offered little to no protection. At least in the apartment, John's windows were reinforced. Her skin had itched all day, and she knew better than to ignore the tension and unease crawling at the base of her skull. One too many times the crawl had saved her life. She'd stepped up her watchfulness, had scrutinized the embassy and the conference room three times, and had scanned the room for extra listening devices. She knew about all the ones already there, and had intentionally left them because if she took them out someone would just sneak in and place more. If she knew they were there, she knew if they changed or if someone had tampered with them again.

If someone got off listening to arguments about medical supplies and crop seed, then good for them.

She took a step forward and touched John's elbow. He only paused in his counterargument long enough to look down at her and nod.

Sergeant Manning took a step back as she stepped into the hall, tucking his hands behind him with his feet set wide at attention. John's heavy accent followed her into the hall, reducing to muffled mumbling when she shut the door.

"What is it, Sergeant?"

Manning was young, probably barely out of whatever rudimentary military training he might have been yanked through in order to give him a pulse weapon and a rank. His red hair was cut tight to his head, but she recognized the slightest hint of a curl to it, and he kept his eyes diverted from her, looking past her shoulder in strict military observance of rank. Ironic, since she technically held no rank. Probably Nick's doing, because she'd noticed similar actions on the part of other military personnel, lower ranked Firebirds included. "Ma'am, there's a problem with the ambassador's transport hover."

"Keep your voice down," she ordered, and stepped closer to him. She would swear a sheen of sweat popped out on his upper lip almost instantly. "What kind of problem?"

"We were prepping the hover for the ambassador's tour, and found . . ." He practically stuttered, blinked hard, and swallowed. "We found signs of tampering along the combustion system outlays and the deceleration mechanisms."

"Damn." Jenifer turned away from him and laid her hand across her forehead. She hated leaving the prep work to a bunch of rookies, but short of dragging John along with her, she couldn't guard him and prepare the craft at the same time. "Anything else I need to know?" She turned back on Manning, who immediately tensed in his stance.

"Yes, ma'am. Doctor Katrina Bauer is running a series of analytical simulations through the long distance lidar systems. She suspects the imaging and auto-response programs may have been altered to project false imagery."

The conference room door opened and John stepped into the hall. She hadn't realized the shouting had stopped, and managed to glance past him to see Claude heft his sizeable gut off the couch with the aid of his wife and mistress. It was lunchtime, after all, and Claude was never late for lunch.

"Is there a problem?" John whispered, leaving the door open a space since Claude was on his slow way toward it.

Manning tensed again, and Jenifer dropped her hand to the pulse weapon strapped to her thigh. The kid's nervousness bounced around him like a force field and made her own nerves twitch. Nervous people made her nervous, especially until she knew the motivation behind their nervousness. Her gut told her he was about to stand at attention right out of his skin because he drew the short straw, and had to be the one to report their findings. She figured if Nick Tanner happened to stroll down the hall right then the kid would snap himself in half. "At ease, Sergeant, before you break something," she said over her shoulder before turning to John.

"Could be," she began, but paused when three uniformed soldiers rounded the corner, talking amongst themselves, walking shoulder to shoulder.

The hairs on the back of her neck bristled.

The halls were short and narrow, the facility having been redesigned from an old structure dating back nearly one hundred and forty years when buildings were built more compact, and apparently more sturdy, because this older block of Alexandria was one of the few still standing after the war. When the soldier's reached them, they fell into single file and Manning stepped back to give them room, standing flush against the wall. Claude chose then to reach the conference room door and waddle his substantial mass into the hall, cutting off the soldiers.

Jenifer cursed under her breath, frustration prickling at her. She shot up a hand and stopped Claude mid-waddle. His murky eyes widened and he huffed with enough ferocity to shake his jowls. She plastered on a smile and planted her hand in the middle of John's chest, pushing him back into the conference room, sidestepped the hefty ambassador. With a flourish, she swept her arm down the hall for Claude to pass.

"Allow me to grant you the right of way, Ambassador," she said more to the floor than him.

He scowled at her, looking both shocked and maybe even disgusted by her audacity to exist within his sphere of reality. He'd yet to really acknowledge her presence in any of the meetings she'd attended, and certainly never lowered himself to communicate with her. Claude passed, followed by his Firebirds and entourage.

"Jenifer—" John began behind her.

She shot up a hand for silence, pointed at Sergeant Manning and ordered him into the room with a jerk of her hand. The soldiers passed, single file, as Manning stepped through the door. With a final glare at the crowded hallway, Jenifer kicked closed the door, gripped Manning's wrist and flipped him around to slam his chest into the wall with his arm up his back, and yanked his pulse weapon from his hip holster—all before Manning could protest.

"Do you have any other weapons on you?" she demanded.

"Wha—"

She shoved his arm up his back. "It's an easy question, Sergeant."

He came just shy of squealing like a girl. "No!"

Panic rolled off him, maybe even downright fear, and for just a moment Jenifer felt a fraction of compassion for the poor kid. What the hell would he do if he ever had to face a real danger? What would he do facing down a mob of Xenos? Or Sorracchi? Geez, he had probably been a pimple-faced pubescent kid when the Sorracchi first attacked. Then again, maybe some good, old-fashioned jolt of fear might do the kid some good.

She took a step back and held the procured pulse weapon out toward John. He took it, giving her a curious look, his brow arched.

She stared back. "What?"

He smirked and chuckled, checking the weapon. "Nothin'."

Jenifer arched an eyebrow.

John laughed outright and held up his hands in a sign of surrender, still holding the weapon. "Nothin', I swear." He glanced toward Manning. "You've frightened the boy, Jenifer."

"May I turn around, ma'am?" Manning mumbled, his cheek against the wall.

Jenifer slammed her body against his back, making him grunt. In barely a whisper, she spoke against his bright red ear. "Tell Montgomery sixteen-thirty in the hanger. Got it?"

"Yes, ma'am," he choked.

The kid scurried out of the room like the devil was on his heels, the door rattling in its frame in his departure. Jenifer groaned and snatched the pulse weapon from John's hand and opened the door.

"Hey! Forget something?"

She gave the kid credit. He managed to turn *and* catch the weapon. Then he was gone.

"Damn kid," she mumbled, shutting the door again. "He'd be dead in a real fight."

John walked to the old plaster hearth built into the wall perpendicular to the windows facing the street and turned to lean his hips against the wall with his hands shoved in his pockets, his feet out in front of him set apart. The way his shoulders slumped and he hung his head made Jenifer pause before crossing the room to him. After a few quiet moments, he drew in a long breath through his nose and raised his head as he released it.

"So, what happened?" he asked not much louder than a whisper.

Jenifer crossed to him to stand in the space between his feet. The way he leaned, his feet away from the wall, set him at about eye level with her. John knew about the surveillance devices planted in the room, and while it drove him nuts to leave them behind, he had understood and agreed with her rationale. She leaned in closer, so close their cheeks nearly touched.

"The secure hanger isn't so secure."

He scowled and sighed, dropping his chin again. The wispy ends of his fine hair brushed her temple and cheek. It wasn't the first time in the last week someone had messed around with his private craft, and this was his *new* one, since the Xenos had blown up the last one. They'd moved the hover to a secret location, but apparently, that wasn't enough to keep away John's biggest fans. "Is it fixable by tomorrow night?"

She shrugged, turning her head toward him enough to see his face. His eyes were cast down when she turned, but he looked up when she spoke. "Sure. As long as you don't mind running into the side of a mountain at a hundred and twenty miles an hour."

The scowl deepened.

"According to what the sergeant told me, I'd bet someone set it to accelerate fast, refuse to stop, and not see anything in its way."

John looked away and lowered his head. An inch more and a slight shift and his forehead could rest on her shoulder. When she signed up for this job she had pegged John as just another politician, an actor and liar at heart. Living in his home, spending every moment with him, she had accepted she had been wrong about John Smith. His desire to help, to fix what had been broken, was absolutely sincere and despite that, every time he turned around someone wanted him dead. And he ached for his son. For the first time in longer than Jenifer could remember, she wanted to say or do something that would help. For most people, her first thought was suck it up and get over it, but not now and not with John. He deserved a frickin' break.

She had no idea what to say or do.

This whole giving a damn thing was new to her.

"So, tell me," she said, and he raised his head, his stare still cast down to look more in the vicinity of her chin rather than her eyes. "What has made you such a popular guy everyone wants you to stay in Alexandria?"

He chuckled, which had been her goal. The only goal she could come up with. Make him smile. He had a good smile. "My sparklin' personality?"

Jenifer chuckled, too, and turned away just in time to see a shadow pass over the wall over them. Though distorted and moving fast, the size and shape immediately sent every sense into overdrive. John stiffened.

"Down!"

Either she grabbed John, or he grabbed her, she wasn't sure, but they rolled together under the old and scarred table as the windows shattered in a spray of old school bullets. In a matter of seconds, the exterior wall exploded in a shower of pulverized plaster and splintered wood. The shooting paused and they both raised their heads.

"More friends of yours?" she shouted.

John looked to the windows and Jenifer toward the door.

"He's coming back!"

The shadow fell across the gaping holes once windows and the assassin opened fire once again. The table provided meager protection, but Jenifer ripped the pulse pistol from her thigh and fired from beneath the splintered edge. She caught the jerk and sway of the attacker and knew she'd hit him, but it didn't stop him. He swayed out of firing range again, and John rolled onto his hands and knees.

"Come on!"

They both scrambled to the door and made it into the debris littered hall before the firing began again.

CHAPTER NINE

Captain Adam Edison was on the street when Connor and Mel arrived, plaster dust sprinkling his hair. The air was thick with debris dust, and shattered glass and masonry littered the steps along the front of the embassy. They hadn't managed to clean away the scorch marks and damage from the attack nearly a month before, and now this.

Connor set down the hover on the other side of the street, and slipped on his sun shields before stepping out of the craft. Even with the shields set at highest protection, his eyes ached from the daylight. It had taken nearly two days for his vision to return after the attack, and several days before his eyes didn't feel like they were full of volcanic sand, but bright sunlight still made them feel like they were being pulled right out of his sockets.

Mel came around the front of the hover, zipping up her jacket. "You okay?"

He nodded. "Yeah. Better every day."

Edison saw them and crossed the street at a jog. "As far as we can tell, the one shooter was the sole attacker," he explained after saluting Connor. He pointed to the limp body hanging from a harness at the second story level. What was left of the second story. Three windows were completely destroyed, and everything in between. Papers billowed out the open space and tattered curtains flapped in the wind.

"Is he dead?"

"No. He's been moaning and groaning, but we haven't attempted to get him down. We've been searching for Ambassador Smith and waiting for more Firebirds to show up."

"Where is the Raxo ambassador?" Mel asked. "Was he hurt in the attack?"

Captain Edison chuckled. "It was lunchtime. He'd already left the embassy for his ship. I don't expect him to be back for another hour."

"Wait, so—" Connor cut in. "No one knows where John is?"

"No, sir. Manning was here when I got here, said he was on his way back to speak with you after passing on some information to John's bodyguard, but he stuck around when he heard the explosion. He said when he left, John and his chick—"

"Captain—"

"Sorry, sir. John and Jenifer were in that room." He pointed upward. "Alone. There's no sign of them now. We've been searching the building, figuring they ran from the room when the firing started, but haven't been able to locate them. Firebirds are canvassing the immediate area. We noted some small blood spattering in the room and the hall, but the trail stopped. One of them is hurt, but we don't know how serious until we find them."

"Damn," Connor cursed, rubbing his thumb across his lower lip as he scanned the street. Citizens had begun to gather in curiosity. Everyone around stared up at the dangling body. "Get him down. Take him for medical care, then take him for interrogation. We probably won't hear anything new, but we can try."

"Yes, sir." Edison jogged back across the street.

Connor walked into the street, glass and rubble crunching beneath his feet. Plaster dust settled on his arms and shoulders, and he tasted it on his lips. He tried to study the scene, but every time he raised his head to look directly at the second story, vicious pain shot from temple to temple and he had to look away. Caitlin assured him everything would be back to normal in a few more days, but frustration chewed at him every time he couldn't fulfill his job duties because of the aftereffects of the flash grenade.

"Where do you think they are?" Mel asked, keeping pace beside him.

He shook his head. "I don't know. I'm dealing with an alien former soldier and an assassin-cum-hired-bodyguard. I don't know how to get into either of their heads."

"What would you do?"

Connor stopped and turned to face her, crossing his arms. The wind whipped at Mel's hair, swishing it across her features. He wasn't sure when he'd realized his 2IC was not only a woman, but a beautiful one. It was a recent development, but other than that, he couldn't say. Maybe he was just slow on the uptake on this one. She used a gloved hand to curl her brown hair behind her ears.

"I'd head for my weapons, but John doesn't carry any and Jenifer tends to wear her arsenal. If she keeps any on the side, they're probably in the apartment." He looked up and squinted against the sun. "Which is upstairs. Edison!"

Captain Edison finished instructing two soldiers who then headed inside the embassy, presumably to cut down the Xeno, then he turned and jogged back to them. "Yes, sir."

"Did anyone check the ambassador's apartment upstairs?"

He nodded. "Yes, sir. We fanned out when we got here. Three sets of boots went upstairs, three down. There's no sign of them after the blood spots in the hallway. No footprints, and no sign of where they went. Some kind of alarm went off when we entered the apartment, but no sign of either one of them."

Connor nodded him off, and he went back to his work. "So much for that," he said when Edison was outside earshot.

Mel shrugged and twisted at the waist so she could bump his arm with hers. "Worth a try. Why don't we cruise around the vicinity a little? See if they've managed to get outside the search perimeter."

"It's worth a shot." He shouted their intent to Edison and they went back to the hover.

They were strapped in and he'd engaged the engine before the dual high-pitched whine of two pulse weapons tightened every muscle in his body. He turned his head enough to look at Mel from the corner of his eye. Each of them had the muzzle of a pulse pistol angled at their heads.

"I don't suggest you make any sudden moves, Montgomery," came a low female voice from the backseat. "I'd rather get out of here without one of those bumbling idiots out there figuring out where we are. Cool?"

Connor turned his head until his cheek pressed against the cold barrel of the pulse weapon. "Fine with me, but is it necessary to call my men bumbling idiots?"

Jenifer cocked a single eyebrow. "If the name fits. Actually, I appreciate their ineptitude. The fewer people who know where we're going, the better."

"We're not going anywhere until you disengage."

"I don't think you're in a position to make demands."

"Lower the weapon off her," Connor said, jutting his chin toward Mel, "or we're not going anywhere."

"Jenifer . . ." came John's voice from the back of the hover, the first he'd heard from the ambassador. A fact which both concerned him and relieved some concern. "Connor will take us."

She glowered at Connor.

"And where are we going?" he asked.

"Hover hanger."

He reached for the ignition, but she tapped his shoulder with her weapon. "Not the *secure* one. I want Claude's."

"Claude's?"

John chuckled. Connor tried to get a view of the ambassador, but the two of them had found a nice little cubby behind his seat that didn't let him see a thing other than her weapon. "Drucillus Clodianus Hiacyntus."

Connor laughed. He wasn't sure what he liked better, Jenifer's nickname or Nick's. "Fine. John's right. You can put the pulse away. I'm just as interested in getting you to safety as you are."

The gun moved away from his cheek, same with the weapon trained on Mel, and Connor heard a hiss from behind him. Then John's quieter voice. "Easy. Come here. Let me see."

"Do I need to make a swing by the hosp—"

"No," Jenifer snapped. "The hover."

*J*ohn had read about the mode of transportation that had been used on Earth for over a hundred years, before hovercrafts and self-renewing energy sources for vehicles.

He'd seen pictures of automobiles, and the hovercrafts used by the Firebirds to travel within the city limits were very much like those automobiles. They were small, compact, easy to maneuver, but left little room inside for more than three or four comfortably, two in front and one or two in back. Assuming you actually sat in the seat.

Which they were not.

John was half inclined on the narrow, short bench with his head against the sidewall, and his feet tucked beneath the back of Mel's seat. Jenifer squeezed in beside him, crouched into the even smaller space behind Connor's seat. No one they passed would see the two of them crowded in the back, and with the exterior privacy tinting, someone could walk right up to the hover and not see them inside. While the position was great for hiding, it was not at all helpful for him trying to do what he could for the gash on Jenifer's upper left arm. A flying shard of glass had cut clean through her thick-weave jacket, cutting downward along her arm from shoulder half way to her elbow. Frayed edges of the cut jacket soaked in the blood seeping from the wound.

"It doesn't seem too deep," he told her, leaning as close as he could to see by the dim light offered by the control dash in the front of the hover. "It's just long. We need to get it wrapped."

"It'll be fine," she forced through clenched teeth.

"Quit your bellyachin'," he ordered, which earned him a scowl. "Connor, do you have a medkit in here?" he asked louder to carry over the hum of the hover.

He caught Connor's glance back in the interior mirror. "For who?"

"Does it matter?"

"No," Connor answered, nodding to his 2IC. She leaned forward and opened a compartment in the front. "Just asking. President Tanner will want to know the details."

"You can tell him Jenifer is doin' her job," John forced through a clenched jaw. "Probably too well."

Mel handed back a small kit and John shifted more onto his back to open the kit on his chest. "How far out are we?"

"Less than a minute," she answered.

"When we get there, I'm going to dock the hover. Stay put, understand?" Connor tossed over his shoulder.

"Yeah," both John and Jenifer said together, and he winked when she looked at him. He found a rudimentary skin weave spray and sterile wrap. It would have to do until he could do it properly.

The hover shifted down and slowed. The interior temporarily darkened as they pulled into the hanger, then brightened again with the interior lighting. Neither Connor nor Mel said another word as he docked the hover and got out, slamming the doors. As soon as they were gone, John tipped his chin toward Jenifer.

"Can you get your jacket off without openin' the wound again?"

"Maybe." She shifted on her knees, leaning over him. "Help me."

He set aside the medkit long enough to push her jacket down off her shoulders. She tucked her arms behind her, and rested her weight on his torso as she wiggled it off, her expression pinching with the pain he knew the movement had to cause. He reached behind her, pulling her closer until he could grip her sleeves. She jerked and hissed, and for a moment she dropped her forehead to his chest, breathing hard.

John chuckled, giving in to the temptation of rubbing his cheek against her braided hair. "In another circumstance, this might be far more enjoyable."

He'd managed to pry a chuckle out of her from time to time, but never a full-fledged laugh. It started as a shake of her shoulders until she inhaled, and then the warm sound of her laughter reverberated against his chest and filled the small space. She lifted her head and looked at him, the smallest of smiles on her lips. Okay, so he managed to get laughter but the smile still escaped him. He knew she would be absolutely breathtaking if she just let herself smile.

The moment passed, and she freed her arm from her sleeve with one final wince. Just like her jacket, the sleeve of her heavy shirt was torn wide open from where the shrapnel had ripped straight through. He helped her ease her arm free of the sleeve to bare her skin so he could treat the wound, thankful she wore a tank under the heavier shirt. In silence, John used an antiseptic dampened swab to clean away the blood that had dried around the six-inch gash on her arm. She made a small sound in the back of her throat only once, and kept her eyes shifted away from him until he finished. Only then did she release a huff and blink.

"I'm sorry," he said softly as he popped open the skin weave. The hiss of the can filled the interior of the hover as he misted her arm with the silk thread spray. An anesthetic infused in the silk would help with some

GAIL R. DELANEY

of the pain, but it wouldn't stop it completely. He wished he could do more, but the medkit was very basic. He finished wrapping her arm in the sterile white gauze just as Connor returned to the hover. The door opened with a hiss and Connor stuck his head inside.

"Okay, we're clear. For the moment, the only people here are the four of us."

Jenifer gingerly slid her arm back into her sleeve, her lips a tight line.

"Sounds like you don't expect it to stay that way," John said as he shifted and sat up, wincing at the kink in his back as he slid from the interior of the hover. He exited first, and offered Jenifer his hand to help her off her kneeling position. She gave him the hand of her uninjured arm, keeping the other tucked to her side. "You alright?" he asked as she gained her feet.

"Fine, now that it's dressed." She inhaled and released.

"President Tanner is on his way here," Connor explained. He held up his hands when both John and Jenifer snapped around to him. "Look, when the President of the World wants to know what you did with his ambassador, you tell him. He gets what he wants."

Jenifer snorted. "I bet that's what your sister says."

John nearly choked and covered it with a cough.

"Nice," Connor came back, looking less offended than his tone implied. He shrugged. "Doesn't change the fact he's my commander."

"I'd rather have him than some of the other schmucks around here," Jenifer said, trying to ease on her jacket over the bandage.

"Did you just call me a schmuck?" came a booming voice through the hanger. He strode in the side entrance, armed guards remaining on the other side. The way Nick saw it, protection was protection, but protection and security weren't always the same thing. Dressed in the same military green as everyone else, he looked just like another soldier to someone who wouldn't recognize his face as ruler of the planet. He was one of the most unassuming and honorable men John had ever met, which sometimes seemed in contrast to his position.

Jenifer just smiled and managed to cross her arms. "Never, sir."

Nick didn't seem bothered, and crossed the cement floor to them, his boot footfalls echoing in the wide, open space. "I was on my way to see you, John, when this went down," he said when he reached them, setting his feet apart with his arms crossed over his chest. One eye squinted

98

slightly more than the other and frown lines bracketed his mouth. Tension pushed off him like a force field, immediately making John's gut go cold. "New intel says you're a moving target, with every Xeno cell in a hundred mile radius lining you up in their sights. Someone, or something, has them stirred up and there's a price on your head."

"More of your sparkling personality, Ambassador?" Jenifer snarked, but a small smile tipped the corner of her mouth. He almost missed it. He didn't, however, miss the contrasting pinch at the corners of her eyes.

"They just can't get enough of me," he said with a grin.

"Apparently."

"The word is they see your tour as an insult. Goal one is to make sure you never reach the first stop, preferably never make it out of Alexandria. Either way, they want you dead by the one-year anniversary of the beginning of the war."

"Next month," Jenifer confirmed. "But, it's not like they're just going to quit if he's not dead by then. Marking the date would drive home their stupid point, but if they make it now or a month from now, they just want the point made."

"You got it," Nick said with a jerked nod.

"So, we can expect a reception like this in every city," John stated.

Nick nodded again. "Pretty much, yeah."

"So, they're watching every hoverport and point of exit from the city. They're watching for your hover," she said with only a tip of her head toward John to indicate she meant him. "Because they're going to assume either we haven't found what they did to the craft, or we have and we removed it. In either case, they're going to track the craft until it goes into a mountain or they blow us up."

"So, we send your hover in the opposite direction of wherever you end up going," Nick said. "We're clear here, right?"

"We're getting the hell out of Dodge," Jenifer answered, then shrugged her uninjured shoulder. "Or, at least out of Alexandria."

CHAPTER TEN

"When is the best time to leave the city?" John asked. Jenifer only managed a derisive snort before he raised a hand and tipped his chin. "Okay, let me try again. When are we leavin', because there *is* no good time."

The five of them had moved from the open space of the hanger to a side room used as a lunch area for the soldiers working this detail. Several round tables filled the space, some showing more wear and tear than others, with a mismatched variety of chairs. President Tanner, Lieutenant Colonel Montgomery and Briggs sat at one of the tables, the president slouched low with his legs stretched out in front of him. John leaned against a low counter, his hands braced over the chipped edge on each side of his hips with his ankles crossed. Jenifer couldn't be so still.

"Shouldn't you figure out where you're going to go first?" Briggs asked. "You've got to know which way to head before you decide when to leave. The first might dictate the second."

Jenifer fought the involuntary tick of her head toward her right shoulder when Briggs asked the question. The woman's voice had a way of digging at the base of her skull like rusted steel dragged over asphalt. Always had, since the first time they met. She covered her twitch by raising her hand and rubbing her right temple, while clearing her throat.

She mentally ran through the list of cities on John's tour, from first to last, mapping travel routes and terrain for each. Every one of them was out of the question. The Xenos didn't want John to live long enough to leave Alexandria, but if he managed to, they would be waiting for him in every city he had slated on his tour.

"The cities on the tour . . . why were they chosen?" Jenifer asked, pausing in her pacing to stand between John and President Tanner, looking at John. "Most of the major cities on the continent were hit in the first wave of attacks, and the point of the tour is to revisit these cities, right? To show even though we're down, we're not out."

"Somethin' like that, yeah."

"Okay, so the Sorracchi hit New York, Los Angeles, Chicago, Houston, Philadelphia, DC, Phoenix, Detroit, Orlando, Boston, Denver, Las Vegas . . . and the tour hits eight of those cities. Why those eight? The District makes sense, too close to Alexandria, but why not Chicago, Philadelphia, and Detroit?"

"Time," President Tanner answered and she turned her head toward him. He drummed his fingers on the table. "Travel routes. Security. Weather." Jenifer caught a slide of President Tanner's dark eyes toward John, then back to her. "We had to consider everything."

Jenifer looked to John, but his chin was tipped down, his attention on anything but the others in the room. He probably had no idea Nick Tanner had just given him up. A noise beyond the closed doors brought Connor to his feet, Mel and President Tanner following suit.

"That's probably the guy I sent out for you, Ambassador."

"Sent out? For what?" Jenifer asked, scowling. When had John asked Montgomery for anything?

"I'll be right back," Montgomery said, completely avoiding her question.

John lifted his head enough to nod acknowledgment, and stilled when he realized Jenifer watched him. She gave him credit. Once their eyes met, he didn't look away. His lips were drawn tight, his jaw tense, but she wasn't going to let him go so easy. She would abide no secrets; especially not the kind that could get him killed.

Briggs was hot on Montgomery's heels, which seemed to be her preferred position, and President Tanner beat them to the door, opening it for them. As soon as they were alone, Jenifer took the single stride needed to bring her into John's space. He straightened slightly, but didn't move to back away from her intrusion. With him leaning on the counter, they were nearly eye level. He inhaled, his jaw working. She just stared, her hands planted at her waist, then arched a single eyebrow.

He actually chuckled and looked down, a humorless grin tipping his lips. "I'm no' hidin' anythin', Jenifer. Yeah, we looked at everythin' Nick mentioned when decidin' where I'd go, but I told him I didn't want to go to Chicago. The other cities ruled themselves out for various reasons."

"Why not Chicago?"

He raised his chin again, but his eyes didn't meet hers. He focused downward, staring at maybe her chin to avoid her eyes. "Silas was supposed to go with me."

She almost asked, "What's that got to do with anything?" but her brain engaged before her mouth and she stopped. Drawing a slow breath, Jenifer nodded. "You didn't want to take him back to where his mother died."

"He still remembers." He did look straight at her then. "He was five years old. He remembers the bombin's, and runnin' with his mother and me to find safety." John paused, his jaw working as he ground his teeth. "He remembers his mother dyin'."

Jenifer forced her shoulders to relax and looked past him, finding a chipped spot of paint on the wall to stare at. Some of her anger drained away, unable to maintain it once she understood the reason for his decision. She'd once pegged John to be just like every other politician she ever had the misfortune of dealing with—egotistical and fake—but the more she shared space with him, the more she learned of him as a man, the less she believed he was the typical politician. Creating a new problem for Jenifer. It was easier to protect someone she didn't like, because every choice and action was based on reaching a final outcome—keeping him alive, whether she thought he deserved to be, or not. The fact she actually *liked* John Smith had the potential of clouding her judgment, and changing her perspective. Caring didn't equate with getting the job done.

If she was smart, she'd walk away now and leave him to his own devices or to the care of Connor Montgomery and his Firebirds.

If she was smart.

"How many people know you sent Silas off world?"

He inhaled through his nose and turned away so she saw his profile.

On any other man, the sharp angle of his features might be considered unappealing, but he pulled it off. There was something about the way he used his entire face to communicate, and she could judge his emotions by the way he held his mouth when he spoke. The more excited, the happier, or the more incensed he was, the more he used every part of his face to make his point—from smiling to shouting. The more thoughtful, the more restrained he was about something, the tighter his lips became and the less he allowed his expression to reveal his thoughts.

"Not many. To protect him, I thought it best to get him away as secretively as possible."

"So, the Xenos shouldn't know Silas is off world, but that doesn't mean they don't."

He nodded and pushed his hands into his pockets. She wondered sometimes if his silent agreement to her suggestions or observations was because he'd already determined the same solution, or because he blindly followed whatever she said. She preferred to think they were on the same wavelength.

Jenifer glanced around the break room, knowing logically they were alone with President Tanner in the hanger with Montgomery and Briggs, and moved close enough to him their jackets brushed against each other. They'd grown accustomed to holding their conversations in hushed tones and tight proximity, one of the few ways Jenifer could assure, if only to a slightly greater degree, their words would be between them and them alone even when it *appeared* they have privacy.

"The fewer people who know where we're going, the better." His only answer to her statement was a shift of his attention to her face. "Is President Tanner the only one who knows why you didn't want to go to Chicago, or was it an open topic of discussion?"

"He's the only one."

"The only one you *told*, but someone else could have figured it out. Your history on Earth isn't exactly a closed book."

"I didn't willin'ly open it." His voice was heavy and he dropped his chin again. He looked tired, worn, not physically—it was deeper than that. The word that came to mind was "done", and she understood the feeling.

She shifted until she could lean her hip against the edge of the low counter he used as support, standing perpendicular to him. He moved his hand behind her, his arm against her side. Voices carried from beyond the closed door, she differentiated President Tanner's from the rest and caught enough snippets to know they discussed gathering a variety of vehicles. They had to have the same thing in mind she did. Scatter focus in multiple directions. Hopefully, by the time the Xenos got wind of their departure, they'd be far enough away from the city and somewhere they could lay low for a while until a better alternative came along.

"You know the president better than I do. Will he give us the keys to the car and let us stay out past curfew even if he doesn't know where we're going?"

His eyebrows slid up as she spoke, a small smile revealing his slightly crooked teeth. "Sounds to me like you have a destination in mind."

Jenifer bit down and swallowed. Not a single choice was favorable, and some of the options playing around in her head were downright unpleasant. "Maybe," was the only answer she was willing to offer.

The whole idea made her gut burn.

She stepped away from him, walked several feet, and stopped to stare at the hanger door with her back to John.

They couldn't go anywhere on the tour schedule, couldn't even risk going anywhere *near* the major cities on the list, and she held no faith in anyone beyond herself, John and Nick Tanner; that included Connor Montgomery, his people, the entire population of Alexandria and anyone within a five hundred mile radius. Which meant any type of military or quasi-military base, outpost or refugee camp was out of the question.

They needed to go somewhere off the grid for *both* of them.

She pivoted on her heel, marched to the far side of the room, and set her palms against the worn walls at about shoulder level, leaning in with her head down. What she wanted to do was hit something, do *something* to burn off the tension twisting her up inside.

Off the grid. One place came to mind. A place no one would ever link to John Smith, Ambassador. A place no one alive would ever connect to her. But, there *had* to be another choice.

The idea of Savannah made her insides go cold, even though she hadn't even set foot in the region in ten years, and hadn't been on the property since she'd first left. Nearly twenty years. Very few things managed to rattle Jenifer, but her acknowledgment of those things gave her strength over them. Didn't mean she willingly jumped at the chance to face them down. The fact she had stayed away, and the only person who had ever known this part of her past was now dead, provided near-absolute surety no one would guess their destination.

Savannah would be her last resort, when everything else went so FUBAR she had no other option. She had one other idea, one other place they could go. She'd never been there herself, and considering all that had happened last time John was there, she figured no one would peg him for a return visit. It wasn't a city, it wasn't a military post—anymore—and it would give them enough time to hunker down and hide out until things settled and not so many people wanted John Smith dead.

Or, she could just walk away.

Yeah, sure she could . . .

*J*ohn watched Jenifer from across the room and, not for the first time, wished he could get some kind of sense of her thoughts or emotions. He recalled Michael once explaining to him how frustrated he'd felt in the months after being freed from his prison in New Mexico. Being so secluded from people and society, he had no concept of reading body language, expressions, and cultural references. He felt lost and simple. Even now, three years later, Michael said he still felt out of place.

He imagined his frustration had to be similar. He believed the etymology of many languages on Earth stemmed from or were born from the languages spoken on Aretu and Raxo, along with the languages spoken on Earth before the arrival of the pilgrims. He had studied and learned all main languages on the planet, so communication was not an issue. But, having lived on a planet where communication happened as much with the senses as with words or actions, he felt blind and deaf, and ultimately dumb.

She wore her apprehension like a force field. Tension pulled at her body, drawing her tight as a bowstring and buffered off her in waves of heat, making his skin tingle. He'd wanted to wrap an arm around her waist when she stood close to him, to see if she would remain so rigid if he held her.

As much as he wondered, he also knew she wouldn't welcome it.

She shoved herself away from the wall she'd leaned on for the last several moments, and paced from one side of the room to the other, her arms crossed and her head down. John stepped away from the counter, but only managed one step in her direction when the far door opened. Nick led the way for Connor and Mel. Connor carried his ready rucksack and set it on the table with a thump. John switched directions and met Connor at the table.

"We couldn't bring much out of the apartment," Connor said as he slid the sack toward John. "As it was, I sent only one of my men into the place to grab what you wanted so no one noticed."

"Thank you." John pulled the rucksack toward him. "Were you able to grab any of Jenifer's things?"

"Not much. My man went in with a small, unmarked bag full of junk, made it look like he went in with a full bag and came out with a full bag, so he could only grab what he could easily find, switch out and leave with."

Jenifer reached them while Connor explained, stopping within arm's reach with her arms crossed and her hips cocked to the side. Her eyes practically flashed when she looked between John and Connor.

"I appreciate that," John said, working at the zipper of the sack.

"You sent them back for your luggage?" Jenifer demanded, slamming her hand on top of the sack. "I'm trying to get you out of the city alive, and you're worried about clean underwear?"

John grinned, wrapping his hand around her hand to lift it away. "Luggage, no. And I'm no' discussin' my underwear in mixed company, thank you."

He rummaged in the pack through the various items he'd asked Connor to grab in addition to the things he kept in the bag always at the ready, Jenifer glaring at him all the while. He curled his fingers around a small case, contemplating for a moment whether he should offer the contents and their purpose, but decided the situation wasn't extreme enough to risk the physical strain of using the hoppers. There was a reason they were considered final acts of desperation rather than a casual mode of travel.

He found what he was looking for at the bottom of the bag, and pulled it through the contents, taking a moment to appreciate the weapon he held: Jenifer's personal weapon. He'd noted it the first time he met her, but she'd stopped wearing it as soon as her protection detail had officially begun. Whoever had modified the pulse weapon had done an impressive job, surpassing the standard three settings of most pulse weapons with at least a full dozen that he was aware of. If asked to guess, John would bet money Jenifer had done the modifications herself. He'd seen her various and sundry gadgets, and she used them with a casual skill born of creator knowledge. With the setting ranges, she could do everything from loosening a lock to a setting so intense it could resonate concrete into dust. A sonic disruption system piggybacked the pulse energy and could disrupt EM fields and deafen anyone within probably a radius of fifty-feet. Based on the lack of apparent power, he would bet on a biolock coding set solely to her DNA and possibly voice initiation.

John held it out to her in the palm of his hand, grinning. "That's an impressive weapon, Jenifer. Did you think I hadn't noticed it?"

"Everyone notices Damocles, Ambassador." Jenifer snatched the weapon from his open hand, and it immediately hummed to life at her touch, a blue indicator light glowing softly at the hilt when the handle recognized her DNA. "I can't believe you'd send someone in there for a gun."

He raised his eyebrows. "Damocles. How fittin'. The value of the sword is no' it falls, but it hangs."

"You get a gold star, Ambassador. I'm impressed you know our myths so well." She removed the standard issue pulse weapon from her thigh holster and set it on the table, slamming Damocles home in the empty holster.

"Who said it was *your* myth?" he kidded, but she didn't even whisper at a hint of a smile.

"You still shouldn't have sent someone back to the apartment for a *gun*."

"Not just that. I sent them for my supply of peanut butter." He picked up her discarded weapon and engaged the safety before putting it in the bag. He zipped closed the rucksack and winked at her. Her cold stoicism didn't crack, but a damnable wall of heat still hovered around her.

Perhaps he *did* sense something from her, just not in any way he'd connected with another Human. "You think I'm travelin' anywhere with you without peanut butter?"

"Ambassador . . ." Connor said.

Jenifer's jaw dropped, but she snapped it shut with a clack of her teeth. "You sent them for peanut butter?"

"Ambassador . . ." Connor said again, stronger than the first time.

"What?" John looked from her to Connor.

"We thought you were kidding about the peanut butter."

John groaned and pressed his open hand to his chest. "Oh, no. Oh, Connor, what have you done? You can't send me out there with this woman without peanut butter."

Connor smirked and Nick chuckled.

"You think you're so funny," Jenifer mumbled, reaching past him to grab the rucksack.

"I *am* so funny," he came back, holding the rucksack just out of her reach. "And I'm also absolutely serious. Among other things, I asked Connor's men to grab some foodstuff, whether it be from the apartment or somewhere else."

"I don't have issues with the food, Ambassador," she ground out. She reached long and grabbed a fistful of the canvas bag, giving it a good yank. She winced, and John looked to her injured arm. She'd covered the bandage when she put on her torn jacket, he couldn't tell if the wound had reopened, or not. "I have issues with you and everyone else being so cavalier about your life."

John popped his eyebrows. "Is tha' what you think I'm doin'?" He pulled back on the bag, but she refused to let go.

"It's what you've always done. From our first night together—"

"You're goin' to bring that up?"

"As they say, Ambassador, if the shoe fits—" She jerked harder on the bag.

"You're goin' to hurt—" Her lips twisted in defiance and she jerked harder before he could finish his warning. He jerked back, with enough force to set her off balance and she came against his chest.

Jenifer relinquished her hold on the sack to plant both her hands on his jacket, shoving him back. "It's painfully clear to *me*, even if not to anyone else, these Xenos know a *hell* of a lot more than they should a *hell* of a lot faster than justifiable without having inside information. As far as I'm concerned, anyone and everyone is suspect. Including the grunt you trusted to go back to apartment and bring that bag here. As far as we know, the Xenos already know we're here and we could be vapor in the next ten minutes. And you're worried about *peanut butter*."

John leaned into her attempt at shoving him back, bringing them nearly nose-to-nose. "I'm no' some impotent milksop who requires you hold my hand and lead me around like a rebellious sprat!"

"You could have fooled me!"

"Hey!" Nick shouted. "Geez, get a room or get in your separate corners of the sandbox, I don't care. But knock it off!"

John stopped short of saying anything else, grinding his teeth together. He huffed hard, angry breaths, clenching his fists at his side. She mirrored his stance, huffing the same angry way. A slow, deep breath through his nose allowed him to tamp down the anger he didn't understand. She frustrated him, but was a far cry from the anger simmering beneath his skin.

Jenifer took a step back and pivoted away. In one smooth motion, she hopped onto the top of one of the round tables and folded her legs beneath her. Almost immediately, John's anger was gone and he straightened, blinking.

"I apologize," he finally said. "Jenifer is right." She raised her head, glaring at him. "What? You don't have to look surprised." John turned to speak to Nick directly. "I understand the threat, but I have spent much of my life under threat from someone or somethin'. Sometimes no' against myself directly, but for who I am either in race or title. I *have* been too cavalier, especially because it's not just my life at risk."

"Yeah, well . . ." Nick waved off John's apology. "Let's get this done."

"We have half a dozen hovers ready to go," Mel said from her nearby chair. She'd barely spoken since they came back into the room. "You just need to tell us where you're going."

"No," Jenifer snapped, unfolding her legs. Her boots hit the concrete floor with a thump and she crossed to them in long strides. "Just hand over the passkey so the ambassador and I can be on our way."

"We need to know where—" Connor tried to argue.

"No," she said again, even sharper. "Here's the deal. We all leave here heading in different directions. I don't care where you go, as long as you don't follow me. No radio contact. No communication. When I'm convinced I don't have a tail, the ambassador and I are on our merry way."

"How are we supposed to contact you?" Mel asked.

"You don't," Jenifer snapped at the woman, and Mel leaned back, her eyes wide at Jenifer's sharp tone. "If we need to, and when I decide, we contact you."

"I don't think—"

"She's right," John interjected, ending Connor's argument. He noted Nick hadn't voiced an opinion or argued Jenifer's plan, like the other two. He suspected Nick understood her plan, at least as much as John himself did. "Until a better plan presents itself, Jenifer and I are . . ." He paused, trying to remember a phrase he'd heard one of the Firebirds use, and he'd asked Nick about it. " . . .goin' to ground."

"I don't want the fastest or the fanciest hover," Jenifer said. She practically stomped across the floor to stand beside him, her arms crossed. "No distinguishing markings or idents, something that will blend into any crowd of hovers. Not one of those passenger hovers we came here in, something we can hunker down in if we have to lay low."

Connor held out a passkey. "Out the door to the left, second from the door."

"Fine." She reached for the sack, but John was too quick and flung the bag over his shoulder before she got hold of it. She slid him a glance, but neither smiled nor frowned. "It's dark now, we leave with no lights of any kind. We fly on lidar only. Everyone splits and no one talks."

"How are we supposed to avoid you if we don't know which way you went?" Mel asked.

"Don't follow me. Not complicated, soldier."

Mel scowled, but said nothing. Especially when Connor looked her way and just barely shook his head in a silent order to hold her tongue. In unspoken agreement, the five of them stood or turned and headed for the door. Connor stopped with his hand on the handle.

"We ready?"

Before anyone answered, Nick turned to John and held out his hand. "Take care of yourself, John."

John took his hand in an action nearly universal. As soon as Nick gripped his hand, John felt the tingle of recognition he always felt around the president. Nick's Talents were increasing in strength, whether he was aware of it or not. A whisper, almost an indiscernible hum, passed through his thoughts and he nodded when he understood. Nick released his hand and Connor pushed open the exterior door, and an immediate gust of frigid cold air hit John in the face. Jenifer's fingers wrapped around his wrist as they crossed the dark space to the hover Connor had designated for them.

A comment about holding her hand crossed his mind, but he decided it best to keep it to himself.

CHAPTER ELEVEN

"*H*ang on, Ambassador."

She didn't wait for his response, or for him to brace himself in the chair beside her, before she jerked the controls and gave the hover one last thrust to drive it sideways into the fifteen foot snowdrift deep in the Alabama woods. With a muffled thud and a jerk, the hover settled in a shower of white as the snow shifted and covered half the front view panels.

John released his safety harness as soon as the hover rocked to a stop, and was out of his chair before the side cargo hatch cracked open. Frigid air whistled through the broadening space, pulling a flurry of snow with it. Jenifer switched the interior heat vents to high, hot air hitting her in the face before she stood and followed John outside.

The sharp contrast between the warm air inside the hover and the raw, biting cold outside stole her breath and made her chest ache. The wound on her arm, aching now hours after John had applied the anesthetic netting, stung from the cold even through the jacket.

"How do we look?" she asked, her footsteps crunching in the ice-crusted snow.

"Fine," John answered from somewhere away from the hover. "Jenifer, come here."

She followed the sound of his voice and stomped through the snow toward the back of the shuttle. John stood a few feet from the back of the hover, his hands set at his waist with his head tipped back to the sky. As soon as she was within a couple feet of him, he reached back for her, and she took his hand. His fingers were still warm, lacing through hers, and he drew her beside him.

"It's beautiful." His breath curled in front of his face. "I haven't seen anythin' this beautiful since I was on Senti Hotha."

Jenifer had stopped looking for beauty in anything, hadn't seen anything that made her pause for nearly two decades. Maybe it was the way John saw the beauty that made her do it now. She'd seen through the forward view panel the clearing they cut through to reach the cluster of trees they hunkered down in, but seeing it through the view panel was nothing like standing on the edge of the field at three in the morning. The landscape was a palate of silvers, blues, and whites with moonlight streaming through the forest canopy. The sky was blue-black, the stars bright and clear with no lights of civilization to dim them, and the waxing three-quarter moon was so bright and clear she swore she could reach out and touch it if she tried.

A gust of wind whipped through the trees and stung her face. Jenifer took a step closer to him, hiding behind his shoulder. "Where is Senti Hotha?"

He looked toward the eastern sky, scanned the stars, then turned into her, wrapping his arm around her shoulders to turn her with him. The wind was to their back, whipping her hair around her face. She looked up at him, watching his profile while he studied the sky. He squinted in the moonlight, his fine hair brushing across his forehead. She knew she was tired when she was so easily distracted.

"There," John said, his smile spreading. He pointed almost straight up to a cluster of stars with two slightly brighter than the others. "No wait. There." He adjusted the angle of his arm by maybe five degrees. "That way about thirty-eight trillion miles."

"Oh, so just around the corner."

He chuckled and looked down at her, his breath warm on her cheeks. "Depends on if you catch the right train, otherwise you end up twenty trillion miles out of the way."

Jenifer let go of a fraction of the tension twisting in her gut, just enough to smile at him. She'd had a lot of time to work over in her head the reality of their destination in the hours since they left Alexandria. For the first hour or two, she watched their rear lidar array waiting for another craft to appear. When none tracked them, she'd split her attention between the scanners and her thoughts. John had remained silent for most of the flight, only speaking to tell her he'd managed to coax another forty-mile range out of the array, leaving her to her plans.

With distance from the decision to head south she'd managed to swallow the bitter aversion to the idea, and now, it was just a destination. After all, there was nothing left there but a shell of a building that meant nothing to her. It had lost its meaning twenty years before, and now it was dead, just like the people who had once lived in it.

"Can we get inside before I lose my toes?"

John nodded, dropped his arm, and took her hand to follow the path they'd both made from the hatch. The air inside the vehicle was hot, despite the open door. Once inside, Jenifer slapped her hand on the control panel and the hatch creaked closed, bringing some of the snow from outside with it, left to pool and melt along the hinge. John shrugged off his jacket, running his long fingers over his snow-dampened hair.

"Toasty in here," he said, draping his jacket across one of the crew chairs in the back of the hover.

"We're going to have to power down except for necessary systems. That includes powering down the internal heating units. If we warm it up as much as possible in here first, we'll be fine catching a few hours' sleep. When the sun comes up we'll head out again."

"How far are we from wherever it is we're goin'?"

"Three hundred miles. We're taking the long road."

John just nodded, hunching beneath the low ceiling to walk the three steps needed to cross the small interior of the transport. He opened a panel between two upper storage spaces and pressed a button inside to drop the single bed plank folded into the wall. The mattress was thin, just enough to provide a cushion for the metal beneath, with a thin blanket tucked around it. Jenifer opened one of the storage compartments and pulled out a folded blanket and small puff of nothing that was supposed to pass as a pillow.

"Why haven't you pushed to find out where we're going?" she asked, holding the spare blanket and pillow against her chest. "I'd be curious as hell."

"Not sayin' I'm no'." He sat on the edge of the plank, leaning over to untie his boots. "I can navigate a planet, given coordinates and trajectories. I've been on two-dozen planets from one end of this galaxy to the next. But, this is your world, Jenifer."

"Does this mean you finally trust me?"

He set his boots down on the floor with a thunk and stood, standing taller than her even in his socks. "I've always trusted you, Jenifer." He grinned and leaned closer. "Doesn't mean it's easy to concede."

She had a great comeback, but it was lost in a jaw-breaking yawn. John laughed and walked around her to the pilot station, switching off systems until everything was dark but some dash indicator lights. The heater vents stopped blowing and the engines fell silent. Moonlight streamed in through the forward view panels, casting enough silvery light to illuminate the planes of his face.

"Make sure to leave the system recoil on, or the engines could freeze up," Jenifer managed to say through another yawn while she unbuckled her thigh holster and set Damocles on the floor between the plank bed and where she intended to lay out her pallet.

"Already taken care of. Get into bed quick before it cools off in here."

She tossed her sad excuse for a pillow on the floor, and snapped open the folded blanket. Before she could lay the blanket out on the metal floor, John walked past her, snatched up the pillow, and tossed it on the bed. Before it bounced, he yanked the blanket from her hands.

"What are you doing?"

"More like what you're no' doin'." John spread the second blanket on the bed and folded them back to expose the thin mattress. "You're no' sleepin' on the hovercraft floor, and don't tell me that wasn't exactly what you were goin' to do."

"Ambassador—"

"If we're goin' to sleep together, the least you can do is call me John." He sat on the edge of the plank and slid under the blankets, putting his back to the exterior wall of the hover. The plank bed was maybe six feet long, a little too short for John, and barely wide enough for one person to sleep comfortably, let alone two. He pulled up his knees and tucked the small pillow beneath his head, extending his arm along the mattress so his hand hung off the edge, a testament to the lack of length and width. "I suggest you get in here before we lose the heat advantage and it cools off."

Jenifer looked down at him, and tried very hard to ignore the warmth in her stomach at the sight of John lying in a bed, waiting for her to lie down beside him. She swallowed and blinked, trying to find some justifiable argument, but the logic of sharing body heat in a situation that could mean death from the cold overrode any other argument.

John raised himself up on his elbow. "Remember what I said about it no' bein' easy to concede? Well, on this I'm no'. I also don't bite." A slow grin tugged up one corner of his mouth.

Jenifer shook his head. "Don't even *think* about saying it."

"Then get in bed."

She swallowed the low sound at the base of her throat, but wasn't about to let him know he'd affected her. No way in hell. He wanted to play 'get a rise out of Jenifer'? No problem, she could do the same. Moving with calculated ease, she turned and sat on the bed, far enough back her hips brushed his stomach. She thought she felt his fingers brush her hip, but ignored it. She leaned forward and unlaced her boots, taking her time but with forethought to the cooling air in the hover. When her boots were off, she shrugged out of the jacket, sliding it off her shoulders and arching her back to pull the sleeves off behind her. She tossed the jacket across the room and it landed on top of John's. When she settled into the bed and tucked her feet under the blankets, she made sure to shift and nestle her body against his, her back to his chest.

His warm breath whispered across the nape of her neck when he draped the doubled-up blankets over them, trapping the heat. Jenifer shifted again, rubbing her cheek against the warm, exposed skin on the inside of his arm, the arm she used as a pillow. He dropped his arm across her waist and his fingers curled into the cotton sheet under them. A small sound, more in his chest than his throat, made Jenifer grin.

"How is your arm?" John asked, sliding his fingers through the slice in the sleeve along the silk mesh over the wound. It stung, but it wasn't intolerable.

"I've had worse, and probably will again."

"That's no' what I asked."

"It's fine, Ambassador."

He drew in a long breath, and released it, once again sending warmth across her neck. "Sleep well, Jenifer Of No Last Name."

She swallowed and shifted deeper into the bed, and closer to John. He flattened his hand against her stomach and drew her closer. Jenifer forced her breathing to stay level, unchanged. She'd never slept beside a man, she wouldn't leave herself so vulnerable. Not even with Elijah. She'd slept near him after she and Jackie had pulled him and Jace Quinn out of the Sorracchi prison, but not beside him. Just close enough to know he was alive. He'd been her lover, and she hadn't slept with him. John Smith was her job.

That had to be why it was so easy.

"Sleep well, Ambassador."

*E*ither they both were too tired to move during the night, or their subconscious minds didn't want to disturb the small huddle of heat they created, because neither moved until the morning sun reflecting off the snow beyond the forward view panels woke John. Jenifer was still nestled against him, her head on his arm with her hair teasing his chin, catching in the full day's growth of beard stubble. One of them had drawn the blanket up higher, covering half their faces, and when he inhaled, the enticing scent of warm woman—warm Jenifer—wrapped around him.

He fought the urge to pull her closer, to tempt fate by spreading his hand across her stomach, only because he knew if he did she'd come awake and he'd lose all contact. He'd pulled her close during the night, when they'd first stretched out beneath the blankets, but then it had been part of the dance. The game they played. He wasn't sure who had won this round, if anyone had won at all. It wasn't about winning; it was about coaxing a smile from her beautiful but far-too-stern lips.

John closed his eyes, knowing the sun would wake her any moment, and focused on every point of contact. He didn't know if he would ever be given the chance to be this close to her again, and he intended to enjoy it while he could. Their bodies fit well together. With his knees bent and legs drawn up so he could fit on the short bed, she nestled perfectly into the shape of his body. It would be so easy to curl his arms and hold her close, and nuzzle his cold nose against the warm nape hidden by her hair.

Somewhere between stolen chocolate candies and licking peanut butter off a knife, Jenifer Of No Last Name became more than a hired gun to keep him alive when his hands were tied and his weapon confiscated. She tested him, she captivated him, and she made him keenly aware of her presence whenever she was in the room. She got in his space, and he didn't mind. She was feminine and strong at the same time, and he found it damn attractive. She was a mystery and a challenge, even beyond his inability to sense anything from her. There was a story behind her eyes, which just added to his wish to find the Jenifer she hid.

She woke with a slow, graceful stretch and a long draw of air.

John stole the chance and tightened his hold on her, matching the stretch. "Good mornin'," he said through a yawn.

She mumbled, threw back the blanket, and swung her legs over the edge. Before he could follow, she picked up her weapon and holster from the floor, reached the pilot chair and fired up the engines. They sputtered at first, churning in the bitter cold, but finally hummed to life. John slipped his feet into his boots with a cursory knot of the laces, grabbed her boots with one hand and both their jackets with the other. She switched from auxiliary idle power to full engine capacity as he dropped into the co-pilot seat. He held out her jacket and dropped her boots on the floor near her feet.

"How are we lookin'?"

"Systems are sluggish," she answered, her focus on the panels and readouts. "This damn cold could freeze lava. Never used to be like this, you know. Around here, we were lucky if we got a couple inches of snow a year and wore short sleeves until Christmas."

John laid her jacket across his lap since she was too focused to take it and pulled on his own. "Are you from this region?"

"Close enough."

Something near the rear nacelles banged and shuttered, immediately followed by a low vibration shifting through the ancient conveyance. A weak, tepid stream of air leaked from the overhead heat vents. It would be a good hour before the chill was gone from the air. John stood and moved behind her chair, holding out her jacket.

"Come on," he said, giving it a shake.

She didn't look at him, but slipped an arm into each sleeve. Her wince when she shifted her injured arm didn't go unnoticed. With it zipped up, she hunched to put on her boots, her attention still on the power readings. "We're not going to be able to move for a few minutes. The engines need to recoup power before they'll be strong enough to free us from the bank."

"Open the hatch. I'll take a look outside, see if we're buried deeper than last night."

At that, she finally looked over her shoulder and smirked, pressing a button on the panel. "Sure, Ambassador. Just don't freeze anything off."

"Funny."

The side hatch cracked and spread open as he turned, and frigid air prickled his face when he stepped outside. More snow had fallen. Not enough to bury the hover, but enough to block the nacelles. The heat thrown off from the circulation units had already melted away some of the accumulated snow, but she was right, it would be a few minutes before they could move.

He headed back to the hover minutes later, stomping his feet on the lower hatch. "Bloody freezin' out there—"

The loud shrill of proximity alarms cut him off, and half a dozen warning lights flashed along the overhead panels above Jenifer.

She cursed, and John took three long strides to reach the seat beside her. "What is it?"

"Heavily armed *something* heading in our direction."

"Intercept course?"

She shook her head, flipping the lidar view from sonar to topographic. "No. They'll miss us by about two miles, heading west. But, I'd bet the peanut butter you're hiding in that bag of yours they're looking for us."

CHAPTER TWELVE

*T*he blare of alarms and the screech of metal trying to stay together under the strain of pulse cannons ripped through Jenifer's head like pinpoint needles through her eardrums. Every jerk of the struggling hover forced her to brace her body against slamming into the console, or the seat, depending on the direction of the blast.

"They've gained another hundred yards on us," John shouted over the wails

"I know! I know!"

She lurched forward, pain shooting up her injured arm when her palm slammed against the edge of the console to keep her from going into the front view panel. Before falling back into her chair, she managed to open the combustion vents into the rear nacelles to eke out a few extra units of thrust. If they took on one or two more blasts, even that wouldn't help them. They'd lost lidar control and she manually flew the hover through the snow-covered landscape. Every crank on the controls to avoid a crash made her gut twist, and adrenaline choked her with a bitter burn in the back of her throat.

"We hit the ocean in fourteen miles." John coughed, waving away the smoke curling out of the burning console, the acrid stench of melting coils and wires filling the air.

Jenifer coughed and blinked through the burning tears from the smoke. The water would be frozen solid. The hovercraft could travel over the frozen surface as well as over land, but she wasn't sure this beaten and battered craft could handle water. If it were in better shape, maybe. If they went down, if they crashed, they'd go through the icy surface and the hover would sink like a rock.

"I'm banking east, try to get us over the mainland."

She twisted the controls and braced with her feet to keep from tumbling out of the chair. They hadn't had time to buckle in before the hover had turned on them, essentially blasting them free of the snow bank hindering their takeoff. For the last two hundred miles, Jenifer had pulled out every fancy maneuver she could manage in the rust bucket Connor Montgomery had pawned off on them. Had she known the Xenos would be this aggressive, she'd have demanded something with a little more speed and finesse. Ambiguity versus speed, the choice could have gone either way.

A ripple of distorted light and energy whizzed by on their right side, hitting and annihilating a copse of trees a quarter mile ahead of them. They shot past it a second later, chunks of wood and ice ricocheting off the forward panel in their wake. Something hit the side of the hover, forcing her to fight with the propulsion controls to keep them from going head-on into another cluster of trees.

"Damn it," she cursed, attempting to boost the rear shields even though defense system power was nearly non-existent, blown away in the first fifty miles of chase. They'd been running for nearly an hour, and she was so off course from being anywhere near where she'd intended to be she wasn't even sure what territory they flew over. They were near the ocean, yes, but beyond she hadn't had time to confirm global positioning. She just flew. Ran. Tried to stay alive.

"Incomin'!"

She braced again at John's warning, the ripple of the blast moving through the hover in a massive wave, squeezing her lungs as it pummeled her. That was the third full blast the hover had withstood, and she wasn't sure how many more both she and the craft could take. She didn't know how the blasts affected John. Maybe Areth somehow could withstand the full ripple better than a Human, maybe not. She couldn't even risk a glance in his direction to judge.

They couldn't keep this up indefinitely. They'd run out of power, and even if the O_2 cyclers could keep up with the demand, the other hover would eventually overtake them and out-maneuver them. Their options fell between little and none, and not one held appeal.

Which seemed to be the theme of her decisions as of late: they all sucked, but which one sucked the least? And which one might they actually survive?

"Rear nacelles are at seventy-five percent power and trajectory thrusters are gone." John slammed his hand on the console, cursing in a language she didn't understand. At least she assumed it was cursing, based on his tone. "We just lost rear shields completely. Another hit and we've got nothin' to disburse the energy blast."

"There's an auxiliary routing system near the thruster unit relays, but it requires manual engagement."

John didn't affirm he understood, but was out of his seat and heading into the rear of the hover before she could explain more. She tried to keep the craft level, but with the trajectory thrusters gone she had little to no finesse in her maneuverability. The controls shuddered in her hands, and the hover shook around her. It wouldn't last much longer. She would bet the backstabbing sons of bitches chasing them knew that, considering she'd also place money on them getting information from whomever sent them this far west in search of John Smith.

All of three people knew they'd left Alexandria, and those same three people knew exactly what kind of hover they flew. She clenched her teeth so hard pain shot to the base of her skull. *Damn it!* No one had followed them out of the city, at least not close enough to slide into the lidar array of the hover, and it had been hours between their departure. The only way someone could have found them was if they tracked them. Since no one had been close enough to either of them to plant a trace, it was in the hover. No question.

The dash dimmed and flashed for half a second, and the rear shield diagnostics stopped blaring just as John shouted "Got it!" from the back of the craft.

They crested a hill and Jenifer's heart jumped to her throat. "Damn!"

At seventy miles an hour, the clustered settlement literally sprang from the snow. Jenifer slammed the deceleration drive and banked hard to the right, practically setting the hover on its side. Crashing and a muffled grunt came from behind her, but she couldn't turn to look. The cushion drive fluttered and she held her breath as she tried to keep her seat long enough to right the hover. Ice and snow exploded in front of them, sending waves of white over the front view panels.

With a gut-twisting wrench of the hover, they leveled off and she tried to wring one more burst of power from the dying engines. The air whistled and one of the buildings to their left exploded in a shower of splintered, smoldering wood. The asses were taking pot shots with civilians in the line of fire!

"Ambassador!" she shouted over her shoulder. No answer. "John!"

Panic flashed over her skin like ice water, and she dared a quick twist in her seat to look into the dark interior of the hover. She caught a glimpse of his crumpled form, face down, on the hover floor and the panic swelled. Okay, that was it. She'd had enough of the damn cat and mouse game.

Jenifer waited until they were at least thirty miles clear of the settlement headed inland, then dropped deeper into the trees, branches and smaller trunks snapping and cracking with the impact. Limbs slapped the forward view panel, snow wetting the thick glass in huge chunks. A tree ahead of her blew up in a brilliant explosion as their pursuers fired, the pulse blast skimming the top of the hover before making impact in front of them. The force shoved the hover down and the runners hit the surface. These crafts were not designed for this kind of abuse, and one way or another the hover was going down in the next few seconds. She could either control the crash or let it happen, and she wasn't a let-it-happen kind of girl.

She cranked the controls hard to the left, engaged the deceleration systems to maximum and punched the O_2 thrusters. The hover dropped hard from over one hundred miles an hour to a third speed and flipped into a hard left roll, landing on its side. It slid for another five hundred feet, plowing its way through the forest undergrowth before coming to a hard stop against the massive trunk of an oak. For the next few seconds, Jenifer's heart stopped and pain pummeled her body. The teeth-cracking wail of tearing metal ripped through her head and she fought to keep from vomiting.

Blackness replaced the flash of lights, for how long she didn't know, but when she blinked open her eyes the hover descended from its side to its runners with a creak and a teeth-shattering thunk. Smoke burned her lungs and a biting rush of frigid air made her gasp. The front panels were blown out and acrid smoke billowed from the smoldering controls. Jenifer crawled free of the twisted remains of the pilot seat, unable to control her cry when pain rippled up her arm. Warm blood trickled from the wound beneath the jacket sleeve, already making the cuff sticky. Morning sunlight reflected off the snow outside, the light amplifying the headache threatening to make her head explode.

She pulled herself over the seething console, the metal hot beneath her hand. Free of the mangled mess, she looked back into the tossed interior of the hover.

"Ambassador!" Panic, raw and vicious slammed her chest. "Ambassador!"

The whistle of a hover moving at high speed whizzed over them and Jenifer looked through the shattered view panel. They were at the bottom of an embankment, several felled trees curled and broken over the crushed hull of the hover. Flames flicked from the rear nacelles. They'd double back in moments, undoubtedly to make sure she and John were either dead or alive.

She and John would be the only ones walking away if she had anything to say about it.

Smoke tainted the air, ripping ragged coughs from her. She stumbled into the dark interior of the shuttle, the only light the red glow of emergency fixtures in the ceiling, three of the four broken and the fourth a harsh glow without an opaque faceplate to diffuse the light. The light flickered, threatening to go out as the power units withered and died a slow and painful death. She had to hurry if she intended to use the lingering O_2 trapped in the nacelles.

Jenifer dropped to her knees beside John, pain screaming from shoulder to elbow through her injured arm as she rolled him partially onto his back. The light blinked out completely before she could make an assessment of his injuries, but she couldn't take any more time. She turned and stumbled to the door, not quite making it fully to her feet before slamming her hand on the control panel to open the hatch. It whined and screeched, but opened with a hiss and pop as the powerful hydraulics forced open the panels. Biting cold hit her, whipping her hair as she turned back to John. Tapping into whatever hidden reserve of strength she had, fueled by pure, raw adrenaline, she pushed her battered body beyond anything she thought possible and threw his body over her shoulder in what she'd once heard Elijah call a fireman's carry.

By the time she cleared the hover and made it the necessary hundred feet into the thick undergrowth of the forest around the smoldering craft her legs burned with exertion and each cold breath sawed through her chest, leaving a thick film at the back of her throat she couldn't swallow away. She tried to lower to her knees and ease John to the ground, but her legs gave way and she dropped hard, both of them tumbling into the snow. Black smoke billowed from the hover, escaping over the tree line to darken the sky. The air vibrated with the approach of their attacker's hover. She almost heard the voice in her head screaming, *Hurry! Hurry!*

Leaving John where he fell, she forced her shaking legs to propel her back to the hover, stumbling once in the snow to land on her hands and knees. The ice crusted snow cut into her palms and burning pain radiated to her shoulder. The silk weave on her arm had long since given way, sticky blood chilling in the bitter cold. She was on her feet by the time she reached the open hatch and ran inside, panting for breath.

Her numb fingers fought every step as she ripped open the access hatch to the nacelles and flipped the recoil switch, forcing the O_2 to churn into a frenzy with no outlet now that the thrusters and trajectory controls were dead. Within less than two minutes the power sources would be miniature bombs waiting for a spark to ignite them. She tripped over parts and various pieces of equipment now littering the floor trying to reach the front of the hover to engage the system ignition. With nothing to receive the power burst, the ignition would soon overload and be the spark the nacelles needed.

There was no way to time the blast. She hoped to get clear, and more than that, hoped their would-be assassins would arrive to investigate the hover before they blew.

Her toe caught something just as she reached the open hatch and she looked down. The rucksack John had so adamantly guarded. She flung it over her shoulder and lurched down the ramp, slamming the control as she escaped. The hatch slowly cranked closed behind her, the hydraulics fighting to draw the last bit of power from the system to complete the task. Snow and smoke swirled around her, choking her. The other craft hung overhead, the smoke camouflaging her from their view . . . she hoped. She ran for the trees, falling when she hit the cluster of undergrowth she'd used to hide John. He hadn't moved, his arm extending out, supporting his head, his face turned away from her. Crimson stained the snow.

She reached for him, but snapped back to the landing hover as a powerful gust of their cushion drive cleared the air of smoke for a brief moment before they settled the military-issue battle craft in the path Jenifer had cut through the trees in her attempt to land, not crash. Jenifer crouched behind the scraggly shrub they hid behind, leaves and foliage gone in the cold of winter. Hatred and anger boiled in her chest, making her nearly oblivious to the cold as she studied the craft that had chased them down. It was definitely military, which put a finer point on her suspicions. The Xenos may claim to be civilian revolutionists, but they clearly had terrorists—because that's what they were, without question—planted in the military service. Maybe even higher.

Three people had helped them prepare to leave Alexandria.

Three people knew they were leaving the city.

Three people knew what they would be flying.

Three people had access to the craft . . . and their supplies.

She looked down at the rucksack she'd grabbed on a whim from the hover. Maybe it wasn't the hover at all. A tracking unit in the sack would narrow down her list of guilty parties. The side hatches of the military hover hissed open, and she shifted her attention between the bag and the two soldiers exiting the craft. Patting down her pockets and belt, she found the tiny device she needed and flipped it on. The scanner, no bigger than the palm of her hand, blinked green as she waved it over and around the sack. The light never changed. The sack had no tracking device, and there was no device within ten feet or the light would be yellow, indicating she should keep looking.

The tracker had to be in the hover.

When all other options are nullified, the remaining option is the answer.

The two soldiers wearing the emblem of the prestigious Firebirds approached the smoldering craft. The engines hummed enough to send a low vibration through the ground, hopefully making them believe she and John might still be inside. Both had their weapons drawn, and one nodded to the other to approach the hatch while he walked around the front of the hover. Jenifer studied their faces, not recognizing either one of them.

The one sent to investigate the hatch attempted to open the panels through the exterior commands, but the hydraulics only whined and the panels creaked open a few inches before slamming shut again. The first motioned him toward the front of the hover, and standing side by side, they both aimed and fired at the already cracked front view panels.

The resulting blast knocked Jenifer backward, sending her sprawling on her back, knocking the wind out of her. She gasped for breath, rolling onto her side. Her hand left a bloody print in the snow from the blood running past her soaked cuff. She coughed and shifted to her knees, crawling back to the bush she'd hidden behind. Some of the branches burned like small matches, the glorious burn of the hover holding her attention. The air practically sizzled now, waves of heat rolling off the ship. The overloaded nacelles had done exactly what she wanted.

All that was left of the two Firebirds were the bloody stains on the snow and the spatter of their annihilated remains across the front of their own hover.

John made a sound, low and strained, and rolled onto his back. Jenifer scrambled toward him, helping him roll. His hand curled into the sleeve of her jacket as soon as she touched him and she leaned over him.

"Oh, god. John . . ."

The right side of his head was matted with dark blood, a gash along his hairline still running bright red. His face was mottled and swollen around his eye and cheekbone, his eye nearly swollen shut. Whatever he'd hit could nearly have bashed his head in if the result of the impact was any indicator. There was no way to know the internal damage until he woke up and spoke to her.

Jenifer crawled forward on her knees to kneel at his side, leaning over him to take his face gingerly in her hands. Her throat tightened so hard it hurt to swallow or speak, and a bitter taste of adrenaline burned at the back of her tongue. Her heart pounded so hard she thought it would come right out of her chest.

"John," she called out. He moaned, rolling his head just slightly in the snow. His skin was cold, and sticky with blood. "John, come on. Please. Open your eyes."

She laid her hands on his cheeks and something violent snapped through her like a bolt of pure energy. John arched off the snow, his arms flailing out to grab fistfuls of her jacket hauling her against him. A low, guttural sound echoed in the air but she couldn't be sure if it was her or John. Panic shot through her. His hands slammed against the side of her head, holding her captive and something ripped free of her soul.

Jenifer screamed and flew back, landing hard on the snow. She choked, gasped, tried to fight for air while the trees over her head swirled and swayed. Her eyes rolled and she fought to stay conscious . . . but lost.

CHAPTER THIRTEEN

*a*wareness came back to John with a pop of sudden sound—a whoosh of air, the sizzle of a burning fire, and a tenacious buzz in his right ear muffled everything else—coupled with a nauseating twist in his gut and a persistent pounding in his head. It took him several deep breaths to quell the urge to vomit, and to realize he was sitting with his knees drawn up and his head cradled in his folded arms.

His last clear and definable memory was engaging the auxiliary routing system for the rear shielding. Then the hover pitched and he braced himself against the shift in angle. He'd held his feet until a case of something heavy came free from the overhead compartment. He remembered trying to deflect the case at the same time the hover pitched again.

Then nothing else.

The ringing made him wince and fight the urge to stick his finger in his ear. He raised his head, his stomach twisted when the smell of blood assaulted his olfactory senses and he squinted at the shiny smear of bright red fluid on his jacket sleeve. He unfolded his arms and raised his arm, the simple action pulling a groan from him when every joint from the base of his neck to his wrist screamed in protest. A ginger touch to his forehead confirmed he'd taken a hard blow, and explained the slightly blurry vision in his right eye. His fingertips came away tipped in red.

John swallowed again, his stomach roiling despite the lack of food intake in nearly twenty-four hours, and he set his hands in the crusted snow to keep from tipping with a wave of dizziness.

He squinted against the too-bright sunlight reflecting off the snow, and realized warmth bathed the left side of his body. Facts and acknowledgments came slowly, his mind not able to fully process each thing he saw with any kind of cognitive speed.

Beyond a smoldering bush, their hover burned in a ferocious blaze, throwing off enough heat to melt the snow and ice off all the trees in a seventy-five foot radius. Another hover sat nearby, both side hatches open, but he saw no one else.

Then the bloody splatters of Human remains across the front of the second hover, and the crimson stains in the melting snow, registered in his foggy brain.

He blinked, and for a heartbeat, the image in front of him was replaced with a burning building against a night sky and warm, salty tropical air hit his face. So real he could taste the brine. The burning hover snapped back into his line of sight and pain shafted through his head from temple to temple.

Something flittered on the edge of his perception, something foreign and intrusive. Intense, choking, smothering sadness and panic. Fear. Regret.

He swayed and caught himself, shifting to his knees, snow soaking almost immediately through his trousers, adding to the overall wet cold permeating his body. Squinting against the raging headache, John looked around again. He felt misplaced in time, out of alignment. He knew he'd only been conscious for a few seconds, at most, and yet he felt like he'd been sitting there for hours.

He blinked again, trying to stay in the right place, and saw her.

She was on her back, not three feet from him. How did he not see her when he opened his eyes? How did he look at everything else and miss her prone body? John crawled forward on his hands and knees, afraid if he tried to stand he'd fall over again. Even the act of crawling set everything at an angle and the topsy-turvy forest threatened to topple him over again.

"Jenifer," he tried to cry out, but her name caught in the raw of his throat.

His eyes stung from the smoke billowing from the burning hover. The short distance felt like a marathon before he finally reached her side. He set his knees wide, sitting more than kneeling to keep from tipping over, and touched her face to turn her head toward him. No visible injuries explained why she was unconscious, other than some small abrasions on her forehead and jaw. Her hands were stained with blood and blood saturated the sleeve of her injured arm, leaving a scarlet streak in the snow. Her skin was warm, but he had absolutely no idea how long either one of them had been outside or how long ago the hover had exploded.

"Jenifer," he forced in a harsh, gravelly whisper. With a hard swallow, he pushed past the raw pain. "Jenifer, *su'ista*, open your eyes." He smoothed his fingers over her cheeks, his thumb over her lips, thankful to feel the warmth of her breath. "Jenifer!"

She groaned, raising her hand from the snow to rest it on his arm. Blue eyes fluttered open, flakes of snow stuck to her eyelashes, and color filled her cheeks. "John?"

A strange, pleasant warmth hit him—completely out of place and inappropriate considering the situation—when she used his name. He smiled anyway, immediately regretting it when pain radiated from the right side of his face.

"What happened?" he asked.

She curled her fingers into his jacket, pulling herself up to a sitting position, pressing red-with-cold fingertips to her temple. "Mmmm . . . we crashed. I blew up the hover. Was checking on you . . ." She squinted, tilting her head, and he wondered if she had the same gap of memory he fought to push through. "I don't know."

"Are you hurt?"

She shook her head, and immediately looked like she regretted it. "I don't think so. Just banged up, nothing serious." Her blue eyes rounded and she grabbed his sleeves, looking him over, pulling a face.

"Do I look as bad as I feel?" he asked, trying to chuckle and ignore the high-pitched buzz in his ear.

"Worse. Come on. Let's get out of this cold snow before my backside freezes solid."

Watching them gain their feet might have been entertaining to anyone lucky enough to watch. As trashed as his equilibrium was, he figured Jenifer wasn't much better the way she swayed when she stood.

They held onto each other, and taking carefully metered steps, made it to the empty and abandoned hover. He diverted his eyes from the severed hand in the snow, a snapped off radius bone extending three inches from the torn flesh where the wrist had once been. He'd seen worse, but the current condition of his stomach advised against dwelling too long.

The interior of the abandoned vehicle was only slightly warmer than outside, the former pilots having left the heat running when they exited. Most of the heat escaped the open hatches, but something was better than nothing. John sank down on a bench hugging the exterior wall of the craft, his vision momentarily blackening.

Just as it'd happened outside the hover, his conscious awareness shifted from the interior of the hover to another place he didn't recognize and had never seen before. Within the confines of the strange setting, he looked through another's eyes to their hands. Feminine hands. Hands soaked with blood. Once again, choking grief seized him as he lived it with her.

Yes, her . . . Jenifer.

That much fell into place.

When reality snapped into place again, Jenifer knelt in front of him a deep line of concern digging between her elegant eyebrows. "You with me, Ambassador?"

He nodded, afraid to speak or his stomach might actually turn inside out. She rose from her crouched position, apparently recovering from her bout of vertigo much faster than him, and sat on the bench on his right side. He closed his eyes, swallowing again to tamp down the nausea. Gentle but insistent fingers worked at the wound he felt but had yet to see. He hissed when she cleaned the source of blood running down his cheek.

"Sorry," she said through her teeth.

The simple apology ripped through his head, her voice a spike driven straight through his ear to the center of his brain. He cried out, the shock of pain so abrupt and fierce he had no defense against it, and covered his ear to shield from more sound. The buzz amplified, his own skull acting like a resonance drum, and tilted his head in a meager effort to ward it off.

Jenifer touched his chin and urged him to look in her direction. When he managed to force his eyes open again, she silently mouthed, "Sorry," again and went back to her ministrations.

"How bad is it?" he asked, keeping his own voice as low as possible. When he spoke, he sounded like he was inside a barrel full of water.

She shifted to face him straight on, apparently figuring out already he couldn't take her speaking too close to his ear. "It looks bad. But, it probably looks worse than it is. You're having trouble with your ears, are you having vision problems?"

He nodded, regretting the action. He hoped the action was enough of an explanation. He doubted she'd accept his explanation of his own vision shifting out to be replaced by some memory she'd transferred to him, and back again. Just "problems" had to be sufficient. He looked away from her face, and his shifty vision focused on the bloody tear in her jacket sleeve. The heavy-duty fabric glistened with blood, and the smell saturated the air. Every one of his senses were on overdrive, from smell to hearing to touch.

"Your arm . . ." he managed to choke out, reaching for her.

She leaned back, widening the space between them. "It's fine. We need to worry first about keeping you mobile and getting us the hell out of here. To *where*, I don't know since any plan I had went pear-shaped when we crashed, but we can't stay here. Once whoever sent them after us—the backstabbing son of a bitch—figures out they're not coming back, the next wave of would-be assassins will come to finish the job."

"You think they were sent after us?" John asked, trying to remember the finer details of their flight.

Anger, raw and clear, shifted across her deceivingly delicate features. "No doubt about it, Ambassador. They were Firebirds."

"What?"

She stood and walked to the front of the hover. Blood dripped from her pinky finger, leaving a trail across the floor. A jacket hung on the back of each seat, and she dragged one free with the hand of her uninjured arm, holding it out as she turned. The red, yellow, and orange emblem of a Phoenix rising from fire—the symbol of the elite military guard— mocked him from the upper sleeve near the shoulder.

"At least the bastards left us dry jackets," she said, tossing the jacket on the bench beside him.

John picked up the jacket, staring at the emblem.

"Cover your ears, Ambassador."

He barely managed to before Jenifer leveled Damocles on the controls console and fired. Wires hissed and sizzled and flames licked from beneath the panel. "What the bloody hell are you doin'?" he demanded.

"Using this hover is out of the question," she said, holstering her weapon. "If they tracked us so easily, you'd better believe whoever sent them knows exactly where they were when they set down. And this hover is military issue; it's got a GPS tracking system built in. The nearest military outpost is two hours away by hover. I wouldn't bet on any more than that before someone shows up, whether they're the bad guys, or not." She yanked the other jacket off the seat. "And since I killed two of their own to save our asses, they're not going to like me very much."

John nodded, dropping the jacket on the bench again. Unzipping his wet and bloody jacket was a chore, but movement was getting easier. The haze in his head was clearing by small degrees and his focus sharpening. He didn't feel disconnected, just uncomfortable with the buzz in his head and the slight off-kilter angle of everything around him.

"Come here. I'll take care of your arm and we'll figure out where we're goin'."

"It's fine."

"I'm no' askin'," he snapped, his patience at an end. Not just with her stoic stubbornness, but the whole bloody situation. His head hurt, his right eye was nearly swollen shut, and the *damn bloody buzzing* in his head was about enough to send him bonkers, and he wasn't in the mood to argue with her. John clenched his teeth and bowed his head, drawing in a deep breath through his nose. "Fine, let's be practical. You're leavin' a blood trail, which might be a bit obvious in the snow. And you're losin' blood. No' even *you* can keep losin' blood without losin' strength."

She worked her jaw to the side, her blue eyes darkening. With a click in her cheek, she unzipped the bloody, mangled mess that was the remains of her jacket and dropped it on the floor as she walked back to him. She didn't say a word, barely flinched, while he removed the now saturated bandage he'd applied the day before and pulled away the pathetic remains of the silk weave left clinging to her arm. The hover, thankfully, was equipped with an adequate medical kit since it was a military transport. He was able to properly clean the wound, apply topical antibiotics, pull it closed with another application of silk weave, and wrap it well with gauze and bandaging.

"Where were we goin'?" he asked, holding another square of gauze half way down the long cut as he wrapped her arm. Her gaze cut to him, but her teeth were clenched and she didn't speak. Was it out of stubbornness or pain? "You said we can't go where we were actually heading because we crashed too close. Where were we goin'?"

She looked away and licked her lips. "Tennessee."

John arched his eyebrows. "The old Phoenix camp? There's nothin' there 'cept what we left behind when the Sorrs attacked."

"Exactly. No activity, no tech, nothing to draw attention. I figured we could have hunkered down there for a while until the *Firebirds*," she said, mocking the entire idea of the elite force, "figured out who headed the manhunt on you and cleared the way home."

"And we're close."

She turned her wrist and read the face of the rectangular device strapped to her lower arm above the wrist. Various streams of information rolled across the screen. "We're not even a hundred miles from the base."

John nodded, but only until the front lobe of his brain slammed into his skull—or so it seemed—and he had to tip his chin toward his chest and close his eyes to combat the wave of nausea. Speaking wasn't an option until his stomach dropped down where it belonged. She stood and walked around the small space, the sound of her boots thundering in his head with the same skull-rattling effect of a sledgehammer inside a steel drum. A wave of sound rolled down his ear canal, popping painfully enough to make him tilt his head and wince when she crouched beside him. John forced open his eyes, squinting to focus on her. She was blurry, and shifted in his vision even though he knew she hadn't moved.

"Doesn't matter where we were going." She shrugged with an unconvincing nonchalance. "We're not going to get any further than we can hoof it before the next wave of headhunters show up. Two smoldering hovers and footprints in the snow aren't exactly subtle."

The pop of sound offered a small respite from the nausea and vertigo. John sat up slightly, bracing himself with a hand on his knee. "I had an option . . . but I'm guessin' it went up with the hover."

"What? A magic carpet?"

He smiled. "Somethin' like that. But it was in the rucksack."

She gave him a funny look, laid her hand on his thigh to leverage herself up from the crouch, and walked back outside. He heard her boots crunch across the icy snow, growing softer as she moved away, then louder as she returned. She stomped up the ramp, knocking snow off her boots, and dropped the pack beside him. "This I gotta see."

Part of him thought he should be surprised she had the bag, but part of him wasn't the least bit amazed at her ingenuity or ability to deliver. He dragged the bag to him and opened it, pushing aside the other items inside. Before retrieving what he sought, he grinned and removed the single jar of peanut butter Connor had indeed smuggled out of the apartment. He tossed it her way, and only allowed himself a moment of pleasure at her wide-eyed surprise before she twisted open the jar and dug in with her finger.

"Leave me some," he joked, removing a small black case from the bottom of the bag. To anyone who didn't know what he held, the case looked like nothing much at all. He set the bag aside and laid the case on his thigh, the whole thing no bigger than his hand. Inside were two black band collars, with two nodules attached to each collar. A small control, the size of his thumb, was nestled in its designated spot between the two collars. He lifted the control with one hand and one of the collars with the other.

"Doesn't look like a magic carpet to me," she said around her finger as she licked it clean of peanut butter.

John refused to focus on her mouth, but set the case aside and removed the second collar, hanging both collars from his index finger. She scowled and took one from him, holding it a few inches from her nose to study it. Sudden anger twisted her scowl further and she tossed the device onto the bench beside him, shaking her head.

"That's a damn collar."

John retrieved the collar. "It's part of a transterran psychoportation device. These . . ." He held up the other collar and the control. " . . .are the rest. It's Defense Alliance standard issue for all soldiers."

"Psychoportation. You mean . . . it's a psychic interface."

He stood, holding the collars between them. "With a limited scope, but yes. This device is capable of almost instantly transportin' one or two people from one place to another, with a range of up to five hundred miles."

"And you didn't mention this before now because . . ."

"Because usin' a hopper should only be an act of desperation. It's dangerous and unpredictable at best."

She stared down at his hands, looking as close to being ill as he had felt a few minutes before. Jenifer drew in a breath and tipped up her chin, looking down her nose at the collars. Her upper lip twitched and she swallowed. "I'd wear one of those."

"We both would. The collar is the most secure way to wear the device. Less likelihood of it fallin' off or bein' ripped off by an enemy. The dual collar lets the controller transport someone else, an injured comrade or . . ." He tilted his chin toward her. "Anyone who can't control the collar."

She laid her hand at the base of her throat, long fingers stroking her skin where the collar would rest. Her pulse jumped rapidly and she drew in a shaky breath. It was all he heard in the cold silence of the hover. He tried to find the connection—however harsh and fleeting—he'd found before, when she opened herself to him if even for a moment, but Jenifer Of No Last Name was once again an impenetrable wall. The effort alone to expand the range of his Talents shot a piercing pain through his temples.

The simple act of reaching out was enough to send spots into his vision. What would happen when he tried to control the collars?

Jenifer drew in a slow, carefully metered breath and pulled back her shoulders, easing away from him by a small degree. "How do you control where we go?"

"That's the hardest part of usin' the hopper. You have to know where you're goin'. You have to have a clear destination. Which is a challenge on a foreign planet."

"Do you have to have been there?"

"No, just have a clear enough understandin' of the destination. I can't just think 'go somewhere safe', I have to know a specific place like . . ." He shook his head, regretting it. "Nick's office or the Tennessee base."

"You want to use this to go to Tennessee."

John winced, a sudden sharp pain shooting through his skull like a white-hot arrow, and took a step back, sinking down to sit on the bench. "No. For every reason you said. It's too obvious now."

She stepped to him and lowered into a graceful crouch so she looked up at him, a deep line digging into the spot between her eyebrows. The touch of her fingertips along the ridge of his brow was gentle and warm in contrast to the cold air. For just a moment the frazzled, sparking, and frayed edges of his nerves calmed.

"I know where to go," he finally said. "I know it isn't much of an answer, but until we're away from—" He looked around the interior of the enemy hover, not wanting to move away from her probing touch. "—possible listenin' ears that's all I want to say."

"Are you going to be able to do this?" she asked. "With a knot on your head."

"I don't see another alternative."

She met his gaze, her eyes shifting only slightly as she studied him. With a tight nod, she pushed up and stood over him. "We're burning daylight," was her only affirmation.

They gathered whatever could be salvaged from the hover that might serve a purpose: dry, blood-free jackets, a few meager supplies from the scavenged med-kit, and John's rucksack. Midday sunlight reflected off the white snow, making him squint. The nausea had eased, and the dizziness had balanced, but his skull felt like a barrel full of lead marbles and broken glass stuck in a centrifuge at maximum speed.

Jenifer stopped at the bottom of the hover ramp and zipped up her jacket. "What should I expect?"

"Like you're flyin' head first into a wind tunnel. You won't be able to open your eyes, won't be able to speak, and you'll feel like you can't breathe. You'll think you're goin' to suffocate, but you're no'. You've got to trust me on that. The trip only takes a matter of seconds, but it feels much longer."

She turned to him, drawing in a breath through her nose. "You always take me on the best dates, Ambassador."

He chuckled, despite the price his head paid. "You should see what I can do when I'm really tryin' to impress you."

Knowing they couldn't delay any longer, John took the two collars from his pocket, snapped open one of them, and slipped it around his neck. It immediately locked and a small hissing sound preceded a slight tightening of the band around his throat. He released the clasp on the other and held it toward Jenifer. Her features flinched, but she

138

immediately hid her gut reaction and raised her chin so he could wrap the band and bring the ends together behind her neck. A simple thought commanded the collar clasp to engage and the fitting system to tighten the collar.

Her body tensed.

"It's a'right," he said low, leaning toward her to see the back of the collar, making sure none of her hair had been caught in the enclosure. "The collar automatically tightens to fit the wearer. It's tight enough no enemy would be able to grasp it and use it as a weapon against you, but no' tight enough to restrict."

She nodded, her throat bobbing when she swallowed. "Let's just do this."

"The key is contact between travelers. The collars are designed to be very selective. Two people can travel together as long as they're together, and as long as both are wearin' the collars. If we're both wearin' the collars, but we don't have contact, only the one with the control—" He slipped the control from his pocket and held it up for her to see. "—goes anywhere. If someone tries to tag along, grabs someone wearin' a collar but they don't have one on, they don't go anywhere."

"You're just gone and they're left with their hands empty."

"More like they don't have hands at all."

Jenifer pulled a face. "Brutal."

"Effective. Now, come here."

Jenifer ticked up an eyebrow and her slow, subtle grin curved her lips. "A couple dates and you think you can get demanding."

He took the bait, liking it more than she probably intended him to, and wrapped his arm around her waist yanking her against him. It wasn't the usual mode of travel between two soldiers, but then again, few of his Areth comrades looked like Jenifer. The landscape tipped and his vision swam, but he held onto her and she kept him upright.

"Hang on." Her fingers curled into the shoulders of his jacket and she leaned into him. "Close your eyes, Jenifer."

As soon as he knew her eyes were closed and her grip on him was sure, he closed his own eyes and wrapped his fist around the small control in his palm. The command was simple, silent, and immediate. The air around them sucked away in a frigid vacuum and the ground disappeared beneath them. John had done this before, more times than he cared to count, but it never got any easier. Tearing a wormhole through a planet's atmosphere and traveling ten times faster than the speed of light was hard enough on the body without the piercing headache he already had and the near-total destruction of his equilibrium. Agony ripped through his head, and flashes of light ricocheted behind his closed eyelids.

Eternity passed in a half a dozen painful heartbeats, and the wormhole spit them out on the other side. His ears popped painfully, and as soon as his feet hit terra firma his knees buckled beneath him. The pain was excruciating.

"Jenifer," he forced through gritted teeth, her name the only word he could get out.

Then the world went black.

CHAPTER FOURTEEN

4 March 2054, Wednesday
First Church of Christ Revival
Tallahassee, former state of Florida
North American Continent

"*B*lessed Assurance, Jesus is mine. O, what a foretaste of glory divine! Heir of salvation, purchase of God . . .*"

Reverend Lieutenant Jace Quinn paused in the back hall behind the sanctuary pulpit, tilting his head toward the sound echoing off the high concave ceilings of the church. Michael's rich, unschooled baritone filled the small building.

"*This is my story. This is my song. Praising my savior all the day long . . .*"

Jace had intended to head for the parish living quarters off the back of the church, where he and Lilly and Jamie, and in the last few weeks Michael Tanner, lived but the sound of singing from the sanctuary had stopped him. He closed his eyes and listened. There was something pure and innocent about the way Michael sang, with abandon and no concern whether anyone heard him or found fault in his pitch or tone. It lifted Jace's soul.

He wished Michael's own soul wasn't so tortured.

Jace doubled back to the door leading to the sanctuary to the right of the pulpit, and eased it open so he wouldn't disturb Michael's singing. The aroma of polished wood, mild incense, and old books mingled in a soothing combination in the peaceful sanctuary, wrapping around Jace in a comforting, familiar embrace. In another few hours the congregation would fill the pews and the sound of their voices lifting in song would reverberate off the ceilings, making the very air vibrate, but right now it was just Michael.

He sat on the floor in front of the first pew, his back to the pulpit, an array of parts, wires, and casings spread out on the pew seat. Jace figured at least three stratum basale stimulators had been dissected and sacrificed in an attempt to give his wife a single working unit. Medical supplies were hard enough to come by, and they had been lucky to get their hands on three malfunctioning SBS units. Michael was a wizard with electronics and had already restored for Lilly two osteoskeletal sonic binders—one of which they'd traded with the doctor manning a small clinic forty miles away for a small supply of liquid antibiotics—and a handheld diagnostic reader.

Michael finished singing *Blessed Assurance* and paused, his hands stilling in his lap. He raised his head and looked up to the ceiling. From his angle, Jace easily saw Michael's side profile and knew he'd been discovered when Michael smiled. His friend looked down again, bringing the disassembled SBS closer to his face, his glasses sliding down his nose. Hair Lilly declared to be too long fell forward and he used the back of his hand to push it out of his eyes.

"I would appreciate the company," Michael said. "I intended to seek you out, but Mrs. Weatherley told me you were counseling Mark."

Jace crossed to the aisle leading between the fifteen rows of pews down the center of the church and sat in the second pew so he could lean his elbows on the front pew, looking down on Michael as he worked. "You don't often seek out company. Is there something on your mind?"

Michael looked up, a smile tinged with sadness tipping one corner of his mouth. "Someone. Jacqueline. Nicole. I miss them."

"More today than usual?"

"Perhaps I'm letting myself feel the absence today more than usual."

Jace drew a breath and ran his fingers across his mouth,

contemplating much like he had dozens of times before in the last couple of weeks, how to broach the subject of Michael returning to Alexandria. Michael chuckled and focused again on his project.

"Am I so difficult to speak with?" he asked.

"Difficult, no. I don't want you to think you aren't welcome here. You are family to us, Michael. You know that—"

"But I have a family waiting for me in Alexandria."

"A family who misses you as much as you miss them."

Michael looked up again, this time with no humor or lightness in his eyes or expression. His jaw set firm in a familiar way Jace had seen on Nick Tanner more times than he could recall to count. Michael, even more than his father, didn't beat around the bush. He didn't know how to be anything other than completely direct, although he had learned in the last two years to take pause before speaking to temper his words.

"To go back before I have full control would be to put them in danger."

Jace huffed and shifted to rub his hand across his forehead. "Michael, what happened before was more than you not being able to control this new . . ." He fumbled for the right word. " . . .ability. You had control over nothing. You died the first time, and you were sick enough this past January you very well could have died. Your body had the ability to protect you, and whether you intended to do it or not, your body did what it had to do to preserve its own life."

"It could happen again."

Jace shook his head. "No, I don't think it will. You have taken this gift —" Michael visibly flinched, and Jace regretted his choice of words. Michael hated the array of manifested skills he'd developed since being rescued from New Mexico to be called *gifts*. It had only been in the last year or so he'd finally admitted they were naturally a part of him, not something thrust on him by the Sorracchi as part of their genetic experimentation. "You've taken this *ability* and learned how to do more than just suppress it. You've learned how to control it, manipulate it. Just like you have with every new ability you've had surface."

"I want to go home," Michael said almost before Jace finished.

Jace barely had time to formulate a response before an intense tingling up his spine made the hair on the back of his neck stand on end.

Michael sat up straighter, his attention snapping to the door at the back of the church.

"Did you feel that?" they both said at the same time.

Jace stood and moved around to the front of the pew, extending his hand to Michael. He pulled Michael to his feet and handed him the knobbed-wood shillelagh Michael had left leaning against the end of the pew. With stiff movements from sitting on the floor, Michael leaned on the Irish cane and they both headed toward the back of the church. The tingling burned like frostbite, pushing him forward. Michael had to feel the same urge because his broken stride picked up. Just as Michael pushed open the double door leading to the vestibule a woman's scream broke through the silence outside.

"John!"

Jace left Michael behind and shoved through the exterior door, the cool afternoon air washing over his exposed skin. A light layer of snow dusted the ground, something never seen a decade before in Florida, but common now since the war. Fifteen feet from the front of the church a woman was on her knees, her back to them, holding a man against her chest to keep him off the cold ground.

A weapon—a pulse gun tweaked out like nothing Jace had ever seen —was in her hand and aimed at him before she even turned. A sharp hum filled the heavy air. The gun was no toy. "Stay back!" she shouted, her hand shaking as she tried to keep him and Michael at bay and hold the man in her arms. Finally, she looked over her shoulder, panic rounding pale blue eyes and recognition made Jace stumble.

"Jenifer?"

She squinted, her body shaking with each ragged breath she took. "Lieutenant Quinn?"

He nodded, trying to see around her to whomever she held. Only one John came to mind, but last Jace knew, he didn't think Jenifer and Ambassador Smith knew each other. Michael stepped beside him, his breath heavy from the strain of rushing across the hard ground. Her attention shifted to Michael, and for a moment her look of panic shifted to annoyance, immediately back to panic. Her hand dropped and the gun clattered to the ground.

"Help him," she begged, looking back to the man she held.

One of the church parishioners ran around the corner of the church. "Rev?"

"Mark, get my wife. Now!"

Jace and Michael reached them together. The shillelagh dropped to the ground and Michael fell to his knees beside them. "John! John!"

The man Jenifer held actually *was* Ambassador John Smith, and Jace mentally told himself he would have to get the story behind whatever brought these two unlikely people together another time. John was nearly as white as the snow beneath him. A vicious cut along his brow appeared to be the source of the dried blood crusting his skin. He was unconscious, limp in Jenifer's hold. Both of them wore a thin, black collar and looked like they'd been through a small war. Jenifer was bruised, her hair tousled and falling free from a braid hugging her skull. She looked ready to either pass out, or vomit, or both, swaying slightly even as she tried to keep John off the ground.

"What happened," Michael asked.

She darted her gaze from Jace to Michael, a brief scowl pinching her features, but she immediately looked back to Jace. Her hand twitched toward the weapon on the ground, the debate clear and obvious in her eyes. Footsteps echoed from around the church and Jace knew Mark was on his way back, hopefully with Lilly. Jace leaned forward, closing the space between him and Jenifer. She tensed, but didn't go for the weapon on the ground.

Yet.

"Jenifer, I have no idea what's going on here, but by the looks of the two of you it's not good. You can trust us. I swear to my God." He pressed his hand over his heart. "We'll send Mark away as soon as we get John inside, but we need to know what happened so Lilly can treat him."

She only hesitated for a heartbeat, the sound of footsteps coming fast. "We were in a hover crash, then he used these collar things to transport us. It's Areth tech, I don't know how."

"I understand the technology," Michael said beside him.

Jace nodded and leaned back when Lilly and Mark reached them.

"Dear God, John," Lilly gasped.

Jace stood before she got on the ground, touching her arm. "Hang on, baby. Let us get him inside first."

She nodded and stepped back. He motioned for Mark to help him, and once they convinced Jenifer to let them help, the two of them lifted John from the ground and carried him back to the small clinic Lilly had set up in a building behind the parish.

*J*enifer couldn't sit still. She couldn't stand still. She couldn't *be* still until she knew John was okay. Her gut clenched every time she let herself dwell on the way he'd crumbled the second they'd solidified in Tallahassee.

She paced from one side of the small reception room of the cramped building to the other in three strides, pivoted, stared at the door leading to the examination room, and paced again. The door from outside creaked open and Jace Quinn came in, carrying a covered plate. He looked a hell of a lot better than the first time she met him nearly two years before, an emaciated and delusional prisoner of war who had no memory who or what he was. His skin had the glow of sun despite the winter weather, and he filled out his black jeans and long sleeved black shirt nicely, and had a slight scruff of dark beard along his jaw.

He looked toward the examination room door. "Have they come out yet?"

"No," she snapped, glaring at the door.

"It's only been a few minutes. I wouldn't worry."

Jenifer shot him a sharp look, and bit down hard on her annoyance when he just smiled and chuckled. He set down the plate on a table against the wall and lifted the napkin draped over it to reveal some cold chicken pieces and dried fruit. "It's not much, but I thought you might be hungry."

Her stomach growled loudly at the mention of food, and she cursed its treachery. It didn't feel right to eat without knowing about John, but a mouthful of peanut butter in the last thirty-six hours wasn't cutting it. The thought of the peanut butter made her stomach clench worse. With another look toward the door, Jenifer crossed the room with three angry stomps and picked up a piece of chicken someone had pulled from the bone and left in small, easy to eat bites. It had some seasoning, but not much, but it was moist and satisfied the hole in her gut. The dried fruit was tart, just sweet enough to make her mouth water.

Quinn set a cup of water on the table, and Jenifer picked it right back up, drinking half. Thirst was never so extreme as the moment water was in her hand. Her stomach only allowed a few pieces of chicken and fruit before it protested and said she'd had enough. Quinn stood near the door, his hips leaned against the wall and his arms across his chest, watching her.

"I've been out of Alexandria for a while, but last I knew you and Ambassador Smith didn't exactly run in the same circles."

Jenifer pushed away the plate and sank into a chair. Indecision fought in her chest and her head whether to speak or not speak. John had said he was taking them to someone he knew he could trust. But, he thought he could trust the three who saw them off in Alexandria and she knew as true as she knew her name—her true name—one or more of them had betrayed his trust. And hers. She stared at Quinn, and he stared back, his gaze never wavering, never flinching. She'd helped Jackie Anderson take him out of a Sorracchi prison, she'd watched Jackie fight to keep him alive, and she'd heard how he forced himself to forget everything and everyone he'd known and loved to keep them safe. He'd nearly driven himself insane to protect his wife, to protect Phoenix, from the enemy. A man capable of protecting with such ferocity was a man of honor, and these Xenos had no honor. On principal alone, her gut told her she had to put some level of faith in him, if only to keep John safe a little bit longer until she knew what to do.

Jenifer drew a long breath and looked to the door leading to the room beyond. "The Xenos want him dead. They tried to kill him twice in Alexandria, the last time driving us out of the city."

"How did you get involved?"

Jenifer pushed her hair out of her face, and doubted she wanted to see a mirror any time soon. Her knuckles were dirty and crusted with dried blood, her pants were stiff from mud and dried gore, and her hair hung in her eyes. She gave Quinn the sixty-second version of the events leading up to and following their flight from Alexandria. He looked righteously enraged when she told him—without a doubt—the last batch of would-be assassins were Firebirds. Before she got too far into the details of their magic carpet ride the door opened, and Michael Tanner came out, a knobby-wood cane aiding each stilted step. Jenifer stood, her heart going from rest to marathon in two seconds flat.

"He's fine," Michael said before she could ask, holding up his hand not braced on the cane. "He has a mild concussion, bruised ribs, and some mild abrasions."

"Then what happened when we . . ." She fumbled for the right word. " . . .landed?"

"Extreme exhaustion," Doc Quinn said, coming out of the room behind Michael. Jenifer shifted her weight on her feet, trying to see past them to the bed beyond. "His injuries had already taken a toll on him, and using the . . ." She looked to Michael.

"Transterran psychoportation device," he provided.

"Yeah, that. Using it took everything he had, especially considering his head injury. He had to have known how dangerous this was for him to try before he ever did it."

Jenifer clenched her jaw and crossed her arms, looking down at her scuffed boots. She didn't like the bitter tang of guilt in the back of her throat, especially since she knew they hadn't had any other choice. Not a viable choice, anyway. "So, he'll be fine?"

"He will be after a few hours' sleep." Doc Quinn smiled.

The relief surprised Jenifer, washing over her shoulders like warm water. She didn't take any time to analyze it and brushed past Michael and Doc Quinn into the exam room. It was a sparse, basic space with three beds separated by patched curtains hanging between them. Glass door cabinets lined one wall, only a meager supply of medications and supplies visible through the metal-mesh enforced glass. The room smelled clean, like disinfectant and rubbing alcohol. John was on one bed, lying on his back. Jenifer crouched beside the bed, gripping the edge to keep her balance on her own tired legs, and took a moment to look at him. They'd removed his jacket and his boots and draped a blanket over him, and the blood and dirt had been wiped from his face. Color had come back to his cheeks and he looked calm.

Her fingers tingled to reach out and smooth some of the damp hair off his forehead, but she clenched her hand to keep herself from acting. John drew in a long, deep breath and rolled his head on the pillow, turning toward her. His eyes pinched tighter for a moment before he opened them. A slow, and surprisingly sexy smile curled his lips. The instant, visceral reaction—a flush over her skin and a jump of the pulse at the base of her throat—was both foreign and a shock to Jenifer.

"Jenifer . . ." His voice was rough, like he'd been shouting.

"Go back to sleep," she said, returning his smile. "Doc Quinn says you need to rest. I just came in to check on you."

"Of course you did." His eyes slowly closed and opened again. "Ever the protector."

"That's what they pay me the big bucks for."

John chuckled and raised his hand. His fingertips brushed her cheek, pushing back some of the escaped hair, then down her throat to the collar she still wore. She hadn't been able to figure out how to get the damned thing off. With just a touch to the strap, it fell away, falling limp on the edge of the bed.

"Thank you," she said, rubbing her throat. "I was beginning to wonder how long I'd have to wear the thing." He didn't say anything, just looked at her with heavy eyes. Jenifer took a deep breath. "I'm going to camp out in the other room and let you get some rest."

She moved to stand, but his hand covered hers on the edge of the bed. He didn't say anything more, and she swore she felt the blanket of sleep shifting over him. Jenifer tried again to stand. He didn't release her, instead he pulled gently on her hand. Jenifer finally gave in to the demand he never made and stretched out on the narrow strip of bed beside him. He draped his arm across her waist and drew in a long breath as she settled into place. She closed her eyes, not realizing until that moment how tired she was. It was like the water, the thirst didn't hit her until she had the water in her hand. The need for sleep didn't smother her until she lay down beside him. She inhaled, exhaled, and let the relative feeling of temporary safety lull her toward rest.

"I'm sorry," John said softly near her ear, pulling her back from sleep with a warm rush.

She shifted her cheek on his arm and looked down at his abraded and smudged hand where it rested on her stomach. "For what?"

"For frightenin' you—"

"You didn't—" she started to argue, but he sought out her hand and laced his fingers through hers. Jenifer closed her eyes. "Just don't make a habit of it, Ambassador."

He chuckled. "We are, however, makin' a habit of this."

She didn't ask "What?" because she knew, although she wasn't sure sleeping twice beside each other constituted a habit, but she was too tired to argue the point. John pulled her closer and his breath warmed the back of her neck. Two deep breaths later he was asleep, and Jenifer let herself follow.

CHAPTER FIFTEEN

*T*he mouth-watering aroma of simmering chicken, vegetables, and bread drew John through the rooms of the small parish living space toward the kitchen. He fluffed his damp hair as he went, unsure which had done him more good, the few hours of sleep or the warm shower when they woke up. Then again, there was something to be said about waking up the second time in less than twenty-four hours with Jenifer Of No Last Name beside him. His hunger and his need to wash away the film of filth were the only things convincing enough to make him leave the narrow bed.

He winced when his fingers hit the sealed cut above his eye. Lilly Quinn had sealed it with liquid bandage, but it still hurt to the touch, the bruise beneath making his forehead and temple tender to the touch. He had a headache, but it wasn't the blinding pain he'd felt back at the hover. He had regained his equilibrium and his secondary senses no longer fizzled like frayed electrical wires.

It wasn't difficult to find the kitchen since the living quarters designed for the reverend of the church weren't much more than thirteen hundred square feet with two bedrooms, a single bath area and a common area for sitting and eating together with the kitchen area at one end. John stepped out of the hall leading to the bedrooms into the common space and inhaled deeply.

"Somethin' smells fantastic."

Jace Quinn and Michael Tanner sat at a long table, with nearly two-year-old Jamie Quinn in a high chair at the end eating pieces of meat, fruit, and bread with her fingers. Lilly turned from the stove, smiled, and tapped her wooden spoon on the side of a pot.

"It's nothing fancy, John," she said. "Tonight is chicken soup with dumplins."

"I'm no' sure what a dumplin is, but if it tastes as good as it smells, I can't wait."

"We already ate since I have service tonight," Jace said, handing his daughter another piece of bread. He slid at look at John. "We figured you and Jenifer can eat together. You shouldn't need to wait much. I doubt she'll let you out of her sight for too long."

"Did she tell you what's going on?"

"In a nutshell, yeah." Jace leaned back in his chair. "She told me she suspects someone close to Nick as being a traitor. What do you think?"

John took a seat on the other side of the table from Michael and Jace. "I think she's right. I don't want to believe it, but everythin' points in that direction."

"Do you know who?"

John shook his head. "No, but the list isn't very long. Problem is, I don't want to believe this of any of them. Only three people knew we were leavin' Alexandria and how. Nick—" Michael visibly tensed and John raised his hand. "No worries, Michael. Your father is *no'* even a consideration."

"Who else?" Jace pushed.

"Connor Montgomery and Melanie Briggs."

"I can't imagine either one of them being traitors." Jace shook his head. "Connor fought with Phoenix through the war, and Mel has been Connor's 2IC since before that. They're both loyal. Are you sure there was no one else?"

John tapped his fingertips on the tabletop and shrugged. "Connor had a couple men return to my apartment for a few things, but to my knowledge none of them knew where we were and certainly not where we were goin'."

"Does anyone know you were coming here?" Lilly asked, setting a steaming bowl of something heavenly in front of him.

John shook his head, but paused to inhale before answering. "None of us ever spoke of Jenifer and me comin' here. It was Nick's idea, but no one else knew." He tapped his temple and each of them nodded in understanding. Nick Tanner's Talents had progressed immensely since his return from Raxo and Aretu, much as his son's own Talents. There was no doubt the son had inherited his gifts from his father, no matter what Michael wanted to believe. "He relayed the information as we prepared to leave."

Lilly laid her hand on his shoulder and leaned over to kiss his forehead. "Either way, it's good to see you, John."

He patted her hand. "I've missed seein' you." John looked at Michael. "I'm not the only one, of course."

Michael swallowed and met his gaze for several moments before shoving back from the table. He stood with obvious effort and crossed the room to a double glass door looking out onto the white landscape. Frustration buffered the air around Michael like a force field, pushing all of them away. John wondered if Jace felt it the way he did, knowing Jace had some level of Talents as well. Without a word, Michael opened the double doors and stepped outside, the warm air inside disturbed momentarily by the fan of the door. When the door closed behind Michael, Jace sighed and turned to focus on John. Lilly lowered her head, her own sadness adding to the frustration Michael had left in his wake.

"No one knows he's here," John said. "At least no' his father, and certainly no' Jacqueline. They're all worried about him."

"I suspected as much," Jace confirmed. "In typical Michael fashion, he hasn't said anything more than he has to and reveals nothing more than required. I didn't make it a requirement for him to stay, but I did make him tell me why he left."

"Why's that? I think Nick has his suspicions, but he never said for sure."

"It goes back to his rescue last year, and then his illness in January."

"The infection from the surgery on his leg," John confirmed. Both Jace and Lilly nodded. "I know he left the hospital without speakin' to anyone, leavin' Jacqueline there. What do the two have to do with each other, other than the point of the surgery was to repair some of the damage from the torture on the ship?"

"You know what happened when he was brought to the *Excalibur*."

John nodded again. "I thought I'd seen every evolution of Talents, but I've never seen anyone capable of drawin' energy from another to survive. But, it was unintentional. I know Michael well enough to know he would never hurt another, even if to save his own life. Let alone the people he loves."

"When the infection set in after the surgery, he could have died again. His body was still weak from the torture, his ability to control the draw completely untrained. Apparently, he began to draw on Jackie again. When he came through the worst of the infection, he learned she was hospitalized, too, for severe exhaustion and dehydration. It didn't take much for him to assume he'd done it again, intentionally or not."

John closed his eyes and lowered his head. He understood now. He remembered Jacqueline being hospitalized, but she had spent night and day at Michael's side and exhaustion wasn't a surprising result. He hadn't thought any more of it.

"It haunted him," Lilly said in a small voice. "The idea he might someday do worse, draw too much, without the ability to stop it." She chuckled, but the sound was humorless. "So, Michael did what he does. He removed himself until he could figure it all out. He's not a coward, he just . . ." She didn't finish.

"Sounds pretty much like a coward to me."

John twisted in his chair at Jenifer's voice. She stood in the arch leading from the hall to the common area, her damp hair framing her face, her arms crossed, wearing borrowed clothing whose poor fit only served to accentuate her hips and the toned lines of her arms. Her blue eyes sparked with what John could best describe as righteous anger.

"Michael—"

"Walked out on Jackie and Nicole," Jenifer cut off Lilly's counterargument. "I don't give a damn what he thought he was saving her from, he left—I'm guessing—without an explanation even to her. Frankly, I don't blame Jackie for leaving, too."

"Jenifer—"

"What, Ambassador?' Jenifer snapped, cutting him off with a glare as sharp as the daggers she shot at the rest of them. "Are you going to defend him, too? Tell me I don't know the situation? I don't know poor Michael and the crap storm he lived through?"

"Do you?" Lilly asked. "Do you have any real idea?"

"I know this, Doc. If he didn't have the testicular fortitude to stick around when things got tough, he had no business convincing Jackie she should give up who she was to be with him."

"Is that what you think I did?"

None of them had heard Michael come back inside, but everyone turned together to face him. He crossed the room, the thump of his cane hitting the floor with each silent step of his sneakers. Jenifer shifted her stance, her hands at her waist, her fingers resting near Damocles. John knew full well she'd never draw here, but he also recognized her stance. She was ready for a fight, whatever kind of fight it might be, verbal or gunfire.

"I know Jackie never had interest in the husband and kid routine. Not that you're her husband. Is that too much of a commitment? Easier to walk away?"

Michael said nothing, staring at her across the room.

Jenifer laughed, but it was cold and humorless. "At least you're not trying to deny it."

"I love Jacqueline and Nicole with everything I am," Michael said through clenched teeth. "I left to protect them. From me."

The air sizzled, practically crackled, and Jamie began to cry, her wails echoing in the small space. Lilly stood and walked around the table, lifting the toddler from her high chair. She left the room, brushing past Jenifer to the bedrooms beyond. A moment later the distinct sound of a bedroom door closing preceded the muffling of Jamie's crying.

"Is this how you show them you love them?" Jenifer demanded, seeming unfazed by the toddler's crying. "You didn't have the decency to tell her where you were going. If that's love, you've a convincing argument against it."

"What did she tell you?"

"Nothing, but it didn't take a genius to see what you'd done to her. And it certainly doesn't take much to figure out why she left."

"Jenifer," John said louder.

She held up her hand. "Oh, no, Ambassador. Let it sink in."

"Left?" Michael's expression fell and he moved closer. "Where did she go?"

John stood, moving into the space between Michael and Jenifer. He held up his hand to her, hoping she would *please* let him explain when he faced Michael. "She's gone to Aretu. With Silas."

Michael's attention snapped back to him. "Aretu? She's off planet?"

"She volunteered to protect Silas, to take him to my brother and Queen Bryony."

"Where is Nicole?"

"With Grandma and Grandpa," Jenifer tossed out. "Now she's not only wondering where her daddy went, but her mommy, too."

"Alright," Jace shouted, silencing all of them. "Nothing is going to get solved like this."

"I have to go back," Michael mumbled, heading for the hall.

"Too little too late, bucky. She's gone."

John took hold of Jenifer's wrist and pulled her out of Michael's way as he headed for a door on the other side of the room. She yanked her wrist free, but John didn't concede, instead lacing his fingers through hers.

"Please," was all he asked.

She scowled but only pulled back momentarily, consenting to follow him out of the parish into the back of the church sanctuary. Aromas of old books, polished wood, and anointment oil tingled in his nose almost instantly providing a sense of calm. A low buzz of scattered conversation carried from the half a dozen congregants mingling in the sanctuary. Jenifer stopped fighting him, letting him lead her to a small, secluded area behind the pulpit with just a couple of benches, stacks of old books, and some sort of red and green decorations. Sounds from the sanctuary were even more muted back here, becoming just a distant muffled sound. Once in the shadows of the space, John released her hand and turned to face her.

"Don't you dare tell me I'm wrong," she snapped before he could say anything.

"I'm no'."

"He should know what he did," she ground out through clenched teeth, pointing an angry hand back toward the door they'd come from. "He—"

John stepped into her space and took her face in his hands, pressing his thumb to her lips. She stilled, her blue eyes wide, her breath ragged against his skin. He moved in close enough their noses nearly touched. "He knows, Jenifer. He knows."

Jenifer closed her eyes, and a thin sheen of moisture gathered along her lashes. Not enough to fall, but enough to justify the heart pounding, heart *breaking* waves she put off. He didn't think she had any idea how much she radiated, how much he felt. John stroked her cheek.

She opened her eyes. Her breath caught when he didn't look away, held her gaze. Jenifer blinked, her lips parting, and John couldn't help but look down at them. She was so beautiful, but so much a mystery. He looked up again. Jenifer tensed for just a moment and tried to move back from him, but John followed, not letting her go.

"No," he said softly. "Don't."

Her eyes turned to hard steel, any sign of the emotions just a moment before completely gone. John practically heard the clank of steel doors closing around her, shutting down any hint of emotion—good or bad— she'd allowed him to feel from her, however unintentional the glimpse into her soul.

"You don't want to know what I did to the last man who tried to give me orders."

"You probably broke his heart."

She snorted a snide laugh. "I broke *something*."

"Why do you pretend no' to care, Jenifer, when I know you do?" Her eyes pinched just slightly at the corners and she pressed her lips together. "You've gotten very good at puttin' up walls. Your mental shields are stronger than anyone I've ever known. I knew you for weeks before anythin' got through."

"You don't know what the hell you're talking about," she snapped, shoving him away.

He didn't resist, letting her pass. John stepped back until his hips hit the wall behind him and he lowered his head, shoving his hands in his pockets. She stomped away, but stopped before leaving the back area completely. John closed his eyes, willing his heart to slow. It had jumped hard in his chest the moment he stepped close to her, touched her, looked into her eyes, and didn't want to slow now.

"Do you know why I was so worn out when we go' here?" he asked when she didn't leave. She turned to face him, her arms crossed. "I had to fight *you* the whole way. I don't know what was on your mind—or, I should say *where*—but it took everythin' I had to keep control of the collar."

John raised his head and looked at her. Her features were shadowed by the dim, broken light but he saw the glint in her eyes.

"You're powerful, Jenifer. And I honestly don't think you even know it. Do you?"

She shook her head and looked away from him, everything about her body screaming *Don't touch, don't get too close, don't know too much.*

"Where were you thinkin' about, Jenifer? Where did you want to go—"

"I didn't *want* to go anywhere," she snapped.

John stepped away from the wall and moved toward her, only until she tensed and leaned back. She didn't step back, not yet. "Okay, maybe it was somewhere you didn't want to go. Somewhere you thought of as a place we could hide?"

She closed her eyes.

"No one would ever guess wherever it was, right? Because in order to guess it, they'd have to know you more than anyone ever had. It was somewhere personal." He was grasping, reaching, tossing out more suspicions than any solid belief, but with each idea the tension around her grew.

"I told you once, Ambassador, you know nothing about me."

"You also said I never would, but that's where you're wrong." He risked a step closer to her. She glowered at him, her lips and jaw set, but she didn't flinch. "I know you love peanut butter and chocolate. I know you're intelligent and probably designed every gadget I've seen you use yourself. I know you feel intensely even if you don't want anyone to know. And I know you never really relax when you rest because I feel the tension in your body when you sleep."

She inhaled sharply, turned on her heels, and marched back into the parish.

CHAPTER SIXTEEN

4 March 2054, Wednesday
Office of the President
Robert J. Castleton Memorial Building – The Castle
United Earth Protectorate, Capitol City
Alexandria, Seat of Virginia
North American Continent

"*H*ow the hell did this happen!" Nick slammed his palms on the desk surface. Caitlin's picture bounced and fell over, echoing unnaturally loud in the nighttime still building.

Connor raked his hands over his hair, pacing between the desk and one of the couches. He spun back around, looking as pissed as Nick felt. "I don't know—"

"Not good enough! We've got two dead Firebirds and a missing ambassador with a woman no one knows beyond her first name. How the hell did those two men even know to be out there? *I* didn't even know which direction they went."

"This was strictly a need-to-know situation—"

"I know!" Nick snapped, jabbing his finger in the air at Connor. "I'm the one who told *you* it was need-to-know."

Connor came across the office in three long strides, stopping on the other side of the desk, punctuating each statement with a thump of his finger on the scarred wood. "No one knew but you, me, and Mel that John and Jenifer were at the hanger. We kept this tight to the chest, Nick."

"So, who's the leak, Connor?"

Connor's eyes widened for a split second before his jaw snapped shut and he looked away, huffing every breath.

Nick pushed away from the desk and turned his back on Connor, shoving his fingers through his short hair. The call had come in hours before: an explosion of decent size had been picked up in northern Alabama near the Tennessee and Georgia borders, followed almost immediately by a perimeter danger signal from a military fighter shuttle in the same vicinity. Ebben sent out a recon team and found the smoldering remains of what appeared to be the shuttle he'd sent John and Jenifer off in the day before, along with the dismembered and charred bodies of two Firebirds. No sign of John or Jenifer other than some footprints near the shuttles, but nothing leading away from the crash. Blood had been found staining the snow away from the shuttle, and preliminary comparisons to their DNA database registered as John Smith's, and another sample was identified as female but with no record in any accessible database, but the trail ended there. No sign of their alien ambassador or his mysterious bodyguard, who for as far as Nick knew, had become his assassin and kidnapper

The unanswered question remained: Why were two Firebirds out there without orders?

Three solid knocks sounded at the door. Nick shouted "Yeah!" clenching his jaw to tamp down the anger rolling in his chest.

Colonel Ebben led the way into the room, followed by Mel Briggs. The pretty brunette exchanged a look with his brother-in-law and frowned, shaking her head once.

"Report," Nick ordered.

"Sir, we've discovered an encrypted message from within the military command center to Captain Guerrero approximately oh-four-fifteen this morning, and they left Alexandria at oh-four-forty-nine heading southeast along the coast. Lidar scans have determined they proceeded along the coast until they reached an isolated area in central Mississippi where they engaged in a high-speed pursuit with another shuttle we now have determined to be the shuttle procured by Ambassador Smith and his . . . companion . . . yesterday evening. The pursuit continued several hundred miles through southern Mississippi and north through Alabama until they approached the borders of Tennessee and Georgia where it is believed Ambassador Smith's shuttle crashed and subsequently exploded. We have determined Captain Guerrero, along with Lieutenant Clinton Williams, landed the shuttle prior to the explosion and it was the resulting explosion which killed them."

Nick waved him off. "Any sign of John or Jenifer?"

Ebben cleared his throat. "No, sir. Other than the damage to the surrounding area from the crash, there is no evidence of their departure either on foot or by any other form of conveyance."

Nick squinted. "So, we're still going on the theory they disappeared into thin air," he ground out. Before Ebben could attempt to form another useless answer, Nick cut him off with a slice of his hand through the air. "Who sent the message?"

"Sir?"

"The message, Colonel! Who sent the damn message?"

"We don't know, sir."

Nick spun on the balls of his feet and shoved his desk chair away from him, slamming it hard against the far wall. "If *one more person* tells me they don't know . . ." He clenched his jaw and closed his eyes, fighting the hum at the base of his skull. He waved his hand toward the door before setting it firm at his waist, never looking at the three of them. "Get out. Find me answers, Colonel. Whether I like them, or not."

"Sir, there's more."

"Oh, good. I haven't gotten *nearly* enough bad news today."

Mel looked down and Ebben flicked his gaze away from Nick. Connor turned to face both of them. Mel glanced at him for only a second before looking down again.

"Speak!" Nick ordered.

"Sir, the Xeno we captured at the embassy yesterday is talking."

"Did he tell us who wants John dead?"

"It's not just one group, it's the mission of every Xeno cell to assassinate John Smith. Or, if they can't kill him, destroy him."

"Destroy him," Nick repeated, grimacing.

Ebben nodded, a sharp jerk of his head. "If our intel is correct, Xeno operatives have left Earth en route to Aretu."

A lead ball dropped hard into Nick's gut and the pressure behind his eyes tripled. "Silas . . ." he managed to force through clenched teeth.

"Yes, sir. He admitted if they can't kill John Smith, his son is the next best thing. They theorize if his Human son is dead, he will leave Earth."

Nick cursed the ignorant stupidity of the terrorist group. Didn't any of the boneheads realize the Earth couldn't be rid of anything Areth or Umani? Every Human being on the planet carried alien DNA. Everyone. Hell, there was so much Areth and Umani DNA embedded in the Human race, they could barely be called alien.

"The only transports heading for Aretu right now are military transports and Defense Alliance."

"Yes, sir."

"How would a Xeno get on a—" Nick stopped short and shook his head, anger burning in his chest like a ball of acid. He held out his hand. "Give me the details."

Colonel Ebben held out his open hand, a data chip in his palm. Nick grabbed it and tossed it on the desk beside his PAC. "I want anything new, I don't care what it is, brought to me immediately. Whatever else he says."

"Nothing more will be garnered from the Xeno, sir. He died an hour ago."

"Damn it." Leaning over the desk, Nick slammed his knuckles onto its surface. "Figure this out, Ebben. I don't want to hear any more excuses."

Three voices snapped "Yes, sir" and all three marched from the room.

In the silence of the office Nick drew in a deep breath and dropped his chin toward his chest. One word echoed in his thoughts . . . *Traitor*.

But who?

And how many?

A three-beat chime sounded from the PAC on his desk.

Nick lunged for the PAC, sending his chair into a spin. He dropped into the seat and pushed the receive button at the same time. Only one person had that particular chime. "Michael."

His son looked back at him through the secure—though secure meant little these days—connection, having the decency to at least look contrite. "Hi, Dad."

Half a dozen questions fought in his head to be the first one out of his mouth. *Where the hell are you? Why haven't you let us know you're okay? Do you have any idea what this is doing to your mother? Do you know what you did to Jackie? When are you coming home?* Nick set his arms out straight on either side of the PAC and dropped his head forward, drawing in a slow and purposeful breath before he looked up again.

"Are you okay?"

Michael leaned back away from the monitor, the sound of a creaky chair matching the motion, and scrubbed his hands over his face. A day's stubble roughed his jaw, and he didn't look gaunt or pale, so Nick had hopes he wasn't in any immediate danger. An aged plaster wall with yellowing paint, possibly once white, served as Michael's backdrop, giving Nick no real indication of where his son might be. Michael raked his forever-too-long hair off his forehead and met Nick's gaze through the computer screen.

He chuckled, a single huff of a sound. "I thought I was, Dad. I don't know."

"Okay. Where are you?"

"I'm with Jace. I have been since shortly after I left."

Nick ground his jaw. He intended to have a discussion with his former top pilot about keeping secrets from the Commander in Chief.

"I didn't tell him you didn't know. He didn't know he was hiding something from you."

Nick nodded, rubbing his fingers across his chin. He had his own scrape of whiskers, felt like he'd been in this damned office for three days instead since just this morning. "I'll save the third degree for your mother. For now, when the hell are you coming home?"

"How is Caitlin?"

Nick almost smiled. Nice diversion tactic. "She's fine. She'll be better when you get home."

It didn't matter, had never mattered, Caitlin was only about five years older than Michael. Since the day Michael was freed from his Sorracchi prison Caitlin had been the only mother to him he ever counted. The shell of a Human possessed by a Sorracchi parasite who had given birth to him was nothing more than a pathetic surrogate as far as the Tanner family was concerned.

Michael looked down and away, taking a slow breath. "I'm coming home as soon as I can arrange transport. It's time I stop running."

Nick struggled to tamp down the surprised look he knew popped out on his face when Michael made his admission. His son was probably the most self-aware person Nick had ever met, but he didn't usually say as much.

"Michael, you should know something. Jackie—"

"Might not forgive me," Michael cut him off. He stared hard at Nick, clenching his jaw, and in that moment Nick knew he knew. Jackie was gone. For now. "I'll do whatever it takes whenever I have the chance."

Nick nodded. "Well, I know of one little girl who'll be happy to see you."

No matter what thoughts rolled through his son's head, the mention of Nicole brought a smile to his lips. It was a restrained, still sad smile, but a father's smile nonetheless. "I've missed her." He paused, barely long enough to consider it a pause. He shifted forward in his chair again, the old parts squeaking loudly. His face, an almost perfect replica of Nick's twenty years before, filled the screen. Dark brown eyes flicked past the screen to his left and back to the screen again. "I've missed a lot of people. I'm looking forward to playing poker with you and John." Michael smiled, but Nick recognized the falsity behind it.

Sensation niggled along the back of Nick's neck. Even hundreds of miles away and through an electronic connection, something tangible and definite connected him and his son. It amazed him to know that kind of connection could exist even though he hadn't known his son lived for the first twenty-five years of his life. He heard the truth as clear as if Michael sat across from him.

He's here.

That was how Michael knew about Jackie. Of course. But how the hell had John—and Jenifer?—made it from Tennessee to Florida in a matter of a couple hours? Not even a fast hover could cover that kind of distance, and even if one could, it would have lit up their lidar like an old fashioned Christmas tree. He'd told John to head for Jace if things went pear-shaped, but traveling that far that fast was impossible with overland transportation.

"Not sure when we'll fit it in," Nick said, keeping his tone casual. *No faith in security.* "I've been stuck in Alexandria pretty late these days. A lot of things going on."

"Caitlin must not like that. Are you going home soon?"

"Not for a while. Damn Xenos are stirring up trouble." Part of him worried about even saying the word, since they were probably the ones listening, but they'd probably wonder more if he didn't. "I'm waiting on news of a few things, then I'll go home. I'll probably be back here before dawn. I'd sleep here, but Caitlin would have my hide. Speaking of . . . when do you think you'll be home?"

"I'd be there waiting for you in the morning if I could." Michael chuckled. "Remember those books you gave me to read? *Star Trek*? Too bad I don't have a transporter."

Nick squinted. *Oookay. We can go with that.*

"I'll be home by the end of the week."

Nick nodded. "It'll be good to have you back."

All play acting slipped away and Michael's features shifted to the same frightened wariness Nick had hated to see in those first few days after he'd come out of New Mexico. Restrained. Internal. Afraid to disappoint. Afraid of the repercussions. "I hope so."

"No need to hope, son. Everybody screws up."

"I thought I was doing the right thing." Michael looked down and away, his light brown hair falling forward.

"You can explain when you get here. We just want to understand." Nick smiled. "And for once we can have a real birthday party for you."

Michael nodded, his hand moving toward the screen. "I'll see you soon, Dad."

"See you soon."

The monitor went black. Nick leaned back in his own squeaky chair and scrubbed his face with his palms. Unless he was completely off base, somehow—and that was a big somehow—John and Jenifer would be back in Alexandria by morning. Undetected. If John could pull one off, he had a new career as a magician to look forward to.

Now, Nick just had to figure out a way to get John on the *Steppenschraff*, the next Defense Alliance ship scheduled to leave Earth for Aretu before an assassin killed his son. Once John knew, Nick held no illusion things would go down any other way.

CHAPTER SEVENTEEN

"*T*omorrow morning," Michael said, pushing the powered down PAC away from him.

"That conversation couldn't have gone better if we planned it."

"I told you it wouldn't be a problem." Michael shoved back from his desk, his back wheels hitting the wall barely after he moved. "Is the device accurate enough to put you in my father's office?"

John nodded, stepping away from the corner of the small bedroom where he'd stayed still during Michael's conversation with Nick. "Absolutely. The trick with the device is bein' familiar with your destination. Knowin' coordinates will work, but havin' been there before makes the trip much easier." John smirked. "If I focused hard enough I could put Jenifer and myself on the couch."

A slow smirk shifted Michael's features.

John chuckled and shrugged. "Okay, maybe no'. Jenifer is beautiful, but like a rose, her thorns can sting."

Michael started to speak, but stopped himself and looked down at his hands.

"What?"

"I was going to say something, but I realized it was very clichéd. And quite possibly hypocritical."

John sank down on the edge of the small bed. There wasn't much in the room: a bed, a desk, a chair, and a small bureau, filling the room to capacity and leaving little space for maneuvering. John wasn't even sure it was actually a bedroom or just a storage closet Jace had managed to set up as a room for his unexpected guest.

"Why don't you tell me anyway."

"Caitlyn once told me I would find it easier to be around people when I learned to read them, to see beyond what they say," Michael said, leaning back in his chair. It squeaked loudly in the tight space. "I find this very difficult."

"I can understand that," John said, nodding his head. "You know I can feel things from people. Other Areth. Most Humans." Michael returned the nod. "When I meet someone I *can't* feel anythin' from, I feel like someone blindfolded me and stuck cotton wool in my ears. Like you, I've had to learn to . . ." He paused, trying to remember the way Nick had put it. " . . .to read people. Figure out what they meant, no' just what they said."

Michael didn't say anything, staring at John, studying. Probably trying to read John just like John tried to read all the silent people around him. John smiled and patted Michael's forearm. "Just tell me."

"You love her."

The words, said so simply, hit John in the center of his chest. He sat back a little.

"Or, you will love her," Michael amended.

"That's quite the observation. But, it doesn't seem cliché to me." Funny how a suddenly dry throat made it hard to talk.

"I was going to say the two of you are a very unlikely couple."

"How is that hypocritical?"

Michael opened the PAC and turned it on with a slide of his thumb, the screen brightening with an image of Michael and Jacqueline, their faces close together—cheek to cheek—with wide, genuine smiles. "I would rather not list all the ways Jacqueline and I are incompatible —"

"Not incompatible. Different. You compliment each other, Michael."

He didn't argue, didn't agree. He touched his fingertips to the curve of Jacqueline's cheek in the photo. A heavy emotion rolled off him, nothing John could define with any specific name beyond the out of place word. John stood and laid his hand on Michael's shoulder, squeezing firmly.

167

"I'm goin' to find her," John said, figuring he didn't need to clarify further. "Tell her what's goin' on. I need to get some rest before I tackle the collars again."

Michael nodded, silent, and John took it as his cue to go.

The house was quiet. Lilly had put Jamie to bed right after the service and retired herself. He returned to the common area, finding Jace at the table with Jenifer. Both looked up when he entered, and Jace moved quickly to his feet. "Coffee?"

"No, thank you—"

"He doesn't drink coffee," Jenifer said at the same time.

Jace stalled, looked between them, and sat back down. "So, what's the plan?"

John swiveled the chair adjacent to Jenifer and straddled it, crossing his arms on the high back. "Nick told Michael he'll be in his office early tomorrow mornin'. I intend to be there before he arrives."

"Okay, this probably seems like a stupid question, but why exactly are you going back to Alexandria?" Jace motioned between John and Jenifer. "You two left the city barely twenty-four hours ago with assassins hot on your tailpipe. Why go back now? You don't think everyone who wants you dead just followed you out of town, do you?"

"We can't stay here," John said. "They're goin' to look for us near the crash site for a while, but then they're goin' to start lookin' in every place they even suspect we might show up. Anywhere either myself or Jenifer have known connections."

"Anywhere *you* have connections, Ambassador," Jenifer said, taking a bite of the doughy, broth-covered dumplins Lilly had made earlier. The aroma drifted to John, and he was tempted to get another bowl. "The only reason any of those damn Xenos know of me at all is because I've been hanging around with your hunted face for the last couple of weeks."

John had to blink to make himself look away from her and focus again on Jace. "The point still stands. They're goin' to come here eventually, most likely under the guise of friendship, but I want no trace of us here. Only one man saw us, right?"

Jace nodded. "Mark. He's an honest and loyal man, former Earth Force himself."

"The sooner we leave here, the less likelihood of anyone else seein' us," John continued. "I figure they could be here as soon as tomorrow, especially if they start figurin' out how far we could get since this afternoon. They might even stay nearby for a couple days, watchin' to see if we show up. If we're already gone, they'll sit here and wait for nothin'."

"Fine, but why Alexandria?"

"We left Alexandria," Jenifer answered, swirling her fork through the remnants of dinner in her bowl. "We'd have to be idiots to go back."

John pulled a slow breath in through his nose and released it just as slowly. Jenifer had made her opinion quite clear about returning to Alexandria when he'd told her, Jace, and Michael after the evening service. On the tail of their argument, for lack of a better definition, in the church she'd been all prickles and barbs all evening.

He caught Jace's smirk as he stood and picked up his and Jenifer's empty bowls, turning to take them to the sink. "You don't think there's anywhere you can go no one would suspect?"

Jenifer tensed, the shift in her body miniscule and nearly unnoticeable if John wasn't keenly aware of her.

"What if you just picked a random place on the planet, somewhere neither of you have *any* connection to, and just go?"

John forced himself to pay attention to Jace, forced himself not to watch Jenifer when she stood and walked away from the table to the bench lounge Lilly had collapsed to make a serviceable sleeping surface. She snatched up her jacket and shoved her arms into the sleeves, shooting a slanted glance in his direction.

"John?"

"I won't run like a frightened child," John said, perhaps more sharply than he intended. Jenifer met his gaze before he turned away and looked to Jace. "There's a line to be drawn, and I'm drawin' it."

The back door closed with a loud thud.

Jace came back to the table, and set a mug on the table with a thunk before he sat. "I get the impression Jenifer isn't thrilled with the idea."

"What gave her away?" John said with a chuckle.

Jace stared at the back door, working the inside of his cheek against his teeth. He tapped his fingertips on the tabletop. Even if John didn't feel the indecision pushing off Jace like beats on a drum, he'd know something sat heavily on the man's mind.

"You might as well just spit it out," John said, sitting back in the chair.

Jace smiled. "As a minister, part of my job is to speak up about what I see in relationships, give my parishioners insight into what they are too close to understand. But, you're not a parishioner."

"I'm a believer in the same God, is that close enough?"

Jace's entire expression changed, shifting away from the tight concern. "I'd love to talk to you more about the New Covenant faith on Aretu."

John chuckled again. "Nice try. Spit it out, and then maybe we can talk."

Jace stood again and went back to the sink, dumping out the coffee he'd made. He shrugged. "If I drink it I'll never sleep." He turned and leaned against the counter, his arms crossed over his chest. "You know Jackie and Jenifer were the two who brought me out of the Sorracchi prison."

John nodded.

"They didn't go into prison for me, John. I credit divine intervention for them finding me and bringing me home to Lilly and Jamie."

"Who were they lookin' for?"

"Elijah Kerrigan."

John sat up straighter, remembering the exuberant, talkative man he'd met in the ruins of Chicago after the initial Sorrs attacks. Eli had been the one to contact General Castleton in Tennessee to bring in reinforcements and bring John—along with the remaining survivors—to the relative safety of their hidden base. John had spent several evenings talking with Eli, and had considered him a friend. Eli loved to tell John of Jenny, a woman he more than loved, he adored.

The skin on the back of his neck prickled.

Jace paused, and nodded the moment he knew John had made the connection. Jace had been with the Phoenix contingent when they came to Chicago, and had greeted Eli with the familiarity of friendship. "Eli was Jenifer's lover. He died in the first day of the war as part of an attack on a Sorracchi base in New Zealand. By what I understand, in Jenifer's arms."

John involuntarily looked toward the back door.

As vivid as the first time the memories flashed to him, he smelled the acrid burn of ion and the stench of warm blood. He saw the glistening red on Jenifer's hands, remembered the pain he'd experienced with her. It all became clear.

"I don't know Jenifer well. I have absolutely no memory of her and Jackie bringing me back to Phoenix, and I've only spent time with her a few times since then." Jace kept talking, but John's attention was more outside than inside. "I know she's loyal to Phoenix, or at least the idea of Phoenix. I know she's a solo flyer. And I'll tell you, I've never seen her express as much . . . emotion for lack of a better word . . . in any time I've been around her as I've seen since y'all showed up here a few hours ago."

"Funny, I've been thinkin' the opposite," John mumbled.

5 FEBRUARY 2054, THURSDAY 00:22
FIREBIRD COMMAND BARRACKS—FORMER HOTEL DISTRICT
"THE NEST"
UNITED EARTH PROTECTORATE, CAPITOL CITY
ALEXANDRIA, SEAT OF VIRGINIA
NORTH AMERICAN CONTINENT

"*D*amn it!"

Connor gripped the back of a metal folding chair and flung it across the break room, taking out three more chairs with a loud cacophony of metal against metal. He wanted to punch something—someone—snap something in two to vent the raging anger bubbling like lava under his skin. "*C'est vraiment des conneries!*"

"Connor!"

He swung around, instinctively bringing his hands up in fists, pulling back his urge to swing in a split second when his brain registered his 2IC's voice. Mel stood near the door, wide brown eyes shifting as she scanned the chaos in the room. Connor tapped his fisted fingers twice against his forehead, while drawing a scraping breath in through his nose.

"When I find who betrayed us—betrayed me—betrayed *Nick*—I'm going to—" he forced through clenched teeth, shaking his head. "I can't . . . I can't even begin to process who of my men could have done it."

The double doors of the former ballroom-turned-dining and rec hall burst open and three Firebirds ran in, pulse weapons drawn. Mel spun around, hands up.

"Stand down," she said firmly and they immediately lowered, but didn't holster, their weapons.

They didn't move fast enough.

"Get out!"

Everyone moved at once in response to Connor's shouted order. The three Firebirds sharply took their leave and Mel slammed the doors behind them, twisting the lock from the inside. She closed the space between them, and caught his arm as he turned to take out his frustration on the coffee station. He tried to shrug her off, but she grabbed a fist of his long-sleeved tee shirt and got between him and the offending stack of chipped and mismatched mugs.

"Hey!" she shouted. "Hey! Listen to me!"

"Just *let* me be pissed, Mel," he ground out, trying again to shake off her insistent hands. "One of *my* men is a damn traitor."

"One of *our* men, Connor. *Our* men. This isn't just your squadron."

"We picked every single one of those Firebirds!" He pointed toward the now closed door with several sharp jabs, punctuating each word. "Handpicked them for their damn *loyalty* to Phoenix and Nick."

"I know."

"He's pissed as hell, and he has every damn right to be. At this point, not even you and I are above suspicion."

"No, Connor. President Tanner knows who he can trust."

"What good is trust in me if the people—" The words sputtered out and he snapped his jaw shut, bitter adrenaline spawned by treason sticking in the back of his throat.

She let go of his shirt and took his face in her hands. The unfamiliar contact from his 2IC snapped Connor's attention back to her. He instinctively grabbed her wrists, holding her hands in place, and tipped his head to touch his forehead to hers, sucking in deep and ragged breaths with his eyes closed. Her feminine scent, a contrast to the soldier personae everyone saw, wrapped around him and scraped away the jagged edges of his anger. He'd caught the scent before—a heady mixture of floral, spice, and cotton—and held no doubt Melanie Briggs was as much a beautiful woman as a competent soldier, but he'd never allowed himself even the thought of being any closer to her than the regular execution of their duties allowed. Sometimes that meant a shared cramped space, or the casual, meaningless touch of a hand on a sleeve, but never being so close they shared the same breath. Never so close the warmth of her palm seeped into his skin.

That was a lie. He'd thought about it plenty.

"And if you keep this up, whoever the traitor is will know we're aware of them. We may not know their name, but they're going to know we're looking for them and they might go to ground. If they think they're still operating in the shadows we have a better chance of finding them because they won't know they need to hide." Her voice carried no further than the space between them, humming over his skin.

Connor clenched his teeth and swallowed, nodding in the hold of her small, strong hands. The movement brushed the side of his nose along hers, and the simple act sent a shot of awareness through him. It was all he could do not to let the groan escape when it lodged at the base of his throat, especially when he heard the tiny catch in Mel's breathing and her fingertips slipped further into his short hair.

Later he knew he'd probably kick himself to hell and back, but in this moment he didn't care. In a single, fluid move he wrapped his arms around her body, lifted her, took two steps toward the counter behind her and set her down with enough force to rattle the stacked mugs. Mel stared at him with wide eyes, rapid breath skimming across his face. Her gaze shifted down to his mouth and the tip of her tongue appeared to moisten her lower lip. It was the only invitation Connor needed or asked for.

He fisted his fingers into the waistband of her utility pants and pulled her hard against him, her thighs bracketing his hips. Body to body contact electrified every nerve ending and his pulse hammered through him. He kissed her hard, covering her open mouth with his and plunging his tongue past her lips to taste her surprise. He couldn't pull her close enough, kiss her deep enough, breathe her in fast enough. If at any moment, for even just a second, he'd thought she didn't want this as much as him he would have stopped. He knew he would have stopped. Told himself he would have stopped. But every pull harder against him was met with an erotic shift of her hips and a moan against his mouth. Her fingers pulled at his hair, trying to draw him closer and every stroke of his tongue was met by one as eager from her.

"*Mon Dieu*," he said against her open mouth, pausing only long enough to catch a few ragged breaths before he kissed her again. "Mel . . ."

She laughed and combed her nails along the back of his head, drawing back only enough to look at him with bright, dark eyes. "If you're going to kiss me like that, the least you could do is call me Melanie."

He groaned and kissed her again.

CHAPTER EIGHTEEN

*W*hen Nick was a kid, before WeatherNet had even been heard of, let alone engaged, he used to love going out on the dock at the cabin when a lightning storm came rolling in across the lake. His father would let him stay out there until the first lightning strike, and then he had to come back in the cabin. But it was that moment, right after the first strike, when the air practically crackled and the smell of ion burned his nose, he loved the most.

He felt the same crackle in the air, could almost smell the sizzle of ion, walking down the dim hall to his office at o'dark thirty. He stopped, looked up and down the long hallway and acknowledged the Firebirds standing at attention on each end. Neither of them gave any indication they felt or noticed anything unusual.

Just as quickly, the crackle passed. Nick scrubbed his palms over his face and shoved his fingers into his hair. He was too damn tired, that was it. He'd been here until nearly one in the morning, went home for three hours of sleep, and was now back here. He hadn't even seen Caitlin awake, but found some calm in listening to her soft breathing and resting his hand on her stomach to feel their child stir.

He shook his head and took the last few steps to his office door. The doorknob hummed in his grip. He glanced sideways to make sure the

175

Firebirds held their post and no one was close enough to see into the office.

"I thought you said it wouldn't be as hard this time," was the first bit of conversation Nick heard when he opened the door. Plain and simple, Jenifer sounded ticked despite speaking in barely above a whisper.

"It wasn't, but it's been less than twenty-four hours since I used the collars. They aren't intended to be used so close together and this time was farther than yesterday."

"And you didn't think to tell me this until now? Damn it, Ambassador . . ."

Nick slipped into the room and shut the door behind him.

"Did you have another way to get here?" John snapped, and dropped onto the couch in a limp slump, with Jenifer helping him down.

"I didn't want to get here *at all*, remember?" She crouched in front of him, one hand resting on the arm of the couch, the other on his leg.

"I'm no' havin' this conversation again—"

"Dropping your decision on me and not listening to reason is *not* a conversation."

Nick cleared his throat. "Am I interrupting something?"

Both turned their heads with a snap, clearly neither having realized he'd come into the room at all. He took quick inventory of both of them, and didn't like what he saw. Both looked worse for wear, John more than Jenifer. One side of his face around his temple and eye socket was mottled and bruised, a cut held together by a small bandage and showing signs of stratum basale stimulator use; which made sense. They'd just come from Lilly Quinn. Which made him wonder what John had looked like before seeing her. Jenifer had a bruise along her hairline, but Nick didn't know what he *couldn't* see on either one of them.

Both wore thin black bands around their necks, nodes on either side of their throats. Considering the fact they'd basically beamed into the office from apparently nowhere, he assumed the collars were one of John's Areth toys. John reached for his and it came off with a snap. He reached for Jenifer at the same time. Before he could touch her, she removed her own collar with an angry grimace, and tossed it on the couch beside him.

"Nothing unusual, just Ambassador Smith being pigheaded," Jenifer practically growled, pushing up to stand over him with her arms crossed.

"And Jenifer bein' her sparklin' self."

"Glad to see you two crazy kids are working things out."

Jenifer scowled at him and John chuckled, rubbing his fingers across his forehead. He looked tired, worn.

"So, who gets to tell me what the hell happened?"

"You've got a traitor in your midst," Jenifer answered before John could speak.

"That much I've figured out. Got any idea who?"

She shook her head. "All we know is we had a Firebird hover up our tailpipe for two hundred miles before we finally crashed. And when they came looking for us, it wasn't to check and see if we had any boo-boos."

"We confirmed communication within the city to the two Fire—two men who chased you down." In Nick's eyes, the two no longer deserved the designation of Firebird or any other rank in his administration. "Someone told them where to find you. We're still trying to figure out who."

"Not many to choose from," John said. "I know full well Connor was careful no' to give us away from the minute we . . ." He grinned and looked at Jenifer from the corner of his blue eyes. " . . .commandeered their hover. He couldn't avoid any contact, no' and get us out of the city, but it was limited."

"I need Connor in here," Nick said, turning toward his desk.

Jenifer stood from the couch, using the leg beneath her to leverage herself to standing. "You sure that's a good idea?"

"If anyone is going to help us figure out who it is, it's Connor."

"Because you're convinced beyond any question he's above suspicion." It was a question, but she didn't ask it as a question, leaving it more like a "so, that's what you're going with" statement. "Sir," she added.

"Yes. I am." Nick made sure his tone left no doubt of his opinion.

Jenifer shrugged and went back to the couch, flopping down beside John. "Far be it for me to question the President of the Whole Frickin' Planet."

Were she anyone else, Nick might have called her on her attitude. Ultimately, she reminded him way too much of himself to dress her down for a little sarcasm. He took his communicator from its spot on his belt and punched the code to call Connor. It was early, but Connor probably didn't get any more sleep than he did.

*C*onnor opened his eyes with the first twitter from his communicator, slipped from his warm bed, grabbed the communicator on the second, and stepped into the adjoined bathroom by the third. He pulled the door shut with a low click, wincing at even that much sound.

"Montgomery."

"I need you in my office. Now."

"Yes, sir," Connor said, pinching his nose to shake off the final tendrils of sleep. "I'll get Mel and we'll be there in half an hour."

"Just you. And make it twenty."

"Yes, sir."

He tossed the communicator on the counter and scrubbed his face with his palms. Exhaustion dragged at him. He had to shake it off and quick. Moving as quietly as he could, he turned on the shower and stepped under the sharp spray, panting through the ice-cold needles until they had a chance to warm. But by then he'd already finished and switched off the water. He dried off just as quick and went back to the bedroom for a clean uniform. He only dared a brief glance at the bed, knowing full well he'd be tempted to return to the warm, naked, sexy woman waiting for him.

Melanie stirred, a soft moan sounding much louder in the still room, and stretched her arms over her head, propping herself up on her elbows. She smiled slow and sexy, her tousled brown hair bringing back vivid memories of the same chocolate curls spread on the white pillow in the wee hours of the morning. Connor grinned back, as he bent over to pull on his second boot.

"Where are you going?" she asked, picking up her own communicator from the side table. With a swipe of her finger, the time came up on the small screen. "We don't have to be in morning briefing for another hour and a half."

"Nick called. I've got about fourteen minutes to get there," he said with a grin. "I'll come find you when I'm done."

"Do you need me?"

Connor finished tying his boot and straightened, taking two strides to reach the bed. He leaned over her and kissed her firmly, moaning against her mouth before forcing himself to pull back. "I do. Absolutely. But not for this. I'll catch up with you later."

Mel pulled her lower lip through her teeth, her eyes sparkling. "Okay."

He went around the foot of the bed, stepping over their discarded clothing from the night before. That was, he supposed, one of the benefits of being housed in a historical hotel in the former resort district of Alexandria. As the elite, Firebirds didn't sleep in cold, utilitarian barracks but converted hotel rooms. The power flickered from time to time, the water never quite got hot, but the beds were comfortable and no one inspected their rooms. As a commanding officer, he had a room to himself. Good thing since he'd broken a two hundred year military statue the night before by making love to his second in command.

He picked up his jacket from the chair closest to the door, slipped his arm into one sleeve and realized it was a good two sizes too small. With a chuckle, he tossed the jacket back where it was and bent over to pick up his *actual* jacket from the floor.

"Connor?"

"Yeah," he said, turning as he zipped up the jacket.

"What happened—"

"Was a long time coming." He gently cut her off, and smiled, waiting until she smiled back. Damn, she looked sexy in his bed.

She nodded. "I'll see you later."

"Later."

He had twelve minutes left.

"*W*hen did we find this?"

Nick Tanner's voice vibrated with rage, so palpable Jenifer would swear she felt it in the air buffering around them. His personal communicator had gone off a few minutes after he'd contacted Connor Montgomery, and by what she could glean from this side of the conversation he spoke with Colonel Ebben.

"Damn it. Transfer the file to my PAC. I'll review it from here." He paused, then shook his head with a sharp jerk. "No. We'll debrief at oh-eight-thirty once I have time to review it myself."

Jenifer had assumed her usual spot in the presidential office, falling quickly into the old habit of standing near the massive hearth across the room from Nick Tanner's desk with the couches between her and the desk, and facing the door. With a turn of her head, she could see through the second story windows to the property outside while keeping the entire room under surveillance. John paced across the front of the couch, having apparently recovered from his temporary fatigue from the hop, his arms crossed over his body and he stared straight down as he walked.

She wondered how much of Nick's anger John *actually* felt, felt in the way he'd told her he could pick up on people's emotions. Probably was why he paced.

John paused at the end of the couch closest to her, raised his head, and his gaze connected with hers. A subtle sensation she refused to call a tingle shifted over Jenifer's shoulders and down her spine. She tilted her head and arched an eyebrow. Two strides brought him to her, closing the space between them until it was barely existent. He leaned into her the way they'd done for weeks. So why did she notice the warmth of his proximity so tangibly?

"A great deal has happened in the last forty-eight hours or so," he whispered, leaning close enough his breath stirred the hair around her cheek and ear. "I've never felt Nick so unsettled."

"The description seems inadequate," she said, turning slightly toward his cheek.

John pulled back to look into her eyes. "You feel it too?"

"It doesn't take a Talent to know he's angrier than a mule chewing on bumblebees."

John's eyebrows shot up and he chuckled quietly, only the shake of his shoulders and low rumble in his chest evidence of his laugh. Jenifer rolled her eyes and tried not to laugh herself. She hadn't slipped into one of her grandmother's colloquialisms in years, but the slip was worth it to see John's face.

"I'm goin' to remember that one," he said with a grin. The grin slipped slightly and the lines tightened around his eyes a degree. "What about you?"

"What about me."

"You've been angry with me since last night."

"With good reason . . ."

"I suppose." He shifted closer, his entire body within a breath of touching her. John bent at the knee the slight degree needed to bring him more eye level with her. "I wonder what made you angriest."

"You want an itemized list?" She tried to stir up the ire again, but couldn't seem to find the well of frustration she'd felt even minutes ago when they arrived in the office. The fury was gone once she saw his energy return.

"Just the top offenders. Was it my decision to come back to Alexandria, because I didn't tell you the trip would probably tap me a bit, or . . ." He paused, and when he spoke again his voice was heavier, almost rough. "Or was it because I dared think about kissin' you last night in the church?"

She looked at him before the logical part of her brain could warn her against it, and the dark look in his blue eyes made her breath still. Jenifer always held to the discipline once eye contact was made, never be the first to look away. Show your opponent who was in control. John wasn't her opponent, not anymore, but she couldn't look away. His eyes shifted down, focusing on her mouth, and he drew in a slow, metered breath. Just as his lips parted to speak, a knock at the office door broke the moment.

John turned and stepped to her side, giving her a view of the office door as Nick marched to answer it. She slipped Damocles partly free of her thigh holster, feeling the instant hum against her palm as the weapon came to life at her touch. John's fingers curled around the inside of her other elbow.

"Probably Connor."

"Or not," she muttered.

"Yeah?" Nick called as he neared the door.

"It's Connor, sir."

Nick glanced at them before wrapping his hand around the knob. He opened the door just enough to look into the hall, probably confirmed Connor was alone, and yanked the door open ushering Connor into the room. "Forty-five seconds to spare."

Connor grinned wide and chuckled, about to say something when he noticed her and John across the room. He practically stumbled to a halt, his mouth hanging open.

"As you were, soldier," Nick said, walking past Connor to stand so he could speak to all of them at the same time. "We'll skip the obvious question, since I haven't quite wrapped my own brain around how John's toy works, and move on to the 'What the hell do we do now?' question."

"Yes, sir." Connor assumed an at ease stance with his feet apart and his hands clasped behind his back. "Am I correct to assume the only people aware of the ambassador's return to Alexandria are in this room?"

"And it damn well better stay that way," Nick snapped and motioned for everyone to sit.

He sat at the end furthest from them on the couch across from John and Jenifer, and Connor sat on the edge of the cushions beside him, hunched forward looking ready to jump into action at any moment. Jenifer re-holstered Damocles and followed John to the other couch, waiting until he sat before she perched on the arm. John shot her an odd look, but she considered sitting on the cushions too passive, especially if they should be discovered. She didn't budge and he eventually looked away to the other two men.

John shifted to lean forward, resting his elbows on his knees with his fingers loosely clasped. "It's abundantly clear runnin' isn't an option, and I'm no' about to hide like a child frightened of shadows. We need to find out who these internal people are and stop this cat and mouse game."

"I agree, and we *will* find who it is," Nick emphasized with a jab of his finger in the air. "But, John, there's something you need to know before you decide what to do."

"What?"

Tense regret made the lines around Nick Tanner's mouth twitch, like the words themselves he had to say tasted sour. "The would-be assassin we retrieved from the embassy attack told us something before he died. These damn Xenos are so intent on convincing you to go back to Aretu and off Earth, they've plan on hitting you where it hurts the most." He paused and swallowed. "Silas."

John blanched. "Explain."

"We can't trust anything we thought confidential before now, but we suspect Silas is also a target."

John lunged to his feet. "How long have you known this?"

"Since last night, just before I talked to Michael. I assume you were with him, but I couldn't very well explain since I have no faith the line was secure." The calm levelness to the president's voice surprised Jenifer, and she wondered if he'd learned the trick or if someone taught him. Reacting to John's frustration with the opposite reaction hopefully would bring John down a notch.

Not that she blamed him.

John paced past her to the fireplace, raking his long fingers through his hair. He stopped at the high mantle and thumped his arms against the edge, head bowed. Jenifer fought the undeniable urge to go to him, and just lay her hand on his back in some form of comfort. The question of where such an urge came from kept her from moving. Instead Nick stood and walked to within a couple feet of John and set his hand on the mantle.

"Colonel Ebben sent me a file this morning he said reinforces our theory. He said it's an audio file they found in the recording database. It popped up after a key word search. The quality is bad, but he said I need to hear it. He doesn't know you're here, too."

"How do we have a recording like that?" Connor asked, standing himself.

"Almost every communication within Alexandria is recorded, coming, going, or within the city. Our system is rudimentary, especially when we don't know what we're looking for, but in this case we did. I had them work on a search last night."

"You think because the Sorrs are gone Big Brother isn't still watching?" Jenifer snarked.

"Play it." John's voice was strained, almost lost across the room.

With a sharp nod, Nick returned to his desk, picked up the flat PAC, and brought it to the table between the two couches. John turned his back to the cold fireplace and leaned his shoulders against the mantle with his arms crossed and his head down. A tight muscle along his cheek jerked with each clench of his jaw. This time, Jenifer didn't fight the urge and rose to move to him. She didn't touch him, but stood by his shoulder until he looked at her. The pain in his eyes made her chest ache. He already planned for the worst.

A few audible beeps behind her indicated Nick accessed the file. "Okay, here it is."

She turned and stayed by John's side. He took two steps toward the table, the tension rolling off him as he waited. She waited with him.

The recording was choppy, low quality, and had a decidedly synthetic sound to it. Nick turned it up enough they could all hear.

" . . .*operatives already en route.*" The first voice was definitely male, though it still sounded "false" in some way. Perhaps it was the program they used to extract the recording.

"*At what point do we call the on-planet efforts a failure?*"

Jenifer's skin broke out in gooseflesh. The second voice could be female. It was hard to tell.

"*We still have people willing to do what it takes. You just need to keep us informed. Don't worry, you'll stay out of the line of fire.*"

"*See to it. You lose me, you lose your best source of information.*"

"*Don't threaten me. You came to us, remember? I can't help it if your need for revenge overrode what you claim to be your sense of loyalty to Tanner.*"

The line crackled loudly and buzzed. Jenifer stole a quick glance at President Tanner, recognizing the twisting turmoil behind his dark eyes. He ran his hand over his upper lip, the scrape of skin over rough whiskers seeming loud in the morning hours. No one relished the idea of having a traitor in their fold, but everything pointed to someone close to Nick, and dug even deeper.

"*I don't like the idea of killing a child.*" The softer voice burst through the crackle.

Jenifer reached out before she considered any other option, and laced her fingers through John's. His grip tightened on hers immediately, almost painfully, but she understood and didn't pull away.

"*Don't get soft-hearted now. You more than most understand the need to get the damn aliens off our world. They brought the war here, they're responsible for the apocalypse we barely survived, they need to get the hell off our planet.*" The first voice they'd heard practically shouted the words, his voice strained with righteous anger.

"*Don't preach to me. I know what has to be done. The end always justifies the means.*"

"*Damn straight. We already have our people in place to move when we send the word. If running for his life doesn't convince him to go home, maybe the boy's funeral will. He has a hell of a lot of nerve to claim a Human child as his 'son'.*"

John released her hand, his arm immediately coming around her shoulder to pull her against him. He cursed in a language she didn't understand, but she didn't need to speak the language to understand the anger behind the words.

"*I get that, but the boy is Human. He knows no better.*"

"*You've seen him as much as anyone and you know he has no close ties to anyone here. No one we can use without bringing down a firestorm we don't want to contend with. His friends are too high up in the chain of command.*"

"*What if he takes a Human lover?*" the female-like voice asked.

"*Do you know if he has?*"

"*President Tanner found him a bodyguard.*" The speaker snorted a strange laugh. "*She lives in the ambassadorial apartment with him, and goes everywhere with him. I've seen them together and they have grown more familiar with each other each time. If she isn't his lover, she will be.*"

Connor raised his head and looked at them, his gaze shifting from her to John, and to his hand curled against her side. She scowled back, daring him to say anything.

The conversation paused as the other speaker probably considered his co-conspirator's suggestion. "*No, the real stake will be the murder of the boy. She's probably no more than a—*"

His fingers curled into the fabric of her shirt. She couldn't move away if she wanted to, but she didn't despite the flash of heat over her skin. The words broke and the rest of the recording was nothing more than buzzed, crackles and half-words. Not enough to decipher. It ended seconds later.

"When was this recorded?" John forced through clenched teeth.

Nick picked up the PAC and squinted at the screen. "Nine days ago."

"They know he's on his way to Aretu." John spun away from her with such violence she swayed in his wake. He was half way to the door before she registered his intent and she ran after him. Nick and Connor stood, but she was faster and she caught him just as he reached the door. She got in front of him and grabbed his arms, pushing him back.

"John, stop!"

"Get out of my way," he ground out.

"No! I know what you want to do, I get it, but you can't do it like this."

"He's my son!"

"I know!" Jenifer moved against him, bringing them chest to chest, and he shifted away from the door. "I know," she said softer. "Breathe for a second and we'll figure this out. Right, sir?" she said past him to where Nick stood behind them.

"A Defense Alliance ship is leaving the planet for Aretu by way of *Gateway* in four hours; been on the docket for weeks."

"What designation?" John asked the question of Nick, but his burning gaze never left Jenifer, and she refused to look away. One blink and she might lose him again.

"*Steppenschraff,*" Nick answered. "You can rendezvous with the *Constellation* at *Gateway*. Jackie and Silas have a scheduled eight-day layover and the *Steppenschraff* should be able to reach *Gateway* before the *Constellation* leaves."

John's arm hooked around her waist when he turned away from her, keeping her close enough she couldn't do anything but move with him. "Tell me where to go and I'll be there. And I want a weapon."

CHAPTER NINETEEN

"*I*'d like to believe once you're on the transport you'll be safe, but damn it, I haven't a clue anymore, John. It was bad enough before the war when the Sorracchi wore our skins. You literally had to be psychic to have a chance in telling friend from foe, but this . . . I don't get this."

John sat again on one of the two couches in the presidential office, one leg bouncing in pent up frustration, fighting the need to move, the need to *go*. A half-eaten breakfast sat on the table in front of him. Nick hadn't eaten more than three or four bites. The only one with an apparent appetite was Jenifer, and she'd eaten the savory breakfast without hesitation. He'd smiled at her obvious enjoyment, and thought again how he would love to see her reaction to some of the more savory culinary creations on Aretu. Regret immediately replaced his appreciation for her abandon. It was a very real possibility he may never see Jenifer Of No Last Name again once he boarded the transport.

Until he knew Silas was safe, nothing was for sure. Whether he would ever return to Earth was even at question.

"Are you going to eat . . ." she asked, reaching for the remains on his plate.

"Go ahead."

The bit of bacon, or something akin to bacon, was between her fingers before she finished asking, let alone his permission given. She leaned back beside him and drew her legs up under her to sit cross-legged on the cushions.

"I've seen a lot of conflicts on a lot of planets, and the common factor in nearly every one of them was the warped vision of someone who either was in power or wanted to be in power. This isn't much different."

"They've killed Earth citizens. How is that supposed to help us?"

"Logic isn't usually a factor."

Three sharp knocks at the door preceded Connor's re-entry. John caught Jenifer's motion to reach for Damocles, but she stopped and reached for a slice of toast when Connor came through the door.

Connor dropped onto the couch beside Nick and set a small pack on the floor at his feet. From the interior he pulled a PAC tablet and held it out to John. John leaned across the table and took it from him. When his finger brushed the touch-responsive screen it lit up with a schematic layout of the *Steppenschraff*, a Defense Alliance transport and travel class ship. He'd been on several similar ships. With a swipe of his finger the screen moved through each deck from the storage bays to the bridge, with several decks of living quarters from the basic for lower-level military personnel to the more elaborate for dignitaries or . . . ambassadors.

"Ninety percent of the compliment is either Areth or Umani, with only a small contingent of Earth Force. The main purpose of the trip is to take a collaboration of Earth scientists to Aretu for a symposium on agricultural recovery with some of your people," Connor explained, although John remembered the details of the trip. He had been asked to go, but because of the anniversary junket he was supposed to be on, he'd reneged on the option. "No Firebirds, which I'd usually be upset over, but in this situation I'm not. As much as it rakes me, I believe the traitor amongst us wears the Phoenix on his sleeve."

"Pisses me off," Nick mumbled.

"This means you'll be surrounded mostly by those we can trust to be allies because they're more your people than ours, except for the scientists."

John winced at the delineation.

"Your quarters are on deck two below the command deck in the dignitary suite. I suggest once you're there, you stay there until you clear

Earth's atmosphere by a good hundred light years. Then you should be safe to move about the transport until you meet up with Jackie and Silas at *Gateway*. From there, you can either stay on the military transport or continue on with them on the ship they're traveling in. I figure it could go either way. If the assassin is on the *Constellation* with them, and you can get on and get off without being seen, I say get them on the faster ship and hotfoot it to Aretu before them. Be ready when they land. Put surveillance on anyone you might find suspect. Either you're going all the way to Aretu, and wait until the next ship back to Earth leaves from Callondia Capitol, or you stay on *Gateway* and wait for the same ship to come back and get you."

"Right now my focus is to get my son. Once I have him in my arms again, I'll worry about my next move."

Jenifer sat silent beside him, no longer nibbling at the remains of breakfast. She watched him, her eyes never shifting from him even when Connor spoke. John turned his head and met her studying gaze. Even then, she didn't look away. The scowl line above her eyes deepened.

"Do you need more than this to use the collar?" Connor asked, tossing his hand toward the PAC.

"No, this is fine. I've been on this type of ship before so I know the general interior layout and I've got enough of a pinpoint to get me there."

Jenifer frowned.

Connor dug into the sack again, bringing out a sleek Areth design pulse pistol cradled in a thigh holster. He held it out in the flat of his hand and John took it, bouncing the weight in his palm. It had been a long time since he carried a weapon in earnest, even longer since he carried an Areth weapon. It felt both familiar and foreign, like a long forgotten memory.

"Security checks all weaponry going onto the ship, but if you're bouncing in no one will be the wiser. I'm sure you'd rather be armed."

"Damn straight." He reached around the end of the couch and gripped his worn rucksack. The thing had been to hell and back in the last couple of days, but he'd managed to hang on to it every step of the way. Someone else might find some of the contents foolish risks just to hang on to, considering his flight, but everything in the bag held importance either to him or someone he cared about. He unzipped the main pouch and put the weapon inside.

"You might want to leave your jacket. It's still Earth issue even if we take off the Firebird badge and it might draw too much attention," Connor suggested.

"I suggest you go as soon as you can, so you're good and settled before the ship leaves," Nick said, standing with a groan. "Departure is in an hour and a half."

"Right." John stood and extended his hand to Nick, who shook it vigorously. "Thank you for everythin', Nick."

"I told you I'd do whatever you needed of me to protect your son. I meant it."

John nodded and shook Connor's hand as well. He fished into the jacket pockets and found the two collars and control node he'd stuffed away earlier and held them in his closed fist as he shrugged off the jacket. He wouldn't need a jacket on the ship and it was summer in Callondia Capitol, or nearing the end of summer when he arrived.

"Do you think you should be hopping again so soon?" Jenifer asked, unfolding her long legs to stand beside him. "And don't give me any bull about being fine."

"This is a short hop," he explained, dropping the jacket on the couch.

"You're going to get over the fact I don't believe you."

He sighed and dropped his arms to his sides, looking down at her. "Fine. Alright. Yes, I will probably want to take a good, long nap when I get there. But I'm fine."

"Did something happen before?" Nick asked behind him and Jenifer toed up to look over his shoulder at the president.

"We landed in Florida and he dropped like a stone—"

"I was injured in the crash," he tried to explain. "And you—"

Her hand shot up in front of his face, one finger raised, and the look on her face would be enough to silence an entire classroom of rowdy toddlers. "I did *exactly* what you said this time."

John wrapped his empty hand around hers and pulled it toward his chest, out of his face. "You did. You were perfect."

"And yet, you could barely keep your feet when we got here."

"I bounced back."

Jenifer snorted and pulled her hand free. "You had hours to rest before, this time it's less than three. How do you know you're not going to plant yourself in the middle of a bulkhead because you're not ready?"

"I won't."

"Again . . . I don't believe you."

"Short of strollin' down to the dockin' bay and bein' seen by every Firebird—friend or foe—between here and there, I've go' no other option."

"That's what I'm here for."

Nick cleared his throat behind them. "Should we step outside so the two of you can—"

"No!" they both said at the same time.

Connor chuckled. John ignored him.

"'Cept *you're* no' goin'."

"There you go again, Ambassador. Trying to tell me what I can and can't do."

"Oh, the Good Lord forbid I actually have an opinion." He worked the collars apart, jerking them away when she went for one of them.

"That goes both ways," she snapped.

"We'll just be . . . over there . . ." Nick mumbled behind them. "Being generally uncomfortable."

John huffed and looked her in the eyes while he fastened the primary collar around his neck. It immediately adjusted and latched in close to his throat. He shoved the other in his pocket with the control node. "You heard the recordin'."

"I heard a lot of things on that recording."

"If you stay with me you become a mark, too."

"Because I'm not already a moving target *as your bodyguard*."

"You're more than that, and you damn well know it."

The words were out of his mouth before he thought better of it, and his confession stopped the argument cold. She glared at him, huffing several rapid breaths. John inhaled, breaking eye contact to retrieve the rucksack from the couch, sliding one strap over his shoulder. When he straightened he caught Nick and Connor staring at the two of them from behind Nick's desk, and both men turned sharply giving him their back. Nick cleared his throat and tapped the edge of the desk. Jenifer crossed her arms over her chest, staring at him with one elegantly arched eyebrow.

"I've made up my mind, Jenifer. I need to do this, you don't. Goin' across the universe wasn't ever part of your job description."

"I'm pretty sure after 'keep your ass alive', the details were subject to change."

"And you did your job. Thank you."

"Don't mock me," she spat.

John let his shoulders drop, feeling some of the exhaustion she apparently knew he felt even if he wouldn't admit it. "I'm no'. Honestly. Thank you."

She opened her mouth to toss out another argument, but he cut her off by taking her face in his hands and stealing her words with a firm kiss. She muffled a protest, trying to pull back, but he refused to let her escape. It only took a few beats of his pounding heart for her to let go and lean toward him the small fraction he needed to know she was in the kiss as much as he was. He parted his lips and shifted the kiss, wanting more. But more was not an option, and he had no right to ask. Part of him didn't dare, dreading she might say no. He ended the kiss before dropping his hands, and met her fury-filled grey eyes.

"Feel better now?" she snarked with another characteristic arch of her brow.

John stepped back and shifted the pack on his back. He rubbed his lips together, enjoying the taste of sweet butter left behind by her kiss. It was a short-lived pleasure. Holding her gaze, he removed the control node from his pocket and held it in his palm. He looked only briefly to Nick and nodded. Nick's return nod was the only communication they needed. When he looked back to Jenifer, her eyes were cold and angry.

"Goodbye."

He snapped out of sight with a blur, leaving a warped field where his body had been and a sharp charge to the air. Jenifer blinked, trying to bring the spot back into focus. It cleared quickly and she rubbed her hands over her arms to ward off the tingle. She hadn't given any thought as to what their departure might have looked like to the Quinns and Michael Tanner that morning, and to see it first hand was unnerving.

Not nearly as unnerving as the audacity of Ambassador John Smith.

President Tanner cleared his throat and she spun around to face the two men. "I want another PAC with the ship schematics and access to John's old apartment. I left too many tools behind."

Connor looked at Nick and Nick nodded, staring at her across the room.

"And quick!" she shouted as Connor left the office. She never broke eye contact with Nick. "I've got a flight to catch and by what I figure, I've got less than an hour left."

Nick's mouth turned into a slow grin, his brown eyes sparking with his amusement. "When I met you I knew you'd be a good thing for him."

"Someone has to keep him alive. He's doing a lousy job of it."

"Yeah, that too."

CHAPTER TWENTY

*T*he trick to infiltrating any facility, Jenifer knew, where one technically didn't belong was to act like you did. No slinking in the shadows. Never, for even a second, look concerned. Walk with confidence, purpose, and a destination even if you didn't know where you're going.

Jenifer stepped out of the central lift onto the main promenade as a lilting voice announced through unseen speakers the ship would seal in three minutes and anticipated breaking atmosphere in seven. The deck was full of passengers, a variety of faces and races. She couldn't differentiate the Areth from the Earth residents, but the Umani were easy to spot since most stood head and shoulders above everyone else. She figured the small group standing near the observation window had to be part of the contingent of Earth scientists traveling to Aretu for a symposium on agricultural recovery. Sounded like a massive yawn-fest to her, but the scientists' presence gave her the blend-in element she needed.

She paused only for a moment, taking in the area. As much as the *Steppenschraff* was armed equal to any Defense Alliance scout ship, it was also equipped as a luxury transport vessel designed to carry dignitaries, ambassadors, leaders of the Umani and Areth people . . . and stowaway bodyguards. The promenade provided areas to sit both near the observation windows and further away in what for all intents and purposes appeared to be a bar and lounge.

Enticing aromas drifted in the air, making Jenifer's mouth water and stomach rumble in protest. They hadn't eaten before leaving Florida, and although she'd nibbled on John's breakfast in Nick's office, it wasn't going to hold her long. For making her come on board through the cargo bay, John would just have to buy her a nice, big lunch.

She slipped her travel bag over her shoulder and headed across the main concourse. In the mad rush to prepare for the trip, she had snagged some of the toys she'd left behind in John's apartment two days before and Connor had provided her with a PAC tablet with schematics of the ship and a change into more appropriate travel clothing for a Defense Alliance ship. A white silk sleeveless blouse—long enough to be more a dress than a top—tailored to her upper body with a high, straight collar hugged her throat nearly to her jaw line. The neckline exposed the base of her throat and perhaps two inches lower, but no more. She wondered if the sleeveless style would draw attention to the healed wound on her arm, and thus raise questions; but just like her theory on breaking into a locked facility, she would act like the mark was nothing so it was nothing. The shirt/dress hit mid-calf with slits from the hem to her lower hips dancing around her legs when she walked. The material clung but flowed, a perfect weight to sway and flirt without being stiff or restricting her movements.

She wore black leggings tucked into knee-high butter soft black boots. The clothing was modest but flattering, and more comfortable than she anticipated when she first saw the folded clothing.

She made the decision to avoid John's suite until the ship had cleared the atmosphere, ultimately avoiding any option he had of finding a way to get her off the ship. Whatever little power play he pulled in Nick's office wasn't going to fly with her.

The air within the ship pressurized by a small degree, but enough to make her ears pop and made the hairs on her arm stand on end. The ship had been sealed. A tingling sensation swept over her bare arms, turning raised hairs into gooseflesh. It had been a long time since she'd felt excitement, or anticipation, about something. Jenifer had never been in space, never broke the atmosphere, and the idea of shooting through the stars made her heart thump a little harder.

The tint in the observation window darkened, blocking out the activity within the transportation hub. Murmurs amongst the obviously Human passengers increased and many moved to stand closer to the massive panels. By what she understood, once they broke the atmosphere the windows would be cleared again so the passengers could watch the Earth disappear and experience the beauty of space jump travel.

Trying not to look like a tourist, she moved to one of the horseshoe shaped chairs scattered throughout the lounge area. A tall Umani approached, with almond-shaped pitch black eyes and dark hair twisted into a knot against his crown. He smiled and blinked, and Jenifer tried not to make direct eye contact. Some Umani had Human looking eyes, she supposed depending on the continent or division of Umani they descended from. Similarly to Earth, the Umani had many variations in their race while the Areth were more similar—more Human—in appearance and biology, But, the Umani with the black orbs for eyes always set her off just a little. It was like looking into glistening inkwells.

"Would you care for a beverage as we depart?" he asked with a thick accent. English and Areth were practically interchangeable, but the Umani spoke seven different languages. She supposed since they were transporting Human scientists, knowing how to communicate with them would be a requirement for the staff.

She considered it, but the empty hole in her gut decided against it. She'd rather wait, too, until John could give her a bit of guidance. That was after she allowed him to speak again.

Jenifer managed to mostly suppress her smirk. "No, thank you."

He blinked and bowed his head, taking a step backward before pivoting and walking away. His movements looked almost unnatural in their fluidity.

Another announcement sounded through the lounge. The *Steppenschraff* would be ascending to atmospheric levels momentarily. A giddy flutter hit Jenifer again and she fought the urge to rush to the window. She knew John's suite had portals, but this might be her one chance to see the Earth shrink away.

Her stomach flipped as the ship rose. The increase in gravity pushed her into the chair as they took to the air. If she closed her eyes, she felt each shift. The ship swiveled to starboard one-hundred-eighty degrees to face east, although she couldn't see the movement outside, the compression against her chest told her direction. She'd spent years tracking where she was without sight; this wasn't much different. With a powerful push back into her chair, the *Steppenschraff* lunged forward, and she opened her eyes at the passengers' collective gasp.

Fluffy puffs of cloud flew by the observation window as they cut through Earth's atmosphere at a sound-breaking rate. The nose of the ship tipped up and several people stumbled to keep their feet. Seconds later the clouds disappeared in a blink and they were in blackness. The ship turned so the port side paralleled the planet below.

Jenifer's breath caught in her throat.

It was the most painfully beautiful thing she had ever seen.

She didn't know the landmasses from this altitude. On the ground she knew where she was at all times, but the continents below weren't the continental shapes she'd learned in school. Not by a long shot. Massive chunks of land were gone, the shorelines misshapen and jagged. But, the planet itself was still beautiful.

Bluest blues hugged land made up of varying shades of green and brown, all swirled beneath twisting patterns of white clouds. As they circled, the light faded to dark and the masses of green and brown changed to almost black. Scattered and thin clusters of light marked some of the most populated areas, but held no comparison to the space images she'd seen in her childhood where entire continents were balls of light. Life.

Her vision blurred and she sniffed, clearing her throat. She had to look away, look down at her hands, to break the hypnotic hold of the planet.

A new voice broke through the intercom, a deep male voice with a soft lilt not unlike John's, though slightly more refined. "I would like to take this opportunity to welcome all our honored guests aboard the *Steppenschraff*. We will leave Earth's solar system in two hours, at which time we will jump into hyperspace. We anticipate approximately ten pauses along the journey to rotate our engine fuel and allow systems to rest and will arrive at *Gateway* in seven of Earth days' time. Please enjoy your journey, may it be a productive one."

They were clear of the atmosphere and that was Jenifer's cue to hunt down one Ambassador John Smith. She stood and slid her bag over her shoulder, taking a moment to allow her legs to adjust to the variant gravity and subtle motion of the ship. Then with purposeful strides, she headed to a different bank of lifts leading to the higher-level accommodations. Nick's people worked quick, she had to give them that. There was no way she would be discovered for not having the right credentials. In a band around her wrist she wore the only ID she needed to move throughout the ship.

The bracelet worked as a security pass to all portions of the ship authorized to her. In order to get on the ship in the first place, Nick told her every door would open to her. But for the sake of her disguise, he informed her the security settings would revise one hour after take-off. Just in case anyone ran a check on the badge, they wouldn't find anything strange. Stowing away on the *Steppenschraff* was the easiest thing she'd done in weeks.

She stepped onto the lift, the doors closing behind her.

"Please verbally indicate your desired destination," an overhead speaker asked.

Jenifer scanned the walls. There were no other means of command. "My suite," she said toward the ceiling.

The motion of the lift was almost undetectable, and the doors swished open moments later onto a brightly lit hallway. According to the schematics, there were only two suites on this level, one to her left and John's to her right. For all intents and purposes, and as far as the ship's security system and data records were concerned, it was her suite as well. Apparently, since John's biosignature was already programmed into all Defense Alliance systems, he was actually traveling as himself. They hadn't had time to override his details. Only the computer knew he had a travel companion, and was to allow her access.

Jenifer moved down the hall to his suite door and paused, leaning toward the smooth portal. No sound came from inside, but then again, the ship could very well be designed to be soundproof. Especially on the dignitary levels. She took a step closer, and with a whoosh, the door opened.

The interior of the suite was spacious and dark, opening first on a sitting area with a lounge and two chairs matching the horseshoe design downstairs. The other suite was designed proportionately for an Umani where this one was scaled down for the average Areth, or so she understood from the schematics Connor provided. A clear panel hung suspended on one side of the sitting area, currently displaying a subtle image of trickling water with the accompanying sound. Past the sitting area was a dining table with four chairs, an overhead light casting a circular glow over the table and the colored glass centerpiece. A counter and some cabinets were tucked into the corner behind the table. The outside wall reflected like observation glass, currently black. She assumed, much like down on the promenade, the tint could be lightened to view space.

To her left the wall curved in a serpentine design, separating the main space from a room beyond. Soft light spilled through the doorless floor to ceiling opening, acting more like a nightlight than any kind of actual ambient lighting. Jenifer set her bag down and walked to the entryway, her soft boots silent on the cushioned floor. The entire suite spoke of a luxury and elegance she hadn't experienced in years, not since she stepped out on her own before the world went crazy.

The room beyond was the sleeping space. A massive bed was situated against the outside wall, with an oblong observation window above the bed's headboard. John's worn, drab clothing draped the foot of the large bed, his boots and socks on the floor at the foot. In the sitting room, Jenifer had heard the ambient sound of falling water created by the holographic screen, but in the bedroom the natural sound replaced the artificial. Another doorless opening led to the attached facilities. Other than the security door leading into the suite, the entire space was free flowing, divided by walls, but open without anything to keep anyone in one room over another.

Jenifer doubled back to the main room, looking left and right. She hadn't noticed it before because of the way it was tucked into the curve of the wall, but another opening led to two other bedrooms with a shared facility between. The bathroom was luxurious, and she was curious to know if the one off the larger bedroom was even more so. A massive bathing closet—though by the size, closet seemed painfully inadequate as a description—walled by glass tiles with jets extending from the walls and what appeared to be spouts from the ceiling itself to create a rain effect took up a third of the room.

The bedrooms were smaller than the larger master room, but still bigger than the tiny apartment she'd used in Brazil. She walked through the opening to the first room. This one was against the outside wall of the ship. A long, narrow observation window, blacked out for the moment, stretched above a deep shelf behind the head of the bed. The room was nicely furnished with storage drawers and an entertainment screen on the wall parallel to the foot of the bed. A small couch and chair nestled against another wall.

An open entrance led to the shared bathroom, but here she found the first actual door in the suite. Perhaps since the room was to be shared by more than one occupant, privacy finally became a factor. She walked through to the third bedroom, much like the first but without the observation window and here there were two smaller beds. The colors in here were a little brighter, more primary and childlike. Instead of a couch and chairs a small table sat to the side with a large bin on the floor nearby, reminding her very much of a toy box. She had a fleeting curiosity if Areth children played with toys similar in any way to the toys Human children played with. They seemed the same in so many ways, but there had to be differences.

Jenifer paused in the hall and rolled her head around her shoulders, fighting a pull of tension across her back. A slight headache pressed behind her eyes.

John had probably finished his shower, but she didn't want to chance walking in too soon. At the thought of John Smith, skin damp and flushed from the warm water, wearing next to nothing, her cheeks flashed hot and she was thankful for the sleeveless blouse. Drawing a slow breath, she continued the circular walk through the two bedrooms back to the small hall leading back to the main room. A left turn brought her back to the master bedroom entrance.

John's back was to her, and she remembered with clarity the first night she'd spend in his apartment when she found him looking out over the Alexandria night skyline. He once again wore deep blue silk, or the Areth equivalent, pants hung low on his hips and loose to the floor, bare feet sticking out from the hem. Bruises she hadn't seen or known about before marked the back of his left shoulder down his side, wrapping around his ribs. He hadn't said a word about them.

He raised his arms to dry his hair with a towel in the same color blue as the pants, his back muscles shifting and flexing with the motion. She had appreciated the restrained strength in his agile, sinewy physique then, and she appreciated it now. Perhaps more.

When his left elbow extended above the height of his shoulder, he hissed and flinched, dropping his arm.

"I'm willing to bet you didn't mention the bruised ribs to Doc Quinn, right?"

John spun toward her, dropping partially into a crouch, his right hand reaching for the holster on the bed. The moment his eyes connected with hers, he stopped, a mixture of expressions shifting over his angular face in a blink. Shock. Too, perhaps, anger. Then to a deep scowl as he straightened again.

"What part of *you're no' goin'* confused you?"

"What part of *yes, I am* confused *you*?"

"How the bloody hell did you get on the ship?"

Jenifer crossed her arms and tilted her hip to lean against the wall framing the entrance. "President Tanner brought me here to do a job, and he didn't think I was done either."

John huffed and strode toward the bathroom. He twisted at the waist to point back at her, the towel still held in his fist. "I don't appreciate bein' undermined."

She drew in a deep breath through her nose and followed. "And I don't appreciate you making my job so damn hard, Ambassador. We can go at this the whole trip, or—"

He stopped short at the door, spinning back to her so fast she almost ran right into his chest. "Or what?"

"Or . . ." Jenifer liked the slight advantage her boots gave her with him in his bare feet. They weren't eye-to-eye, not quite, but a bit closer. She grinned. "You can get dressed and take me for something to eat. I'm starving."

He didn't move for several pounding beats of her heart, and neither of them looked away. Jenifer wanted to grin the moment she sensed his concession, but she managed to refrain.

"Fine," he said on a sigh.

Then she did grin. "I'll let you get dressed," she said as she turned away, but looked back at him over her shoulder. "Unless, of course, that's appropriate travel attire."

She laughed and ducked the towel flying toward her head.

CHAPTER TWENTY-ONE

"*H*ow do we order something if we don't know what they have?"

John shifted his attention from his quick scan of the intimate dining room to Jenifer seated on the other side of the table from him. He had tried to maintain his fury after he dressed and they left his suite, tried to remember he should be angry with Jenifer for defying him, but the more he watched her take in the new discoveries of the *Steppenschraff*, he couldn't keep up the guise of frustration. He should have considered how different a ship like this would be to her. He didn't know if she had even been in space.

"You can have anythin' you want," he finally answered.

One elegant eyebrow arched. "But, I don't know what they *have*."

John chuckled and leaned back in his chair, crossing one leg over the other. "I suppose then I have a unique opportunity to introduce you to Aretu first through our food."

"Is it any good?" she teased, smirking.

"We like to think so."

"I've tasted some *local delicacies* I wouldn't feed to my dog, so I'm not sure your opinion on your own culture counts."

"How about this . . ." He leaned forward again and pushed aside the light filigree centerpiece so it wouldn't block his view of her. All he had ever seen her wear was the functional, utilitarian uniform of Earth Force and to see her in the softer civilian clothing of Aretu elicited a deep reaction in him he knew could be very dangerous. "I'll order a variety of foods, you can try everythin'. But—" He held up a finger. "Save room for dessert. Trust me on this. We'll do one dessert at a time because each one should be savored on its own."

A slow grin tipped one corner of her lips. "Now you're speaking my language."

An Areth man dressed in the uniform of service approached them and John requested both a soup and a root dish to begin the meal, then three different main courses focusing on three different types of meat and four different side dishes. She could pick and choose what she wanted. The dessert he ordered was pure decadence, and usually too sweet for him to enjoy, but he had a feeling it would be perfect for Jenifer's taste. The young man taking the order had a bewildered look in his eyes, but he didn't question. John added a blended fruit drink with the meal, knowing it would complement any of the dishes they ordered.

Her attention kept drifting to the blackened observation windows. A slight pinch at the corner of her eyes made him wonder if she might have a headache or felt ill from travel. With experience, the Areth had learned some—even some of their own people not accustomed to space travel— had difficulty when moving at high speed but short of wormhole travel. The flash of stars passing in and out of view caused space sickness, but for most it usually dissipated once they broke the travel barrier. The swirling color of the wormhole was soothing to most and hid the illusion of travel.

"Are you feelin' ill?" he asked and she immediately shook her head, turning back to look at him with a smile. "We'll be jumpin' in another hour," he said, answering the question he saw in her eyes.

"Why don't they jump while still in the solar system? The reports around the war said the Defense Alliance ships jumped a hundred light years to get away from Earth."

"They did," he answered, taking a sip of his juice. It had been months since he had any kind of *real* juice, not a powdered concentrate used for mass production. "But that was an emergency situation and very risky. The risk of no' jumpin' outweighed the risk of jumpin' inside such a tight cluster of planets."

She nodded and looked back to the windows.

"Have you ever been in space?" She just shook her head. "We'll try to be back to the suite before we jump. You'll have a better view without crowdin' for the window."

She nodded absently, looking around the room.

"Are you lookin' for trouble, or just lookin'?"

Jenifer finally brought her attention back to him. "Just looking. It's been a long time since I saw something new." She reached for the juice she probably hadn't even realized the server had brought and took a sip. He swore her eyes fluttered, and she hummed in appreciation. "That is good."

By the end of the meal, he had a good idea of what Jenifer liked. Intensity. She didn't care for the bland root dish, but the savory soup had her licking her lips and polishing it off without looking at the seasoned roots again. Of the three main courses, comparable to a poultry dish, a fish, and a free-range red meat, she seemed inclined toward the red meat and the white fish in a seasoned cream sauce. She wasn't turned off by the poultry, but it didn't elicit the same satisfying response. Of the four side dishes, she liked the roasted vegetables over the mashed roots, and the ricegrain balls in peppered sauce over the leafy steamed vegetables.

His mouth watered over the red meat and ricegrain balls, but he willingly ate the poultry and the remaining sides she passed over in favor of the richer compliments. Going forward, he felt confident he could judge her taste.

With one final, deep moan that made his blood warm Jenifer leaned back in her chair and wiped her mouth with her napkin. "I haven't eaten food this good in—" She seemed to stumble over the rest of the sentence, then cleared her throat. "Actually, I don't know when I last ate like this."

"I'm glad you liked it."

"You're getting better at showing a girl a good time."

The weight of her voice made him look at her, across the table directly into her eyes, and uninvited memories of the brief kiss they'd shared in Nick's office made his blood heat more. John worked his lips together and smiled a slow grin. "You haven't seen anythin' yet."

The server chose an untimely moment to return with the single dish of dessert. Sharing a dessert was considered a publicly acceptable intimacy between lovers, and while Jenifer didn't know that element of his culture, it served two purposes. One, he could enjoy her meal with her and two, to anyone observing it drew a distinct line in the sand. Call him possessive, call him jealous, he didn't care. If he was going to spend the next week on a luxury trip with a woman as beautiful and alluring as Jenifer Of No Last Name, he intended to make the most of it.

Somewhere along the way, he wasn't sure when, Jenifer had inexplicably and irrevocably become more to him than a bodyguard or even a comrade in arms. Well before he kissed her in Nick's office, he knew he wanted more. Before Jace told him about Eli Kerrigan, he understood something held her back, and even now he knew there was more than just a dead lover in her past. Before he finally felt a touch of the emotions and gifts she suppressed, he knew she was far more than she appeared. And from the moment he first met her, he knew she was one of the most beautiful women he had ever seen, of any race.

The plate the server set between them immediately drew her full attention. The common name for the dessert was *God's Ambrosia*. The core of the dish was candied rassafruit, a plump and juicy berry encased in a sweet glaze made of boiled nectar, baked in a moist cake of pomman and coacao, so close to the chocolate on Earth they could have been the same thing; although the coacao on Areth held a slightly sweeter inherent flavor than bitter cocoa. Poured over the cake was a warm coacao sauce infused with rassafruit essence and hot chia berry to contrast the sweetness.

Jenifer reached for a utensil to dig in, but John reached across the small table and covered her hand. "Let me," he explained. "You don't know the secrets this food holds and I want to make sure you experience it properly."

She smirked. "Are you going to make me close my eyes?"

"You can if you want to."

He understood the trust it took for Jenifer to release the hold on the utensil and close her eyes. She leaned forward enough to inhale the decadent steam curling above the dish. Swallowing, John cut into the cake and revealed the candied rassafruit, the coacao sauce pouring into the space to coat everything. He carefully assembled her first bite, consisting of fruit and cake and sauce. He had to swallow again to moisten his throat before he could speak.

"Open your mouth, Jenifer."

She parted her lips. John's blood rushed, thumping in his veins. He cupped her chin with one hand, his thumb brushing her jaw, as he slid the food between her lips. Her mouth closed over the metal tines and he pulled it free as she bit into the ambrosia, her tongue making a brief appearance to lick the last of the coacao sauce from her lips. Her eyebrows raised and he heard the barely audible pop as she bit into the rassafruit, knew the sweet juice spilled into her mouth to mix with the cake and the coacao sauce, contrasting with the hot chia berry. Something akin to ecstasy softened her features and she moaned low and deep in her throat, working the flavors together.

"Oh my god," she mumbled around the food still in her mouth and opened her eyes. John still leaned close, close enough to enjoy the bloom of color in her cheeks when she covered her lips with her fingers. "I've never tasted *anything* like this."

"Perhaps I should have started with somethin' more basic . . ."

She was shaking her head before he could finish, swallowing the bite in her mouth. "No, this is a *great* start."

"*A*ttention, esteemed passengers. We are now five thousand Earth measured miles from the edge of the solar system and are preparing for our first jump. For those passengers experiencing travel related illnesses, it is advised you do not observe the initial jump process. For all passengers, please prepare yourself for jump."*

"Are we going to make it?" Jenifer asked as the lift doors opened.

John grabbed her hand and pulled her inside. "We will if I have anythin' to do with it."

The lift immediately engaged and headed up toward their suite, John mentally willing it to go faster, knowing even Areth Talents couldn't speed it along. The lift stopped and the doors opened. He pulled her with him, having never released her hand, and they jogged together toward the suite door.

"*Interstellar jump in twenty seconds.*"

The suite door opened a second later than he wanted, and he pulled her into the dark interior of the suite, heading straight for the outer wall past the dining area. The observation glass was tinted, only the slightest sign of the stars beyond visible if he stared long enough. He pulled her along, putting Jenifer between him and the glass when they reached it. Jenifer laid her hands on the smooth reflective surface, squinting to see space beyond.

"Jump in ten seconds."

"Are you ready?" he asked, and she nodded, her body shifting with each rapid breath she took. John reached past her to touch the glass behind her hand, sending out the slight mental command the majority of the suite technology functioned from. The glass shimmered and cleared, revealing the blackness of space beyond.

The *Steppenschraff* sat still, its engines preparing for the burst forward into the wormhole. The process was much simpler than this, but the light show was for the sake of the travelers. John knew it, but he felt no need to spoil the moment for her. She stared wide-eyed and parted lips into the black.

"Even this is beautiful," she said softly.

"Absolutely." He watched her, never focusing on the starscape.

He felt the change in the ship, having flown in enough single pilot and battle cruisers to anticipate the shift in air, in gravity, in vibration. Taking an opportunity he knew wouldn't come often, John stepped close behind her and set his hands around her hips, his feet wide apart outside her own.

"Four — Three — Two — One."

Jenifer sucked in a sharp breath and John pulled her back against him. The darkness disappeared in a flash of vibrant colors swirling together like a brush twirled through a painter's palette. Blues. Pinks. Purples. Varying shades of white. The engines twenty decks below them coiled to life, and with a slight lunge, just enough to make Jenifer stumble and give John an excuse to pull her closer, the *Steppenschraff* snapped into hyperspace.

Stars flew by so fast they were nothing more than white lines dragged through the swirling color, now more like oil dancing on the surface of a whirlpool, the colors becoming almost indistinct in the miasmic blend.

Jenifer's hands brushed his arms, and it was all he could do not to react with his whole body to the touch. She never looked away from the new wonder outside, and he didn't look away from her. Elegant yet strong fingers weaved between his own. She squeezed and held on.

"Is it what you imagined?" he asked, leaning in enough to speak close to her ear.

She turned her head and tilted her chin back to look at him. In that instant, he was rewarded with the one elusive moment he'd sought since the day they met. Jenifer smiled. Not a smirk, or a grin, but a beautiful smile lit her face and made her eyes shine; a smile that transformed her entire face from simply beautiful to completely devastating.

"Could anyone imagine this before seeing it, John?"

His heart pounded viciously against his ribs, his chest ached with the beauty the glow he had tried to imagine, but just like Jenifer and the wormhole, his imagination held no comparison to reality. He had to draw a slow, shallow breath. "Never," he finally managed to answer.

CHAPTER TWENTY-TWO

Thursday, 5 February 2054
Robert J. Castleton Memorial Building — The Castle
United Earth Protectorate, Capitol City
Alexandria, Seat of Virginia
North American Continent

a bang of the conference room door made Connor look up from the PAC tablet he'd been scrolling through waiting for the upper echelon of command to file into the private meeting. He'd been so focused on the data, scrutinizing every fact and detail, he hadn't realized how many people had filled the room. Nick had just entered, and stood at the far end of the table with Vice President Surimoto seated to his right and Colonel Ebben seated to his left, between Nick and Connor.

The seat on Connor's left was empty, waiting for Mel to arrive as his second in command over the Firebirds. Across the table sat Colonel Conrad Corchan and Colonel Helen Bertrand, the two top commanders of the Earth Force Terra. Further down on Connor's side sat Colonel Bobbie Castleton, granddaughter of the late General Robert Castleton and now commander of Earth Force Sphera, and her second, Lieutenant Colonel Merin St. John.

The only ones missing were Mel and Lieutenant Curt Kelly, the training officer standing in for Jackie Anderson while she was off planet.

The door opened again after a short knock and Curt entered, followed immediately by Mel. She scanned the room quickly, her gaze settling on him. The snap of warmth was familiar, but today it was intensified. He hadn't seen her since he'd left her in his bed that morning.

My 2IC is my lover.

It wasn't a revelation, but perhaps just a way to confirm to himself the reality. Melanie Briggs had been part of his unit for years, his second in command for five, and when he took on command of the Firebirds there hadn't been a moment of hesitation to bring her with him. They were a unit in and of themselves. Some part of him wondered why it had taken them this long to get here.

Her smile was warm, and beautiful, but gone in a flash as she resumed her military face and walked around the table to reach his side. She leaned slightly toward him as she scooted in. "What's going on?"

"The president will cover it better than me," he said.

"Is this why you missed the morning meeting?"

He nodded. "New developments overnight."

"Guess everyone had a busy night."

Her tone was non-committal but the glimmer in her eyes warmed him. Connor grinned slow and indulged in a brief moment of studying her lips when she smiled back. "We'll have to get back to that, too."

Her gaze shifted past Connor toward the head of the table, and Connor turned his head as Nick assumed his stance at the head of the long table.

He tapped the table twice with his knuckles, scowling. "We've got a problem, people. The focus from here on out is to fix it before we get bit again."

Shared shock and anger rolled through everyone at the table who didn't already know about the suspected traitor somewhere within the military force, probably a Firebird, and suspected to be a woman. It was no surprise when every head in the room turned to look at every female in the room. It was human nature.

"We will make *no* assumptions, but we're not leaving anyone off the suspect list," Nick snapped before the roll of discussion began. "There are *no* hard facts, only pieces of facts. Hell, we're only basing the woman thing on a scratchy voice on a bad recording. The one thing we know is this person has access to information not known by the general public and not much past the command structure. Either they're close enough to know it first hand, or they have a source. Both options are unacceptable."

Nick played the recording he and Connor had listened to that morning with Jenifer and John, and while no one made a sound, many shifted uncomfortably at times and the looks of anger spoke volumes words didn't. Nick said nothing about John's presence, or his current destination heading for Aretu to meet up with Jackie and Silas.

"Where is Ambassador Smith now?" Colonel Castleton asked when Nick finished.

"His exact whereabouts are unknown," Nick answered. "The last location of John Smith and his detail confirmed by long scan lidar was at the explosion yesterday where Captain Horatio Guerrero and Lieutenant Clint Williams intercepted his hover. Guerrero and Williams are dead and no sign of either John or Jenifer were found at the explosion."

Connor kept his face neutral, but mentally he was impressed by Nick's answer. There wasn't a word of lie in it. Although they knew where John had gone, the information hadn't been lidar confirmed and without trying to plot their route, neither Connor nor Nick knew exactly where the *Steppenschraff* might be.

"Have we considered the woman with him is the assassin?"

"Until we know otherwise, everyone is considered." Nick's hard stare shifted from person to person in the room. "Everyone."

"What resources are being utilized to find Ambassador Smith?" Corchan asked.

"None," Nick answered, earning him a confused look. "Providing aid to Ambassador Smith could have already gotten him killed. Until I know *exactly* what we're dealing with, we let sleeping dogs lie. Right now, John is outside the radar and I'm of the opinion that's the way to keep it. When and if we figure this out, we'll work on getting John back to Alexandria."

He fielded a few more questions, but never even hinted at John's destination or the fact Jenifer still traveled with him. At least they assumed she had made it onto the *Steppenschraff* before it took off since she hadn't contacted Nick to say otherwise. After a final order to get him answers, and get him answers yesterday, the gathering of command was dismissed.

"Connor," Nick barked over the noise of departure.

Connor turned to Mel. "Wait for me in the hall. I'll be right out, then we'll head back to the nest and start working on this."

Mel nodded and saluted the president on her way out the door.

Nick waited until everyone else had cleared the room. "I know you don't like this," he finally said.

Connor clenched his jaw and looked toward the door. "I understand the necessity for secrecy, sir, but if I can't trust my second in command—"

"Trust me, right now the fact I can't look every one of my men and women in the eye and know without question I can trust them pisses me off," Nick said, cutting Connor off mid-argument. "There are very few, *very* few people I know are above suspicion. You are one of them, but I have to draw the line."

Connor nodded. "Yes, sir."

"She'll understand when the time comes."

"Of course she will."

Connor headed for the door and Nick called after him again. "Make sure your trust in her is for the right reasons."

Connor worked his jaw before answering. "I can tell you half a dozen times when she's been the reason I'm alive. My trust is for the right reasons."

"Good enough." The tight lines around his eyes softened and he smiled. "Michael is coming home tomorrow. Come to the house for dinner. We're having a double celebration."

"Double?"

"Nineteen hundred hours. You'll find out."

Connor smiled back. At least there was *some* good news out of all this crapstorm. "I'll be there."

Mel waited twenty feet down the hall, leaning against the wall with her ankles crossed and her head down. She looked up as he approached and smiled, falling into step beside him as they headed toward the stairs.

"So, what's the plan?"

"First," he said, holding a door for her, "we get something to eat. I'm starving."

"You're always starving."

"Then, we go back to the nest and hunker down for the next several hours studying personnel files."

"Sounds stimulating."

Connor winked. "We can probably work that in."

Her blush was his reward.

Frustration pushed Jenifer to pace the suite from one end to the other without finding a place to settle. They'd been in flight only a few hours, and already she was going stir crazy. John showed her how to access the entertainment files, and he'd been amused by the array of Earth film archives someone had been thoughtful enough to download to the ship's database for the use of the Human passengers, but she couldn't make it through more than thirty minutes before she was up again.

The only thing she found to hold her interest was the swirling color and light display of the wormhole outside their observation windows. It was hypnotic, and the closest thing to soothing she'd ever known.

The only problem was whenever she stood there she remembered John's hands on her waist and his arms around her when they jumped. She remembered with tactile clarity the feel of his breath on her cheek when he spoke near her ear, and the curl of warmth in her stomach his voice elicited.

With the memory, her frustration flared again.

She'd fallen too easy into the idea they might be safe here for a while. Maybe assassins didn't lurk around every corner. For a while she might be able to sleep soundly without one eye open and an ear to every little noise. For a while, she had allowed herself to enjoy the close proximity of a man.

She chalked it up to a long dry spell. Eli had been gone nearly a year and it had been months before his death since they'd seen each other long enough to share any time.

Jenifer slammed the heels of her hands against the thick sill around the observation window and pushed herself away. She would *not* think about Eli. Not here. Not now.

Hot tears burned her eyes, and she blinked against the foreign reaction. She hadn't shed a tear since the day he died, and even then she hadn't allowed herself more than a moment before tamping down the sorrow and moving on. Always moving on. Never look back. There was a reason the past was in the past. It was not worth the effort.

So why now?

She marched through the sitting room, past the open doorway into the master bedroom where she heard John moving around down the hall to the larger guest bedroom. The room was in darkness, the observation window blacked out and none of the ambient lighting turned on.

"Lights," she said, hating the slight waver in her voice. Nothing happened. The room remained dark. Jenifer pivoted back to the doorway, the silk tunic flaring around her. She ran her hands along the wall looking for some kind of switch or control, and found nothing. "Lights, damn it!"

She was half way across the room before John stepped into the doorway. "Jenifer, what's wrong."

"This damn ship!" she shouted, flinging her arms out away from her body. "I can't turn on the lights. I can't access the files. I'm amazed I can even open a damn door!"

The lights came on, dim but slowly brightened and Jenifer barked a mocking laugh. "Great, just great." She swiped at her wet cheeks, refusing to turn and face John. "You did that, right?"

"It's the way the ship is designed," he said, his voice too low and calm. He may have intended it to keep from angering her more, but the roughness scraped across her last nerve. "This suite is of Areth design, so it's assumed—"

"It's assumed you wouldn't bow so low as to share the space with a backward, lesser Human who can't turn on the lights with a frickin' thought," she snapped, stepping deeper into the room away from him.

"I can have—"

"No!" Jenifer did spin around then, and immediately regretted it.

John's eyes pinched and he took a step toward her. She shot her hand up to stop him, and he halted. "I don't need the room dumbed down for my sake. I'll sit in the dark first."

"Is that what you're angry about? Because the lights won't come on?"

"I'm not angry," she snapped.

"You're no'."

"Don't patronize me, Ambassador."

John sighed and pinched the bridge of his nose. She turned away from him, crossed her arms over her body, and walked to the ledge of the observation window. She wished she could see out, but that required the Areth Jedi Mind Trick to clear the panel.

"I'll teach you."

Jenifer shook her head. "Don't start again, Ambassador."

"Why don't you believe me?"

"Because if I could do what you do—" Her voice faltered again, and she bit down hard. Why was she all over the place? Why was she weeping over Eli? And why were memories she buried so deep in her psyche she swore they'd never see the light of day again suddenly flashing in her mind with such clarity she smelled the foul body odor and felt the bruising hands from twenty years before? "I can't. You're wrong if you think I can."

"You can."

She was going to fly apart any moment. Her head pounded and her heartbeat thrummed hard in her ears. All her senses were on overdrive. The air pressed in on her like another quarter extra gravity. Jenifer jumped and thrashed when John's warm hands, more like branding irons, wrapped around her upper arms and he turned her to face him.

"Jenifer!" he said sternly. "Look at me. Look at me!"

She had to blink to clear the haze, her vision spotty. "What the hell did you feed me, Ambassador? I feel wrong . . ." Her voice drifted to her, but didn't sound right.

"It's no' what you ate. I never considered this . . ."

"What?"

Her head was heavy. His voice was muffled, like speaking underwater. He snapped his fingers at the end of her nose, the sound like a firecracker, and Jenifer jerked. Just for a moment, the noise cleared and the thudding dimmed.

"Jenifer, I need to get you focused."

"Don't you dare kiss me," she mumbled, trying to keep her head from swaying.

John smirked, the shift of his face happening in slow motion. "'scuse me?"

"Isn't that what they did in all the old movies?" Where were her thoughts going? Where were her hands going? She stared at her own hands fisting in the soft sleeves of John's sweater. So soft. His body heat smoothed over her. "Kiss the hysterical woman to make her stop?" Her tongue felt thick.

"Noble idea, and I might save it for later, but no' right now."

"Too bad . . ."

She scowled. Her mouth said things her brain hadn't thought of yet.

"I feel sick."

"Jenifer . . . Jenifer, listen to me."

"I am."

Did her mouth move?

He moved his hands from her arms to hold her head, his palms hot against her cheeks. She swayed but his hold kept her in place. Gentle thumbs tipped her head so she had to look at him, even though she had to blink to keep him in focus.

"I'm sorry," he said. "If there were another way, if I'd thought this could happen, I would avoid it. But I've got to—" He shook his head. "I'll explain later."

Explain what?

He closed his eyes and her body jolted, nerves sparking and going numb in an instant. White light blinded her. She gasped and floundered for something in the nothingness, instinctively wrapping her arms to the one solid force she found. Just as quickly, in the same blinding flash, the light blinked out and the room appeared again. Jenifer sucked in deep lungfuls of air, her face pressed to John's shoulder, her arms around his neck. He held her in a firm embrace, and she realized she was trembling. Her legs were weak, her knees buckling under her own weight. John held her firm, keeping her from falling.

"What. The hell. Happened?" she asked, fighting with every ounce of depleted strength she had left to stop the trembling.

Before she could argue, though she didn't try because she felt about as able to fight him off as a kitten could a bulldog, John bent and scooped her up behind her back and knees and carried her from the room back to his bedroom. He set her on the edge of the bed, her vision still swimming. She kept hold of him even when he tried to pull away, because she was pretty sure she might just topple forward and fall on her face if he moved too far.

John laid his hand over hers and crouched in front of her. His eyes squinted at the corner while he studied her, and as much as she didn't like the scrutiny, she didn't feel much up to arguing.

"You with me?" he asked.

She almost nodded, but the idea of doing it made her dizzy. "Yes. Explain."

John huffed and shifted his position so he was still in front of her, but could rest his arm on his bent knee and still stay close enough for her to use him as an anchor. His grin was compassionate but satisfied at the same time. "Every argument you had against no' havin' any Talents was just proven invalid."

"Bull. I got dizzy."

"You've got to let down the walls, Jenifer. Otherwise, this is goin' to be a very bad trip for you."

The frustration began its slow roll all over again and she clenched her jaw. John took her hand from his shoulder and held both hers within his in her lap. "Stop it. Don't fight, Jenifer, just listen."

She drew in a slow breath, forcing down the annoying crawl before it took over again. "I'm listening."

"The *Steppenschraff* is an Alliance ship, it's designed to work fluently and efficiently for any and all races who might be aboard, with the exception of Humans, I'll admit. If you look in the main lounges, there is seatin' appropriate for Areth and larger furniture for the Umani. The Umani suites are different than the Areth suites. Controls throughout the ship are designed to be used by all races. And the structure of the ship is designed to serve as a resonance conductor for the Areth."

Jenifer squinted, swallowing against the lingering nausea. "Resonance conductor?"

"For our Talents. In a way, it's a form of relaxation for us. Every curve, every control, every design, especially here in the suite, is engineered to magnify and ease our ability to use our Talents. Whatever they may be. It's why the lights came on so easily when I stepped into the room."

"And to make me sick?"

"Think of it like . . ." He looked away, the familiar squint of his eyes pinching at the corners, then back to her. "Sonic feedback. Your mind is fightin' against your underlyin' abilities, bein' here where everythin' is designed to enhance them, is an assault on your system. Instead of resonatin' your Talents, it's amplifyin' your emotions and your senses."

The more she tried not to think about what she didn't want to remember, the more the memories taunted her. The maniacal laughter of a sadistic man with painful hands who made her cry and scream, made her hurt everywhere. She suddenly felt very small, and very helpless, trapped in the past.

She shuddered, gripping harder to his hands, hot tears rolling down her cheeks. She felt each slide, felt the splash when it hit their joined hands. "Memories . . ." She couldn't quite give her voice enough lilt to make it a question.

John rose up, pressing a long kiss to her cheek. She leaned into the contact, focusing on it and the chill pushed back.

"I'm sorry, but yes," he whispered, kissed her cheek again and returned to his position in front of her.

"What did you do?" Exhaustion hit her hard, and her limbs felt tied down. "To make it stop, what did you do?"

John took her hands and spread them to her sides so she braced herself against the edge of the bed. Keeping his attention on her face, he cupped one large hand behind her left calf and lifted her leg, pulling off her long boot. "In essence, a power surge. Things were sparkin' and overloadin', and I cranked up the energy, then snapped it off. It realigns everythin' . . . for now."

She stared when he repeated the act of removing her boot on her right foot. She was aware of every brush of his hand, how close her toes came to his thigh when he drew up her leg, and the rush of cooler air on her skin with the boot removed. But, she couldn't manage to move herself. It was like having an illicit buzz. A high.

It had been many years since she'd used substances to bury the memories, right up until she decided she'd rather wield a gun and take out her frustration in other ways.

"I've never heard it described that way."

Jenifer blinked and focused on his face rather than his hands. "What?"

"A buzz. Granted, I've never been on your side of it."

"Did I say that out loud?"

John grinned and stood, going to the head of the bed to pull back the blankets. He returned to her and lifted her off the bed again to hold her against his chest. "Yes. I think it's time you get some rest. Tomorrow, Jenifer, you learn to open your mind."

"Don't carry me. I can walk," she mumbled, some part of her mind acknowledging she curled against his shoulder even as she said it.

"Where are you goin' to walk to?"

She didn't have an answer. As soon as he laid her on the bed and her head touched the pillow she closed her eyes. Sleep felt as heavy as the blanket he pulled over her, and she thought to herself she'd never been in such a comfortable bed.

Somewhere on the edge of her senses she heard John chuckle. She vaguely registered the shift of the bed and the movement of the blankets, then what little light slipped through her closed eyelids was gone and she sank into blissful darkness.

CHAPTER TWENTY-THREE

February 2054, Friday
Presidential Residence
United Earth Protectorate, Capitol City
Alexandria, Seat of Virginia
North American Continent

*N*ervousness like he hadn't experienced in years now fluttered in Michael's chest when he reached for the front door knob to his father's home. No, nervousness wasn't right. Michael closed his eyes and rested his forehead on the door, hot tears burning his cheeks.

It was shame.

When he left Alexandria he had believed with his heart he'd done the right thing. He left to protect Jacqueline, to protect Nicole. To keep his traitorous mind from stealing from them more than they had to give, more than he wanted to take, but didn't know how to stop it. Since then he'd learned the ability to control all aspects of his abilities, but in learning, he'd had to face what he'd done. Even before John and Jenifer appeared at the parish, Michael had known it was time to go home.

Drawing a fortifying breath, Michael raised his head and swiped at his cheeks. Tonight he would make amends with his father, daughter, and his friends. Someday he hoped to make amends with the woman who shared his life. If it were possible. He was the one who had asked her to stay with him, forever, and he was the one who left. Jenifer's words had rung true. He'd asked Jacqueline to be something she wasn't by nature just to be with him.

He turned the knob and opened the door. Normally it wouldn't have been unlocked, but his father knew he was coming and the security detail standing just a few feet away at the bottom of the porch steps had told Michael to go straight in. He saw the two Firebirds, but for every two he saw, he knew another half dozen lingered unseen.

The inside of the house was warm and smelled of burning wood and . . . he inhaled . . . roast. Voices mingled with bits of laughter from the kitchen at the back of the house. Michael set his bag on the floor and shut the door behind him. The click of the lock must have echoed enough to catch the ever-watchful attention of Dog, even for his advanced years. The shaggy pile of fur came loping down the hall, his nails clicking on the hardwood, his exuberant barking echoing off the walls. The moment he rounded the corner, his barking changed from one of a warning to the rest of the house to excitement.

Michael crouched to Dog's level, laughing as Dog jumped and clawed at his jacket, trying desperately between whines to lick Michael's face.

The talking paused in the other room, followed by the sound of chairs scraping across the floor. The rapid tap-tap of tiny feet preceded everyone else, and Michael's chest tightened the moment before Nicole rounded the corner, running at full tilt. Her blond hair was pulled into a floppy ponytail at her crown, forming tight ringlets with tiny curls escaping to frame her precious face. Her cheeks were bright from play and she held a familiar afghan of multiple colors to her chest.

"Daddy!" she cried and tossed aside the beloved blanket to run to him, not slowing a step until Michael wrapped her tiny, warm body in his arms and hugged her tight. Chubby arms wrapped around his neck and she hugged him back with pure joy only a child could muster.

"There's my beautiful girl," he choked, inhaling her familiar scent.

Tears burned his eyes again and he squeezed them shut tight, willing them away so his daughter wouldn't see and wouldn't be frightened. She wiggled free of his hold to stand in front of him, immediately launching into a long story made mostly of gibberish, but highly animated, as she pointed down the hall and up the stairs and back to the cluster of people standing a few feet away.

Michael looked up and met his father's gaze. He saw no censor, no anger, not even disappointment, just a welcoming smile. Nicole gripped his hand and pulled at him, forcing him to stand and walk with her, holding her tiny hand. At not quite eighteen months old, she walked well, ran better, and talked a mile a minute, even if she was the only one who knew most of the words. He caught Gumpa and Lumpy, her versions of Grandpa and Grammie, and a great deal about Dog. When they reached the end of the hall, she let go of his hand, apparently satisfied she'd given him the full rundown of the last several weeks, and picked up her beloved blanket from the floor.

Michael had lost any words he thought he might say then, standing before his parents—a father he'd only known a couple years and a woman who didn't birth him, couldn't have birthed him, but loved him unconditionally—and his friends. Victor and Beverly stood with but behind them, Victor's arm around Beverly's shoulder, her emerald eyes glistening when she smiled. Connor, his uncle for all intents and purposes though they were no more than two years apart in age, stood further back with his shoulder leaned against the doorjamb leading to the kitchen.

In the end, no one needed to speak. His father opened his arms and pulled Michael into a hard embrace. As soon as he released Michael, Caitlin toed up and wrapped her arms around his neck, her damp tears slicking the contact of cheek to cheek.

"Welcome home," she whispered against his ear. "We've missed you so much."

Michael could only nod, his own emotions running so high he couldn't force his throat to work. When living in terror of the Sorracchi and the wrath of the monster who had formed him, he had learned to suppress his emotions. Especially his most intense emotions. They fueled her fire. But in the years since his liberation he'd found it harder to keep it all in control, the suppression of twenty-five years flooding forward to make up for lost time. Or so it seemed.

Both Victor and Beverly embraced him as well, Victor patting him hard on the back. And Connor shook his hand. He and Connor had yet to find the connection he held with everyone else, although Connor was family. He had helped bring Michael home when Kathleen had captured him again and nearly brought him to death, and Connor had been one of the first to fall victim to Michael's uncontrolled energy draw. Perhaps the reason Connor held his distance, Michael didn't know.

They showered him with questions. How was the trip back? How were Lily and Jace? Had Jamie grown? How was he feeling? Caitlin's watchful eye frequently took in the cane he kept in his hand to help him navigate the simple act of walking. The cold, worse here than in Florida, made him ache and strained his weakened muscles.

They made their way to the kitchen and the dining room beyond and Michael sat, Nicole immediately tugging at his sleeve to be in his lap rather than the highchair positioned beside his seat. At least he knew he had his daughter's forgiveness. She acted no different than if he'd left that morning, happy to see him no matter what. It wasn't until Caitlin brought the food to the table and everyone sat did Michael feel some of the real tension ease away. This was familiar, his family and friends gathered around a meal. The only one missing was Jacqueline.

A heavy ache bloomed in his chest at her absence. For the first time, despite his knowledge she was gone the empty space left behind was real. He tried to keep the smile on his face as he put Nicole in her chair and took his seat.

His father's hand came down on Michael's arm, drawing his attention. "It'll be awhile before she makes it back, but she'll be back."

Michael looked to Nick, at the same time holding a fork of potato to Nicole to eat. She accepted it with a toothy grin and bounced in her chair.

"How do you know that's what I was thinking?" Michael asked.

Nick looked down the table to Caitlin, his smile widening when she met his look. "I'd be thinking the same thing if your mother wasn't here."

"I pray you're right. I need her, Dad."

Nick nodded. "I get it." He sighed and went back to working his fork through his dinner. He kept his head down, only his eyes shifting back to Michael. "You ready to tell us why? It'd be a good start for explaining to her."

Michael set down his fork, and gave in to Nicole's insistence to be in his lap. She was content to sit and nibble at a roll, but he needed to have her close. "I acted impulsively, I realize now, but at the time all I could think to do was separate myself from Jacqueline and Nicole. It was the only way I saw then to protect them."

"It happened again," Caitlin said, her voice firm without question.

Michael nodded. "When I woke in the hospital after the surgery, and you told me Jacqueline had collapsed, I knew I was doing it again. Drawing energy from the people I loved the most." He looked down at Nicole and she tipped her head back to smile at him, wide with only four front teeth. She went back to chewing on her roll. "If I could do that to Jacqueline, what could I have done to my daughter if I didn't find a way to control it? I could have killed her."

"But you didn't," Victor said across the table from him.

"No, not then. I had to find a way to control it somehow."

"So you went to Jace?"

"Not at first." He took a bite of meat and held it out to Nicole. She pulled it off his fork with her fingers and popped it in her mouth. "I went to the cabin. I thought I couldn't hurt anyone if no one was with me. I waited until I was stronger, when I was sure I wouldn't draw from anyone else, then I went to Jace. He was the only person I could think of who could help me find focus."

"How are you now?" Beverly asked, and Michael smiled at the improvement in her speech.

"You're doing great," he said and signed at the same time, the signing purely out of habit. "I have control over all the abilities I had previously discovered, and I've learned of a few more. I believe myself to now be in *full* control."

"Like what?" Nick said around a mouthful of food. He swirled his fork at Michael. "What else can you do?"

"Nicky, is that important right now?" Caitlin teased.

"What? It's cool," he said with a shrug.

Michael smiled at the warmth in the room, not from the fireplace but from the people. As much as he loved the Quinns, and would always consider Lilly one of his closest friends, these people here were the people who meant family to him. He chuckled, and the laughter felt good.

"It's okay," he said, shifting Nicole to his other leg. "I'm not sure I can adequately explain all of it. I'm not sure there are names for what I can do."

"Can you read minds?" his father asked.

"Not in the common understanding, but I believe my skills align more with what John Smith has described. Having a sense of people, not their thoughts and not necessarily their exact emotions, but a level of intent. Honesty versus deception."

"Like a living lie detector."

Michael nodded. "I suppose. It's not random and I can't turn it off and on. I need to be exceptionally focused on the person, and I find it has been more accurate when I have no personal knowledge of the person or predetermined opinions."

"Good to know." Nick went back to cutting his meat, and Caitlin cleared her throat. He looked up again and shrugged. "In my job, something like would be handy."

More of the tension eased between Michael's shoulders. It felt good to talk and laugh and hold his daughter. "I've also learned to harness my previously uncontrolled *draw* on other's energy. I can focus it, begin it and stop when I wish, and I've learned not only to take but to give. I was able to help Lily with patients on occasion by giving them the extra strength they needed."

"Michael, that's dangerous," Caitlin scolded, standing. "You need to keep your strength."

"I'm careful."

She came out of her seat and moved around the highchair to stand beside him, leaning over to kiss the top of his head. "It's good to have you home."

Michael took her hand and kissed the back of it, squeezing gently. "Dad said this was a double celebration. What else are we celebrating?"

His father and Caitlin exchanged looks and Nick held out his hand to her, drawing her beside him as he stood. "Caitlin and I have an announcement."

Comprehension hit Michael a moment before his father spoke. The way she stood, the fit of her clothing, the glow in her eyes. And the sparkle in his father's eyes when he looked at her. Michael was already on his feet and pulling Caitlin to him when his father said, "We're going to have a baby."

EARTH TIME: FRIDAY, 6 FEBRUARY 2054
DEFENSE ALLIANCE STATION GATEWAY
27,000 LIGHT YEARS FROM EARTH

"*H*ow many more days are we here, Miss Jackie?"

Jackie looked up from the book she read on her PAC tablet, smiling at Silas where he played on the floor of their on-station quarters. They had to move off the *Constellation* while it was restocked and maintenance performed in readiness for the final leg of their trip to Aretu.

"Seven."

Silas sighed and worked with the stack of blocks to make a tower. "I wish we could go tomorrow. No, today."

"I know. I'm bored, too."

"I wanna get to Artoo fast because then Papa will come and we can go home." He said the words softly, perhaps because they were meant more for the universe in general than actually for Jackie. But she understood his sentiment.

"Are you looking forward to seeing your cousin?"

Silas shrugged. He had fleeting moments of excitement sandwiched between much longer moments of quiet sadness. He missed his father. It had taken her days to convince Silas his father had spoken the truth when he said it wasn't Silas' fault he had to go away. He hadn't done anything wrong. He was going to Aretu because his papa loved him and wanted to keep him safe. She wasn't sure Silas had actually accepted her words, or if he just pretended to so she didn't talk about it anymore. He was a good boy, very well behaved, but sadness was a constant in his big, dark eyes.

"Did you have fun the last time you visited Aubrianna?"

Silas shrugged and nodded. "Sure." His entire face brightened and he turned on his knees to face her. "Papa took me to this really big farm. He said as far as I could see would be mine someday because it was his family's farm. They had horses and cows and dogs. Did you know even though Artoo is a completely different planet, they have animals like us? 'Cept their horses are really, really big. So big three people can sit on their backs! And Papa said when the horses have their babies one year, I can pick one for me. I've never known anybody who had a horse."

Jackie set aside her reading. It was a rare moment when Silas was so animated, and she didn't want to lose it. "I've never ridden a horse, have you?"

He nodded, grinning so wide she saw the space between his lower front teeth where he'd lost a tooth on the way here. "Uh huh. Papa said he was a little horse, but he was *so big*. Papa let me sit on him until he said Jacob knew me. Jacob was the name of the horse. Do you think that's a funny name for a horse?"

"No, I think it's a great name."

He kept on going, barely pausing. "Then, Papa got on another horse that was even bigger than Jacob and we rode together. It was the coolest thing ever!"

"It sounds like you would like to live there."

"I would . . ." Just as quickly as the smile had come, it was gone and the distant sadness was back. "I'd like to live there with Papa. It doesn't matter, though, if Papa isn't there."

Tears prickled Jackie's eyes and she offered the best smile she could muster. Her heart ached for the boy, while suddenly missing Nicole with such a smothering need it made it hard to breathe. She missed Nicole, and she missed Michael. She missed the life she'd created with him in less than a year. A life she'd never expected or wanted, and now didn't want to think she might never have again. Especially now . . .

Silas returned to his melancholy game and Jackie leaned back on the couch, her hand moving of its own accord to her lower stomach. If her math was right, she was just about twelve weeks along. Soon she'd be evident.

A new wave of anger hit her and she stood from the couch, marching to the small kitchenette area in the compact living quarters to find something to eat. She had figured it out while Michael was in the hospital after his surgery. At first she'd assumed it was stress worrying about him that made her tired and stole her appetite. A fever had set in a few hours after the surgery, and he'd failed to wake up from the anesthesia after two days, a vicious infection taking over his body. She'd stayed with him night and day, held his hand and talked to him just like she had on the *Excalibur* a year before. Then she'd passed out, and when she woke, the doctor had informed her first she was pregnant, and second Michael was gone.

She'd gone home to their apartment to find a note. Just a note. He told her he loved her and he would be back. Nothing more.

It was after the war ended, when life had settled again and she and Michael took Nicole to the cabin in Maine, before Michael said he found the words to tell her what the Sorracchi had done. The last time they'd held her prisoner, just weeks before the war began, they had taken from her one of her ovaries, for what reason no one knew. The chance they could ever conceive could have all but been stolen away from them.

He told her he wanted to be with her for the rest of his life. Now, she carried their child and he didn't even know.

The door chime sounded, making her jump. Silas didn't budge, barely responded to the sound. She stepped carefully over the toys on the floor and motioned her hand over the side control panel, the hydraulic door swooshing open. In the hall stood an Earth Force officer, one of the few commissioned to serve on the ship alongside the Areth and Umani officers of the Defense Alliance. He wore the insignia of an Airman First Class, and bowed his head in greeting.

"I have a message for you, ma'am. Encrypted for your eyes only."

"From who?" she asked, taking the small chip he offered.

"Unknown, ma'am. I only know the message came from Earth."

"Thank you," she said absently, staring down at the chip.

He dipped his head again, saluted, and turned on his heels to stride down the hall with long, floor eating steps. Jackie motioned for the door to close and went back to the couch. She sat and slid the chip into the side port of her PAC. A red Phoenix flashed on the screen, rotating as it waited for her passcode. The code would both open the message and decipher the encryption. To anyone before her who saw the message, it would see nothing but gibberish, and the code was in effect undecipherable. Nick and Michael had worked up the program with a young computer programmer named Katrina Bauer, creating an individual code for each person with access to the program. There were perhaps twenty people total on the planet with access. Jackie being one of them.

She typed in the twenty-seven digit access code and waited for her PAC to run the decipher program. With a series of twittering beeps, the rotating Phoenix flashed away and a message appeared on the screen.

Jacqueline

We are en route to Gateway, and will rendezvous with you there. We anticipate arrival prior to your next departure, but if we don't make it, please remain on Gateway until we arrive. Try to do so without detection.

Don't tell Silas. I would like to surprise him, and I know he would be disappointed if we don't make it when we say.

There have been major developments, none of which I dare speak of even here. We will explain when we arrive. I can't express to you how much it has meant to me for you to protect my son, and I can't wait to see him again.

With respect, John Smith

Jackie tapped the screen and an icon appeared to revert and destroy the message. She accepted and the wording disappeared. She looked up, watching Silas pretend to play, pretend to hide the sadness in his eyes. Jackie smiled and rested her head on the back of the couch. At least soon, for whatever the reason may be to bring them together again, Silas would soon smile with his papa again.

CHAPTER TWENTY-FOUR

EARTH TIME: 7 FEBRUARY 2054, SATURDAY
DEFENSE ALLIANCE SHIP STEPPENSCHRAFF
APPROXIMATELY 17,000 LIGHT YEARS FROM EARTH
ESTIMATED TIME TO GATEWAY: 3 DAYS

"*T*ell me what to do!"

John pressed his palms together and touched his index fingers to his lips, closing his eyes against the cacophony of mental sound bouncing off the exercise room walls. Her mind screamed as loudly as her voice, but he knew she had no idea the volume she projected. "I can't just tell you. It's a process, Jenifer."

Anger and frustration smothered the air around him, radiating off Jenifer like a force field. She fought for control, he also felt that, but the resonance harmonics of the ship weren't letting her. She had to be going mad.

She screamed, long and throaty, pushing away from the wall from where she squatted. Sweat made her shirt cling to her body and ringlets of damp hair framed her face. She'd been pushing herself in the on-ship gym for hours, wrangling demons she didn't understand, while John tried to find some way to help her. But he only knew what he had been taught, and his education had begun as soon as he could speak. Children of Aretu learned to control their Talents right along with learning to read and write.

"You're lying to me!"

He tried to stay calm, attempting to balance against her incoherent rage and confusion. Her confusion was almost as palpable as her anger, and John understood her enough to understand the two fueled each other like layering dry wood and liquid fuel on an already burning bonfire.

"Jenifer, it would serve me no purpose to lie to you."

"No!" she shouted, pivoting to kick the padded wall. She turned on him, stabbing an angry finger in his direction. "You're trying to get in my head!" The same angry finger jabbed her temple, leaving red marks. "You told me you couldn't feel anything from me. Is this your way of getting in? Get my thoughts? My memories?"

"I could never hurt you like this—"

"Don't. Mock. Me," she ground out through clenched teeth, glaring at him with such ferocity he knew if she had harnessed the mental skills to back it up, he'd probably be a writhing lump on the floor.

Her emotions were wild, erratic tangents yanking him from one extreme to another. At the mention of memories, panic and overwhelming terror took his breath away when it billowed out of her like shockwaves. Since the day he met her, he'd wanted to find a way to reach her and now all he could do was put up walls against the flood or follow her into the rage.

"You have to tell me what's in your head, *Su'ista*, so I can understand. I need to understand."

A ragged sob ripped from her and she slammed her arms against the wall over her head, dropping her forehead against the black cushioning. Her shoulders shook with the weeping.

Rage he understood. Anger was as much a part of Jenifer's personality as her eye color was a part of her face. She always bristled like an angry porcupine. Tears, weeping, were so foreign to her makeup their presence squeezed his heart to the point of pain. What in her memories could possibly draw enough pain to break her so completely?

She'd lost all ability to rein it in, to control it, and since he'd helped her two nights before she'd refused to let him help . . . wouldn't allow him to even touch her. She hadn't slept, had barely eaten, and hadn't

GAIL R. DELANEY

stopped *moving* since she woke the morning before from the forced sleep he'd pushed on her. With every hour she pushed she grew more exhausted, and her exhaustion dragged her further away from control.

She dropped to her knees, dragging her arms down the wall until she knelt like a supplicant at an altar. Pathetic, mewling sounds echoed in the empty expanse of the exercise room and John's heart broke for her. Against her demands, he slowly approached her, set his hand on the wall and lowered himself to kneel near her without touching her. Her face was hidden behind her raised arms, her weeping muffled against the wall.

"Don't make me live it again," she pleaded. "Please, John."

His name on her invocation forced him to close his eyes and swallow hard, fisting his hands to keep from touching her. "*Su'ista*, you need to *let* me help you."

She raised her head, tears wetting her cheeks, unfathomable sadness in her eyes making her a pale shadow of the strong woman he'd known for the last few weeks. Yet, the weakness made her somehow whole, something greater and more complete than she had been before. Her strength was the greater part of her, but her weakness could destroy her.

"No one will help me."

Her voice sounded so small, so defeated, he stared at her to make sure she hadn't been replaced with a child. She dropped her arms and wrapped them around her body, pivoting to put her back against the wall. She curled into her raised knees, becoming small for such a strong woman. Jenifer trembled, her lips quivering from a cold he didn't feel.

"No one will help me. No one will believe me. Stop crying!" she shouted the last sentence, dropping her voice low and deep as if mimicking a man. She kept the voice, and each new demand chilled John's soul. "No one will hear you. No one will help you now, you pretty little thing. Stop fighting! Stop fighting! Stop fighting!" Jenifer shouted each order louder, louder, until she propelled herself off the floor to attack one of the weighted dummies set up in the center of the room. With each word, she pounded and kicked. "Stop! Fighting! Stop! Fighting!"

"Dear God . . ." John whispered and slowly gained his feet. A reality still no more than a shadow hit him hard in the center of his chest. He'd thought the memories she fought were of Elijah Kerrigan and his death

232

Jace had told she'd witnessed, but these memories were darker . . . deeper. Older.

"What's the matter, pretty thing?" she asked no one, still speaking in cold, mocking voice. "Not big enough to hurt me?" She backhanded the form with her bare hand, the slap loud enough he thought she split skin. "You'll do what I tell you!" She used her other hand to backhand the form again. Blood streaked the leather covering as her skin finally broke under the assault. "Stop fighting!"

Her voice cracked. Her knees buckled but she stopped herself from falling, shoving away from the form to begin her assault all over again. "Stop fighting!"

"No!" John shouted now, running to her. He grabbed her arm and yanked her around harder than he would ever consider in any other time. "Fight!"

Jenifer spun, her arm connecting solidly against his chest but she'd pushed herself to exhaustion. John grabbed both her elbows, forcing her to face him. "Fight! Come on, Jenifer! Fight me!"

She turned into a wildcat, an instinctual, trained, killing machine. The only thing saving John from serious injury, and he held no illusions otherwise, was her weakened state. Otherwise, she might well have been able to kill him in moments despite his own deeply engrained survival training. Again and again, she assaulted him, kicking and swinging, grunts of exertion and impact the only sounds in the room. John met every assault with trained countermeasures, not to hurt her but to save her.

Again and again he demanded of her. "Fight! Fight!"

She swung a fisted hand, streaked with blood and John ducked it, lunging forward to wrap his arms around her torso, shoving her backward. Her legs wrapped around him as he slammed her back hard against the wall, pinning her there. All air whooshed from her chest and she fought to breathe, lashing out again with her hands. He leveraged his weight to hold her between him and the wall, gripping her flailing hands to slam them over her head. Nose to nose, their heaving breath and sweat mingled.

"Come on, Jenifer! Fight me!" he ordered.

She fought harder, her weakened body still desperate to shove him away. She screamed and thrashed, nearly knocking him loose.

"You can't use your hands, Jenifer. You can't hit me. You can't kill me. You have *nothin'* but your mind. Fight me!"

Equipment rattled behind him, machines weighing hundreds of pounds rattling against the bolts holding them in place. The air vibrated with power. Again she screamed, throaty and feral. Jenifer bucked with her hips, her legs tightening around his ribs with nearly enough force to crack his ribcage. Pain radiated up his side from the bruises still left behind from the crash. He slammed her hands over her head again, taking away any leverage she had. Her eyes were wild, heat radiating off her body like a furnace.

John leaned in, speaking close to her face. The words were bitter in his mouth, like vomit. "For once, fight me."

A massive metal resistance machine on the other side of the room ripped free of the thick bolts holding it in place and flew across the room. John flung them to the left, dropping them both the floor with a loud "oomph" seconds before the mangled machine slammed into the wall and fell to the floor just short of landing on their legs.

As soon as she was free of his hold, Jenifer drew up her knees against his torso and shoved him away, scrambling back at the same time. John covered his head and managed to avoid a ball weight as he rolled to his feet. By the time he raised his head to find her, she'd crossed the room with her back to the wall, wild eyes shifting from one rattling or flying object to another.

John took a step toward her, breathing hard. Even in her current physical state she was a powerful opponent. She was the perfect soldier, and John thought a quick prayer of thankfulness the Sorrs hadn't discovered her when they held power. Strength, endurance, intelligence . . . they could have made her into a machine.

"Do you feel the power, Jenifer?" he asked, once again leveling his voice. "Do you feel it thrummin' in your veins?"

She panted hard, her wide eyes never leaving him.

"This is all you, Jenifer. All you. Look around. Look at the havoc, the damage. The *power*," he stressed again.

Metal rattled, and he split his focus between her and the rest of the room. He wasn't positive she saw *him* yet, and knew he could be dodging projectiles at any moment. The air vibrated with the capacity of a mind unleashed, empowered and magnified by every angle and structure of the ship carrying them.

"Can you imagine now what you are capable of?"

He took a step forward and she took a step back, her spine hitting the wall. A force as solid and real as a hand pushed against his chest, holding him back. John smiled. She learned quickly, and he wasn't the least bit surprised.

"You hold the power, Jenifer."

Her shoulders relaxed, some of the panic eased around her eyes. John shifted his gaze from her long enough to scan the debris of the exercise room. It had been a long time since he'd showed off, but the moment called for it. A metal rod, broken clear of one of the many machines, lay on the floor not far from her feet. John looked at her again, found her still staring at him, and pointed toward the rod.

"Let me teach you control."

With ease born of a lifetime of experience, John held up his hand palm out to her. The rod flew from the floor toward his hand, stopping just short of making contact. Her eyes widened, but she didn't speak, and never looked away from the rod. It was completely for show, the act of kinesis requiring nothing more than focus, but he twirled his fingers and the rod spun rapidly clockwise like a child's pinwheel.

He splayed his hand and the rod stopped short, perpendicular to the floor. John laid his palm out flat and leveled the rod so one end rested in the flat of his hand, fingers open. He then made it bounce, end to end, again and again, as if he were juggling it even though his hand never moved.

John hid his smile of satisfaction when she took a step toward him, still watching the rod. This was all play, nothing more strenuous than a child tossing a ball, but he knew she saw now the potential. The power she could gain with this kind of control.

He wondered if he was waking a sleeping giant.

John brought his hand up and flipped it to hold his arm out at shoulder length, palm down, the rod hovering a few inches below his hand parallel to the floor.

"Take it."

She reached for it.

"No. Don't touch it. Take it."

Jenifer shook her head, looking away from the rod to him. The wild panic was gone, the trembling had stopped. He no longer felt her frustration buffering the air. They'd broken through, and now they just had to rebuild again.

"I don't know how."

"Yes, you do." He took a step toward her, drawing his arm back so the rod stayed equally between them but he could be closer to her. "Jenifer, look around. If you can do all this, you can take a small rod from me without touchin' it."

She nodded, just a slight dip of her chin, and he knew she was back in focus. The chaos of whatever memory tormenting her minutes before had once again been tamped down into the dark corners of her mind and Jenifer was ready to take control. She would probably sleep a full day when this was done, but she'd wake a different person.

She raised her hand, and he flinched at the bloody splits across her knuckles, her wrists already mottling with bruises from the grip he'd been forced to take with her. He'd ask her forgiveness later, he promised. Jenifer mimicked his position, hovering her hand parallel to the floor, palm down, over the rod. For several long beats of his heart he felt nothing, no change.

"Don't think about the rod, Jenifer. Think about what you want from it."

She nodded, not looking away from the metal.

Then he felt it, an almost indiscernible tug away from his hand as if she'd taken a grip on it and tried to pull it from his hold.

"Yes, that's it."

Her eyes pinched and her lips drew together in concentration.

The rod tilted, angling sharply toward her hand and she pulled back.

"No, you've got it," he urged. "Don't let go."

She steadied her hand again and the rod leveled, the pull away from him growing stronger. John slowly let go his hold, and the rod held its position. John smiled and withdrew his hand. Her eyes only shifted for a second, noting his withdrawal, before she focused again on the metal.

"Yes," John proclaimed, trying not to let his pride overwhelm his voice and break her concentration. "You've done it, Jenifer. You've done it!"

She looked up and dropped her hand, the rod clattering to the floor, and the smile on her lips was the most beautiful thing he'd ever seen. He'd thought the smile when she saw the wormhole had been amazing, but this smile . . . this smile topped it with ease. John threw out his arms and laughed. He lifted her feet off the ground and turned them one-hundred-eighty degrees, her arms wrapped around his neck.

"I knew you could do it!"

She wobbled a bit when he set her down, so he kept his hands at her sides. He knew he grinned like a fool, but despite the destruction around them and the bruises he knew he'd have tomorrow, he couldn't have been more proud of her. Of anyone.

"My head is killing me," she said softly, and John winced.

"I'm sorry. It might for a bit, but it'll get better. I promise."

Jenifer lifted her head and looked at him, her cheeks a little too pale for his liking but her eyes no longer looked haunted. "If you say so."

John took his hands from her sides to hold his palms against her cheeks and kissed her brow. She curled her hands around his wrists in a weak hold and leaned into him. John rested his forehead against hers, his eyes closed.

"I am so proud of you."

She leaned back, breaking the contact, but didn't move away, her gaze shifting in tiny degrees as she stared up at him. John opened his eyes and looked down at her, his chest hitching at the shine in her eyes. He swallowed and took in the fine details of her face.

"You amaze me, Jenifer," he said softly, his voice needing to carry no further than her ears.

He intended for the kiss to just be a touch to her lips, a symbol to her how precious she was to him despite the bruises and split lip she'd left him with. She'd fought through more than he wanted or could imagine. He held his lips to hers, not asking for anything more than to allow him the chance to somehow show her, and when he pulled away he smiled.

Her light eyes shifted from meeting his gaze, to what he knew was a split lip, and back to his eyes. The air shifted, and his heart immediately pounded hard and needy in his chest. Jenifer released his wrists and laced her fingers into his damp hair, pulling him down to her again.

She kissed him hard, stealing whatever moment he had to prepare for the demanding intensity. His lip stung, and the salty taste of dried tears mingled with the slight copper tinge of blood but he could no more stop the kiss than he could push her away. Open mouths fought for dominance in the kiss, her deep, throaty purr mingling with his groan. Need flashed hard and hot through him, fueled by her own wrapping around them both. His traitorous body wanted her, demanding, pounding, pushing him to take more.

They turned together, neither leading, neither following, until her back hit the wall and he lifted the back of her knees to draw her legs around his waist. The position minutes before had driven her to break through her walls, had been vicious and hard, but now his only thought was the feel of her body wrapped around him.

John pressed his palms to the wall on either side of her body, holding her in place with the pressure of his hips. Her pulse throbbed against his lips when he nipped and kissed the salty skin along her throat, her head tossed back against the wall. Eager hands tugged at his clothes, and with a flash of clarity, John groaned in frustration and dropped his forehead to her shoulder, sucking in deep, hard breaths.

"No' here," John said against her skin, letting his lips brush the warmth. He still kissed her throat to her ear, unwilling yet to give up the contact. "No' in this chaos."

"One place is as good as another," she said in a throaty voice, taking his face in her hands. "Come on, Ambassador. I know you want it."

A bucket of ice water couldn't have quelled his desire any faster than the rasped sound of his title, not his name. She tried to draw him in for another kiss, and he allowed the contact, but refused to deepen it. Passion turned to a dull ache when he stepped back and eased her to the floor again.

"I want *you*," he said, swallowing hard as her feet met the floor again. "There's a difference."

She scowled, the light he thought he might have awakened in her eyes gone in a blink. John fought to temper his breathing again and looked down. Her hands hung at her side, no longer reaching for him. He inhaled slowly and reached for her hand, lacing his fingers through hers. She didn't comply, but didn't pull away either.

"Come on," he said, hearing the weight in his own voice. "You should rest, and I have some explainin' to do to the captain."

Jenifer tried to pull her hand free, but he tightened his hold a tiny degree and she stopped. She could have easily stepped free and he wouldn't have stopped her, but he wanted her to know he wished she didn't. "I can clean up my own messes, Ambassador."

John raised his head and looked into her eyes. "Perhaps you can, but you don't have to."

He stepped away and started for the door, thankful Jenifer followed, her hand still in his.

CHAPTER TWENTY-FIVE

*I*n the spring of 2033, eleven-year-old Genevieve Moffett went riding in the gardens surrounding her family's antebellum estate in Old Savannah. Her father, Fullerton Lee Moffett IV was a very important man, she heard people say it all the time, and she knew he had to be important because he spent a lot of time working with very important people.

No one thought to look for her until the sun had set and her pony came back to the stable for dinner, a stirrup broken on his saddle and his reins dragging on the ground.

Fullerton Lee made a public plea for the safe return of his precious daughter, offering a huge reward for information leading to her return and the arrest of those responsible.

No ransom demand ever came. No information ever led them to where she had gone.

When Genevieve was found two weeks, three days, and seventeen hours later there was no remnant of the frivolous girl who wore pink, curled her hair, and rode ponies. She had been alone in the dank basement of one of the many outbuildings of her father's estate for three days, cold, starving, and sick.

The man who took her didn't know who she was, who her father was, and he didn't care. He'd taken what he wanted and left her behind when he was done.

Her father would have paid any ransom to someone who thought him important enough to steal his only daughter, he would have publicly thanked anyone who came forward to bring her home. But the man who took her wanted nothing more than her innocence. Fullerton Lee made an announcement his young daughter had run away, and now she had returned home, they wanted and needed privacy to help their troubled daughter.

She was told to put it behind her.

She was told to forget it.

She was told to stop fighting about it and just move on.

She was told to tell no one.

At thirteen, Genevieve disappeared again. This time she intended never to be found. On that day, Genevieve Moffett died.

And Jenifer was born.

he lights were on when John entered the suite and he headed straight for the bedroom, knowing the service droid would arrive soon. He took two steps into the bedroom, and the lights turned off. John paused and turned them back on to keep from banging his shins on the foot of the bed.

He walked around the bed, dropping the small kit he'd brought with him on the cover, and headed for the large bath and walk in shower, since Jenifer had been showering when he left the suite. The bathroom door was open, the air still heavy with the scent she'd chosen, but she wasn't there and the room was dark. He turned back to the bedroom and made it to the foot of the bed before the lights blinked out.

John stopped short and closed his eyes, drawing a slow, steadying breath.

And he waited.

A few seconds later the lights came on again. The whisper was so subtle he hadn't noticed it the first time, but when he stilled his thoughts the shift was like a breath on the back of his neck. He opened his eyes, grabbed the kit, and left the empty bedroom to the sitting area.

"Jenifer?"

"I'm here." Her answer was muffled and faint, coming from the lounge. He'd walked right past her. Just before the lights went off again he saw her lying on her back, one foot still on the floor, with a bare arm draped across her eyes.

A small light over one of the chairs cast enough glow to allow John to cross to the lounge without running into anything and find his way to her. He crouched beside the lounge and waited. A second later the lights came on again and a familiar whisper brushed the back of his neck.

"Does it help?"

She made a noise that sounded something like an affirmation.

He rose from his crouch and glanced around the sitting room until he spotted a wide footrest, and with a gentle mental tug, the piece of furniture slid across the floor to where he stood. He tugged it into place and set the small kit he carried on the floor beside his foot. Jenifer harrumphed.

"You're just showing off now, Ambassador," she mumbled, but he caught the small smirk just before it slid away again.

He chuckled and sat on the edge of the footrest to be as close as he could to the lounge, and to her. "Actually, I'm testin' a theory."

Jenifer blinked and brought her arm down to rest across her stomach. "I think I've had enough of your theories, Ambassador."

Her usual snark tinkled in her voice, and he knew the intent of her words wasn't to chastise, or give him a hard time, as he'd once heard Nick say, but he felt the jab of guilt nonetheless. She had been in pain of some kind almost as soon as she set foot on the *Steppenschraff*, and while he hadn't even intended for her to be here, John carried the weight on his shoulders. He bent down and opened the kit he'd brought from the medical wing, removing a pair of black gloves woven with tiny disks within the knit.

The lights turned off as he slid on the gloves. He winced at the sting across his knuckles, and was glad the lights were off so she didn't see. John took her hand nearest him and let it rest across his lap.

"What are you doing?" she asked, pulling away from him.

He pushed aside his personal anger at the mottled bruises around her wrists. Other bruises marred her upper arms and elbows, but he knew those were offensive wounds. The circle of bruises above her hands were defensive, testament of what he'd done. "I studied preliminary medicine before choosin' military service—"

She snorted and the lights came back on. "If this is where you say you want to play doctor—"

"Hush," he said with a chuckle and drew her arm back into his lap. This time she didn't fight or resist. "I think you'll be able to leave the lights on for a bit once I get started here." A simple mental command engaged the gloves with a subtle hum. John began with the center of her hand and worked a slow massage toward her wrist. Jenifer hummed low in her throat and her arm relaxed across his legs.

"Okay, I take back the whole playing doctor thing."

John smiled and continued the massage. "These gloves create a low level psychic field controlled by the wearer, and with this field, I can speed along the healin' process for bruises and achin' muscles through massage.

"This is what they taught you in medical school? How to give a massage?"

"Among other things." He circled his thumbs around her wrists, keeping the touch gentle but effective to keep from hurting her.

The gloves were designed to allow him full contact sensation so he could feel the warmth of her skin, or heat that might be a sign of an inflammation, and the give of her muscles to let him judge knots and tension. He guided her arm to lie across his thighs, the inside of her elbow facing up, relaxed and pliant. She moaned softly when he pushed the palm of his hand from her wrist nearly to her shoulder.

"I had a professor who had a theory about the development of Talents in such a large percentage of our population. The degree and definition varies from person to person, but the presence of Talents is almost complete. Ninety-seven percent of our people have a marked Talent." He shifted his attention away from her arm to her face. She watched him, looking more aware than when he'd sat down. "He theorized Talents could be enhanced and improved solely by the presence of others with Talents."

"Are you trying to say all this . . ." She swirled the fingers of her other hand near her temple. " . . .is happening because I'm around you? You've never struck me as the arrogant type, Ambassador."

John paused in the massage and leaned forward, holding her arm between his legs and his body as he closed some of the space between them. "Perhaps, but you've left the lights on for nearly four minutes."

Jenifer stared at him, neither smiling nor frowning, and John took it as the closest thing to a concession he would get. He leaned back and drew her other arm toward him, over her body. The angle wasn't as ideal, but he could still provide some benefit to the healing process. The gloves worked best within three hours of the injury, and hopefully he would be able to relieve the pain if not erase the bruises completely. He repeated almost the entire massage on the opposite arm before she spoke again.

"It felt like pressure," she said after a few minutes of silence. "Like vapor building in an O_2 cycler. Each time I flipped the lights on or off it let go of some of the pressure."

John nodded and returned to the first arm still draped in his lap. This time he began at her upper arm near her shoulder and worked downward toward her elbow. "Vapor is a good description. Think of this ship like the cycler. The entire structure is designed to create more power, more vapor, so those who use it can access it easily. If power isn't used, isn't drained, it builds up. It doesn't matter who or what drains it, as long as it's used."

"You're releasing the vapor for me," she stated.

She didn't say anything more while he finished the massage. Once he was convinced he'd done all he could, he leaned back and let the gloves go still, tugging them off his fingers. "How are you feelin' now? Any pressure?"

Jenifer shook her head. "None."

"What I did here should help for a while. Long enough for you to rest."

A chime sounded and John looked toward the door. Because every act of thought helped Jenifer, he fell back onto habits he had shied away from for years. Kinesis was too easy, but for her, he had no problem with opening a few doors and moving a few pieces of furniture without touching them.

He opened the door and the automated droid carrying their dinner slid into the room, hovering four feet above the floor. He instructed the droid to move to the table across the room and stood, shoving the footrest out of his way.

"And to eat," he added, holding his hands out to her to help her to her feet.

She gripped his hands and groaned as she rose. "Do those gloves work everywhere?"

Heat rose up John's neck and he cleared his throat. "Yes."

Jenifer chuckled. "Look at that. I made an ambassador blush."

John clenched his jaw and looked down at their still joined hands. He'd accepted the title of ambassador months before when Bryony asked him for his service, but in the last week the sound of it grated on his nerves like barnacles on raw skin. But he was determined to not allow Jenifer to see, if possible. He drew in a slow breath and lifted her hands to chest level, turning them so the faded bruises were visible.

"I will never ask you about what happened in that room," he said, keeping his focus on her hands. "If I ever know it will be because you choose to tell me, and once I say this it will go no further—"

"Ambassador—"

"Forgive me," he said, raising his head to look into her face. Frown lines pulled at the corners of her lips and between her eyes. He raised her hands a little higher so her own wrists entered her view. "If I had thought there was any other way . . ." He trailed off, not sure what other justification he could offer.

She met his gaze for several moments, drew in a slow breath through her nose, and offered nothing more than a small nod before easing her hands free of his. Jenifer stepped away and walked slowly toward the table, every movement revealing the hidden injuries all over her body.

"So, what did you get this time?"

CHAPTER TWENTY-SIX

"*M*ichael!"

Michael stopped short in the hallway, turned on his heel and leaned heavily on his cane to watch Victor jog down the hall toward him. Victor smiled widely, an expression Michael had grown used to on his friend in the last year. Since being freed from the Sorracchi consciousness that had tormented him for decades, Victor had become a new man with a ready smile and a joy in life Michael hadn't seen in anyone else before. Perhaps it was because Victor understood, more than anyone else, the chance he had at a life he never before imagined.

Perhaps it was because he'd wed the woman who had loved him even before he knew who and what he was. A sentiment Michael knew well, and hoped to know again if he could gain Jacqueline's forgiveness.

"I was hoping you would be in today."

"Did you need something?" Michael asked as Victor fell in step beside him, his hand setting firmly on Michael's shoulder.

"In a way. I want to talk to you about a discovery we came across late yesterday and get your opinion. Come talk with my team."

Michael had been on his way to his own office, but turned right instead, and they headed down another hallway to a wing of the facility Victor and his team had taken over. While they had no official name, their focus was accessing, deciphering, and utilizing any and all Sorracchi technology, records and equipment located in the recovery process. Victor's extensive personal knowledge of Sorracchi science and culture made accessible to him when the Sorracchi consciousness was removed made him the one single and undeniable expert on the goals and motivations of the race. Since the war, he had gathered a small but exceptionally skilled group of scientists, researchers, and simply geniuses to work with him.

They reached the security locked double door leading into Victor's area, and Victor placed his hand on the bioscan reader, waiting while a green line moved from top to bottom and back again, confirming his identity. With an audible click, the lock disengaged and Victor pushed open the door for Michael to precede him into the large space. The room was set up partially as a lab on one end, partially as a storage area for various pieces of machinery and technology they'd brought for study, and the opposite end of the lab was an area of desks for the team. A door at the back of the room opened into Victor's office, the wall between the main space and his office made up of large windows. Another similar office sat empty other than storage of more equipment.

Michael had met the members of Victor's team before, so he immediately recognized the brother and sister computer expert team of Katrina and Karl Bauer hunched over a data board spread out on a table along the far wall. Two of the three medical members of the team, xenobiologists Doctor Averill Jones, an Areth doctor on loan to Victor's team, and Doctor Agatha Corbin, worked in the sealed section of the laboratory. Agatha raised a gloved hand and waved in greeting. Njogu Anini, a citizen of the Bagdaghir sovereign on Raxo, worked on something large and disassembled near the Bauer siblings. Missing were Carmen Ellis, a woman assigned to assist Njogu with reverse engineering and repair, Horatio Vasquez the team linguist, and Doctor Corin Lordahl their theoretical biologist. Corin was traveling to Aretu to confer with some of the Areth's top xenophysicians to bring back knowledge helpful to the team.

"Trina, come on in my office," Victor said, heading to his right.

Katrina looked up at her name with an attractive smile on her seemingly far too young face. When she saw Michael, she immediately looked down and away, saying something to her brother. He nodded and continued with whatever he had been working on, and she picked up a PAC tablet from the table, heading toward them with the PAC hugged to her chest. Michael stopped to wait for her, and noticed the bright bloom of color in her cheeks when she was close enough.

"Good morning," he said.

"Good morning," she answered so softly he barely heard her.

She walked one step ahead of him into Victor's office, sat in one of the two chairs facing Victor's desk, and set the tablet in her lap. Victor motioned for Michael to sit in the other chair and took his own seat. Michael eased into the chair and leaned his cane against Victor's desk. He took the moment to watch Katrina. He had learned enough about body language and what Caitlin called "tells" to know Katrina Bauer was exceptionally nervous around him. She never looked him in the eyes, never raised her head more than she had to, and fidgeted incessantly. Her chestnut hair waved in thick chunks around her cheeks when she stood straight, but when she bowed her head the curls fell forward to block her face. Michael had run through every time the two of them had been given opportunity to talk, and couldn't think of anything he might have done to make her so opposed to talking with him.

"Tell Michael about your discovery," Victor urged.

Her dark eyes shifted to Michael for a brief moment before she cleared her throat and activated the PAC screen. "Karl and I were deciphering some of the Sorracchi logs and we found reference to a ship called the *Abaddon*." Her voice was so soft he almost couldn't hear her, and he leaned closer to catch each word. "We have no record of this ship in our inventory of either destroyed or confiscated ships, so I dug a little further and found out the ship had been left derelict after one of the main compulsion units failed. By what I've seen, I think the ship was a scientific vessel."

"Averill believes this may have been one of their off-world experimentation vessels based on some of the records Trina translated for him. There could be a wealth of information there about what they did to us, in detail, and even what they may have done to other worlds and races," Victor added.

"Do you remember anything about this ship?"

Victor shook his head and shrugged at the same time, his movements so much more casual and natural than the man Michael had known nearly his entire life. Michael liked this new Victor, although he considered both sides of the man his friend. "Only in passing. I wasn't ever stationed there, but I heard Kathleen refer to it a few times."

Michael wondered how many years would have to pass before the name of the Sorracchi who'd birthed him wouldn't make his skin crawl and his stomach turn. He bit down the distaste. "Do we know where it is?"

Victor looked to Trina, who had raised her head, but as soon as Michael turned toward her she looked down again. "I believe it is currently floating dead near Proxima Centauri."

Michael leaned back and raised the ankle of his injured leg to rest on his other knee. "Should we find it?"

"That's what I wanted to talk to you about. I'd like your opinion."

"Any records we find could prove beneficial."

Victor nodded. "That's the way I see it. Even if we find nothing more than details on a single experiment, it's more than we had before. We have no idea what we might find until we go."

Michael smiled. "It sounds to me you've already made up your mind."

Victor chuckled and leaned back in his chair with his elbows resting on the arms and his fingers steepled in front of him. "I can't deny that. I still need to present the idea to Nick and get clearance to take at least a portion of the team to Proxima Centauri."

"I don't understand why you needed to speak to me."

His friend stared at him for a long moment before he hitched up his chin and dropped his hands. "How do you feel about going with me?"

"I need to be here when Jacqueline comes home," Michael said without hesitation.

"And you will be. If everything is on schedule, Jackie is at *Gateway* now. It will be weeks before she will be back here, Michael. She still needs to reach Aretu, get Silas settled in the palace, then wait for a transport back here. If we get clearance, I want to be off world within the week. With the Areth ships at our disposal, it's a thirty hour flight to Proxima Centauri, we're too close to jump, but we can go at top speed. We would only be there a few days, then back. We'll be gone at the most two weeks, and that's with an extended stay on the *Abaddon*." Victor laid his arm on his desk and rapped his fingertips on the wood. "I have a feeling about this ship, Michael. I can't explain it, but I don't think we'll leave there empty handed."

Michael looked past Victor to the window behind him, at the rays of bright sunlight twinkling off ice covered trees. "I have to think about it."

Victor rose quickly from his chair. "Fair enough. I'll be speaking with Beverly and Nick this afternoon about it. You can let me know in the next couple of days."

Michael smiled. "Beverly will be the harder sell than my father. You've only been married a few months. Do you think she'll be pleased with you going off world?"

Victor smiled at the mention of his wife. "I think you are right, my friend. She'll understand, though, and it won't be long." Njogu called from the other room for Victor's attention. "I'll be right back."

Michael nodded and shifted his weight forward, leveraging himself out of the chair. He couldn't rely on the strength of his legs to help him, and winced at the stab of pain near his hip when he gained his feet. Gripping the edge of the desk, he reached for the cane but Katrina already had it in her small hand, holding it out to him.

"Thank you."

She withdrew her hand as soon as he had the cane. "You're welcome," she said softly, keeping her gaze cast down. "H-how are you feeling?"

"The cold makes it difficult," he answered honestly.

She nodded and shifted away from him to escape the confines of the desk and two chairs. "I hope you feel better soon, Doctor Tanner."

"Call me Michael. Please."

Her dark eyes met his for a brief moment, and he wanted to ask what he'd done to make her so nervous, but she looked away too soon and nearly bolted from the room, the PAC hugged to her chest and her head down. Once clear of the office, she looked up and jogged across the large room to her brother. Michael stepped to the doorway and watched Karl look up and give his sister a devious smirk. He said something and laughed, and she slapped his shoulder, glancing back to where Michael stood. Karl laughed again and went back to his work.

Victor returned from speaking with Njogu and leaned his shoulder against the doorjamb outside the office, looking over his shoulder at Karl and Trina. "That girl is likely to explode from embarrassment one of these days."

Michael looked to Victor. "I don't know what I did."

"So, you've noticed?"

Michael looked toward Katrina again. Her back was to him, her posture more relaxed with more distance between her and Michael. "I've done nothing to harm her."

"You think that's why she won't look at you?"

"What other reason would there be?"

Victor laughed and laid his hand on Michael's shoulder. "She's smitten with you, Michael."

Michael scowled and looked at Victor. "I don't know what that means."

"She's attracted to you." Michael opened his mouth to protest, but Victor held up his hand. "I know exactly what *you* are thinking, I've known you far too long not to. No, you didn't do anything wrong. She knows you are with Jackie, but that doesn't mean a young girl's heart can't flutter."

Michael looked across the room again. "She's so young."

"Do you know what your problem is, my friend?" Victor squeezed his shoulder. "Your soul has outlived your body. God never intended for one so young to be so old on the inside."

CHAPTER TWENTY-SEVEN

EARTH TIME: 11 FEBRUARY 2054, WEDNESDAY
DEFENSE ALLIANCE SHIP STEPPENSCHRAFF
APPROXIMATELY 27,000 LIGHT YEARS FROM EARTH
ESTIMATED TIME TO GATEWAY: TWO HOURS

*T*he whisper of silk against soft sheets and the slight shift of the bed drew Jenifer from her sleep. She inhaled through her nose and blinked open her eyes. The shimmering, shifting light of the wormhole outside the bedroom observation window danced across the walls and ceiling of the bedroom, casting a luminescent rainbow across John's bare torso as he walked around the foot of the bed.

"Something wrong?" she asked, sitting up enough to lean on her elbows. The decadently soft silk of the sleeping clothes John had gotten her stretched across her body, cool on her skin.

He came up her side of the bed, his bare feet silent on the cushioned floor. His slow smile made her exposed skin flush warm. "I didn't mean to wake you," he said in a low, husky voice despite the fact they were alone in the suite.

"I notice when you leave."

John leaned over her, bracing his hands on the bed on either side of her body. "I like the idea you miss me beside you in bed."

"Don't get too full of yourself, Amb—" She didn't finish the jab before he covered her mouth in an open-mouthed kiss that switched the warm flush to a slow burn, heating her blood from the center of her body out.

Never taking his mouth from hers, John pushed aside the heavy blankets covering her lower body and urged her to lie back, joining her again on the bed. Jenifer pushed her fingers into his soft hair which had grown a little too long since she met him, but it gave her something to grip to pull him closer. His hungry moan brushed her lips and vibrated through her. The erotic sensation of their silken night clothing whispering against each other when he moved over her made her skin tingle.

The kiss was slow, thorough and deep, but more powerful than any kiss of seduction she'd ever shared. John savored her kiss, his tongue sliding slow and firm against hers. Long fingers shifted the fabric of her nightshirt, pushing up the hem until his palms found the bare skin of her stomach.

Jenifer woke with a jerk, and in the moment before she opened her eyes, she knew without looking and without reaching out the bed was empty beside her. She blinked open her eyes and let them adjust to the dim light from the clear observation window above the bed, casting a dancing array of colors over the walls and ceiling.

The blankets stifled her, a smoldering heat simmering beneath her skin, and she kicked them off, trying to slow her rapid breathing and ignore the ache of need the vivid dream had created. She glanced to the left side of the bed, and confirmed what she already knew. John wasn't there.

The first night on the *Steppenschraff* Jenifer had slept in the large bed beside John because the exhaustion of John's reset had worn her out and the choice hadn't been hers. She couldn't have walked to the other room if she tried and she doubted he would have let her. The second night, when she so violently fought the chaos and couldn't calm the noise in her head, she hadn't slept at all. The third night, she'd been determined to break the cycle of sleeping beside John but after three hours of restlessness in the next room she accepted it wasn't just what he did to release the psychic pressure, it was his nearness. He hadn't said a word when she'd come into the room in the middle of the night and slid between the blankets. With each day, and night, the pressure was less noticeable and she saw herself grow more proficient each day with the lessons he taught her. They stuck to the basics, but John repeated often he knew she was capable of much more.

In the nights since, she'd slept better than she could ever remember, except for the dreams that gave her in her sleep what she refused to consider when awake. After the intense kiss in the gym, the kiss John had stopped and walked away from, Jenifer had convinced herself she could walk away and forget it, too. She did when awake, just not sleeping beside him at night.

This was the first time she'd woken without him there.

But, she knew why.

Jenifer waited until her heartbeat slowed to a normal rate and the flush cooled before she sat up and swung her feet over the side of the bed. The memory, and the ache, remained.

The sitting room was dark, too, but the lights of the observation window in the eating area drew her along the curved wall. John stood with his back to her, his arms crossed over his chest, his head down. Tension pulled across his shoulders, defining the lines of his muscles. The swirling lights of the wormhole danced over his bare arms and shoulders. He twisted at the waist just enough to look back at her as she approached.

"Is something wrong?" she asked.

"I didn't mean to wake you. I'm sorry."

She caught herself before repeating the conversation they so clearly had in her dream. Jenifer shook her head and brushed past him to curl up on the bench seat along the window. From her perch she could look to her left out the window and to her right at him. She focused on the lights outside the ship. "We'll be dropping out of the jump soon."

"Another fifteen minutes. We have to approach *Gateway* at cruising speed."

"Did you confirm with the captain the *Constellation* is still docked?"

John raised one hand to stroke his thumb across his lower lip, taking a step closer to her so the silk of his pants brushed the bench. She felt the warmth of his body against the bare skin of her arms. Jenifer swallowed and tamped down hard on the curl in her stomach.

"As of his last communication with *Gateway* the ship was still there, and didn't intend to leave for another couple days."

She looked up at him, and found him watching her. Jenifer smiled, hoping she could ease his worry, surprised she wanted to try. "You'll see your son soon, John."

John drew in a long, deep breath, never looking away from her. His eyes were dark, and she pegged the dim light in the suite to be at blame. "My plan is to have Jackie join us and continue on to Aretu on the *Steppenschraff*."

She nodded. "I assumed."

"I'm anxious for you to know my son, Jenifer."

The weight to his voice skimmed across her shoulders almost as tangibly as an embrace. She had to look away and drew her knees toward her chest. What the Areth lacked in functionality of their clothing —none of it would work on a battlefield or in a fight—they made up in comfort. Things on the *Steppenschraff* were too comfortable, and she constantly reminded herself why they were here. Someone wanted Ambassador John Smith dead, and just because they were on a Defense Alliance ship didn't mean he was out of danger. Him or his son.

"I wish I had met him before he left. It might make me being here less uncomfortable for him."

"He knew I would have someone protecting me when he was gone." A strange hitch in his voice made Jenifer look at him again. "I think perhaps he'll be very glad to meet you."

She remembered the first time she'd seen John in Alexandria, watching from the shadows while he said goodbye to his son. That day, she had questioned whether his show of sorrow had been for someone's benefit. She knew now, without question, his pain had been real.

Jenifer twisted, lowered her feet to the floor, and stood. John stood close enough she brushed against him and clenched her jaw against the intense awareness. "Since we're both awake, and we've got a good hour and a half, why don't we go get something to eat before we dock?"

He chuckled and smiled, some of the tension finally easing around his eyes. "Between you and Silas, I'm no' sure who has the greater appetite."

"As long as he keeps his fork to himself we'll do just fine."

His laughter followed her as she headed for the bedroom to change. Just before she rounded the corner into the room, Jenifer stopped and turned back to him. John hadn't moved from the window, but had turned to watch her retreat. "I have a question about the ship and . . ." she swirled her fingers near her temple, the only way she referred to whatever it was John had released in her. She wasn't in denial anymore, but she wasn't fully accepting either.

"Ask," he said, taking a step toward her. "Are you feeling all right?"

She nodded and waved off his worry. "I barely feel the pressure anymore."

"Good. You're gaining more control. It will get easier from here on. And once we reach Aretu, you'll notice a marked difference. You won't have the ship affecting you."

"That's what I wanted to know. The first day or two everything was magnified, and I wanted to know—"

"Not magnified, Jenifer. Clarified."

"What's the difference?"

"Your emotions, sensations . . . memories . . . weren't made greater. They weren't stronger or more intense."

"Sure felt it."

John smiled. "I'm sure it did." He finished closing the space between them, stopping within reaching distance with his arms crossed over his bare chest. "Imagine wearin' dark glasses your entire life. You saw everything, and you thought you saw it all clearly. Those of us who were raised with the knowledge of how to use our Talents don't wear those glasses. The ship took off those glasses for you. Everything is the same as it was before, but you see it—feel it—remember it—with clarity rather than shadow."

"And when I leave the ship, I go back to wearing the glasses?"

"No' if you don't want to." John tilted his head, watching her. "I promised you, Jenifer, I would help you."

Jenifer took a step back, trying to process his explanation. If he were right, then she had to change her entire perspective on the last few days. She assumed once free of the ship everything would go away, and part of her wanted it to. She wasn't accustomed to the pull toward someone, the instinctive want to be closer. When they were just a side effect of the ship, she was willing to shove them aside; if that wasn't the case, she had to find a different way to deal with it.

"You must enjoy this, Ambassador," she said, dropping her voice and bringing up her guard. "This is your element, not mine. You're in control."

"Do you honestly think I enjoy watching you struggle?"

She didn't intend to look at him, but she did, and the disappointment she saw in his light blue eyes dug deep. What was wrong with her? She didn't depend on others, she didn't back off, and she didn't regret. She didn't enjoy sleeping beside a man every night. She didn't get used to the presence of another person. She didn't wake from vivid dreams of intimacy seeking the person in her dreams. She didn't learn the difference in someone's smiles.

She didn't take on jobs to protect a politician just because he risked his own life to save the life of a kid she didn't know.

But . . . she had.

Jenifer held up her hand, mentally shoving away the ideas, and turned away from him. She caught him leaning back from the corner of her eye and realized she actually *had* shoved him back. She clenched her jaw before an apology escaped.

"Jenifer," he called before she made it around the corner into the bedroom. She struggled with ignoring him or stopping, and in the end, she stopped in the doorway and looked over her shoulder at him. "Not everything has to be a fight. There doesn't always have to be a winner and a loser. We can just . . ." He held out his arms, hands up and away from his body. " . . .*be*."

Jenifer walked away, leaving him alone in the room.

$\mathcal{A}$ constant stream of announcements carried through the massive promenade on *Gateway* Station. At least, Jenifer assumed they were announcements of some kind because the languages were completely foreign, some lyrical and almost beautiful and others guttural and harsh, sounding more like a broken voice recording than a spoken language.

"The announcements remind all visitors their weapons are dampened on the station, deemed useless."

"Wanna bet?" Jenifer said under her breath and lowered her hand to Damocles. She hadn't worn the weapon in days while on the

Steppenschraff, but wasn't about to walk around a massive space station filled with hundreds of potential enemies without her gun on her thigh. The weapon was a sharp contrast to the soft, casual tunic in blue and dark blue leggings she wore, but the tunic was long and hit mid-thigh with a slit on the side that allowed the panels of the tunic to camouflage the weapon.

John chuckled and took the hand reaching for the pistol. "Let's no' find out if that beautiful piece of weaponry can or will bypass the dampenin' field. Better to leave it be, trust me."

They had docked at *Gateway* three hours before, but it had taken that long for all the necessary declarations, inspections, and procedures to be completed before they were allowed off the ship. The team of scientists originally scheduled on the *Steppenschraff* were carefully herded and guided by their Defense Alliance chaperones in the other direction, all of them bumping into each other as they walked because their heads were tipped back and their mouths hung open.

"You are one of the few Humans to set foot on *Gateway*, Jenifer. Try no' to look too much like a tourist."

"Shut up," she said, unsuccessful in disguising the laughter lacing her words.

The promenade was full of people . . . aliens . . . or was she the alien? The ceiling was at least three stories high and built of glass and steel. The promenade extended from the docking bays where they had disembarked for the entire length of the station. Restaurants and mercantile shops popped up every fifty feet or so, and the air was filled with a mix of aromas she couldn't even begin to identify but made her mouth water. The spaces between the shops were sealed in glass and beyond she saw the tops of trees and other plants. John had explained the station had an entire garden, equivalent to what had once been Central Park in New York City, at the core of the station. People lived here, worked here, and just passed through. It was a city within a massive floating ship.

In a single span of the area she saw no less than a dozen different and easily designated races, varying from what could be Human—probably more Areth—to hooded and cloaked humanoid forms hidden from view. She saw many Umani, and had begun to recognize citizens of the various sovereigns by the clothing they wore and the slight variations in appearance. One race wasn't much larger than a toddler, with skin bearing just the slightest blue tint. A group of three women walked together, more like glided, with skin so pale it was almost translucent, white blond hair and eyes so striking they overwhelmed the delicate features of the three women. They offered shy smiles to those they passed and spoke to each other in hushed tones. When he pointed out the Zibala, the three women, the heaviness in his voice brought Jenifer's attention back to him. The smile was there, but strained, and his eyes had lost their spark.

"Come on, Ambassador. This is a big station," she urged, trying to shift his attention. She looked forward and nearly choked at the sight of the behemoth of a creature lumbering down the walkway toward them.

He was massive, at least eight feet tall and nearly as wide through the shoulders. At least she assumed it was a "he". His skin looked like tanned brown leather, barely indiscernible from the dark brown of his clothing. A swatch of spiky black hair topped his head and shiny black eyes, like stones of obsidian, blinked as slowly as his stride.

With a tug on her hand, Jenifer realized she'd stopped and she stumbled to fall in step with John again. He leaned sideways to speak close to her ear. "That is a Pehemau. No' very technologically advanced beyond basic space travel, but they're good to have in a ground fight. Their skin is as tough as leather, and almost impenetrable. Other races make the mistake of thinkin' they're just clumsy giants, and often underestimate their intelligence. Actually, they are wonderful composers. Their music will make you weep."

She looked up at him, ready to give him back the same jab, but saw no teasing in his eyes. He was serious.

"You know I'm not going to be able to keep all this straight, right?" she asked, hoping to pull him back from where he'd momentarily gone. She preferred the smile.

"You'd better. There's a quiz later."

"Do you know *all* these races?" she asked as they resumed the walk. There were shifting panels in the floor to move them along faster, but she found she enjoyed taking it all in. It had been a very long time, if ever, since Jenifer had experienced something so completely foreign.

John nodded. "As an officer in the Defense Alliance, I was required to know the names, customs, and languages of every race we came into contact with."

Jenifer slowed her step and he slowed with her, looking down at her from the line of his shoulder. "How many languages do you know?"

"Speak or read?"

"Both."

"Forty-two, includin' nine Earth dialects."

Jenifer blinked and started walking again. "I didn't think Earth still had nine dialects, everything has merged so much in the last few decades."

"I studied some of your ancient languages: Greek, Hebrew, Latin."

His voice trailed off with his step and Jenifer stopped again with him. She followed the line of his gaze. Twenty feet down the promenade stood Jackie Anderson, dressed in a cream suit common amongst the more humanoid travelers, her dark hair plaited down her back. At her side was a dark skinned boy leaning over the railing so he could see the park below. He spoke animatedly to Jackie, pointing at something they couldn't see, and Jackie responded with genuine enthusiasm. Silas took her hand and dragged her further down the promenade away from them to get a better look at something.

John's hold on her hand tightened, and so did Jenifer's throat. She looked from Silas and Jackie to John, thrown a little off balance at the waves flowing off him. She couldn't put a word to the emotion, but it made her chest flutter.

Silas turned to pull Jackie in their direction, and Jenifer's heart jumped almost painfully when she felt as much as saw the moment the son saw his papa. John took a step forward, his hand still wrapped around hers, but she didn't move. He only afforded her a quick glance, so she could smile and slip her hand free, before he headed for his son.

"Papa!" Silas cried and broke free of Jackie, running with the clumsy speed of a child.

John dropped to his knees as Silas reached him, just in time to snatch the boy up and Silas wrapped his arms around his father's neck. Tears streamed down the boy's cheeks. Jenifer drew in a fortifying breath before she took the few steps needed to reach John and his son. Jackie did the same from the other direction.

"Oh, my boy," John said, his voice cracking. "I am so happy to see you." John kissed Silas soundly on the cheek and cupped his hand around the back of the boy's head. "I love you."

Jenifer looked up at Jackie, catching her wiping tears from her cheeks. Jackie shrugged and smiled unapologetically. Jenifer nodded and blinked back the hot irritation in her own eyes. She sniffed and turned away to walk to the railing, stealing the few moments she had left to somehow find a way to build stronger walls around her heart. The moment was short-lived and not nearly long enough.

"Jenifer."

She made one quick swipe of her cheeks before turning her back on the beatific scene below to face John and Silas. John stood just a foot away, Silas in his arms. He made no effort to disguise the wet tracks on his cheeks, nor did his son, who sniffed loudly clinging to the fabric at his father's shoulder.

"Jenifer, I want you to meet my son. Silas, this is Jenifer. She is the person I promised you would keep me safe until I came for you."

"Hi, Silas," Jenifer said after clearing her throat. "It's very nice to meet you. Your papa has told me so much about you."

She extended her hand to shake the boy's in what she considered to be an acceptable greeting for the situation, but had to react fast when Silas all but launched himself from his father's hold into hers, his skinny arms and legs wrapping around her in quite possibly the fiercest hug she had ever received.

"Thank you," Silas said softly, hiccupping.

Jenifer wrapped him in her arms to hold him in place, patting his back because she couldn't say anything at all. She watched John embrace Jackie, listened to him thank her for all she'd done, but until Silas wiggled free of her hold minutes later she completely lost the ability to speak. John turned from talking with Jackie when Silas wrapped himself around John's leg, and he smoothed Silas' thick, curly hair. When he looked at her, something bloomed in her chest, a low, pleasant ache.

"Have you eaten breakfast yet?" John asked, tipping his son's head back so Silas looked up at him. Silas shook his head, a wide, bright smile spreading his features. "Good, because I've made a bet with Jenifer she can eat more than you can."

"Never!" Silas shouted, the tears of moments before completely gone. "Come on, Papa. I'll show you our *favorite* restaurant."

Silas took John's hand and tugged him down the walkway. John looked to Jenifer again before taking a step, smiled, and held out his hand. She took it before she gave herself a moment to consider otherwise.

CHAPTER TWENTY-EIGHT

*J*ackie came out of the bedroom she'd be sharing with Silas for the next three days as they finished their trip to Aretu, a trip that would have taken another three weeks on the *Constellation*, and stopped at the end of the short hallway to watch her charge.

At no point in the entire trip from Earth had Jackie seen the little boy so animated and happy. She didn't think he'd stopped smiling since he'd turned around and saw Ambassador Smith, and he'd only stopped talking long enough to chew his food.

Now he sat on the lounge beside his father, curled snugly to John's side, while John read to him from one of the books Silas had brought from home. Silas' attention was far from the story, his big, dark eyes barely wavering from his father's face.

She fought the urge to point out it was past Silas' designated bedtime, accustomed to guiding the boy's schedule, and let him enjoy having his papa back. The thought made her eyes prickle and she looked away, trying to focus on anything else.

Jenifer sat in the far corner of the suite, the entire space easily three times larger than the quarters Jackie and Silas had shared on the *Constellation*, tucked into the shadows at a small table. She sat beside the table, not so much at it, slouched in the chair with her legs crossed and her arms laced loosely over her body, her full attention on John and Silas.

Jackie had been trying to figure out the dynamics between the two since they'd connected on the promenade. She'd noted the hold John had on Jenifer's hand, and the way Jenifer reacted to the reunion between father and son. It was an emotional response Jackie never would have expected from the other woman.

She had known Jenifer for years, having spent time with her on and off working various missions for Phoenix before the war, and other than the pseudo-relationship Jenifer had with Eli Kerrigan, she'd never known Jenifer to be anything more than a hard, emotionless soldier. Jenifer liked her guns, liked a good fight, and liked a stiff drink. The Jenifer she saw now was a parallel to the Jenifer she'd known, but not the same woman she'd met with in Brazil.

This woman watched John when he wasn't looking with a softness in her eyes, a softness she purposefully hid whenever he paid her attention. She held her distance but stayed close. And every once in a while, with a word or smile from John, the firmly set in place façade slipped.

Jackie crossed the room to the table. She opened their small refrigeration unit and removed a cold fruit juice beverage and slid into one of the chairs. Jenifer spared her a quick glance before looking back to John.

"I'm all moved in with Silas," Jackie said. "This is definitely the way to travel."

Jenifer looked over her shoulder. "Why are you in his room?"

"Where should I sleep? On the lounge?" Jenifer joked, motioning toward where John and Silas sat.

"No, in the other bedroom."

"Don't you . . ." Jenifer turned away before Jackie finished, and Jackie grinned. "Oh."

"Don't assume anything," Jenifer said in a low voice.

"Wouldn't dream of it." Jackie took a long drink of the juice to hide her smirk.

They sat in silence for several minutes, watching Silas fight sleep while John read. She couldn't quite make out the story from here, and figured John could read a manual on cleaning the grease from a hydraulic ramp and Silas would listen. John looked up once, his eyes settling easily on Jenifer, and he smiled before returning to the book. Jackie almost felt like an intruder.

Jenifer shifted and cleared her throat. "We saw Michael."

A cold flush skittered up Jackie's spine and her heart skipped. She hated the immediate and intense reaction her traitorous heart had at the mention of his name. "Did he finally return to Alexandria?"

"No," Jenifer said flatly. "Though I think his plan was to head back once we were gone. He was in Florida with Jace and Lilly Quinn."

A heavy sense of betrayal squashed the flutter in her chest and she pushed away the bottle of juice. "I can't believe Nick didn't tell me."

"Don't blame him. As far as I saw, he didn't know. No one knew, and Quinn didn't know he'd taken off on you."

Jackie slid her arms beneath the table to hide her hands resting on her stomach. Her eyes prickled and she looked down. "Did he say . . ." She stopped talking just before her voice faltered.

"I think he told John, or Quinn did. I figured whatever excuse he offered was just that, an excuse." She shifted again, rubbing her fingers across her forehead. "I told him if he didn't have the testicular fortitude to stick around when things got tough, he had no business convincing you to be with him and give up who you are."

Jackie's first reaction was a flash of anger, but she forced herself to tamp it down. She drew in a slow breath and reached again for the juice. "I know you don't believe it, Jenifer—hell, sometimes I don't believe it myself—but I like the life Michael and I have together."

John eased himself up from the lounge, shifting at the same time to pick up the now sleeping Silas. He disappeared down the hall, carrying the boy.

"*Had* together," Jenifer said as John rounded the corner.

She blinked. "No, have. I have to believe we're not over."

Jenifer stood and marched across the suite, stopping half way to crouch and pick up some of the other books and toys Silas had left on the floor. "Why stay? You've got no strings, no commitment. Just walk away."

"You're wrong. I have Nicole."

Jenifer swiveled on the balls of her feet to look back at Jenifer. "She's not your kid, Jackie."

"She's my daughter," Jackie said through a suddenly tight throat. "I'm her mama, Jenifer. I didn't have to give birth to her . . ." Her throat cracked and she looked down, reining in the wave of smothering sadness. Sometimes, like now, she missed her little girl so much it hurt. "When Michael introduced me to her, and explained how he came to have her, he told me biology has very little to do with being a family."

Jenifer didn't say anything more, only the sound of her cleaning up filled the dead space. When Jackie felt in control again, she lifted her head and saw Jenifer holding one of Silas' toy gliders. She turned the glider in her hand, all the other books and toys now stacked on the table in front of the lounge.

"Have you ever seen anyone love someone so completely as John loves Silas? And Silas loves John?" Jackie asked. Jenifer's answer was a silent shake of her head. "Try telling John that boy isn't his son."

Jenifer bounced the glider in her hand, the toy hovering for an unnatural few seconds over her palm. "It goes both ways."

"What goes both ways?"

"You can be a good parent without being blood, and you can be blood and be a damn lousy parent."

Before Jackie could say anything more, John came back into the room, walked straight to Jenifer, and dropped into a crouch, mirroring her so he looked her in the eyes, tension pinching his features. "Why didn't you say somethin'?" he asked.

"I'm fine."

"What's wrong?" Jackie asked, rising from her chair.

Jenifer sent John a scathing look when he started to speak and he shook his head, rising to stand again. He offered Jenifer his hand, and she took it, letting him help her balance as she rose.

"Nothing is wrong," she said firmly. She leaned over to set the toy glider on top of the stack of books. "I think I'm going to the exercise room." The look she gave John convinced Jackie she was definitely being left out of a silent conversation.

"Jackie, do you mind stayin' here with Silas?"

"Sure—"

"Stay here with your son, Ambassador," Jenifer interrupted, moving around John to head for the suite door. Her voice wasn't harsh, wasn't angry, just resigned. "I can deal with this myself."

John caught her arm. Jackie half expected Jenifer to swing around and lay him out, but she didn't, she just stopped and looked back at him.

"Like I told you before, I know you can. But you don't have to."

"What is going on?" Jackie demanded, pushing up from the table.

"The ambassador will fill you in," Jenifer said, pulling her arm free of his hold. She looked John square in the eyes, unwavering, but without any sharp edge. She spoke in a voice so soft Jackie almost didn't hear her, and her entire body gave a small jolt, as if speaking the word alone was a physical reaction. "Please. John."

He closed his eyes and clenched his jaw, turning his face toward Jackie before opening his eyes again. Jenifer was out the door of the suite before he blinked.

Jackie crossed her arms over her body, gripping her elbows as she walked toward John. He scrubbed his face with his hands and moaned against his palms.

"What's going on with her?" Jackie asked when he dropped his hands to his waist.

"I bloody well wished I knew," John mumbled, then huffed. "I'm sorry, Jackie. I'm just . . . everythin' is a bloody battle with her."

"You noticed that, huh?" she said with a smile, trying to lighten the mood.

He chuckled. "Yeah, I caught on to it early. I'm brilliant."

"Is she okay?"

"No' yet, no' fully." He sighed again. "But she will be. It's hard to explain, but Jenifer is learnin' to control her Talents and it's difficult."

Jackie raised her eyebrows. "I didn't know she was a Jedi, too."

John scowled. "Jedi . . ."

"Like Michael," she clarified. Holding out her hand, she wobbled it back and forth. "She uses the Force."

"Oh, right. I've heard Nick use that reference before. It's some Earth folklore."

Jackie smiled. "Somethin' like that, yeah. I didn't know she could."

He looked toward the door, frowning. "Neither did she until a few days ago. I suspected, but she denied it. This ship is designed to make it easier for an Areth to use their Talents, which would be fine for someone like Michael, for instance. But when you're suppressin', it's more like feedback."

"She going to be okay?"

John nodded. "I'm going to make sure of it."

*J*enifer didn't know when exactly she decided not to go to the exercise room, only that when she stepped off the elevator she was on the *Steppenschraff*'s main promenade. For the purpose of socializing it was still early in the evening and nearly all the seating in the promenade lounge was taken.

She contemplated briefly wandering out onto *Gateway*, but accepted she didn't know enough about the lay of the land and the variety of races she'd encounter to mingle without John. She'd learned early on it was one thing to ram headfirst into an unknown situation, it was another thing entirely to be an idiot.

The long tunic and leggings were a bit casual in comparison to some of the evening socializers, but she'd given up dressing for the occasion twenty years earlier. She didn't intend to socialize anyway. Exerting herself to the point of exhaustion wasn't the only way to relieve the slight pressure in her head. Relief by association worked fine, too. And the headache building behind her eyes wasn't the only reason she'd needed to get out of the suite. She needed to share a space not occupied by John for a little while, she needed to be able to think clearly without his nearness distracting her.

She also needed to stop thinking about how natural he looked with Silas. Until today, the concept of John being a father hadn't gone any further than the image of him putting Silas on a ship. She had been able to keep herself separate from it. Since John had dropped to his knees to embrace his son she hadn't been able to smother the ache in the center of her chest.

She wanted to be part of what she witnessed.

And the entire thought of wanting such a thing was crazy.

Impossible.

Would and could never happen.

Not for her.

Wasn't worth it, and Jackie Anderson was proof. Jackie was still a soldier, still someone Jenifer would fight side-by-side with, but she'd lost her edge. She'd given it up for middle of the night feedings, dirty backsides, and someone to call her Mama. She'd given it up for a man who didn't have the decency to consider her when he decided it was time to leave. Now, what did she have but a broken heart?

No, thank you.

Jenifer weaved through the various chairs and tables, not even attempting to decipher the variety of languages and dialects mingling as she passed, and found a single chair alone in a back corner. She no sooner sat when a blond haired, Human-looking man in the uniform of the service staff approached with a too-big smile. He had to be one of the Areth contingent, which she was glad for because she wouldn't have to figure out how to communicate.

"How are you tonight?" he asked, bowing slightly.

"Just great," she mumbled, but forced herself to attempt to look cordial. "I had a drink the other night, foamy white top layer, kinda blue green in the middle and clear purple at the bottom."

"Of course. Would you care for something to eat?"

"Sure, surprise me. Something I can eat with my fingers."

He bowed his head and smiled before walking away. Jenifer had finally grown accustomed to the subtle brush and nudge somewhere near the base of her skull whenever an Areth was nearby. She didn't pick up on them the same way she did John, feeling more exact sensations from him, but it was enough to make her aware.

From her seat she was able to see out the massive observation window she had originally viewed Earth through when they left orbit. Now she saw some of the other docking harnesses for other ships at *Gateway*, ships of varying size, shape, color and condition, and beyond the ships the stars. Not a single one looked even remotely familiar.

She wondered how many races across the galaxy were represented by the ships she saw, and how many ships she didn't see, how many other races she had no idea about. Here on the *Steppenschraff*, she realized she was filtered from the vastness of reality beyond. John had given her a taste today, but the immensity of potential wasn't lost on her. When she'd decided to follow John, she only saw the one goal: don't let him go to Aretu alone. She hadn't considered the larger picture: she was traveling across space to an alien planet.

The young man came back with her drink and a plate of something that immediately made her stomach wake up with the savory aroma.

Cylindrical finger foods wrapped in a crust of some kind, golden brown and crunchy, held a mixture of seasoned meats and soft cheeses. Or at least she assumed meats and cheeses. By what she could tell thus far most of the foods John had chosen for her had some kind of correlation with food on Earth. They ate meats, vegetables, fruit, cheeses, sauces, rice and grains, everything she'd find on Earth, just with a slightly different flare. A flare she found she liked.

"Thanks," she said, picking up the glass for her first sip. The drink—whatever it was called—started out with a sour, hot bite that warmed the back of her throat. As she moved through the layers it shifted to warm and fruity and finally to sweet and light.

"Be sure to advise me should you need anything further."

Jenifer waited until he walked away before she picked up one of the tubes. One thing she had to give John's culture; they knew how to cook. The meat inside was slightly sweet with a mild glaze, and the soft cheese was pungent and savory. A few small, dried red fruits filled the tube, mingling amazingly well with the meat and cheese.

"May I join you?"

Jenifer closed her eyes for a brief moment, preparing in her head her blow-off speech. Men were apparently the same everywhere. A woman sitting alone just had to be in desperate need of their company. She raised her head, ready to shove him off, but anything she had to stay stuck in her throat. He took her silence as apparent consent and pulled a nearby chair to her low table.

He could have been Elijah Kerrigan's brother.

Tall for a Human or Areth, maybe just over six feet, he was lanky and lean with brown hair the color of rich chocolate waved back from his forehead. He had blue eyes, so did the majority of Areth, or so it seemed, and sharp bone structure defined his cheeks and jaw with the same angular clarity she had found appealing in Elijah. He wasn't Eli's twin, but close enough to make her stumble.

"You're traveling with Ambassador Smith, aren't you?"

She regained her composure immediately; until she knew his intent, she wasn't about to show her hand. "Yes."

He smiled, deep dimples popping in his cheek. Another similarity he shared with her dead lover. "I'm sorry, I'm being incredibly rude." The accent was the one clear thing separating Eli from this alien stranger, a contrast to anyone on the North American continent, certain consonants harder or softer than she was accustomed and a prolonged rounding of the vowels. "My name is Devon."

"Jenifer," she answered.

He watched her mouth in a way that made her hairs tingle and her defenses slammed up hard. "I hope you can forgive my bold question, but am I correct in assuming you are Human?"

"Depends on why you need to know."

His blue eyes shifted up to meet hers. "I've never had the pleasure of meeting one of our distant relatives until this voyage, and I find the similarities between your race and mine fascinating. Intriguing." The weight he pressed on the last word, and the uncomfortable push—no, more like a mental grope—he sent out left no margin for confusion about what intrigued him. "I'm inclined to learn the differences."

"Good thing I'm not the only one on the ship." She made sure her tone brokered no confusion.

Devon leaned back and draped his arms along the horseshoe shaped arms of the chair, crossing his legs. "Perhaps you aren't different after all. I can feel your Talents buffering around you. They're raw, untrained. Is Ambassador Smith assisting you with harnessing your abilities?"

Jenifer's skin crawled, and if she weren't in a position where a low profile was an absolute must, she would have discovered by now if Areth had their larynx in the same place as Humans and how Devon liked his crushed.

"If you're concerned about my relationship with the ambassador, you might heed common sense and keep your thoughts to yourself." This being polite and behaved crap sucked.

Devon smiled, one eyebrow jerking up in acknowledgment. "Understood." He sighed and shifted his position in the chair, glancing toward the observation window. "I have a great deal of respect for John Smith. He's a decent fellow. I wouldn't want to encroach on an area I clearly don't belong."

The hair on the back of Jenifer's next stood up, and her breath hitched. A memory that might have otherwise been a casual thought flipped through her mind like a clear movie scene; Elijah sat beside her at a table in some back alley dive that had managed to survive the attacks. The food was lousy, but always hot. The liquor was always watered down, but it was warm and they had rooms in the back. Nothing classy, but clean.

"I met him in the ruins of Chicago," Elijah had said with a chuckle. *"Says his name is John Smith, but hell, who am I to question? I really respect him for everything he did for those people. He's a decent guy, Jenny."*

"Did I say something to upset you?"

Jenifer blinked and realized she was on her feet, Devon standing in front of her.

She veiled her reaction and looked down at the plate of food. "Enjoy a snack on me," she said, skirting the low table to make her way out of the lounge.

He called out her name, but she kept moving.

Names . . .

At the core of everything was a name. In his dying breath, Elijah had confessed to her he knew her name, and knew what happened in Savannah. Cold dread hit her gut like a ball of ice, making her feel sick.

Twenty years and she hadn't so much as breathed the name. She would never know how Elijah found out, would never know how long he knew, and would never understand how he went on like nothing had changed. How could nothing have changed when he found out the truth? Right now, she needed to know if Elijah had confided in a man he respected . . . especially if he thought the chances their paths ever crossing were nearly unfathomable.

Jenifer walked confidently into the lift, but as soon as the doors closed, she braced her hands on the walls and slumped.

Two words rolled through her head, the thought incomplete and yet encompassing in one plea everything she wanted to deny.

Please, John . . .

CHAPTER TWENTY-NINE

*T*he woman who marched into the suite an hour after she left was far removed from the Jenifer he had grown to know in the last few weeks. She might not be wearing the military issue uniform or have a weapon on her thigh, but the cold, untouchable soldier had returned. Her expression bordered between anger and no emotion at all. Her gaze was cold when she scanned the room and settled on him as he stood from the lounge.

She was a blank wall. He felt absolutely nothing from her.

A lead ball hit his gut.

"You knew Elijah Kerrigan," she stated. It wasn't a question, and she was in no way asking for confirmation.

And probably not justification.

"Yes."

Jenifer planted her hands on her hips, more aggressive than defensive. "At least you have the good sense not to deny it."

"Why would I deny his friendship?" he asked, wishing he had a clue what fine line he was about to walk. "He was a good man."

"I don't need to be told he was a good man," she practically growled.

"No, I don't suppose you do." John took a step toward her. "His death was—"

"Pointless?" she cut off. "Save me the platitudes, Ambassador."

"What is it you need me to say, Jenifer?" Before she could say anything, he kept going. "Yes, I knew Eli Kerrigan. I considered him a friend. No, I had no idea you were the Jenny he spoke of when I met you. I didn't know the connection until we were in Florida and Jace told me."

Her eyes widened slightly and he caught the almost imperceptible tension ratchet up in her entire stance. She practically hummed she was pulled so tight. "You should have told me."

"Perhaps, but when exactly in the last several days do you think I might have brought it up? Jenifer, when I left Alexandria I wasn't sure I'd ever see you again and frankly, as I was leavin' mentionin' your former lover wasn't exactly foremost in my mind." By the time he was done, even he heard the edge that had crept into his tone.

Walking on paper shells was getting old.

"And since then?"

John spread his arms out away from his body, palms toward her. "Again, I'll ask . . . when would I have slipped into casual conversation?"

"You could have tried."

John scrubbed his face with his palm. "Yes, you are right. You are absolutely right. I should have, and I won't continue to make excuses. Regardless, I should have told you. And so as to no' exacerbate the situation, what else would you like to know?"

"You said you didn't know I was the Jenny he talked about."

John nodded. "He always referred to you as Jenny, and even if he had called you Jenifer, I doubt I would have thought it was you. Jenifer is almost as common a name here as John."

She crossed her arms over her body, shifting her weight to lean slightly away from him. *From the offensive to the defensive.* "What did he say?"

John shook his head and paced away, turning back again before he spoke, holding out a hand in a plea. "Are you really askin' me what your lover told me about you? Jenifer, don't you think it's bad enough I know how he felt about you and feel practically the same thin's myself?"

Her body jerked, a small action, almost imperceptible, but a definite visceral reaction to his confession. Whether good or bad, he didn't know. The words had been out of his mouth before he could deny himself speaking them.

"I need to know."

Her voice indicated a plea or a woman teetering on the edge of rage, he wasn't sure. She'd slammed up her walls and wouldn't let him through. John took a step toward her, lowering his hand. He took a deep breath before trying to navigate what could be a verbal minefield.

"Jenifer, *su'ista*, you need to let go. You're goin' to undo all the good we've done in the last week. Please."

The shake of her head was little more than a jerk. "Tell me."

John took a sideways step and dropped into one of the chairs, shoving his fingers through his hair. "Fine. He talked about you with . . ." He had to pause, taking a deep breath as the memories of Elijah Kerrigan rolled back to him. He could smell the stench of burned out buildings and the bonfire burning, felt the warmth on his face and the cold against his back. He remembered the way the firelight made the sharp angles of Eli's face seem sharper, made the shine in his eyes brighter. " . . .with admiration as much as adoration." John's throat tightened as he saw Jenifer through the words of Eli. "He told me you amazed him, and he couldn't figure out how such a beautiful, strong, independent woman came to be with him."

She made a small sound, a tiny whimper choked behind her staunch resolve. John raised his head and looked at her, and his heart nearly broke. She still stood firm and defensive, her features set, her lips a tight, straight line . . . with tears shining in her eyes. She didn't look away. Didn't blink.

"He loved you. Very much." John smiled, hoping she would see in his eyes the truth of his words. "Once I knew you were his Jenny, it all made sense because you *are* everythin' he said. I understand how he loved you so much."

She started shaking her head as soon as John began to speak, and by the time he finished her hair was falling over her eyes. John stood and she took a step back.

"*Su'ista*, you want to hear somethin' from me but I don't know what it is. You need to help me understand."

Her head snapped back and wide, shining eyes studied him. "What does that mean? You've called me it before, what does it mean?"

He blinked, hanging on to the sharp turn in the conversation. "It's Zibalan. Their language is beautiful. In a single word they can encompass an entire sentence of meanin' in any other tongue." He took another step toward her. "*Su'ista* means beautiful soul and precious treasure. I suppose it's like . . . sweetheart . . . but it means much more."

She stared so long he wondered when she would blink, and when she did, a single tear pressed free from her eye, rolling down her cheek. She didn't move to wipe it away, and John had to fight the urge to brush her skin with his fingertips and dry the damp line.

"He didn't tell you . . ." she said softly, her voice raw and rough.

He felt the walls slip, and the first brief brush of her inner turmoil gave him the enlightenment he needed. A volatile mixture of panic and relief stirred with intense sorrow and insecurity. She wasn't sure she could believe him, and for a moment, he considered lying to her. It was what her head wanted to hear, but someday her heart could hate him if he wasn't honest with her.

John finally did what he'd wanted to do since she'd come through the door. He raised his hands and gently laid his palms against her flushed, damp cheeks. With a slight touch to her chin he urged her to look up and into his eyes. His own throat restricted tight, and he hoped he could say the words without breaking.

"He knew what happened to you." Her entire body tensed and she tried to step back, but stopped when he didn't lower his hands. He wasn't forcing her to stay, but he hoped she felt in his touch how much he didn't want her to leave. "No, he didn't tell me, only he had learned somethin' so devastatin' it broke his heart. He said he wouldn't speak of it to anyone, ever, and hoped someday you would trust him enough to tell him yourself." John stroked her cheek with this thumb, her tears slicking the contact. "If you wondered if it mattered to him, yes, it did. But *only* because he wanted vengeance for you. Just as any man would for the woman he loved."

Her entire body shook with tiny tremors, everything inside her wound so tight he felt it ready to lash out and strike at the slightest provocation. John took his hands from her cheeks and wrapped his arms around her, drawing her against him. She never unfolded her arms. John pressed a long kiss to her temple and closed his eyes, drawing in a long breath.

She touched her forehead to his shoulder and let him hold her, though not giving any more to the embrace than her compliance. In the grand scheme of things, John saw even that small consolation as a gain.

"Would it matter to you?" she asked in a small voice he almost didn't hear.

"*You* matter to me, Jenifer. Perhaps someday you'll share with me whatever it is you keep locked so deep inside, maybe you never will. Whether you do, or don't, you will always matter to me."

She unfolded her arms from the tight space between them and wrapped them around his sides, warm palms pressed to his back. John's heart pounded, swelling in his chest. The monumental shift in the moment wasn't lost on him, and he wanted to cheer. But he relished instead the moment Jenifer decided to be in his arms. She turned her head and rested her cheek over his heart, her face away from him, and sniffed softly.

John bowed his head, resting his cheek against her hair, and prayed this might finally be their first step.

She hadn't had Bahsco Liquid Fire in nearly sixty years, well before the Sorracchi elite decided to seek revenge on their enemies by subjugating their descendants. The foreign tongue and throat of her stolen Human body burned when she swallowed, and she reveled in the immediate flush of intense heat through her limbs.

The potent drink had reacted differently with her last body, perhaps not as intensely, and she welcomed the slam to her system in this body.

A Human slid onto the stool beside her, his gaze darting around the sub-level establishment. "I'm glad I found you. I just found out something really big."

She let her façade slide into place and turned to him with abject interest feigned in her eyes. Neither he nor any of his pathetic rebellion groups knew her true identity, and she never intended to let them think anything other than she was a Human comrade in arms working for the same goal. She found it ironic the band of Humans who had managed to send her brethren running and hiding had been called a rebellion group, and now their downfall would be an even smaller mass of stupid Humans they had deemed rebels as well.

GAIL R. DELANEY

"Tell me, Isaac."

"A Defense Alliance ship named the *Steppenschraff* docked here several hours ago. You'll never guess who was on it."

"Just tell me." She tried to keep the irritation from her voice, but even simple conversations with these simple-minded idiots always wore on her patience. She forced a smile. "Please."

Isaac smirked, an expression she had learned to recognize as sexual interest. She'd never lower herself to be defiled in such a way again, but if it worked to her advantage, she would play along. She leaned toward him, meeting his eyes. The slight shift in position gave him a better view of her substantial cleavage. His attention shifted down and he licked his lips.

"Ambassador John Smith," he said in a husky whisper. Tiny bumps broke out over her pale skin, an odd sensation she'd only ever experienced within this species. "And some woman listed as his assistant." He looked around then scooted closer to her so his legs touched hers. She managed to suppress the shudder of disgust. "I heard a porter say they were moving everything for his kid and the woman sent along to babysit him from the *Constellation* to the *Steppenschraff*. They're all continuing on the Defense Alliance ship to Aretu."

She leaned back and motioned for the big Torrilac behind the bar to bring her another drink. "Then I suggest we do the same."

"Do you think we should change the plan?"

The Torrilac set down another small glass of liquid fire. She waited until he walked away. There were far too many weak-minded races in this part of the galaxy sympathetic to the Areth, it would do no good for any of them to overhear their plans. This would be the first of many blows to destroy the fragile alliance building between the Humans and the Defense Alliance. If they destroyed it now, the Earth could still be the territory of the Sorracchi.

"Only slightly. Considering the ambassador's relationship to the Aretu queen I am willing to assume there will be some event in honor of his glorious return." This time she didn't try to hide her disgust, knowing Isaac would accept it as enthusiasm for his cause. "If a Human force of power is held responsible for the assassination of not only the Areth ambassador and the Human child he's forced into his servitude, but the queen of the Areth as well, then I have no doubt the Areth will cut all ties

278

with Earth. When the Areth leave, the rest of the alliance will follow suit."

"How do you know so much about these aliens?" Isaac asked, a slight hint of suspicion pinching his eyes.

She leaned toward him again and laid her hand on his leg, purposefully brushing firmly against the bulge in his pants—an indication her sexual ploy had succeeded. He made a groaning sound and gripped her hand, holding it against him. It was all she could do not to snarl and yank her hand free.

"You follow my lead because I have made it my business to understand our enemy, Isaac. Don't begin to doubt me now. We have far too much to accomplish."

"When this is done, I say we celebrate." His voice was deep and rough and he moved against her hand.

"Absolutely."

When this was done, she would celebrate. If all went as planned, Isaac would be dead along with John Smith.

"*P*apa?"

Jenifer jerked her head up from her pillow and squinted toward the bedroom doorway, where she saw Silas standing, rubbing his eyes. She looked over her shoulder at John, even though she knew he was asleep. She'd been lying beside him for two hours listening to his steady breathing. Moving as carefully and quickly as possible, Jenifer slid back the blankets and swung her feet to the floor.

"Your papa is sleeping, Silas," she said in a whisper, crossing to the little boy. "Are you okay?"

He nodded but she heard his slight hitched sob. She knelt on the floor in front of him so she could see his face in the dim light cast by the holographic wall in the sitting room. His full lips were turned down in a frown and streaks of tears glistened on his chubby cheeks. Jenifer smoothed her hand over his thick, coarse curls.

"What's wrong, Silas?" she said softly.

"I had a dream about when my mama was taken away," he said in a rough little voice, sucking in his lower lip on a sob.

Jenifer swept him into her arms and stood up. His arms wrapped around her neck and he pressed his damp face into her throat, his legs wrapping around her body. She carried him down the short hall to the bedroom on the left, her heart clenching when she saw how torn apart the bed was, most of the blankets pushed to the foot of the bed and onto the floor. She turned the lights on, but only low enough to see him better. Silas sniffed loudly and she rubbed his back, sitting on the edge of the bed so he could be in her lap.

"Will you tell me about your mama?" Jenifer asked, hoping to divert his memories from the sad to the happy. "I bet she was a wonderful mama."

He nodded and sat back, his legs still wrapped around her hips, and wiped his cheeks with the back of his hands. "She made me waffles on Sunday," he said with a soft choke. "And she made really good hot chocolate."

Jenifer smiled, stroking her thumb across his cheek. "I love hot chocolate."

His frown turned up into a small, hesitant smile and a tiny spark of mischief sparkled in his dark eyes. "Papa said you like everything."

Jenifer dropped her jaw and gasped. "Your papa is making trouble."

Silas chuckled, a low belly laugh but just as quickly, he was serious again. "Papa is an important man. Miss Jackie told me."

"Yes, he is," Jenifer said with a nod. She finished drying his cheeks with her fingers.

"Miss Jackie said there are mean people who don't like him, and that's why he sent me away." His breath hitched. "Cuz he didn't want me to get hurt."

She hummed her affirmation.

"Did somebody try to hurt Papa again?"

Jenifer debated for half a second about lying to the boy. Children shouldn't have to face the horrors they had in the last few years. But, he was the son of an ambassador, and this wouldn't be the last time John's life would be threatened. It was better he understood than not.

"Yes," she finally answered. "But, your papa is just fine. I won't let anything happen to him."

Silas tipped his head. "Cuz you love him like he loves me?"

An unfamiliar, disconcerting sensation vibrated up Jenifer's spine and made her skin tingle. She smiled and looked the boy in the eyes. "Silas, nobody could love anybody the way your papa loves you. But, I promise you—I *promise* you—I will do my very best to make sure no one takes your papa away from you. Is that what you're afraid of? That someone will take your papa the way they took your mama?"

He nodded, his lip pouting again with new tears in his eyes. Silas fell against her, his face against her shoulder. Jenifer hugged him tight and stroked his back, shushing softly in his ear. Then his tiny voice grabbed hold of her heart, a heart she'd forced to be cold and untouchable for years, and squeezed tight.

"I love you, Miss Jenifer."

She kissed his cheek and held tight until she felt the steadying of his breathing beneath the strokes of her hand. Slow breathing turned into a funny snore, and she eased him back into the bed, tucking the blankets back around him. The lights dimmed as she left the room and she made her way back to the large bedroom she'd shared with John since they came aboard.

John was on his back, his arms spread away from him with his bare chest exposed, the blankets covering him to mid-stomach. His face was turned toward her side of the bed, his features relaxed. Instead of sliding under the blankets again, Jenifer sat on the bed facing the wall, her arms wrapped around her bent legs, to watch him sleep.

He had taken away from her everything she thought she was. He might not have meant to, but he'd effectively ripped the ground out from beneath her and left her floundering for purchase. Indecision hadn't been a part of her being for two decades, and while in some part she wasn't indecisive about what she wanted, it was such a left turn from who she was it felt like indecision on a deeper level.

She wanted this.

All of this.

Clarity . . . John had told her she had gained clarity.

With the curse of clarity, Jenifer looked back on the last several years. She wanted to put the blame solely on John, but now she accepted Elijah Kerrigan had had a hand in changing her, even if she hadn't seen it at the time.

"Don't you want more, Jenny?"

He'd asked her more than once. And every time she had answered him with derision. No, and if he wanted to keep sharing her bed he'd live with it.

He had deserved better.

She understood now because she wanted more, just like he did back then.

She felt the tug of sleep again, so she pulled back the blankets and tucked into the warm bed, facing John. She fell asleep listening to the sound of his breathing.

CHAPTER THIRTY

Earth Time: 13 February, 2054, Friday
Derelict Sorracchi Cruiser Abaddon
Near Proxima Centauri
Approximately 4.2 Light Years from Earth

*M*ichael had thought most of the memories from his imprisonment a year before were lost, too broken to be clear. He had flashes on occasion, the stale smell of the air, the cold of the slab he slept on, the bright lights in Kathleen's torture chamber. But, stepping aboard the *Abaddon* turned on every vivid memory like throwing on a switch. He remembered the scrape of metal against his feet as he was dragged through the low-ceiling hallways, the smell of his own body after days of torture, the taste of vomit and blood after being sick again and again, and the claw of hunger in his gut.

This ship was constructed much like the ship Kathleen had kept him on, designed for war as well as the sadistic practice the Sorracchi called science. Laboratories and storage facilities filled three decks, the lowest being one deck above the cells where their test subjects, prisoners like him, would have been held.

They hit the holding cells first, moving parallel to the docking bay they'd accessed for landing. The small scout ship was large enough to carry Victor's crew, Michael, a small military contingent, and the pilot staff, but small enough to land inside the docking bay without any issue. From there Victor's team moved as a unit, deciding not to split up until a thorough search of the *Abaddon* could be completed and the Firebirds could report back all was clear. One Firebird remained with them while the others dispersed.

The ship had held its integrity, and they had tested the air before docking. It was breathable, but not for long, so each of them wore environmental suits and carried O_2 cyclers on their backs. If they needed to stay for any longer than a few hours, the mechanics would find a way to draw some power and give them basic life support.

Michael hoped they didn't stay long. The plan was to determine whether the ship was salvageable, or even worth salvaging, and if so a ship with towing capacity would be dispatched to pull the hulking mass back to Earth. Such a trip would take weeks because they wouldn't be able to move with any kind of speed, let alone jump.

The ship had been floating derelict for at least a year, so there was no hope of finding life, but the Sorracchi could have sabotaged the ship before their hasty retreat. A masochistic need drew Michael into the cell area. It was dark and cold, the hand torches they carried barely chasing away the heavy shadows, as if they were living things unwilling to hide from prying eyes.

"You don't need to come down here, Michael," Victor said, stepping beside Michael to lay a firm hand on his shoulder. His voice was muffled by the environmental suit, but amplified by the external speaker system, a strange combination of sound "There's nothing to find."

"I think I do," Michael answered, stepping down the dark corridor.

Some of the cells had solid doors with only small slots at eye level to allow guards to look inside, the kind of cell he had been held in. Others had bars so the entire cell was exposed. Michael clenched his jaw and curled his hand around the cold bars, sending a silent prayer for the poor soul left to die alone in the cell. His decayed remains, the process slowed by the cold, curled into a tight ball on the floor probably in a desperate attempt at staying warm.

Many of the cells had been occupied when the Sorracchi retreated, their prisoners forgotten and considered disposable.

They moved up a level using the access tubes and ladders connecting the decks. Most of the computers were destroyed, smashed or burned by weapon fire. The Sorracchi had made a meager attempt at hiding their perversion by destroying their databases.

"We can salvage some of these," Trina announced after examining one console with slightly less damage than the others. "It would take a while though, maybe days."

"We can disassemble the equipment when we haul this back to Earth," Victor told her. "Keep track of decks and rooms you want focused on."

Trina nodded and moved on to continue her exploration.

The short-range radio wired through all their helmets crackled slightly in Michael's ear before he heard the voice of Sergeant Colburn. "Sir, we've tracked down the low level power draw we picked up when we docked. I think you need to see this."

"Where are you?" Victor asked, his voice feeding through the radio as well.

"Two decks above you. It's a hell of a thing, sir."

The line crackled, indicating the wideband communication had closed and Victor waved everyone toward the door. "Come on. Let's go see what the sergeant found."

Michael's hip and thigh throbbed painfully by the time they'd climbed the ladders the two decks up, and wished for his cane to lean on. He hated the weakness, but had accepted on his search for clarity that his broken body was as much a part of who he had become as anything else. Victor climbed the ladder above him, and offered a gloved hand as soon as Michael cleared the tube, helping him onto flat floor again.

"Thank you," Michael said tightly, limping toward the wall to lean on it for a few minutes rest.

"We'll hold here for a minute," Victor said to the team and many helmeted heads nodded. It was difficult to determine who was who unless they faced him and he could see their faces through the helmet visor.

Katrina was easy to spot simply by her diminutive stature in comparison to the others, and she hurried down the hall toward them, a bent piece of piping in her hands. She approached Michael, holding it out.

"It's not perfect, but it might help . . . sir," she said softly, her voice barely projecting through the suit.

Michael offered a smile, not even sure she could see it, but nodded and took the pipe. It was a little taller than his shillelagh, but the curve of the pipe gave him a place to grip. "Thank you, Katrina."

"Are you ready?" Victor asked.

Michael nodded, clenching his jaw against the jab of pain when he took his first step. The light atmosphere helped some, but the climb up the ladder would stay with him for days. They moved down the hall and as they rounded a corner, Sergeant Colburn stepped out from one of the side chambers.

"In here, sir."

A soft glow of light created a crescent glow on the floor outside the room, indicating there was definitely some type of power pull, even if small. Victor and Michael led the way except for the one Firebird with them, the rest of the team coming up behind. Michael couldn't shake the sense of evil lurking in every shadow. It made the air heavy and made his senses practically spark.

"Damn," the Firebird leading the way cursed as he entered the room, making Michael quicken his step.

He and Victor entered the room side by side, and both stopped at the same time. Michael's gut clenched.

"Dear God," he murmured.

Six pods sat in a half circle, facing inward to each other in a horseshoe, sitting at acute angles to the floor. Two of them were dark, their once suspended inhabitants pressed against the glass in horrid, nightmarish screams, frozen forever as they must have tried to escape before their oxygen ran out. The sealed chambers had slowed decomposition, leaving them looking gaunt and gray, withered lips curled back from open jaws and hollow eyes staring out into nothing. One had been a woman, with long blond hair hanging in stringy clumps from a shrunken scalp, her forehead pressed to the glass, bowed as if in prayer.

The other four pods still had power, a slight white-blue glow circling the observation windows. Dials and screens on the front of pods gave biological readings on each occupant. As Michael approached one, he noted there was also a readout for brain activity. Each of them showed only low-level activity, even deeper than a deep sleep. More like a coma state.

The first pod he approached with Victor held a man Michael would put in his late thirties. He was muscular, though possibly slightly underweight probably due to lack of complete nutrition in his suspended state. Based on estimations on the height of the pod and the space inside, he'd place the man under six feet but still a sizeable man. His hair was dark, as was the beard growth covering his jaw and cheeks. Only having a conceptual understanding of the science of cryogenics, he figured this man had been kept in this state for years, possibly a decade or more based on his hair and beard growth. The act of suspension didn't halt aging, but did slow down the process by vast degrees.

Victor scrubbed away some of the ice crystals coating a plate beneath the observation window. The writing was Sorracchi, a combination of angled lines, swirls and dots once mistaken to be Areth before the truth had been revealed.

"Human Male," Victor read then cursed under his breath. "Based on the Sorracchi date inscribed here, if it's right, this unlucky bastard has been in this state since 2011. Almost forty-five years."

"That would have been three years after the Sorracchi came," Michael said. "There's no name provided?"

Victor shook his head. "According to these readings, he's dying. Granted, it would still take months, but his body isn't surviving under these conditions. Perhaps if the pods had been at full power, but I doubt the Sorracchi even realized they'd left these things with any power at all."

"Check the others."

They turned toward the other three pods, all side-by-side on the other side of the half-circle. Katrina stood in front of one, her head tipped back to try to see in the windows. She was too short to see directly in like Michael or Victor. She'd already rubbed away the ice and revealed the identification plates.

"I'm not so good with translating their dates," she said when they approached. "But, the plates call them the Triad. All three of them."

"Triadic, actually," Victor corrected. "But very good, Trina."

"Thank you, sir." Michael could almost hear the blush in her voice.

Victor pointed at each pod, moving left to right. "They're designated Alpha, Omega, and Beta, and according to the dates they've been in these things for about seven years."

Michael moved closer and stared into the first pod. The man inside was considerably younger than the man in the first pod, probably no older than his early twenties. Light brown hair spiked away from his scalp, having grown out slightly from a very short, almost military type cut. He was designated Alpha. The next man was his twin with the exception of a scar on his upper lip, cut at an angle from below his left nostril to almost the center of his upper lip, creating a crease. He was Omega. The third was a repeat of the first two, which explained part of the Triadic description. He was Beta.

"Alpha, Beta, and Omega," Victor repeated. "The leader, the follower, and the balance."

Michael looked to his friend. "Do you remember something about them?"

He could only make out some of Victor's profile through the helmet, but he recognized the pinched look around Victor's eyes. "Not directly, but I had heard them referenced from time to time. They were a pet project of one of the military commanders, but Kathleen was involved in part of the process. She assisted in building their DNA code." He looked to Michael. "They were in New Mexico for a short time perhaps fifteen years ago. They would have been about your age then if the dates on the pods are accurate."

Michael looked at the one closest to him, Omega. There was a slight familiarity in the angle of the jaw, and perhaps the ridge of the brow, but he would have known the three as younger men, less mature. He couldn't be sure.

"It doesn't give them a race designation. Could they be husks?" Agatha Corbin asked, coming up behind them.

Victor shook his head. "I doubt it. Their brain activity is low, but singular. No indication of a second consciousness. I doubt the Sorracchi would suspend one of their own minds like this, let alone three. Perhaps we'll find some record of them in the computers."

"They're so young," Katrina said in a quiet voice.

"Looks can be deceiving," Victor said with a heavy voice. "I'm willing to bet these three are creations of the Sorracchi in some capacity. And if that's the case, they could be almost anything."

"I don't think we should wait to haul the ship back to Earth to deal with these men," Doctor Corbin said, leaning forward to read the biological readings on the pods. "Victor is right, they're dying. These pods aren't sustaining life properly, and we have no idea how much power they can draw from the ship's reserves before they shut down completely."

"And they face the fate of their two friends." Karl Bauer shuddered. "Not a good way to go."

"Carmen and Njogu, can you two work on determining if we can get these pods off the ship and into ours to get them back to Earth? Maybe use some of the portable power cells we brought. At this point, I say we head back and get these four taken care of. We can have the ship hauled back for everything else."

The two engineers nodded and left the chamber, Michael assumed to return to the scout ship for the power cells and tools. Trina turned away from the pods, her eyes visibly wide.

"I'm going to see if I can access any data on these computers that might help."

Victor gave out more commands, and his efficient team immediately went to work. The respect they all held for him was apparent, and Michael felt pride for his friend considering where he had been just two years before. He had been a broken man, seeking purpose and denying himself love. Now, he was a leader, a husband, and a new man.

Michael envied him on some levels.

He went back to the solitary man with no name and studied him through the window. He was Human, if the plaque was true to fact. Who was he and why had the Sorracchi taken him in a time when they still so carefully hid their agenda? What about him would inspire them to hide him away for forty years and not kill him outright?

Perhaps when he woke up, he could tell them.

"*H*ow long do you think you can keep this up?"

Connor looked up from the notes and files spread out on the table in front of him. He'd resorted to printed files and records just to make it easier to categorize and either eliminate or set aside for further consideration. The resulting stacks of papers, folders and handwritten notes probably made no sense to anyone else, but he knew what everything meant. He offered a tired smile to Mel, and enjoyed the warmth spreading through him from the center of his chest when she sat beside him.

She didn't touch him other than where her knees touched his thigh when she scooted to the edge of her seat and leaned forward to see what he worked on. "You're going to wear yourself out if you keep going. How productive do you think you'll be if you can't keep your eyes open?"

"The president wants answers. Or, at least, ideas."

"Do you have any? Ideas, that is."

Connor shook his head and rubbed his fingertips across his brow. It was nearly 2400 hours and he'd been going over the files since after the evening meal. He'd been in his chair for seven hours, coming off a long day of meetings with Nick and overseeing some buildings being cleaned out in preparation for making them habitable for refugees. He'd been up before o'dark hundred and such had been his days for the last week; alternating between his leadership commitments, tasks assigned to him and his people, and playing detective for Nick.

He was running just about on empty and didn't have much to show for it.

"Nothing is anything more than circumstantial evidence or presumption. I don't even want to keep my scope to just women who would have access to the leaked information, because voices can be disguised. I mean, given the criteria we've got, just about anyone could be suspect." He motioned toward her. "Even you, Mel. High in the Firebird chain of command, access to information including the day John and Jenifer left Alexandria, you're a woman—"

"I was beginning to wonder if you remembered that detail."

Connor chuckled. "Trust me, that detail is one I cannot forget."

The dining hall was empty, but was also public and open to any Firebird who wanted to stroll in, so as much as Connor wished he could lean just a few inches to the side and kiss Mel like he hadn't been able to in days, he forced himself to refrain. She looked over his arm at the file he'd been reviewing. Connor sucked in a tight breath, his body coiling when her hand slid over his upper thigh, hidden by the tabletop. She looked at him from the corner of her eye, a tiny smirk curving her lips.

"You're playing with fire, soldier," he said low.

"Maybe I'm looking to get burned."

Connor scanned the room, noting only two men seated at the far end of the room slumped over a late-night meal. Mercado and Lopez had been assigned the late security run at the Castleton building, and would have been relieved an hour before. Just enough time to come back to the Nest and grab some grub before racking up for a few hours.

He turned back to her and smiled. "You go. I'll . . ." He grinned wider. " . . .clean up here and then I'm heading to bed."

One elegant eyebrow arched and her lips pursed slightly. "Will do."

Her hand slid higher, brushing against the reason he needed a few minutes before he could get up from the table, and she made a small purring sound in her throat. The sound was like fuel on a fire. She'd just added another five minutes before he'd be able to stand. Melanie pushed back her chair and stood, the sexy, flirty grin gone. She was good. She was very good.

As soon as she left the room, Connor worked on restacking and reorganizing his notes and files. He'd have to present Nick with something soon, but right now all he had was smoke and no fire. By the time he was done organizing, it was safe again to stand and he headed back to his room.

And Mel Briggs waiting for him in his bed.

CHAPTER THIRTY-ONE

"*A*ubrianna thinks she's the boss because her mom is the queen," Silas told Jenifer around the mouthful of breakfast tucked in his cheek. "Sometimes she gets really bossy, but I still like it there. Nobody shoots anybody and there's always food, and it's never cold—"

"It gets cold," John interjected. "You've just never been there durin' the winter. Please chew your food and swallow before talkin'."

John caught the tiny tip of Jenifer's smile even though she kept her face turned down to hide it. Silas had been talking non-stop since they all woke that morning, and Jenifer had become his target because Jackie had apparently already heard all his stories. He had a new, captive audience.

"Yes, Papa," Silas said and took a long drink of his milk. He started to wipe his lip with his sleeve but John shot him a glance and shook his head. Silas picked up his napkin and wiped his face. "Do you know what green smells like, Miss Jenifer?"

She raised her head and turned her focus on Silas. "I think so. Like when someone cuts the grass or when you're in the middle of the forest all by yourself."

Silas nodded. "That's what the whole *planet* smells like. Nothing is burnt up and you can walk right out into Papa's field and pick an apple. Well, it's kind of like an apple but not completely. They don't call them apples, but Papa said if I called it an apple he'd know what I was talking about so I can call it an apple. You can pick one right off the tree and bite right into it."

Jenifer smiled, a pure and genuine smile sparked in her eyes. "That sounds wonderful. It's been a long time since I ate an apple right off a tree."

"I'll pick one for you, Miss Jenifer. I'll climb all the way to the top and get the good ones. You too, Miss Jackie."

Jackie smiled too, but her expression was strained and John noted once again she had eaten very little of the morning meal. She caught him watching her and took a bite of fruit. John let it go for now, but intended to ask her how far along in her pregnancy she was. It wasn't long, since she still hid it well, but at just the right angle he saw the physical signs of the baby she carried. He knew Human pregnancies were very similar to Areth pregnancies, varying only by a few weeks, which meant she was early in when Michael left. And if he knew Michael at all, the man didn't know.

"Do you know how to ride a horse, Miss Jenifer?"

Jenifer dropped her fork and it clattered loudly against her plate, drawing the attention of several other diners. Everyone looked away right away and she picked it up again. "It's been a very long time since I rode."

"Papa has these *huge* horses. They're so big more than one person can ride them at a time, and Papa said I could have a baby horse all my own someday. I already told Miss Jackie all about it."

"That's wonderful."

Silas barely paused to eat, and John barely controlled his chuckle. Silas had fixated on Jenifer nearly from day one, and each time he found the two of them deep in conversation or playing together on the floor, something warm grew larger in his chest. Jenifer was a different woman with his son. She had changed since the first night they'd arrived and she'd let him hold her. She wasn't prickles and barbs, didn't push to argue rather than just talk, but she didn't talk much at all. At least not to him.

It wasn't antagonistic. He didn't sense any anger from her. But she had withdrawn and become distant in a way he hadn't experienced with her before.

Except with Silas.

The ship announcement system chimed and the captain announced they were approaching Aretu, with an anticipated entrance to the atmosphere in five minutes. Silas' face lit up and he bounced in his seat.

"Do you wanna see the planet, Miss Jenifer?" he asked, already out of his seat.

She glanced John's way and he nodded. He knew she wasn't one to ask for anyone's permission or approval, but in regards to Silas, she hadn't done anything or gone anywhere with him where John didn't say okay first. The ironic thing was if there were anyone anywhere he would trust his son with, it would be Jackie Anderson and Jenifer. John nodded and she took the hand Silas offered, letting him lead her away from the table. Silas stopped short and turned back.

"Do you wanna come too, Miss Jackie?"

Jackie smiled and shook her head. "No, you go ahead."

He grinned wide, his slightly crooked teeth a slash of happiness across his dark features. Silas led Jenifer through the crowd toward the massive observation window currently revealing black space and the shine of stars. They had left the jump tunnel an hour before to approach the planet at travel speed.

"Silas really likes her," Jackie said, leaning back with her hands in her lap. "I guess I'm not surprised. If there were ever a soft spot in her hard armor, it was kids. It's how I got her to come help you."

"I don't understand."

"After the attack on you outside the embassy, there was a little girl you made them take with Silas to the hospital. Do you remember?"

"Of course."

She nodded. "I showed her the video of the attack, and just like I knew she would, she picked out the woman assassin *before* she attacked. But, I let her watch until the camera showed you saving the little girl."

"You manipulated her." The idea stuck in his throat and he set down his fork.

Jackie shrugged. "Maybe. Or, I showed her the kind of man she'd be protecting."

John looked across the lounge to where Silas had led Jenifer. The two of them knelt on the floor to peek over the bottom edge of the window and Silas pointed, talking animatedly to Jenifer. Her smile was wide and genuine, and a warm spot in his chest stirred more. She was so beautiful when she smiled.

"I've heard the mornin' illness only lasts the first few months."

Jackie snapped her attention to him, her dark eyes wide.

"Michael doesn't know about the baby, does he?" he asked, not looking away from Jenifer and his son.

Jackie cleared her throat. "He didn't stick around long enough to find out. How did you know?"

He looked to her then and offered a small smile. "I'm eighty-six years old, Jackie. I've seen a few pregnant women in my time."

Her olive-toned skin glowed with a deep blush and she fidgeted with the edge of the cloth covering the table. "I suppose you think I'm wrong for leaving Earth knowing I was pregnant."

"Only in that I worry for your health, no' for your reason for leavin'," he said with a single-shoulder shrug. "I would imagine you've been hurtin' for weeks."

Jackie swallowed hard and looked away, her eyes glistening. "Jenifer is right. She told me I gave up who I was to be with Michael and Nicole, but not because he made me. I wanted to. I've been wondering if I did the right thing."

John reached for her hand, tugging it away from toying with the cloth, and squeezed gently until she looked back to him. "I've told you what I know about Michael's choices, and I'm no' about to defend him. I believe what he did was wrong, and so does he, Jackie."

She nodded, her lips pressed together.

*A*s soon as they broke through the atmosphere and white, fluffy clouds obscured the observation windows like bundles of candy wool, Jenifer and Silas turned and sat on the floor with their backs to the wall.

"You were right, Silas," she said, smiling at him. "It did look a lot like Earth. The oceans are so blue."

He nodded. "I told you. You're gonna like Artoo, Miss Jenifer."

"I think you're right." Jenifer rolled forward and gained her feet, offering the little boy her hand.

There was something unexplainably calming to her to hold a child's hand, but Silas more than most. He was such a happy child, and she knew it was absolutely and without question because of John. Jackie was right. In every way that mattered, Silas was John Smith's child.

She looked across the lounge as they neared the table. John had stood and Jackie was returning from down the hall, probably after stepping away for a few minutes. He smiled when their gazes connected, and for the sake of Silas, she smiled, too.

For the first time since she had left Georgia at thirteen, Jenifer couldn't find her footing, couldn't maintain an equilibrium, and didn't know who she was in relation to someone else. Until John Smith, she didn't care if someone liked what she did. She didn't care if she ticked them off. She didn't seek out their approval or company. Perhaps with Elijah in some small degree, but she often went months without seeing him and barely thought of him. The truth of the fact made her heart heavy, because she now understood how much Elijah did love her and while she had granted him access to her body, she had firmly held him back from her heart.

She had been cruel, and overly so.

Silas dropped her hand and bolted for his father, and John crouched in time to sweep up the boy and hold him on his hip. Silas was a growing boy, and quite possibly too old to be carried by his father. But neither of them seemed to care, only that they were together.

"We'll be able to disembark in about half an hour," John told her when she reached them. "I've already arranged for our things to be taken off the ship." John set Silas down beside Jackie. "Why don't the two of you go to the shops and see if you can find a gift for Aubrianna?"

"Can I get something, too?" Silas asked.

"Yes, as long as you choose your cousin's gift first."

Silas nodded and walked away with Jackie, now firmly holding her hand just as he had Jenifer's minutes before. He trusted, and considering what she knew of his young life, trust was a symbol to Jenifer of the love and protection John had poured out on the boy. He was so lucky.

Jenifer raised her head and looked John in the eyes. "You're a good father, John."

His smile was slow but changed his entire expression, right to warming the blue of his eyes. "Thank you. That means a great deal to me. Before Silas, I had no idea how one would even begin to be a parent."

"You're a natural."

"Walk with me," he said, and stepped to her, placing his hand against the small of her back. Her skin warmed at the subtle touch. "I want to watch your reaction when we approach the city."

He led her away from the lounge toward the front of the ship to a bank of windows that wrapped the front of the *Steppenschraff* so the view was forward, rather than as they passed. Clouds came at them and split as the nose of the ship cut through them and she felt the slight dip in her stomach as they descended. The windows wrapped all the way to the floor so she saw the mountaintops they flew over as they lowered from the clouds. From space the greens had been the greenest and the blues the bluest she'd ever seen, and their brilliance was just as amazing at this altitude.

"It's a beautiful world," Jenifer said, stepping to the railing as she leaned forward. "How have you kept it so pure and unspoiled?"

"We didn't keep it this way, we've recovered it." She looked up at him and he squinted one eye. "My people aren't without our disastrous past, Jenifer. We nearly destroyed our own world with war and misuse. At one time our leaders considered enclosin' our major cities and lettin' the rest of the planet die."

"This world?"

He nodded and stepped closer so he stood beside her, one hand on the railing near her own. "This was hundreds of years ago. But someone had the good sense to suggest instead of closin' off our cities we use our resources to recover our environment. The scientists from your world are comin' here to learn from the students of the scientists who pioneered our recovery."

Jenifer turned away and watched the passing landscape.

"Jenifer . . ."

His voice was rough, heavy and danced over her senses. Long fingers curled around her arm and slid down until he wrapped them around her wrist. She stared at the point of contact, memorizing it.

"You've let me in again only enough for me to know you're in turmoil, and I fear I'm causin' it somehow."

297

Jenifer raised her head. "I've hated you for the last several days, John."

His lips straightened and deep lines dug into his brow. The intense need to make him understand pushed her to continue.

"In a matter of a few weeks you have completely destroyed everything I thought I was, and you've made me question my thoughts, my memories, my feelings. I hate you for destroying me. I don't like it, and yet . . ." She sighed in frustration and looked out the window. "I do."

"Why do you like it?"

"Because I like how it feels, even though it frightens me." She focused on him again, unable to keep from watching the change in his eyes when she spoke.

"What are you afraid of?"

"That when I leave this ship I'll stop feeling the way I do. I'll stop being so aware of . . . you. I'll . . ." She swallowed. "I'll go back to wearing dark glasses. And at the same time, I'm afraid it won't stop. I'm afraid it's like you said, I'm seeing clearly what I've known or felt all along and now I know, I can't go back."

"Why didn't you talk to me about this before now?"

Jenifer laughed, but even she heard the lack of humor in it. "I don't know if you've noticed, but I'm not much for in depth personal conversation."

He laughed too, a short chuckle just enough to shake his shoulders. Jenifer dropped her head and looked down at her wrist. He tugged her hand away from its grip on the railing and slid his palm along hers to lace their fingers together. Jenifer drew in a shuddered breath at the warm sensation the touch sent growing up her arm.

Jenifer swallowed and struggled to rein in the war of emotions in her chest. How could she explain any of this when she didn't understand any of it herself?

"Do you still hate me?"

"No," she answered quickly, probably too quickly. "I want to, a part of me wants to, but I can't. I can't be angry, either, or resent you for it. Whatever happens, you've changed me." She chuckled and cut her eyes to him. "Don't you dare tell Jackie. She'll never let me live it down."

"Your secret is safe with me."

Jenifer nodded and drew in a slow breath. "I know."

"Forget about what may or may no' happen, Jenifer." John reached across and touched her chin, urging her to turn her whole body to him so they were face to face. "Tell me what you want. And it's yours."

Her heart had never pounded so hard in all her life as it did at that moment, threatening to break free of her ribs. Heat radiated beneath the surface of her skin so profusely even the sleeveless tunic felt smothering. She realized with a jerk behind her breastbone she was tired of being frightened, tired of wondering, and if she were to remain true to herself she had to be the woman she'd created. Go forward, react, take what she wanted.

This time it would be different.

Jenifer drew her hand from his and raised her arms until she could comb her fingers into his hair. She could barely breathe, already feeling lightheaded, but when he laid his hands at her waist and drew her closer, she sucked in air with a sharp jerk. Jenifer looked from his eyes to his mouth and licked her lips. John's fingers curled tighter into the fabric of her tunic and a low sound rumbled through his chest.

Her eyes fluttered closed of their own free will and she drew him down to her. Their first kiss had been his parting gift, the second born of fire and frustration, but this one was because she didn't want to deny anything anymore. His lips brushed hers in a slow, tentative exploration making her breath hitch again. She'd pass out soon if she couldn't take a normal breath. She trembled, opening her lips beneath his.

John wrapped his arms around her, his large hands pressed to her back, and he pulled her against him, delving full force into the kiss. It was slow and deep and complete, and unlike any kiss Jenifer had ever shared. It wasn't hard and taking, it wasn't demanding, but she gave like she hadn't ever before. Kisses had always been a prelude—a *short* prelude—to the final act of sex, intended to inspire a reaction and to convince her partner to get it over with.

In this moment, she would be happy if the kiss never ended.

John released his hold long enough to take her face in his hands and she wrapped her arms around his body, drawing him close just as he had for her. His thumbs stroked her cheek, teasing the corners of her lips as he kissed her, urging her to open deeper for him. Her nerves danced like champagne bubbles beneath her skin and her stomach tumbled low and thrilling.

Far too soon, John broke contact with her lips and rested his forehead against hers, their rapid breath mingling in the small space between them. He still held her face in his hands, his fingers massaging just within her hair.

Jenifer smiled and tipped back her head so she could look at him. His eyes were closed, and she waited until he finally opened them. They were so dark, so intense, so inviting she wanted to begin the kiss all over again.

"Was that clear enough?" she asked, answering his question at last.

John inhaled through his nose and nodded, a sexy and satisfied grin spreading his lips. "Oh, yes. Perfectly clear."

CHAPTER THIRTY-TWO

*J*ohn had prepared all of them for the arrival on Aretu, letting them know the district of Callondia was nearing the end of summer, and while the sun was bright the air would most likely have a nip. If the breeze kicked up, it could be downright cool.

Nothing in comparison to snow drifts and sub-freezing weather in a hover, but cool enough they should consider a jacket over the usual sleeveless tunics worn on the warm ship. Jenifer decided she could get used to the Areth fashion sense. Everything they wore was comfortable, allowed her to move freely, and the long black coat fit snug to her torso but flared just enough at her hips to give her freedom of motion and hid Damocles strapped to her thigh.

John had made the decision to approach Queen Bryony still active in the roll of ambassador, which meant he wore no weapon. His jacket was also long, but cut much straighter to accentuate his height and build with a straight collar hugging the column of his throat. He wore it well, and Jenifer didn't even try to hide her smirk of appreciation when he caught her studying him.

"And you call Michael and me embarrassing," Jackie mumbled before she crouched to talk with Silas.

John winked at Jenifer and she looked away, doing her best to place firmly back into place what Elijah had once called her "game face."

Whatever she and John were behind closed doors, she was still the person responsible for keeping him alive.

For the quarter hour she'd felt a crawl at the back of her neck that told her something was wrong.

Someone was watching, and they weren't friends.

"Hey, Jackie," Jenifer said, motioning for Jackie to step away from Silas. Jenifer moved close to John to include him. "You're armed, right?"

Jackie nodded and put her hand against the bump strapped to her thigh. Just like Jenifer, Jackie wore a jacket with a flare cut effectively hiding the weapon to the casual observer.

"What's wrong?" John asked.

Jenifer shook her head, holding her attention on Jackie. "Keep Silas close to you. If something goes down, you stay on him and I'll take care of John and try to keep this from getting ugly."

John curled his fingers around her arm above her elbow. "Jenifer, what's wrong?"

"Someone is watching, waiting for us," she said frankly.

She saw the question spark in his eyes, but just as quickly so did understanding. Perhaps this whole clarifying of her Talents would prove to be more useful than she anticipated. He clenched his jaw, a muscle jumping back near his ear, and he looked to Jackie.

"Protect my son," he said simply.

Jackie nodded. "Of course, Ambassador. I told you in Alexandria I'd protect him with my life."

"Except it's no' just your life you're riskin'."

Jenifer scowled and looked between John and Jackie. "What's that supposed to mean?" John and Jackie stared each other down, neither speaking. Jenifer crossed her arms. "Speak up, people," she snapped.

Jackie released a long breath bordering on a growl and looked away from John. "I'm pregnant."

"Are you frickin' *kidding* me?"

John laid his hand on her shoulder. "Jenifer—"

"Don't." She shrugged him off. *Damn it!* "Keeping you alive is one thing, John. Now I've got a kid, a baby, and *stupid idiot* to watch out for."

"What the hell is that supposed to mean?" Jackie snapped.

"You know what it means. What the hell were you thinking coming here at all?"

302

Jackie pressed her lips together, but said nothing more.

"Good answer," Jenifer ground out. "If this goes south just keep your head down and get Silas under cover. *Do not* play hero, just keep him safe. Got me?"

"Fine," Jackie hissed.

"I need a weapon," John said to neither one of them in particular and took a step toward one of the Areth guards standing near the disembarkment ramp.

Jenifer grabbed his arm, stopping him. "You're still an ambassador, John. You can't go out there carrying a weapon. Let me do my job."

Before he could counter argue, an Areth dressed in an elegant jacket of red and gold ascended the ramp, and bowed to John. "Queen Bryony has greeted the Human scientists, Ambassador, and we're ready to escort you from the ship. If everyone could follow me, please."

John nodded without speaking, his jaw set so firm Jenifer expected to hear his teeth crack and the anger buffering off him was tangible to her. At least she garnered enough from the waves the source of the anger—those intending to do harm and his impotence to protect his son.

Silas, oblivious to the conversation between the three adults, took John's hand and smiled up at his father. John put on an impressive act, smiling down at his son and took a step toward the ramp. Jackie took up the place on the other side of Silas, her hand on his shoulder. Jenifer decided now wasn't the time to hide, since the queen knew exactly why she was here and what she intended to do, so she chose to lay down her cards. She released the two lowest buttons on the jacket closing the garment over her hips and lower stomach, giving her enough leeway to flip back the long skirt to reveal Damocles against her thigh. Jenifer curled her fingers around the grip and Damocles hummed to life beneath her touch.

They stepped into the sun, a cool breeze flowing across the docking harbor. The *Steppenschraff* was settled into a docking harness, firmly resting on the flat stone-like surface of the bay area. A long two-story building stretched in front of them with at least one hundred Areth in attendance, lining a long carpeted walkway of a rich royal blue. The reception had been initially set up for the visiting scientists, but with his unexpected arrival, Ambassador John Smith would also be honored.

She would rather slip out the back. Less show meant less chance for being blindsided. Their boots echoed with solid thuds as they descended the ramp, and were met half way by two uniformed Areth guards on each side.

The crowd erupted in cheers; whooping sounds pushed from deep in their diaphragms, and held their hands over their heads clapping. A slight twist on an Earth custom, but enough to cause a lot of noise and make it hard for her to focus. Jenifer scanned the crowd, looking with her eyes what she felt with her mind. The tingle on the back of her neck turned to a burn.

"Eyes wide, Jackie."

"Understood."

At the far end of the walkway she saw a man and woman step just into the edge of the sunlight. The woman was beautiful, with golden hair plaited at each side of her head to hang forward, draping past her waist. Alabaster skin like cream practically glowed, accentuated by the pale yellow dress she wore with gold cord elaborations. The full skirt shifted forward and back as she approached. The man beside her had rich brown hair, but from here she could tell little else. He wore a jacket much like John's but in a beautiful royal blue with gold cording and held the queen's hand as they walked. He had to be Conrad, John's brother and the prince consort. A girl a little older than Silas walked a step in front of them and Jenifer couldn't remember ever seeing such a beautiful child.

"Good lord, what kind of gene pool does the royal family work from anyway?"

John chuckled, but the tension in his body was palpable.

"I don't like she's within view," Jenifer said, scanning the crowd again. Her hand itched to pull Damocles free and carry him at the ready.

"Neither do I, but without shoutin' 'get down', there's no' much I can do until we reach her."

Normal protocol would keep her walking either beside or in front of John, but instinct practically screamed at her to step behind him. She fell back half a step so her shoulder no longer aligned with his. He glanced her way but kept moving.

They were deep into the crowd, the whooping and clapping filling the air in a full cacophony. If she were lucky at all, which she wasn't about to bet on, whomever wanted John wouldn't risk attacking in such a highly armed and public place.

Queen Bryony and Prince Conrad stepped forward, Bryony holding out her arms to them. She started to crouch to welcome Silas first when something so real and substantial hit the back of Jenifer's skull she stopped short and spun around, Damocles alive and ready in her hand.

"Down!" she screamed before she found her target.

She didn't have to see him to know he was there.

Several people screamed at once and the crowd scattered. Jenifer pushed hard against John's shoulders, ducking with him, just as an ion blast sizzled through the air. She didn't take the time to check on Jackie, putting her trust in the woman who had saved her butt more than once. John went down and Jenifer dropped to one knee, swiveling to track the area where the blast had originated.

Another blast fried the air, past them headed for the queen. More people screamed.

"Get the queen out of here!" someone shouted. "Now!"

"Go! Go! Go!"

"Face your executioner, Areth!"

Jenifer snapped her head in the direction of the voice, her senses on fire with awareness. A strange, unfamiliar instinct called her, pulled her to his position rather than her seeking out the source. She shifted to her right, blocking Jackie from the man dressed in a drab green jumpsuit she'd seen worn by crew on the *Steppenschraff*.

"On my mark, you move," she said only loud enough for Jackie to hear. "Now!"

Jenifer fired at the Xeno, because only a damn Xeno would be stupid enough to come this far to prove his ignorance. He dodged and rolled from the blast, but his countermeasure gave Jackie the seconds she needed to drag Silas away, despite his screaming for his father.

Another blast came from behind her. Jenifer crouched deep, trying to see where the blast had come from. It wasn't Earth issue, and by the sounds of it not any Areth weapon she'd seen, but she knew she hadn't seen everything. The angle could have been a poorly aimed shot at the attacker, or an equally poor shot at John. People ran everywhere, at least they were smart enough to run *away* from the fight, but it made it hard for her to find her target.

Blasts thrummed in the air, pinged off the hull of the *Steppenschraff*, and blew chunks off the reception building. The coward Xeno hid within the harnesses and supports of the ship.

She felt him, but she couldn't see him.

"Leave Earth to Humans!" the Xeno shouted from his hiding place, one of his blasts hitting the structure behind them. Glass shattered and rained down on the remaining crowd.

Jenifer risked a glance to where the royal family had been and found the space empty. Her gut twisted at the carnage spread out over the tarmac. Most had escaped but at least a dozen Areth citizens lay strewn across the ground, not moving. The weapons destroyed mass and structure, but killed without bloodshed. The lack of gore didn't make the death any less gruesome.

Her neck tingled and she twisted back in time to see the Xeno jump clear of his hiding place, a volley of blasts coming their way. She turned and wrapped her arms around John, throwing both of them several feet to land together with a breath-jarring crunch. For a moment she couldn't pull in air, her lungs painfully hollow and lights dancing in front of her eyes. Ion blasts peppered the ground where they had been.

The arrogant bastard stood in the middle of the ramp, his weapon trained on the two of them, a self-satisfied smile on his face. "Stand up, Areth, face your death like a man." He fired over their heads to hit the building again, then twisted and fired off to his left at a group of fleeing people.

"No!" John shouted.

John lunged to his feet, and Jenifer scrambled after him, trying to pull him back down when another volley of alien weaponry filled the air. The Xeno dropped to the ground and rolled, firing wildly into the crowd.

"Stand! Or others die!"

Jenifer raised Damocles but John lunged forward, setting his hand on hers to angle her weapon downward.

"Get back," she hissed.

"No, I'm no' worth more dyin'."

"Ask your son if that's true," she snapped before thinking, and his eyes darkened. Her chest tightened and her throat went dry. Jenifer swallowed hard. "Ask me if that's true, John."

John looked her in the eyes and shook his head almost indiscernible. "Trust me."

Jenifer clenched her jaw and lowered her hand.

"Tell your bitch to put the gun on the ground!"

Jenifer lowered Damocles to the ground and let go. The weapon immediately went still and silent. John touched her jaw with the pad of his thumb before he straightened his legs and stood, facing the Xeno.

Weeping and wailing echoed through the docking area, the sound of cracking power and creaking supports threatening to give way from the assault. One zealot had done all this.

Jenifer watched the Xeno, picking up every detail. He was nervous and kept looking around, perhaps expecting another attack. The hand holding the pulse weapon shook when he waved it at her.

"Move away from the weapon, bitch."

"I *really* don't like being called names," she said in warning.

"I don't care. You're protecting an alien against your own people, sure makes you a bitch in my book."

"Is the title of your book *See Dick Run?*"

"Shut up and move!"

Jenifer stood slowly, keeping her hands away from her. She took one step forward toward John. An unfamiliar pitch whined behind her, coming from somewhere near the roof of the long reception building, and in the same second she heard John shout "Hold your fire!" and a searing, scrambling sensation hit the top of her head. She flew forward, landing on her hands and knees, in total blackness. Her skin sparked like live wires and she fought the sudden urge to vomit.

The more familiar sound of the ion pistol answered the Areth weapon. Jenifer curled to the ground and covered her head. A loud buzz in her ears muffled all normal sound. She worked her jaw in an attempt to clear it, but the whine only fluctuated. There was shouting, voices, more firing and screaming, but it all sounded so far away.

"Bloody hell, hold your fire!" John shouted.

Hands touched her shoulders and she jerked back, floundering to fight off the unseen assailant until her instincts reacted to the familiarity of the presence as much as the touch. She slumped in John's hold.

"I can't see, John."

Her ears popped and noise rushed in, shooting pain around the inside of her skull like a ball bearing in a barrel. "Get away from her!" She heard the assassin laugh and tilted her head to the sound. "She gets one chance, or she dies with you."

"No thanks," she spoke to the general area of the sound of his voice, her own echoing hollowly back to her. "I'd rather die than live as a moron."

"On your feet!"

Jenifer gripped the sleeves of John's jacket and let him help her to her feet. Her equilibrium was shot. "What the hell was that?"

"It's called a disarticulator. Intended to immobilize rather than kill."

"Good job." She swallowed to keep her stomach where it belonged.

"Stop talking and face your accuser!"

"Arrogant son of a bitch," she said loud enough to make sure he heard her.

John wrapped the arm closest to the Xeno around her waist and held her firm against him. He linked the fingers of her other hand with hers, just so she knew the hand was there. He leaned closer to her, close enough she felt his breath on her cheek when he said softly, "Trust me. I'll be your eyes. Down but no' dead."

"You better be a good dancer," she said under her breath.

"Very good," he whispered, then said, subtly, "Now."

In one fluid motion, he separated their hands and with a thought—either hers or his, it didn't matter—Damocles hit her palm and she gripped firmly, the weapon alive and ready again. John's hand closed over hers and the weapon hilt. With what at least felt like an effortless move for him, he lifted her feet from the ground and spun them both one hundred eighty degrees. A split second later Damocles fired and she heard the satisfying thud of the Xeno hitting the ground.

Right after that, so did she.

CHAPTER THIRTY-THREE

*S*urety officers ran forward as soon as the Xeno hit the ground, scrambling to secure him before he came to, and John eased Jenifer to the ground, cradling her against his chest. Her head was back, her eyes closed, but he suspected the effects of the disarticulator would be temporary. He hoped.

"Get medics out here now!" he shouted to surety officers running past. One pulled up short, nodded and turned around to run back the other direction.

The need to get Jenifer under cover should the Xeno have friends, coupled with the equal need to find Silas, pushed John to sweep Jenifer into his arms and stand again. He headed for the entrance to the reception area, met at the door by one of Bryony's personal guards.

"Follow me, Ambassador," he instructed, holding the door with one hand and motioning down the hall with the other. "We've moved the royal family and your son's guard to a safe room and physicians are with them now."

"Thank you."

"Is she hurt?" he asked over his shoulder, guiding John into the inner chambers of the reception hall, designed both for meetings and conferences with visiting dignitaries as well as security for those visitors.

John had been here numerous times and was familiar with the layout, the question only remained which room.

"Temporarily only. I want a physician to examine her regardless."

"Of course."

They stopped at a locked door and the guard pressed his hand to a security scanner, a blue light reading his palm print as well as his silent mental command to release the door. A hiss and click indicated the lock had disengaged and the door slid open, allowing them entry.

"John, thank the Almighty," Bryony declared, rising from the lounge where she and Conrad sat with Aubrianna between them. Her eyes widened when she looked at Jenifer in his arms.

Conrad swept his daughter into his arms and moved them both out of the way. "Lay her here, John."

He wanted to do so many things at once: assure Jenifer actually would be fine, find his son, check on Jackie, and embrace his brother and queen all at the same time. His heart pounded furiously and the bitter taste of adrenaline tainted the back of his throat. Forcing himself to be calm for the sake of the children, John crouched beside the lounge and eased Jenifer down on her back.

"Papa!"

Jenifer free of his arms, John spun on the balls of his feet in time to catch his son running across the room. He only allowed Silas a moment of holding on before he eased the boy back to look into his tear-streaked face.

"Are you hurt?" he asked, running his hands down Silas' arms.

Silas shook his head and drew a trembling lower lip into his mouth as he sucked in a sob. "I was scared, Papa. Miss Jackie picked me up and ran and told me you'd be safe because Miss Jenifer was with you."

"She was right," John said and pressed a kiss to his son's forehead. "Miss Jenifer took good care of me." Silas' dark eyes shifted to Jenifer lying on the lounge. John set his hands on Silas' shoulders. "She'll be just fine. She's restin'."

Silas nodded but didn't look convinced. John took the moment to stand and turn to his brother, who immediately pulled him into a hard, back thumping embrace. He was barely free of Conrad when Bryony drew him to her in a much gentler, but no less intense hold. She kissed his cheek twice.

"You have such a way of frightening us, John," she whispered near his ear, the strain on her voice revealing a hidden strain. *Will your friend survive?*

Very few Areth possessed the ability to express thoughts silently, but as the ruler and of a Talent bloodline known to be the strongest in the history of the royal family, Bryony did it effortlessly. John nodded, holding her close a moment longer. *She was hit with a disarticulator. Enough to blind her, but not harm her.*

Even in her stillness I feel her power. She is amazing, John.

He withdrew to look his sister in the eyes. "In more ways than you know."

Bryony smiled, her eyes shining with tears she wouldn't allow to fall as queen. Later, in their solitude, she would release her pain. "Even as you stepped off the ship, I saw the truth between you. She is far more than a guard."

John looked down at Jenifer and his chest tightened. He clenched his jaw and turned to scan the room, finding Jackie seated a bit away with a physician standing nearby. He took several steps toward them.

"She's with child, please make sure—"

"I told them," Jackie interrupted, shooting John a look. "Everything is fine. A little running never hurt anyone."

"Now it's your turn to be checked, John," Conrad said, laying his hand on John's shoulder. "You were the target, after all."

Anger, raw and vicious, flashed through him like a reactor fire and he stepped clear of his brother's touch.

"John, please don't shoulder this," Bryony said in her most soothing voice, and he had no doubt she'd felt the wave of fury. "You aren't to blame for what happened today."

"Aren't I?" he demanded, turning to face his queen. "Bryony, these . . . Xenos . . . have dogged me, threatened me *and* my son, they've attacked me, chased me now across one planet and to another. How am I no' to blame for this? It's *me* they want, and their zealousness brought them here. *Killed* those citizens out there!" he shouted, pointing to the door and the carnage beyond.

"There you go, Ambassador," came a rough, welcome voice. "Assuming everything revolves around you."

John dropped back into a crouch beside the lounge, smoothing a bit of disheveled hair from Jenifer's cheek. When her gaze connected firmly with his he knew at least her vision had returned. How clear, he couldn't know. "How do you feel?"

"Like someone scrambled my brain," she groaned, trying to roll forward to sit.

John helped her get upright and sat beside her, studying her profile. "I'm sorry about that. Most likely usin' your Talents so soon after the blast caused the blackout, but I saw no other way."

Jenifer leaned forward, her elbow set on her knee and her forehead in her hand. She held up the other. "Just tell me it worked."

"It worked," Bryony said, coming forward to kneel before Jenifer, a sign of respect few people ever had bestowed on them. John knew Jenifer didn't understand the significance of having the queen kneel before her, but John did. "Your act stopped a madman from hurting anyone else."

John took Jenifer's hand and rested it on his thigh, squeezing gently. He leaned closer to keep his voice low, knowing her head had to hurt. "Jenifer, I'd like to introduce Queen Bryony the Fourteenth, Ruler of the Areth."

Jenifer made a noble effort to raise her head and offer a respectable smile, but the way her eyes pinched at the corners confirmed for him the headache she had to be fighting through. "It would have been nice if we'd met under calmer circumstances, Your Majesty."

"Of course," Bryony said with a warm smile. "This is my husband, Conrad, and John's brother. Aubrianna has apparently already happily reunited with her cousin Silas," she said, looking to the far side of the room where both children sat close together in deep conversation.

Jenifer tried to look up at Conrad, but John's brother raised his hand. "Please, don't. When you're feeling better."

She swallowed and lowered her head again. "Thanks."

"Bryony, I need to speak with you about my position—"

"No," Jenifer interrupted, her head coming up with a snap. A sickly grimace immediately followed.

"You don't know—"

"Yes, I do." She looked him in the eyes and sat up straighter, despite the effort he knew it caused her. "You think if you resign this will stop. The Xenos will grow some brain cells and get some common sense. They won't. It doesn't matter who serves as ambassador between the Areth and Earth, they will be a target."

"Do you wish to no longer be ambassador, John?" Bryony asked.

"People are dyin'—"

"And more will die before it's all done," Jenifer said.

"How am I supposed to accept that?"

"You are the best man for the job," she argued. "John, you're not a politician." She looked to Queen Bryony with a wince. "No offense intended, Your Majesty." Coming back to him, she leaned her shoulder against his and he wondered if it was to help her keep herself upright. "I know I accused you of being an opportunist and not giving a damn, but I was wrong."

"I can't carry a weapon, how am I supposed to protect—"

"That's why I'm here," she said, her voice gentler than it had been.

Conrad came to his wife's side and helped her to her feet. "We'll all talk more once everyone has had a chance to recover from the day. Go to the palace, John. Accompany my wife, please. I'm going to see to events here and I'll follow later."

"We'd intended a celebration in honor of your return," Bryony added, smoothing her skirt. "I hope you don't mind, but it wouldn't be appropriate now."

"Of course," John said, gaining his feet. Jenifer moved to stand, but he laid his hand on her shoulder. Her lack of resistance spoke louder to her physical state than the visible pain on her face. He motioned for the physician to approach. "Bryony, I truly am sorry for what happened here today."

She laid her hand on his cheek. "As are we all, dear one."

$\mathcal{J}$enifer woke as daylight shifted to twilight, casting a dark blue haze over the massive bedroom where she slept. She remembered the ride from the docking harbor to the palace, but only through a clouded haze of pain. At least the headache was gone and she could see with clarity.

She rolled from facing the center of the big bed to face the edge and eased herself up into sitting with her legs hanging over the side, tossing aside the light, silken, cream colored blanket draped over her. With a sigh of relief, she enjoyed the total lack of nausea. Maybe not at one hundred percent yet, but she was probably functioning at about ninety-five percent. She took the moment to look around the room, and without doubt she was in a palace.

Apparently, palaces were the same everywhere.

The room was decorated in cream and gold with rich wood furniture. The large bed had a cream and gold brocade canopy with heavy drapes tied at the thick posts. Mesh hung from within the canopy and could cover all four sides of the bed. In front of her was an open double door leading to a balcony, and from the view beyond, she guessed she was on a second or third story. A light breeze drifted in, dancing through the mesh curtains over the doors, carrying a heady mixture of floral scents and the elusive green Silas had spoken of.

Two globe-shaped lights brightened the room sitting atop bases that could have been from a bygone era on Earth, hand painted with floral designs and gold accents. The light inside the room shadowed the balcony and it took her a moment to adjust and see John's straight, still form standing at the balcony wall, his arms crossed and his head dipped forward.

"Why don't you come join me?" he said, his voice carrying a tangible weight. "Callondia Capitol is beautiful this time of the day."

Jenifer slipped from the bed, her bare feet hitting the cool wood of the floor. He'd taken off her shoes and her jacket, leaving her arms and her feet bare. She crossed the floor and stepped outside, the air even more brisk without the walls of the palace, and the internal heat, to buffer the breeze.

"The city is quiet tonight, in mournin' for those lost today, otherwise you'd be able to hear music and people. Callondia is full of life most of the time."

He hadn't moved from his spot, looking down on the city below. Jenifer reached the railing and confirmed they were on a second story but the palace sat on a hill above the city, looking down on the streets and buildings. There was nothing particularly alien about the city, nothing to make her feel odd or out of place. To compare to Earth architecture,

Callondia Capitol didn't appear modern in the steel and metal sense. The buildings were brick and stucco, some wood. Many were two or three stories. It was hard to tell much more detail from where they stood, but he was right, the lights made the city shine. It was like when she was a child and they still celebrated Christmas.

There was a thickness to the air, despite the coolness, that wrapped around her and sat on her skin, saturated with the smells of life.

"You should put shoes on. The stone is cold."

"I'm fine," she said, forcing herself to hold back the snarky response she found so instinctive. She wasn't sure how long she could fight against her nature, but for John she was willing to try. For a while. Either she'd get over it, or she'd kill him.

She smiled and chuckled.

"Somethin' amusin'?"

She didn't have to look at him to hear the smile in his voice.

"Just considering my options."

He made a slight "Hmph" sound. Jenifer folded her arms on the high balcony railing, nearly level with her shoulders, and set her chin on her hands to look down on the city. Darkness was falling quickly, making the stars almost as bright as the city lights. A river ran to their right, the water reflecting back the lights of the buildings along the water's edge and the strings of lights illuminating wharfs jutting into the waterway. A large barge floated slowly down the river, with the moving shadows of a few people moving around on it.

"This could be Earth," she said softly. "Your city reminds me of Old Paris, before the bombs came. Or London. I went there a few times before the war. Everything felt old, ancient, but still beautiful because it hadn't caught up with everything else yet."

"We're a contrastin' culture." He moved closer to stand beside her, his hands pushed into his pockets. "These old cities managed to survive the near destruction of the planet at our own hands. There are cities on other parts of the planet in sharp contrast to Callondia Capitol. Ships like your hovers carry people wherever they want to go, and anythin' can be obtained with minimal effort. People who want simplified lives, no' simplicity. Does that make sense?"

She nodded against her hand. "The quick fix. I think that's what got us in trouble when the Sorrs came. People were too willing to accept the luxuries the Sorrs provided in your name. Better health. More wealth. Easier lives. Better Humans."

"You're a very insightful woman, Jenifer."

She grinned without looking at him. "I can do more than built fancy guns and kick your butt from here to *Gateway* and back."

He chuckled again, but she felt the lack of lightness, of amusement, in the sound.

They fell into silence again. She thought to ask about Silas and Jackie, but figured if there was something she needed to know, he would tell her. She let him stay in his own head for a while.

From somewhere in the city a bell rang. It had to be a massive one for the sound to carry so far with such clarity. Moments later, the beautiful sound of voices raised in singing carried on the breeze to them. The harmonies curled in her chest and made her heart tense with the beauty but inherent sadness of the sound.

"They mourn for the people who died today."

"Is it a church bell?"

"Yes."

"Huh . . ."

"What?" The gentle touch of his hand across her shoulders surprised her at first, but she didn't move away or jump. He brushed the edges of her hair with the back of his hand, a slow, soothing action and she wondered just who it was intended to soothe.

"Church bells. I guess I never considered a race so old as yours would have something as archaic as religion."

"Our religion is the structure on which we have built the revitalization of our culture, and I think you would be amazed at the similarities between our faith and the faith of your ancestors. The faith findin' revival on Earth now you don't have the Sorracchi whisperin' words like 'archaic' and 'antiquated' and 'mindless'."

"Maybe you can tell me sometime?"

"Any time you want."

Jenifer turned to put herself between the railing and John, the city behind her, and looked up into his serious face. His attention was fully on her, his head tilted a tick to the side, his eyes shining with the reflective lights behind her. He raised a hand and laid his knuckles against her cheek, stroking her skin with the pad of his thumb. It was going to take some time for her to get used to his tactile affection, she'd never sought it out or allowed physical contact before. But then again, she'd never wanted it before, and for the first time in her life, she did.

He drew in a slow breath through his nostrils, releasing it just as slowly.

"The *Constellation* won't be here for another eight days, and will remain on Aretu for another eight days in preparation for returnin' to Earth, but there is another supply ship leavin' here in four days."

"Okay," she acknowledged, waiting for the rest.

"The *Steppenschraff* will be returnin' to Earth in twenty days with the visitin' scientists. Because of its faster engines, it will be back to Earth before the *Constellation*, but no' by much but the ship leavin' in four days will reach Earth before either one of them."

She nodded, the motion making his knuckles caress her cheekbone.

"I have until the *Steppenschraff* leaves to decide if I intend to go back to Earth as ambassador, or no'." He shifted closer the couple of inches needed to allow his chest to brush against her body and raised his other hand so her face was cradled in his hold. His study was so intent on her, she wondered what he saw when he looked at her like that. What he looked for. "Jackie has chosen to leave on the next ship to return to Earth as soon as possible. She won't admit it, but I think she needs to see Michael and she doesn't want to risk their baby bein' born anywhere but Earth."

"You're going to get to a point somewhere here, right?" She smiled, and caught the slight tick of his lips.

"It's your choice, Jenifer. You can return to Earth with Jackie . . ."

"Or?"

He winced, his eyes pinching at the corners. "I want you to stay, Jenifer."

"Okay."

"Just like that?"

She nodded. "I know what you'll choose to do, so I might as well stay until we both go back on the *Steppenschraff*."

"How can you be so sure when I don't know myself."

"You do know. You just haven't accepted it yet."

"Are you ever unsure about anythin'?" he asked with a smile, finally some life sparking in his eyes again.

"Never . . . until I met you."

"Is that a good or a bad thing, Jenifer Of No Last Name?"

"I'll let you know."

His expression shifted back to the serious, the stroke of his thumb moving closer to the corner of her mouth. His gaze shifted down to watch his own touch and in a flash, heat shifted over her entire body just beneath the surface of her skin and her heartbeat skipped faster.

"If you stay," he finally said, his voice rough and heavy. "I don't want you to stay as my bodyguard. I want that clear. I'm no' your *job* anymore."

"Until we go back."

"I'm talkin' about the next twenty days, Jenifer." The weight of his tone wrapped around her.

She raised her arms and wrapped them around his shoulders, lacing her fingers into his hair to pull him to her. The kiss wasn't the hesitant, unsure kiss on the *Steppenschraff*—that kiss had been a test to see if she could be with him in a different way than she'd ever been with any other man—but now she knew and she wasn't going to hesitate again.

John wrapped her in his arms, pulling her to him so tight she almost couldn't breathe, and she let herself be lost in the kiss. No fighting for control, no demand, just reveling in the lightness.

She slid her hands from his hair to lay her palms against his rough cheeks, drawing back to look him in the eyes. His lids were heavy, his breath warm and rapid against her face.

"I will stay here with you until you get your head on straight and figure out you're going to go back to Earth and show these idiot Xenos you're not going to be scared away by their threats and blinding ignorance. I will still wear my weapon, and if you are very lucky, I might even let you fire Damocles once or twice. On your own." She grinned at the spark in his eyes he couldn't hide. *Men.* They were the same everywhere. Shiny toys always got their attention. "But I will be here because I want to be here. With you. And Silas."

"I guess you don't hate me anymore?" he said with a chuckle.

"I haven't decided yet."

"If this is how you kiss me when you hate me, I can only fantasize how you'd kiss me if you actually liked me."

She answered with another kiss.

CHAPTER THIRTY-FOUR

17 FEBRUARY 2054, TUESDAY
ALEXANDRIA HOSPITAL, SECURE WING — MEDICAL RESEARCH FACILITY
UNITED EARTH PROTECTORATE, CAPITOL CITY
ALEXANDRIA, SEAT OF VIRGINIA
NORTH AMERICAN CONTINENT

"*W*e've managed to stabilize the triplets. Their system degradation isn't nearly as severe as John Doe," Areth Doctor Averill Jones explained. "But, we've got to bring him out of the suspended state soon or risk sudden and complete system failure."

"How long?" Michael asked, reading over the report Doctor Corbin had provided him and the rest of the medical team assigned to the four stowaways they'd brought back to Earth four days before.

"Your guess is as good as mine. Frankly, I'm surprised he hasn't crashed already. Despite the claims in the late Twentieth Century about cryogenics, the science is completely untested and unknown in Human technology. The Sorracchi have more knowledge than us, and they built these machines. Or, they stole them from another race. Either way, we don't have any firsthand knowledge or resources to assist us in reviving him."

"Have we found anything in the records?" Victor asked Katrina, who only offered a quick glance over her glasses before she looked down at her tablet.

"None to identify him. I found a file dated 22 December 2011 after we translated the Sorracchi calendar to ours that speaks of a Human male found within one of the early research facilities established by the Sorracchi after they began working with the United States government in power at the time under President Bart Woosley. He was armed with a projectile weapon but no form of identification." She ran her finger across the screen to move to another page of data. "I also found a report written within a day of this report from a scientist who designated herself as Kathleen."

Michael's gut clenched, but he forced himself not to react outwardly. Victor looked to him, but Michael shook his head enough for his friend to know he could let it go. Kathleen was dead and gone, killed by his own hand. Or, in truth, his mind. He'd crushed her bones and thrown her against a steel bulkhead with enough power to crumple her stolen body.

"What did the report say in reference to John Doe?" Victor asked.

"Um . . ." She scanned the screen. "We're pretty sure she's talking about the same person, but she instructed the security detail to have him taken to the *Abaddon*. It was she who decided to place him in suspended hold. As she worded it, he was a 'prime example of advancing Human evolution' and would serve their purposes well in the future." Katrina looked up, her cheeks flushed crimson. "She references his body mass and muscular strength, as well as bone density, intelligence, and inclination toward violence because of the weapon he carried. Apparently, she saw him as some type of breeding stock."

"Are there any indications he had been used to that end?" Doctor Corbin asked, her casual tone a sharp contrast to the obvious embarrassment young Katrina suffered through discussing the matter.

Katrina cleared her throat and looked down again, fidgeting in her chair. "Um, it's hard to be sure. Since he's never given any specific designation, I can't run a scan through existing files to locate references to him. But, um, the pod he's in doesn't appear to have been opened in years."

"We may be able to determine if any experiments were performed on him once we are able to open the pod and have access to his person."

In the distance, the sudden and blaring sound of sirens echoed through the hospital halls. Everyone stood, chairs scraping across the floor, but before anyone made a move for the door it burst open. Michael recognized Doctor Iris Soursa, her face panicked and her breathing hard from the run.

"We need you now," she said to the room in general. "John Doe is crashing."

EARTH TIME: THURSDAY, 19 FEBRUARY 2054
SMITH ESTATE — DEVON ON THE HILL, CALLONDIA DISTRICT
ARETU

"*A*re you ready, Miss Jenifer?"

John smiled as he walked, squinting against the sun with his flat hand above his eyes to shield them. Across the yard Jenifer stood beneath one of the morelfruit trees, looking up into the branches.

"I'm ready," she answered Silas who was somewhere in the upper branches.

John reached them as Jenifer held up her hands in a cup and a large, deep purple morelfruit fell into her waiting palms. She brought it to her nose and inhaled, looking to him with a smile.

"It smells like an apple, but spicy. What did you call it?"

"Morelfruit. But, we just call it an apple for Silas."

Leaves showered them as Silas worked his way down from the upper branches. He had been promising Jenifer a warm apple since they arrived at Devon on the Hill the day before, after seeing Jackie off for her return to Earth. John laughed and picked a red and yellow leaf from Jenifer's hair. She still had the morelfruit held to her nose, her eyes closed as she inhaled deeply the strong scent of the fruit.

Silas reached the bottom branches and John held his arms up for the boy, swinging him down with a wide swoop before setting Silas on his feet. Silas laughed and tugged his shirt down into place, watching Jenifer with the innocent intensity of a child.

"Go ahead, Miss Jenifer. Try it! It's the best *ever*."

She smiled before opening her mouth and sinking her teeth into the purple skin with an appetizing crunch and snap, a squirt of juice landing on her cheek as she bit through the yellow meat. Jenifer tried to chew and lick her lips at the same time, a low and satisfying groan humming in her throat made John's blood come alive. He wasn't sure how long he would be able to continue spending all his time with this woman—in his home, in his bed—without making love to her. He liked the Human words for the intimacy he wanted to share with her.

Make love.

"Wow, that's good," she said around the meat in her cheek. "It tastes like apple pie without the crust. Like the cinnamon and spices are part of it."

"Told you it was good," Silas said with smug satisfaction.

"Why don't you head to the stables? Anson is waitin' for you. He wants your help with somethin'. Very important, I hear."

"Okay!" Like a rocket, Silas was off and running toward the large building set several hundred feet away from the main house.

Jenifer held the morelfruit to him, having taken another large bite. John accepted and bit into it, sucking up the juice before it ran down his chin. She laughed at him and ran the back of her hand across her lips.

"It's a messy fruit, but worth it."

John nodded, too much in his mouth to speak. He offered his free hand and she took it, and they walked together across the field at an angle away from the house. The weather had warmed enough Jenifer wore one of the sleeveless tunics he'd purchased for her on the *Steppenschraff*. He appreciated the view of her well-defined arms, and wondered if she would ever tell him where the few but noticeable scars came from. The only one he knew was the one on her bicep, now mostly healed, from the attack on the embassy what seemed like months prior. It had only been two weeks in Earth time.

He also enjoyed her willingness to let him simply hold her hand. When he'd met her in Nick's office, he never would have imagined them here, walking hand-in-hand on his family estate on Aretu. They reached the top of the hill and sat on the warm grass, turned to face down to the house.

No matter how often he came back, or how long he'd been away, John always welcomed the sense of being home that came with looking down on the farm. Generations of Smiths had lived here. The main house had been built thirty years after planetary recovery had begun and the ground was deemed fertile enough to produce food and maintain animals. The house had burned down once, and the new two-story building had been constructed to replace it. Stables had come and gone, the final being the massive structure housing all the animals, feed, and supplies. The property spread further than anyone could see with the naked eye from anywhere within view of the house.

Some of his ancestors had farmed the land, others had chosen professions that took them away from Devon on the Hill, like John and his choice to join the Defense Alliance. His mother wanted him to finish his medical education and stay on Aretu, stay near her, but he had been young and determined to go his own way. At least Conrad had stayed close to home, even if his home ultimately became the royal palace.

"You're very quiet," Jenifer finally said, snapping off the last bite of morelfruit she'd taken back from him.

"I came here to think. That's what I'm doin'."

She chuckled. "You're overthinking."

"I doubt that's a bad thing."

"John, I spent days overthinking on our way here. I *knew* what I wanted, and if I'd just accepted it I would have realized I had no doubt. Instead, I tried to convince myself I didn't want to be any different, I didn't want to change, and I didn't want to accept I'd been wrong."

John looked at her and tilted away. "That may be the most I've ever heard you say at one time."

"Keep pushing it and you won't hear it again," she jabbed.

He chuckled and sat straight again. "Okay, fine. I suppose no matter how much thinkin' you did, I'm glad you're here."

Jenifer tilted her face into the sun, a soft breeze blowing her dark hair back from her cheeks. She smiled and hummed. "Do you know the last time I just sat in the sunshine and enjoyed a day?"

"A long time."

She nodded. "A lifetime."

"Then I'm also glad I could give this to you."

Jenifer turned her head enough to meet his gaze, her eyes shifting slightly as she studied him. Without breaking the connection, Jenifer rolled and shifted onto her knees and slid her body across his to sit astride his lap. He gripped the fabric wrapping her hips and settled her against him, reaching up to find her lips.

The kiss curled like smoke in his gut, bringing him to life. Her weight across his hips was a subtle tease, but enough to make him ache for wanting her. She sat back on his thighs, leaving him needing more, with a teasing grin on her moist lips.

"You're very darin' with a young boy just down the hill."

She winked and slid her hand down his chest to his stomach. His muscles hardened and jerked of their own mind beneath her touch. "Do you think Silas would be upset to see us kissing?"

John chuckled and tried not to think about the thrumming in his ears and the dangerous whisper in his head suggesting he turn her and lay her down in the grass. "Us kissin'? No. I don't know if you noticed, but my son adores you."

Her expression softened and a tentative smile replaced the teasing one from the moment before. "He's a special kid. And lucky."

John stroked her cheek, opening himself to her in hopes of experiencing some of whatever thought had chased away the teasing vixen of a moment before; only to know one more small piece of her made her both happy and sad at the same time. That was all he felt, a mingling of light happiness and old sadness.

He loved her, just as Michael had predicted, and wanted to destroy whatever had stolen her joy. He had to wait until she trusted him enough to reveal her past to him. He had to wait until she was ready to accept his love, because if there was anything he knew for sure, he knew love was something elusive and foreign to Jenifer. Despite the love Elijah Kerrigan had confessed to her.

For now, he hoped she would feel his love even if it had no name.

Jenifer shifted from his lap but drew him with her so they both stretched out in the grass, her curled against his side with his arm as her pillow. She inhaled deeply and closed her eyes. John wrapped her in his arms and squeezed tight.

I love you, Jenifer Of No Last Name.

She stood at the edge of the tree line, watching the bastard child play with some old man just inside the doors of the large stable. Her hair clung to the back of her neck in a clammy blanket, the damn heavy air of Aretu making her overheated and her Human skin slick. Her world had been humid, but not this oppressive heat making it hard to breathe.

The boy ran off, chasing a creature she couldn't name in the Areth language but the Humans called dogs. The boy squealed and dropped to the ground so the creature could jump on him and lick his face.

Disgusting.

The Areth ambassador and Human whore had walked up the hill away from the house. Skirting through the trees, she spotted them at the top of a hill, the whore atop him as they kissed.

Her stomach churned and memories of Nick Tanner filled her thoughts, the ways she had allowed him to defile her body in the pursuit of her brethren's research to bear a Human child. It had been a punishment for failure, and she had accepted her fate knowing she would receive a new, perfect husk once the child was purged from her body.

And she'd had twenty-five years to eke out her revenge on the boy designated Michael. Nick Tanner had apparently chosen the name, despite being informed the thin was dead. She hated Nick Tanner, and she would have her revenge again.

Beginning with the death of Ambassador John Smith. Isaac had failed to kill his targets, including the Areth queen. She made sure before she left Callondia Capitol he wouldn't reveal her presence and had watched him choke on his own tongue in a pool of blood.

She would bide her time, but not for long. Only long enough to assure she had a means of escape off this dreaded planet once John Smith and all he held dear was dead. No one knew this body and she would remain safely hidden until the time was right.

Once Smith was dead, she would return to Earth and kill the two men who had humiliated her to High Command: Nicholas and Michael Tanner.

CONTINUED IN
PHOENIX RISING BOOK TWO: TRIAD

PLEASE ENJOY THE FOLLOWING PREVIEW

Alpha. Beta. Omega. The Triadic.

They were created by the sickest, most twisted mind of all the Sorracchi to be super-soldiers – mindless, emotionless, A-moral killing machines – but something went wrong. Compassion, affection, and curiosity are born in the human psyche and if it is strong enough it cannot be denied. But it can be punished. The Triadic were placed in stasis for nearly a decade until their "teacher" could figure out how to strip them of their human hearts.

Before the War Katrina Bauer had spent her life tucked away from the world, hiding her intelligence and her skills to avoid the seeking eyes of the enemy. Now in Alexandria, working with men like Victor, Michael Tanner, and an elite scientific team reporting directly to President Nicholas Tanner, she and her brother Karl have found purpose and a sort of family.

In the dead of night she is snatched away and now must find a way to teach three powerful, frightening men they no longer need to live as slaves. The leader, the soldier, and the balance. They are lynchpins to each other. As their personalities are allowed to emerge, one will grow to be a man Katrina no longer fears, but might even love.

PHOENIX RISING BOOK TWO: TRIAD

TRIAD: CHAPTER ONE

19 FEBRUARY 2054, FRIDAY
ALEXANDRIA HOSPITAL, SECURE WING – INTENSIVE CARE
UNITED EARTH PROTECTORATE, CAPITOL CITY
ALEXANDRIA, SEAT OF VIRGINIA
NORTH AMERICAN CONTINENT

42 YEARS LATER . . .

"We're losing him!"

Michael ran as quickly as he could, using his cane to help propel himself forward. Victor and Doctor Corbin led the way down the hall to the intensive care rooms set up for the four nameless souls they'd found in stasis aboard the *Abbadon*. The shouts of doctors and wail of alarms mixed in a confusing cacophony. Victor shoved open the door first, and the sound amplified.

The room was in chaos, doctors, nurses, and attendants rushing around the prone body of John Doe, the one of the four they knew had been held in stasis the longest. He had been yanked from the pod when they realized he'd shut down and rushed to the surgical room. He now lay on a table, his arms hanging limp away from the narrow bed. His upper body was laid bare, electrodes stuck to his sallow skin wherever they had found space amongst the variety of mechanical and technological interfaces that had been infused with his flesh. An oxygen mask covered his lower face. His vitals had been the weakest when they were found, but they'd hoped to have more time to find a safe way to wake him from his deep slumber.

Hope had failed them.

"What have you tried?" Victor demanded, slipping the loops of a sterile mask around his ears.

Michael had already put on his mask and worked on gloves.

"Once we had him clear of the pod we put him on forced pressure oxygen and injected adrenaline and atropine and performed chest compression to restart the heartbeat. We've picked up a rhythm twice, and lost it twice, never long enough to defib and get a steady beat," Doctor Lois Maybourne shouted over the alarms. "It's hard, sir, to work around the hookups, but we didn't see any of them until we cracked the pod." She paused. "Many of them are integrated into his system, sir. We can't remove them."

Michael looked to the heart monitor. The line spiked and plummeted in random patterns. The line dropped to red and didn't move.

"He's flat lined, Doctor," a nurse Michael didn't know announced over the din. "His brain functions are decreasing rapidly."

"Damn, we really are losing him," Victor cursed, and leaned over the still man's body. He laid his hand across the man's forehead, a motion so familiar it brought to Michael a flash of memories from his earliest years on to the day he left New Mexico. Memories of Victor, even when he was tormented by the Sorracchi consciousness haunting him, caring for Michael and bringing him back to life. "I'm so sorry," Victor said softly, spoken only for the man slipping away.

Michael pushed through the group surrounding the table, yanking the gloves free from his hands. "I can help."

Victor raised his head and looked at Michael, his forehead pulled in speculation. "We've done everything we can medically. He was in stasis too long. His body is worn out, we—"

"I'm not talking about medicine," Michael said in dismissal.

Very little color tinted the unknown man's face, and the only color to his torso was an angry shade of red where the interfaces had been joined with him with clearly more speed than precision or care. His flesh had grown around them, just as the doctor said. Metal plates with light indicators, now dark with no power source, merged with him over his heart, from each side near the lower lobes of his lungs, and some hanging off the edge of the table from beneath him like tentacles. A cord, reminding Michael of an umbilical, came from the back of his neck at the base of his skull. Michael laid his hand on the man's chest over his still heart, the metal plate sliding into the space between Michael's fingers and thumb, his skin already cool to the touch, slightly clammy. His chest didn't rise and fall with even the slightest of breaths, his body more dead than alive.

"No," Victor shouted, yanking Michael back from the bedside.

"Yes!" Michael shoved away his friend's hands. "I've learned to control this both ways, Victor. I can give as much as I take."

"I know you can," Victor argued, holding Michael away from the bed with a grip on the front of his shirt. "You pulled *me* back from death, remember? It nearly killed you."

"Bringing you back didn't nearly kill me, Vic. Kathleen nearly killed me." Michael took hold of his longest friend's wrists and tugged them away from his shirt. "He's important enough to try."

Victor pressed his lips into a tight line and he released Michael's shirt. "Don't make me regret this."

Michael offered a short nod and turned again to the bed. He drew in a long breath, closed his eyes as he released it, and rested his palm again on the still chest. It had taken weeks of prayer and meditation to harness the power Michael had finally accepted he possessed, and with that control had come the ability to turn the power outward. This would be the first time he'd tried to save a life since he'd yanked Victor back to the world of the living, just over a year before, but he was a different man now. He only hoped it was enough.

He turned his focus inward and blocked out the sounds of alarms and murmured voices around him. Slipped deeper until all he heard was the steady rhythm of his own heartbeat and the rush of blood in his own veins.

Give me the strength to bring him back.

He visualized a sparking, electrified ball of blue/white light spinning in the center of his chest, tendrils of power branching outward like an electromagnetic sphere. Michael drew in another breath and with a mighty mental shove, pushed the energy away and toward the cold, still hole where this man's life should be.

David was in the same dream.

Somewhere along the way he'd accepted everything happening around him was just a dream, but since he never actually woke up, he couldn't get himself free. He was doomed to live the same day—a day he never actually lived—over and over again like some bad Bill Murray film.

He blinked and brought the room into focus. Seated on the right side of the couch, he faced the Scotch Pine Christmas tree he had bought with the boys and brought home to the townhouse he had once shared with them and their mother—his ex-wife—in the nice-but-not-too-nice part of Manhattan. The lights twinkled through the thousands of strands of silver tinsel the kids had tossed on the tree so thick they hid most of the ornaments. The smell of coffee and pine permeated the air.

David counted to five, and right on time, he heard his sons thundering down the stairs with squeals of excitement. They tore into the living room and headed straight for the tree and David watched, his heart aching. Trapped in this purgatory, he both knew everything was a lie and hoped it never stopped.

"Say good morning to your father before you open those gifts," Kelly said from the doorway leading into the front hall.

David looked to his left. She stood where she always stood, a cup of coffee in her hand, dressed in the pink chenille robe he'd bought her three years before. Her blond lightened hair was piled on top of her head in a white scrunchie, as always, and the smile she sent him was as flat as ever. *For the benefit of the boys.* His psyche couldn't be so kind as to at least give him the wife he'd loved for so long, the one who smiled at him with open love rather than resolved indifference.

The boys scrambled from the floor to race to the couch in a bid to see who could get in his lap first. As always, they tied. Little Anthony, at seven, still wanted to sit on his father's lap. He wore his favorite

SpongeBob SquarePants pajamas he'd had so long his toes poked out through the feet, and his light brown hair stuck up in odd directions. He perspired in his sleep and his hair always dried in crazy ways. Davey, his namesake, was too old at ten to sit in his lap so he knelt beside David and hugged him. He wasn't too old for that yet. He opted for fleece pajama pants with a camouflage pattern and a black tee shirt because he said it looked like the clothes David used to wear when he was in the Army.

David hugged them both, and kissed each forehead, inhaling the smell of his boys. Even though he had lived this morning more times than he could count, he lived each one as if it were his last . . . just in case it was.

After hugs and kisses, both boys bolted off the couch to the stockings hung in front of the cold fireplace. Davey dumped out his stocking first, and his "Whoa!" made David smile, just as it always did.

"Mom! Check it out! A signed Papelbon Red Sox card!" Davey looked to his father, his eyes wide and his jaw open. "Thanks, Dad!"

"Daddy didn't give it to you, stupid. Santa did," Anthony argued.

"You're such a baby. There's—"

"Davey . . ." Kelly warned and Davey went silent, his smile never wavering.

David loved that moment. When he saw pure glee on his oldest son's face. In another five minutes Anthony would open the Spider-Man Dual Action Web Blaster David had gone to four toy stores to hunt down.

The air crackled and the lights dimmed, flashing back on as bright as before. David looked around. That hadn't happened before.

"The wind must have kicked up. I heard we might get snow," Kelly said.

"Maybe . . ." he mumbled in response, edging forward to stand. The jeans and sweater he'd worn every other time were replaced by a simple pair of cotton pull on pants like he'd wear in a hospital, and his shirt was gone.

Something wasn't right.

The lights dimmed again and a pounding sounded at the door.

"Who on earth could be here on Christmas morning?"

David suddenly felt sick and lunged for Kelly to stop her, but she was already down the hall. She looked at him over her shoulder and scowled before reaching for the door. On the other side stood two men in dress greens, hats set low over their eyes, misted with the fine snow falling outside.

"Can I help you?" Kelly asked.

"Kells, shut the door," David demanded. She didn't even respond. The boys ran from the living room, right past him. "Kelly, shut the door!"

Kelly was still, silent.

"Mrs. Forté?" the sergeant asked.

"Forte," she mumbled, an automatic habit to correct the pronunciation of the name. "The e is useless." The correction seemed out of place.

David took the three long strides needed to put him between her and the two officers. The bite of the winter air outside tingled against his bare back. She looked right through him, tears in her eyes.

"Mrs. Forte, the necessity to deliver this news today is unfortunate, but we felt it couldn't be delayed. We regret to inform you your ex-husband Lieutenant Colonel David Forte has been killed in the line of duty. "

The mug fell from her hand and shattered on the floor, splattering coffee on her pink chenille.

"Where's my daddy?" Anthony cried. "Where's my daddy?"

Davey stared, eyes brimmed with tears, his mouth pulled into a tight, silent frown.

"No!" David dropped to his knees in front of his sons. He tried to touch them, but his hands had lost their substance. "No, boys. I'm right here."

This was it. No more looping. He'd lived his last day. What waited for him now? Heaven? Or Hell?

The house disappeared in a flash of white light and David turned toward the open door, shielding his eyes with his raised arms.

"Are you crying?"

Katrina Bauer swiped at her cheeks with the back of her hand and sniffed, avoiding her brother's taunting smirk. She kept her chin down and blinked to clear the haze, freeing another tear to run down her cheek.

"You are. You're crying."

"Shut up, Karl," she mumbled.

"Why are you crying? Geez, you seriously need to get some sleep. I never knew you to be a weepy female."

Katrina slammed her soldering tool down onto the stainless-steel table tray beside her, the other tools and parts bouncing with the force. She glared at her older brother, silently wishing he would just leave her alone to her work. All he did was tease and poke and distract her.

"You want me to go get Doctor Tanner?" He wagged his eyebrows and winked. "I bet he'd be willing to—"

"Shut. Up. Karl," she said again through clenched teeth. She shook her head and picked up her EM calibrator. How could she explain if he didn't already know?

John Doe lay completely still in his infirmary bed, living more off machines than his own body's need to survive. In the hours after Michael Tanner had—in a way Katrina couldn't even begin to comprehend—pulled him back from death, Katrina and Karl had worked frantically to interface the alien technology that had maintained his body in the stasis pod with their Human technology enough to keep him alive. Running on just a few hours' sleep, Katrina logically understood her emotions and comprehension were compromised, but how could her brother not be affected by the butchering inflicted on the man?

Karl pushed back from the computer console he'd been working at, a mix of Sorracchi and English scrolling in various windows on his screen and stood. She refused to look at him but registered in her peripheral as he came around the foot of John Doe's bed and to her side.

"I get it," he said, the teasing gone from his voice. "I guess I try not to think about it."

"You're not the one working on him," Katrina whispered, wiping again at her cheeks. "He's alive, but what did they leave him with? What if I do fix all this . . ." She motioned with the tip of her calibrator to the tangled mess of life support and electronics surrounding the bed, " . . .and all they left was a shell?"

"You tried, Trina. That's all you can do."

Karl squeezed her shoulder and leaned over to kiss the top of her head. "I need to run a diagnostic on the sub-system, but the access program is set up in the lab. I'll be there for a bit. You going to be okay?"

Katrina nodded but couldn't find a voice enough to say anything. He left her alone again, with only the sound of electronics and the synthetic push and pull of oxygen through John Doe's lungs. In perfect rhythm, his chest rose and fell and the heart monitor never wavered in its constant beep-beep. Everything perfectly timed, perfectly controlled, without falter.

"What kind of sick minds did this to you?" Katrina mumbled, shaking her head. She glanced toward John Doe's still face but looked away just as quickly. He hadn't moved in two days, since the doctors had yanked him from the stasis pod, and for two days Katrina and her brother had worked around the clock to keep him stabilized and find a way to remove the invasive tangle of mechanical interfaces brutally thrust into his body.

Fatigue dragged at her, but with each system interface she bypassed or stabilized, another broke down and threatened to take him with it. The intricacy of the machinery fascinated her, but the way the connections violated his body and organs went beyond butchery to sloppy cruelty. He'd been joined to his stasis pod with meshing of machine to flesh, without consideration of the damage the violations would cause.

Katrina hunched over the thick cable protruding from his left side beneath his arm. She did her best to be careful, to avoid irritating the flesh-to-metal connections, but despite her caution, the skin around the interface had split and wept a thin line of blood. Blinking against a new wave of hot tears, Katrina held the cable in place the best she could and twisted to reach back and grab a few squares of gauze from the table behind her.

White light surrounded him. The townhouse was gone. His children were gone. He spun on the balls of his bare feet, looking for something in the blank whiteness. David flinched and hissed, looking down at his side. Blood wept from a circular wound beneath his left arm, the skin stinging. He touched the blood with the fingertips of his right hand and held the bloody tips in front of his eyes. The blood was warm, slicking his skin.

"I'm sorry," she whispered and sniffed. Her hands trembled, making it hard to tuck the gauze beneath the wound. "I'm trying . . ."

"You're going a great job."

Katrina jumped and looked up, her cheeks flushed hot from embarrassment at not hearing Michael Tanner come into the room. She blinked and focused again on the bleeding wound.

"I'm afraid I'm hurting him more than I'm helping him." She couldn't force her voice to be any louder than a rough rasp.

Michael took three limping steps, leaning heavily on his cane, to retrieve Karl's chair and drag it back to settle beside the stool she sat on, pulled to the side of John Doe's bed. He took away the gauze she'd used to dab at the torn skin and leaned forward to examine the small wound. "I'll treat these to avoid infection. His wounds aren't your fault, Katrina."

She folded her hands in her lap and slid back a few inches, giving Michael room to work. The respiratory system interface was now connected to the reverse-engineered support system computers banking the bed, and his lungs had begun pulling in air again, even if only because they were forced to do it. The alien machines kept his systems going, for now, until Katrina and Karl found a way to disconnect him. Her focus had been in deciphering the system and the commands so his body didn't go into shock from losing the only functionality it had known for decades.

Butchers.

The hum of a stratum basale stimulator joined the low-frequency mechanical buzz of the computer systems and the steady rhythm of John's life support system. The SBS would knit the skin and stop the bleeding . . . until she jostled him again. Katrina closed her eyes, letting Michael do his work as a healing physician, a gift she could only admire.

A strange buzz drowned out the silence, he couldn't identify the source, couldn't recognize the sound. David looked up, looked around, but the sound stopped as abruptly as it began. He focused on his hand again, and the blood was gone. His side was healed, no sign of the bleeding wound.

She lost awareness until her body tipped and she jerked awake just a second before Michael Tanner caught her from falling off the stool. "I'm sorry," she stuttered, shaking off the tendrils of sleep hazing her senses.

Michael gripped her elbows and pulled her to her feet, supporting her while she blinked through sandy eyes. "You are doing a great job, Katrina. You need rest before you do any more."

She nodded, knowing he was right, even though her mind wanted to keep going. She didn't want to leave John—or whatever his name was—

like this. It felt cruel, wrong, and she didn't want to be as thoughtless as the masochists who did this to him.

"He shouldn't be alone . . ." she mumbled.

"I'll come back once I know you're resting."

She nodded, her head feeling light and heavy at the same time.

Michael led her out of the room, her resistance shot. Katrina paused at the door, glancing back to the prone stranger on the bed, as much machine as man. "Why would someone—" She couldn't even finish the thought.

"I don't know," Michael answered. "We'll find out."

He led her a few doors down to what had, for lack of imagination, been named the pod room. The other three pods, housing the three men they knew only as The Triadic, were hardwired to power units and spliced to Katrina's computer system that had been temporarily migrated to the room. Michael pushed open the door and leaned on his cane to let her step past him. The room was in darkness except for the eerie blue glow from her monitors and the array of lights and screens on the fronts of the pods.

"I had them bring you a bed."

Her sleep-deprived brain wouldn't let her form an actual question, all she could manage was a long, tired stare at Michael. He smiled and touched her arm, urging her forward.

"I wouldn't want to be far away if it were me."

She managed a nod, moved past him, and made it to the bed on the other side of the room before he eased the door closed and left her alone. Katrina collapsed on the bed, toed off her shoes, and rolled onto her back to stare at the ceiling. A low electronic hum lulled her with white noise, the combined power system of the three pods and the computer systems constantly working on deciphering, cataloguing, and coding the various files she'd downloaded from the *Abbadon*'s database.

Katrina yawned and flopped her arm over her eyes, already halfway to sleep.

She could have been there an hour, she could have been there thirty seconds, when her decipher program twittered with three distinct beeps, yanking her from sleep. Katrina groaned and willed herself to ignore it, but the insistent program twittered again. She rolled out of bed and didn't quite make it upright before she got to the desk, dropped into the chair, and tapped the key interface to open the data file the program had translated.

It was a video-based file, the angle and immobility of the shot indicating it was probably a standard surveillance and observation recording. The room it recorded looked familiar in that it reminded her of the design of the rooms on the *Abaddon*, dark and cold and low ceilings in comparison to a Human or Defense Alliance ship. A man and a woman were in the shot, and despite the slightly grainy quality from the translation program, they struck Katrina as familiar. If she were rested, even more awake than asleep, she might be more cognitive.

She rubbed her aching eyes and contemplated just watching the video in the morning, but her curiosity wouldn't let her, no matter how enticing the siren call of her bed. Slumped over the desk with the lead weight of her head supported against the knuckles of one hand, she tapped in the command to play the recording.

The woman shouted at the man, her hands waving wildly. She was tall, slightly taller than the average Human woman, with dark brown hair twisted into an intricate coil around her head. The familiarity Katrina felt was frustrating, but she couldn't get a clear view of the woman's face. She shouted in Sorracchi, guttural and harsh. Katrina paused the video, backed it up, and played the shouting again. She couldn't get it all, and syntax and exact translation didn't coincide between English and Sorracchi, but what she got was the woman demanded to know how someone, a plural because the word was equivalent to "they," had found some sort of record she never wanted them to see.

By the time Katrina closed the file two hours later, she had watched and looped the video enough to know the Triadic, the three men silent and still in the pods behind her, had discovered some sort of information the Sorracchi wished to keep secret; specifically, the woman who appeared responsible for their training, and possibly their creation.

Kathleen.

That single name incited any member of or person associated with the Tanner family to a deep and righteously justified rage.

Kathleen: the Human name chosen by one of the most advanced, and most sadistic, minds of the Sorracchi race.

Kathleen: the Sorracchi slug who had stolen the body of a Human woman no one knew how many centuries before and used that stolen body to birth Michael Tanner as part of an experiment for a purpose they had yet to fully understand.

Kathleen: Michael Tanner's tormenter, the woman who brought him near death, and *to* death, more than once and left him nearly crippled. The traitor who had tricked Nick Tanner in his youth to father a child with the woman he thought was his Human wife, who had contrived to make Nick believe he had lost his wife and his infant son, and the woman who had held the child for over two decades as her personal lab rat.

Kathleen: killed by the hand—or the mind—of the boy child she had birthed, tortured, and pushed to the breaking point when she threatened not his life, but the life of the woman Michael loved.

Even though she was dead, the destruction she left behind seemed never ending.

Katrina pushed away from the desk and forced herself to stand. Before she stumbled to the waiting bed to steal whatever precious hours of sleep she could, she crossed the small space to the three pods, and stood in the center of the half-circle they formed. Low level lights within the edge of the observation window let her see their faces, still and unchanged, relaxed in a forced sleep. The powers that be planned on cracking open the pods in the next day or two, to see if the Triadic had been butchered during the process of implanting them in the pod, if their flesh-to-tech interfaces were as sloppy and scarring as it had been on John Doe. But, tonight, they stayed still in slumber.

Now that she knew Kathleen had some hand in these three men, a sense of dread settled in Katrina's stomach. Nothing touched by Kathleen survived unscathed.

"I'm sorry," she said to the still room. "Whatever it was, I'm sorry."

END OF SAMPLE

ABOUT THE AUTHOR

 Gail R. Delaney is a multi-published, award-winning author of romance in multiple sub-genres, including contemporary romance, romantic suspense, and epic science fiction romance. She always wrote stories as a kid through her teens, but didn't decide to write 'for publication' until her early twenties after the death of her mother. While helping her father go through her mother's papers, she found a box her mother kept with everything Gail had ever written—from book reports to short stories. It was then she realized her mother saw her as a writer, and it was time to live up to her mother's vision.

You can find out more about Gail R. Delaney's body of work at:

http://www.GailDelaney.com

ALSO BY GAIL R. DELANEY

Baker Street Legacy

Baker Street Legacy is a romantic suspense series with a Sherlock Holmes bloodline.

Book One: My Dear Branson

Book Two: The Empty Chair

Book Three: Indefinite Doubt

Coming Soon

Contemporary Romance

Something Better

Precious Things

Feel My Love

Fools Rush In

A Love at First Sight novella

CPSIA information can be obtained
at www.ICGtesting.com
Printed in the USA
BVHW031733231222
654917BV00021B/598/J

9 781949 705638